BETWEEN TWO WORLDS II.

"Wandering between two worlds,
one dead, the other pow er less to be
born."

- Mat thew Arnold

Each vol ume is pub lished in two parts: I and II.

BETWEEN TWO WORLDS II.

Upton Sinclair

LCCN: 67120285

ISBN: 1-931313-14-8

Dis tributed by Ingram Book Com pany

Printed by Light ning Source Inc., LaVergne, TN

Pub lished by Si mon Pub li ca tions, P.O. Box 321 Safety Har bor, FL

When I say "his to rian," I have a mean ing of my own. I por tray world events in story form, because that form is the one I have been trained in. I have sup ported my self by writ ing fic tion since the age of six teen, which means for forty-nine years.

... Now I re al ize that this one was the one job for which I had been born: to put the pe riod of world wars and rev o lu tions into a great long novel. ...

I can not say when it will end, be cause I don't know ex actly what the char - acters will do. They lead a semi-independent life, being more real to me than any of the people I know, with the single exception of my wife. ... Some of my char ac ters are peo ple who lived, and whom I had op por tu nity to know and watch. Oth ers are imag i nary—or rather, they are com plexes of many people whom I have known and watched. Lanny Budd and his mother and fa ther and their var i ous rel a tives and friends have come in the course of the past four years to be my daily and nightly com pan ions. I have come to know them so in ti mately that I need only to ask them what they would do in a given set of cir cum stances and they start to en act their roles. ... I chose what seems to me the most re veal ing of them and of their world.

How long will this go on? I can not tell. It de pends in great part upon two pub lic fig ures, Hit ler and Mus so lini. What are they go ing to do to man kind and what is man kind will do to them? It seems to me hardly likely that ei - ther will die a peace ful death. I am hop ing to out live them; and what ever happens Lanny Budd will be some where in the neigh bor hood, he will be "in at the death," ac cord ing to the fox-hunting phrase.

These two foxes are my quarry, and I hope to hang their brushes over my mantel.

In the course of this novel a number of well-known per sons make their ap pearance, some of them living, some dead; they appear under their own names, and what is said about them is fac tu ally cor rect.

There are other char ac ters which are fic ti tious, and in these cases the au thor has gone out of his way to avoid seem ing to point at real per sons. He has given them un likely names, and hopes that no per son bear ing such names ex ist. But it is im pos si ble to make sure; there fore the writer states that, if any such co in ci dence oc curs, it is ac ci den tal. This is not the cus tom ary "hedge clause" which the au thor of a *ro man à clef* pub lishes for le gal pro tec tion; it means what it says and it is in tended to be so taken.

Var i ous Eu ro pean con cerns en gaged in the man u fac ture of mu ni tions have been named in the story, and what has been said about them is also ac cord ing to the records. There is one American firm, and that, with all its affairs, is imag i nary. The writer has done his best to avoid seem ing to in di cate any ac tual Amer i can firm or fam ily.

...Of course there will be slips, as I know from ex pe ri ence; but *World's End* is meant to be a his tory as well as fic tion, and I am sure there are no mis takes of im por tance. I have my own point of view, but I have tried to play fair in this book. There is a var ied cast of char ac ters and they say as they think. ...

The Peace Con fer ence of Paris [*for example*], which is the scene of the last third of *World's End*, is of course one of the great est events of all time. A friend on mine asked an au thor ity on mod ern fic tion a ques tion: "Has any body ever used the Peace Con fer ence in a novel?" And the re ply was: "Could any body?" Well, I thought some body could, and now I think some body has. The reader will ask, and I state ex plic itly that so far as con cerns his toric char ac ters and events my pic ture is cor rect in all de tails. This part of the manu script, 374 pages, was read and checked by eight or ten gen tle men who were on the Amer i can staff at the Con fer ence. Sev eral of these hold im por tant po si tions in the world of trou bled in ter na tional af fairs; oth ers are col lege pres i dents and professors, and I promised them all that their letters will be con fi den tial. Suf fice it to say that the er rors they pointed out were cor rected, and where they dis agreed, both sides have a word in the book.

Contents:

BOOK EIGHT: LEAD BUT TO THE GRAVE

BOOK FIVE

The Valley of the Shadow

22

How Happy Is He Born

I

LIFE settled into its old routine for Lanny Budd. He practiced his music and danced with his little half-sister, who was now seven, a fairy creature, a wellspring of gaiety bubbling incessantly. He attended to his growing business; somebody was always telling him where there were art treasures, or introducing him to someone who loved paintings and might buy something special if it was brought to his attention. Zoltan would give him tips, and also his many lady friends were helpful; this occupation was ideal from the point of view of that buxom butterfly his mother, providing excuses for buying clothes, going to parties and receptions, and meeting the wealthiest and most elegant people. Everywhere she told the wonder-tale of her son's successes, nor did she forget her former husband and the astonishing way his fame was spreading. So Lanny promoted Detaze and Detaze promoted Lanny, and the widow and mother basked in the warm sunshine of celebrity.

It was a way of keeping Lanny entertained, and out of the hands of the dreadful Reds. Of course the tactful Beauty and Marie and Emily didn't say that; they would never find fault with their darling, never let him feel that they were putting pressure upon him; they would just surround him with other interests, flatter him, marvel at his achievements, make him feel that a big picture deal was the most exciting thing in the world. Lanny knew what they were doing; he knew that when he went off to Cannes to give some money to a pitiful Italian refugee, or to meet some friend of Lincoln Steffens just returned from Red Russia, they guessed it and were whispering their fears behind his back. Because he was kind and hated to keep them in a stew all the time, he would do what they wanted, and for the most part refrain from doing anything else. That is the way men are managed, and is one reason why the world changes so very slowly.

There was Kurt Meissner also to be guarded; and Lanny had to be taken into that conspiracy. They knew that Kurt was always brooding over the state of the Fatherland, which he said was in pawn to Britain and France, and could no longer move hand or foot without their consent. Living in the enemy's country, Kurt had to be persuaded to see Bienvenu as a little island of neutrality, a shrine set apart for the worship of the sacred nine. Beauty, who really knew very little about music, had to try to understand her lover's; she would ask Lanny about it, so as to have something to say that wouldn't sound fatuous.

She would devise elaborate intrigues to force a new *Komponist* upon the attention of a heedless public. After many delays, due partly to his meticulous care in reading proofs, the *Spanish Suite, Opus 1,* and the *Piano Concerto, Opus 2,* had been published; Beauty would send copies to friends, asking that they be brought to the notice of critics and conductors; if a letter was received or a comment made in print, she would bring it to Kurt without mentioning her part in the matter. She kept a mental cardfile of musical people who came to the Riviera, and if she heard that one had noticed Kurt's compositions, she would contrive to have that person come to tea and meet him. Sometimes Kurt would be bored, and then Beauty's feelings would be hurt, for that was her idea of how reputations are made and she was ready with numerous instances to prove it.

II

In December Kurt and Lanny made their annual pilgrimage. In Berlin Kurt went to see his brother, also his publisher, and buried himself in the reading of more proofs, while Lanny went to stay in the Robins' nest. Kurt still held to his determination not to go there, and of course the Robins knew the reason, and it hurt their feelings; but Johannes wasn't giving up his business and the boys weren't turning against him. They still lived quite simply in their apartment with two old servants; what Johannes enjoyed was getting things done, and he was surely doing that, for he had offices downtown that occupied a couple of floors of a large building. Nobody but himself and a couple of trusted employees knew how many properties he had acquired in Germany, but he was being mentioned in the newspapers as one of the "kings" of the new finance; like most of the "kings" Lanny had met in his life, he looked harassed and tired. The old mark had been wiped out, and there was a new currency called the "rentenmark"; it was being kept stable, which was a great relief to everybody in that harassed and tired land.

Amazing the way young people grew up! Here was Hansi, now twenty, an inch taller than Lanny. He had grown so fast that he hadn't had time to fill out; he looked frail, but really wasn't, for playing the violin is vigorous exercise. Not that Hansi was one of those performers who toss themselves around and act as if they were conducting an orchestra; he stood as still as he could, and let the music do the talking. He said that the day of the long-haired and theatrical musician was past; with his well-trimmed black hair you might have taken him for a serious young student in a rabbinical school. He had beautiful large dark eyes and a gentle voice, and more and more he seemed to embody all that was noble and inspiring in the tradition of the Jews.

Nobody was promoting Hansi Robin; he knew how it was done but didn't want it. Having the good fortune to have a rich father, he was helping several poor students at the conservatory. What he wanted for himself was to play the best music as perfectly as possible, and he said that when he could do that he would make a public appearance and wouldn't need any promotion. He was learning Joachim's great *Hungarian Concerto*, which he said would delight Zoltan. He played difficult things such as Paganini's *Moto Perpetuo*, but he didn't love technique for its own sake—he spoke with scorn of "finger gymnastics." He and Lanny played Mozart's sonatas, and he extracted loveliness from them just as diligently as if he had had several thousand people listening. Lanny couldn't be sure how much was Mozart and how much was Hansi, but he felt sure that some day audiences would throng to hear this playing; and of course he had only to say this in order to transport all the Robins into their Jewish heaven. Lanny didn't know just what they had in that heaven, but he knew that Elijah—or was it Elisha?—had been taken up there in a chariot of fire. He was sure also that the residents there would play Ravel's *Kaddisch*, and Ernest Bloch's *Schelomo*, which Hansi had transcribed for violin.

One interesting discovery for Lanny: this young virtuoso had turned into a full-fledged Socialist. He had carried out his promise to study the movement, and announced his conviction that it held the hopes of the future. He wasn't ever going to put a party label on himself, but he would play his music for the people at prices they could pay, and he would play their kind of music if he could find it. Lanny asked what Papa Robin thought of this, and Hansi said that Papa wanted his boy to believe what seemed good to him. Whether this would hold if Hansi should ever leave his studies and get into a conflict, say with Generalissimo Balbo, Lanny ventured to doubt; but he didn't suggest it, not wishing to trouble the soul of a sensitive and noble-minded youth.

III

Lanny and Kurt went on to Stubendorf, in company with Emil; the Reds had been definitely put down, so army officers could have Christmas leaves. At the Schloss things were much the same, except that one of the two young widows, Kurt's sister, had been married to a middle-aged official of the neighborhood; not a love match, but men of her own age were scarce, and this was a well-domesticated gentleman who would be kind to her children. Lanny loved German music, German cheer and *Gemütlichkeit;* how he wished there might be some way to extract and eliminate from these people those aggressive qualities which caused the rest of Europe to fear them so greatly!

Among those they met was Heinrich Jung. He too had grown several inches and was a grand and sturdy forester; he was going to school for two years more, to make himself a real expert; Germany was setting the world an example in the conservation of her forest treasures, and the blond and blue-eyed Heinrich studied with a sense of consecration to the Fatherland. He talked with fervor about the National Socialist movement, to which he was still devoted, in spite of the debacle it had sustained the year before. The leaders of that putsch had all been tried, and Adi, their favorite orator, had delivered a masterpiece of oratory in court. He and his associates had been convicted and sentenced to several years' "detention" in the fortress of Landsberg, but a few days ago they had all been let out on parole.

During the period of their incarceration Heinrich had traveled to the fortress to take gifts to the captives, and he was full of the ardors inspired by this visit. He reported that the prisoners had been well treated, it being recognized that their motives were patriotic; they had had better food than most of them had ever enjoyed previously. The young forester was a serious acolyte, with no trace of a sense of humor where his cause was concerned; he had no idea that he was amusing Lanny when he explained that Adi's oratory was adapted to audiences in large halls and not to the confinement of a cell, so his companions had suggested the writing of his memoirs as a means of keeping him occupied. Heinrich reported that he had produced a massive manuscript, and that some of the others were helping to revise it. Lanny said it ought to make an unusual book, and Heinrich promised to send him a copy when it was published.

IV

The story of these martyrdoms produced in Kurt Meissner that state of melancholy for which the German soul is celebrated; he was led to pour out his feelings to Lanny after a fashion which he had not used for a long time. It was agony to the ex-officer to see the Fatherland despoiled, dismembered, and helpless in the hands of its foes. All the country's financial affairs and most of its economic affairs were now under the control of the Reparations Commission, and Kurt said it was evident that they never intended to release their stranglehold. Germany was down; and how could the German soul develop while the German body lay bound and gagged?

Lanny thought: "Certainly not gagged, for it's making an almighty clamor." But he didn't say this. He pointed out to Kurt that reversals of fortune were no new thing in Europe. A little more than a century ago Napoleon had held the great part of Germany and Austria; a little more than a half-century ago Germany had conquered France. "You have to allow a little time for the passions of war to cool off, and the balance will right itself."

Kurt argued that balances had no such power. Whatever happened would have to be done by men. "Germans have to make an effort; they have to struggle against oppression and enslavement. The intellectual and spiritual leaders have to supply the courage and devotion to country."

In short, Kurt was in a mood of martyrdom, and Lanny knew what that meant. The ex-officer's conscience was troubling him about going back to the land of his foes to live in peace and comfort with a beautiful blond mistress. He was too polite to say this to the son of that mistress; he wouldn't even say it symbolically, by referring to Samson and Delilah, to Antony and Cleopatra. But he talked about Wordsworth's "Stern Daughter of the Voice of God," and Lanny in return reminded his friend of the fact that all through the struggle against Napoleon the serene Goethe had continued his labors as thinker and artist.

"But he was a much older man," argued the German. "He couldn't have fought."

"He could have gone into the political struggle, and have tried to inspire the Germans to resistance. But he really believed in the importance of art, and he left us products of his genius which are still working when the political problems of the time are forgotten."

"I know, I know," Kurt said—for Lanny was speaking his own language here. "But the suffering is so dreadful, it throws me into a state of despair whenever I think about it."

"I dare say that happened to Goethe also. It is your problem as an artist to find a way to embody those feelings in the art which you have chosen." Not for the first time, Lanny quoted Goethe's verses to the effect that he who had never eaten his bread with tears, who had never sat by his bed weeping, knew not the heavenly powers. Not for the first time in his struggles with his friend, Lanny thanked God for Goethe! He had even taught Beauty about the august Olympian of Weimar, and about the ladies who had comforted him—so that she might be able to present herself under a more dignified guise than that of Delilah or Cleopatra.

V

They came back to Juan, and Rick and his family arrived in a few days. Rick was planning a play, and intending to devote himself to it all winter and permit nothing to interrupt him. Exciting to the impressionable Lanny to know that a masterpiece of music was being composed in one corner of the estate and a masterpiece of drama in another. It never troubled the young lord of the manor that he had no masterpieces of his own to contribute. Perhaps one might say that he was producing masterpieces of friendship, giving two artists a place where they could work unhindered, and providing that sympathy and admiration which appear to be essential to their functioning.

There was the estate with three pairs of lovers and four assorted fruits of love—Lanny counting in both classifications. Rick and Nina had the only marriage certificate on the premises, and there were people outside who turned up their noses at Bienvenu, saying, like Kurt's aunt, the Frau Doktor Hofrat von und zu Nebenaltenberg: "*Unschicklich!*" But such persons didn't really belong on the Coast of Pleasure. Those who stayed permanently came to realize that morals are a matter of geography, and that love and kindness in the heart count for more than any legal document stuck away in the bottom of a trunk. So, at least, it seemed to Lanny, and he was content to choose his friends among those who agreed with him; in fact he hardly knew that the others existed.

February was the month for Kurt's annual recital at Sept Chênes. This was really a favor that Emily Chattersworth did him, but she insisted upon sending him a check for two thousand francs; it provided all the pocket money he needed for a year, and thus helped to preserve his self-respect. There was always a rumbling and thundering of piano practice for this event, for Kurt was the most fastidious of virtuosi, and every phrase of one of his compositions was sacred to him. A week or so before the event he would begin worrying as to whether his selection of pieces was the best. He would ask Lanny's advice, and Lanny would point out the danger that, loving his music so intensely, Kurt was apt to give his audience more than it could carry away. To most fashionable people a musicale was an occasion for displaying their finery, and for exchanging chit-chat with other prominent persons. They wanted the music to be cheerful and brief.

Kurt's certainly wasn't either of these. He was packing sorrow and revolt into his work, more of it than could be contained within the classical forms he favored. Pretty soon people would be calling him a "modernist," and that would distress him; he would go off and shut himself away more persistently than ever. Kurt wanted to tell the world that the German soul was in chains; while what the world wanted was to eat, drink, and be merry, and not be reminded that there was suffering anywhere. Dressed in his tails and fresh white tie, Kurt remarked on his way to Sept Chênes that he was Wagner producing *Tannhäuser* before the members of the Jockey Club of Paris.

He rendered a new composition of his own to which he had given the old title *Inner Life*. Most of those present were reducing their inner lives to the minimum, and didn't like the idea of having them exposed even to themselves; but they couldn't get away from the realization that something tremendous was going on here, and a few led in vigorous applause, and made it quite an event. As a result, the conductor of the orchestra in one of the Riviera casinos invited Kurt to give his piano concerto, and actually offered to pay him five hundred francs, at the prevailing rate of exchange about twenty dollars. As the orchestra would have to have all the parts copied out for the various instruments, they were really doing an unknown man, and a German, a great honor.

Of course it wasn't a first-rate orchestra, but all the same it was a chance for Kurt to hear his own orchestration for the first time in his life. He was as much excited as Beauty could have wanted him to be; those musicians who had to play regularly for the entertainment of gamblers and dancers were asked to come overtime and rehearse with an unknown genius—and strangely enough many of them caught his enthusiasm and tried to become a good orchestra. Lanny would drive Kurt in, and sometimes Rick would go along, neglecting his own *chef-d'œuvre*. A fire came from somewhere—the Greeks said from heaven—and entered the hearts of men; it came unannounced and in unexpected places, perhaps after you had given up hope of it and had even forgotten its existence; it overcame men's jealousies and suspicions, and they began to run here and there and whisper excitedly; there was a rustling and a murmur, as of the wind stirring in the myriad leaves of a grove sacred to the Muses.

VI

Robbie Budd came along on one of his business trips. He stayed for several days with Lanny in his studio, and told Beauty to "blow herself" to the grandest possible party. She gave her vote for an *al fresco* luncheon on the lawn at Bienvenu; caterers would bring it from Cannes, and there would be an orchestra and dancing, or tennis, or bridge—whatever people wanted. The weather proved friendly and it was a delightful occasion; Beauty's friends came to meet her former husband—so he was called—and speculate as to whether she was taking up with him again. Since the alleged "music-teacher" from Germany was on hand, they supposed not, but hoped for the worst.

Robbie always brought something from America, usually some new gadget of the sort for which the Yankees were famous: electrical irons for curling ladies' hair, or a device that you could put on the breakfast table to make your own toast—what wouldn't they think of next? Last year he had brought a thing called a radio-set; an extraordinary invention—the air or whatever it was all around you was full of music, and there was a tube with two prongs which

you stuck into your ears and you could plainly hear a whole orchestra. This time the traveler brought a bigger and better one,
having a horn like a phonograph, so that you could hear the music
anywhere in the room, and could dance to it. You could even listen
to a man making a speech in Paris! Robbie said this invention
might provide a new method of controlling public opinion; you
could tell the people whatever you pleased and they had no way
to answer back! He had bought a patent and launched a company
to manufacture a set that didn't have to have batteries, but could
be plugged into an electric light circuit, and you could make it as
loud as you pleased. Imagine thousands of people sitting in a hall,
and a great voice roaring to them about the dangers of voting for
the other fellow's candidate!

Robbie appreciated this idea, for his native land had just passed
through a red-hot Presidential campaign. There was what Robbie
called a demagogue by the name of La Follette who had come near
to ousting Robbie's prize President, the "strong silent statesman."
Robbie got fun out of that phrase, for he had met "Cautious Cal"
during the campaign and put up a lot of money to elect him, and
might have become ambassador to France if he had been willing to
give up his lucrative contract with Budd Gunmakers. Robbie said
Cal was the funniest little man that had ever come out of the Green
Mountains. He was so cautious that he didn't talk even to his wife.
She told a story about how he went to church, and when he came
home she asked him if the sermon had been good, and he said yes,
and then she asked what the preacher had preached about and he
said: "About sin." The wife asked: "What did he say about it?" and
the answer was: "He was agin it."

The opposite of the silent Coolidge was the overtalkative Scotch-
man, Ramsay MacDonald; at about the same time that Cal was
elected, Ramsay was ousted, and once more there was a Tory Prime
Minister of Britain. Robbie said that was all to the good, for now
the two countries could get their affairs on a business basis. Robbie
listened politely to the "liberal" ideas of Lanny's English chum and
didn't argue with him, but when he was alone with his son he said
that the British "liberals" and all others were in for a sad disillu-

sioning as to the conduct of the United States. The first thing Britain had to do, if she expected any sort of co-operation in future, was to get busy and pay the debts she owed. Robbie had spoken to the President on this subject, and the country storekeeper's son summed up his attitude in six plain Yankee words: "They hired the money, didn't they?"

Lanny had been hearing a lot about those war debts in Geneva, and he asked by what means they could be paid. Robbie was ready with an answer—he always was. He said that British citizens owned billions of dollars' worth of American stocks and bonds, and if Britain wished to she could tax those citizens and buy those securities to be turned over to the United States government. The reason the British wouldn't do it was plain enough—they were afraid for their world position in the face of intensified competition, and if they kept their claims upon American industrial plants they were sure of having some income anyhow!

VII

One of the purposes for which Robbie had come south was to see Zaharoff, so Lanny drove him to "Monty" and sat in at one of their sessions. The munitions king of Europe had at last obtained that prize which all his wealth had been unable to buy him—the wife for whom he had had to wait thirty-four years. The madman in the Spanish asylum had passed away, and just before Lanny had set out for Geneva the seventy-five-year-old Knight Commander of the Bath had escorted his lady-love, the Duquesa María del Pilar Antonia Angela Patrocino Simón de Muguiro y Berute, Duquesa de Marqueni y Villafranca de los Caballeros, to the *mairie* of the small town of Arronville, near the great estate of Château de Balincourt which Zaharoff owned. There the duquesa, now in her sixties, was made Lady Zaharoff in a strictly private wedding, the crowds being kept at a distance and the shutters of the *mairie* closed so that people with opera glasses couldn't see in. Lanny had read in the Paris *Temps* an account of the event, somewhat playful but still respectful, giving no hint of the fact that the elderly couple had been living together all over the continent of Europe for more than a generation.

Lanny listened while the two businessmen discussed oil company reports, bond issues, expansion plans, the personalities of executives, and of statesmen whom they considered as executives somewhat more tricky and difficult to control. Lanny was again surprised to realize how deeply his father was involved in money transactions with this man whom in former days he had described by names such as "old spider" and "lone gray wolf." *Pecunia non olet* was one of the few Latin phrases which Robbie had brought away from Yale—perhaps because it was associated with a slightly off-color story which had caught a college youth's fancy. Certainly Sir Basil's money now smelled sweet to the Connecticut Yankee, and the smear of oil which ran all through their conversation didn't offend his aesthetic sense.

Lanny listened to many things which the world would have paid a high price to know; among them the financial difficulties in which the enormous institution of Vickers was involved. The old Greek trader was withdrawing from the company, and hinted that he had unloaded a lot of his securities, but he didn't give any figures; he had been scared by all this peace talk, and had seen what was coming to the munitions industry in a world which scrapped its battleships and talked about boycotting aggressor states. He and Robbie discussed the subject in detail, and differed about it, for Robbie had got some small contracts for Budd's and hoped to get more on this trip; Zaharoff said that such contracts might help out a small concern like Budd's, but not Vickers.

Lanny never heard these two men of large affairs say that they hoped for the spreading of distrust among nations, in order that their own business might thrive; he never heard them say that they hated pacifists and pacifying statesmen because they kept Budd's and Vickers "in the red." But that was the attitude to which they were automatically driven; it was the underlying assumption of their talk. Lanny knew that many people hated them, and wrote books attacking them bitterly; he had started to read one of these, but it had made him unhappy. He knew that the "merchants of death" were the product of forces beyond their own control. It was a game they played, and they lost themselves in the excitement of it. He told himself that it wasn't so different from the thrill of selling pictures. He won thousands, while his father won hundreds of thousands and Zaharoff millions; but the feelings were the same.

VIII

Robbie told his son that Esther was going to bring the family to Europe for the coming summer. This was a part of every young person's cultural equipment—that is, among those who had the price. Lanny's stepmother didn't approve of Europe or of Americans who lived there, but she knew that Europe was history, Europe was art, and she couldn't deny her children their share. So they were coming, along with a million other tourists, as soon as school closed; reservations had been made and tickets paid for.

Also Zoltan happened to be passing, and gave his opinion that the time had come to let an eager world see the work of Marcel Detaze; they would rent a first-class gallery in Paris and have a "one-man show," not letting any dealers in on it; they would put extremely high prices on all the works, not with the idea of selling many but of lending glamour to them all. The latter part of the season would be best; Zoltan suggested June, and Robbie said: "Keep it open into the first days of July, so that the family can see it, and they'll help to advertise it in America."

Soon after that came a letter from the Robins. They too were interested in culture; they too were working hard at their studies and earning a vacation. Papa had promised to let them come to Paris and learn all they could about French music. They knew that Lanny was accustomed to spending his summers in or near Paris; might they see something of him, and perhaps visit art galleries with him? Would the kind Mrs. Chattersworth care to have Hansi play music for her? And so on. These two virginal youths had never got any hint of the real reason why Lanny spent his summers in or near Paris, and could have no idea that they might embarrass him by an offer of intimacy. Lanny didn't worry about it, for the pair were old enough to know their way about; he would say to them quite simply: "Madame de Bruyne has been my *amie* for the past few years." And that would be that.

Gracyn Phillipson, alias Pillwiggle, showed up on the Cap at the height of the season. Did she come on account of the delightful Lanny Budd, or was she too seeking culture? "Pillwiggle" of course wasn't any name, just an absurdity that Robbie had invented for a high-school girl presuming to act in a play at his country club. Since then she had made herself a name that even the flippant munitions man could remember. Her show had run in London for the better part of a year, after which she had gone back to New York and starred in a "triangle" play which hadn't done very well—but everybody agreed that it wasn't the fault of Phyllis Gracyn, whose acting had been brilliant. Her producer had given her a rather repulsive play, in which she had set out to carry off another woman's husband, and the man was such a dub that nobody cared very much who got him or what they did with him.

To be sure, the star might have gone to Florida for her rest; Florida also had a "season." It had alligators and palmettos and gambling-palaces, but it didn't have culture; except for St. Augustine it had no history, no romantic-sounding names that highbrow people talked about. So the ambitious young actress took the warm Mediterranean route, which brought her via Gibraltar and Algiers and Naples and Genoa; at this last port she parted from a young man of wealth whom she had been fascinating for eleven days, and took the train to Antibes and put herself up at the expensive hotel on the Cap. From there she wrote a note to Lanny; her friends now called her "Phil," but to him she would always be "your grateful and admiring Gracyn."

Naturally, he went to call on her. He had found her good company in London, and she had helped to bid up the price of the Detaze. She had asked a lot of questions about the Côte d'Azur, and he had said: "Come and see it." Now he decided—out of the vast knowledge of the heart of woman which he had acquired at the age of twenty-five—that he would tell Marie where he was going, and all about the Broadway celebrity whom so many people adored, but not he. Gracyn might be ever so expert at creating "triangles" on the stage, but she wouldn't make Lanny a part of one, and would Marie please not worry because he was polite to her? Marie promised, and Lanny kissed her to seal the compact.

IX

There were other celebrities on the Cap; it was coming to be a rendezvous for them, and they preferred one another's company, looking down on the uncelebrated as not worth bothering with. Already there were several at the hotel who called Gracyn "Phil," but when Lanny appeared she shook them all off and strolled with him to a quiet seat in one of the nooks with which the grounds had been thoughtfully provided. She was only a year or so older than he, but she had matured with surprising speed, and was nothing of the crude small-town girl who had been so excited over playing the part of Puck in *A Midsummer-Night's Dream*. She was the same small sylph-like creature who had been dowered with charm; but now she had made a study of it, both on stage and off, and could exercise it when and where she pleased—just as Hansi Robin could pick up a fiddle and a bow and extract melancholy or rapture from it. It didn't matter what Gracyn had been in the past, any more than it mattered that the bow was strung with horsehairs, and the fiddlestrings made from the intestines of a pig.

Her way of charming Lanny was to be his old pal, with whom it was a delight to be simple and straightforward. He, the old-timer, could come into her dressing-room and see her with her grease paint off and her wig on the dressing-table. Not literally, of course, for she wore a gay spring costume of white organdy and a wide floppy hat with pink poppies, and if all that color in her cheeks was real her sea voyage had certainly done her good. She chatted about old times, and what funny young things they had been, and how little they had guessed what was coming to them. He told her about the picture business, and about his friend who composed music, and how Rick was writing an extraordinary play. "Oh, has it got a part for an *ingénue?*" she asked.

Lanny, who had learned something about worldly arts himself, had meant for her to put that question, and he answered that it surely had. "I want a good play the worst way!" exclaimed the actress. "Could I read it?"

"I don't know," said the other. "Rick has always been fussy about getting his work just right before anybody sees it. He says that first impressions are permanent."

"You know how it was with us in the old days—we worked over a play and we all helped to get it right."

"I know, but Rick has ideas about literature. He wants to write something that will be published in book form and be permanent; and then he wants it produced just the way he writes it."

"That makes it very hard," replied the actress; "but anyhow, will you bring him to see me?"

"My mother wants you to come to our home, and he'll be there. Also you'll meet my *amie*."

"Oh, have you got an *amie*?" On the stage great ladies of fashion met unexpected situations with perfect *savoir faire*, and Gracyn had learned the phrase and what it meant.

Lanny explained that he had been for many years in love with a married lady who didn't live with her husband. Gracyn found that romantic, if disappointing; she said that she would feel exactly as though she were on the stage. Lanny laughed and said: "Don't behave as you did in your last play!" He had read reviews of it, and told her that he would always follow her career. Friendship was a pleasure, memory was a pleasure, and by means of art both could be extended.

"Oh, Lanny darling, you do say such lovely things!" exclaimed the star. "Why didn't I stick by you when I had you?"

"Because you wanted to go on the stage," he replied, gravely. "Don't say you aren't satisfied!"

"Who is ever satisfied, Lanny? Are you?"

"Indeed I am!" he replied.

X

Phyllis Gracyn came to tea, and there were the three embattled ladies of Bienvenu, each prepared to guard her own. But the actress kept to her role of an unpretentious small-town girl, grateful for an opportunity to observe life in a villa on the Riviera about which she had heard so much. She wanted to know an artists' model who had married a munitions king and borne him a son; ditto a French lady who didn't love her husband but did love a shining art expert; ditto the young wife of a crippled English aviator turned playwright. The Prussian artillery officer turned musician didn't often show up at tea parties, but Gracyn had heard about him, and it was her thought that if she proved herself a perfect lady, attentive, considerate, and in no way dangerous, she might have a chance to study all these fascinating types. It was what the French called the *haut monde*, which the actress learned to her great bewilderment sounded like "Oh Maud!" It was "high life," which the French pronounced the way it looked to them—"hig leaf!"

What are the emotions of a mother who meets for the first time a woman who seduced her son at the age of eighteen years? Well, it depends upon the mother, and also upon the son. Lanny laughed at Beauty's idea of the episode, insisting that Gracyn hadn't done him any harm, but had taught him to look out for himself. Seven years had passed, and bygones were far gone, so be a woman of the world, and maybe Gracyn would get interested in Rick's play and make a fortune for both author and star. Nina was not indifferent to that argument, and was quite sure that nobody was going to run off with Rick. As for Marie, if she had any anxieties she was too proud to reveal them.

Gracyn found the lame playwright difficult to deal with. He didn't show himself sufficiently eager for the attentions of a leading lady of renown. He told her that if ever he wrote a play that he thought would please the great public, he'd be happy to let her see it, but the one on which he was working was an attempt to portray the spiritual problems of the youth of his generation, and he thought that only a few were as yet awake to them. The story had to do with a young writer who had made a success, and whose socially ambitious wife looked forward to moving on to the next one; but the writer had become troubled with the problem of poverty *versus* wealth. His questionings were embodied in a girl of the ruling class—the scenes of the play were laid in England—who didn't appreciate her high social position, but wanted to help the workers to pull down her own class.

When Rick outlined this story, Gracyn looked worried. "It sounds as if it was going to be a 'radical' play."

"Stupid people will call it that," answered the playwright; which might or might not have been impolite.

Gracyn noted that it was going to be another "triangle," a theme which has been thoroughly tried out on the stage. She begged Rick to read her the first act, and he did so, with Lanny listening, and afterward they had a discussion, Lanny still listening. It carried him back to those old days which Gracyn called "funny," when he had been driving a real *ingénue* about the roads of Connecticut, she plying him with naïve questions about the world of fashionable society to which she looked up as if it were heaven. Now she had managed to climb there, by what sacrifices she would never tell; and here was a young man to that heaven born, assuring her that the place was "phony," its scenery *papier-mâché*, its glory tinsel and gilt, its dwellers spoiled and silly children, playing on harps out-of-tune music which they had got from degraded savages in the jungles of Africa!

To Gracyn all this sounded crazy; but if it was the latest thing, of course she wanted it. Rick quoted the phrase of an American philosopher: "the worship of the bitch goddess Success." But what did that mean? Didn't everybody want to succeed? And what was wrong with succeeding? You worked hard and got on top and then somebody told you it was all nothing. But how did Rick know? If everybody and everything was bad, who was going to judge? Said the darling of Broadway: "The way it seems to me, you and Lanny have had success all your lives and you've got bored with it. But I've just got mine, and, believe you me, I like it."

The fastidious young Englishman was amused and somewhat

touched. It was a statement of the *arriviste* attitude. It seemed characteristically American—because in that "land of unlimited possibility" the classes were in a state of flux, and it was possible for a girl who had been brought up in rooms over a decorating-shop to find herself at the age of twenty-six at a de luxe hotel, diving off springboards into the same water with the sons of German barons, Rumanian *boyars*, and members of the old French *noblesse*.

Lanny, who had watched the birth of this dancing star, now listened while the baronet's son patiently explained that modern society was based on commercialism, and therefore many of its values were open to suspicion; there were a great many people trying to hold onto their money, and making whatever pretenses were necessary to that end. Lanny wondered: Is Rick going to make a "radical" out of Gracyn? Or is he just going to get his play turned down?

He guessed that the latter would be easier, and so it proved. Gracyn didn't give up her stage career and become a crusader for social justice. What she did was to tell Rick that his ideas were interesting, and that she was grateful for the explanation; she would think about his play, and do what she could to find a manager who was interested in modern ideas; but it wouldn't be easy, because managers also worshiped the bitch goddess, who was known in the theatrical world as Box-Office.

To Lanny the actress said: "Your friend is a very bright man; but he doesn't realize what an advantage he has over the rest of us. You can't look down on things until you've got above them." Lanny said that was a good "line" for Rick's play.

XI

The lady from Broadway and Forty-Second Street made herself so agreeable that Beauty decided she was a real celebrity and gave a tea in her honor. The members of the smartest sets came, and Gracyn liked that a lot better than listening to talk about the woes of the poor. These ladies and gentlemen wore such elegant costumes and had such smooth and easy manners that it was hard indeed to believe they were *papier-mâché*, tinsel and gilt, spoiled and silly. Even those who criticized these people went on playing their game; Rick's wife wore a lovely tulle frock to this tea party, and her sweet little children were dressed up and showed off their perfect manners along with Baby Marceline; Lanny wore a simple sport-suit, but somebody had seen to it that it was freshly laundered. To a poor girl from a near-slum in a New England manufacturing town it appeared that the sons and daughters of the rich had had things far too easy.

There came a cablegram from a manager in New York who had a play for Gracyn, so she went to Marseille to take a steamer. Lanny offered to drive her, and invited Marie to go along, but Marie found an excuse for letting them go alone. Maybe an old friend might have something she wanted to say to Lanny; and so it proved.

"Darling," she began—it being the stage formula—"are you sure you are happy?"

"Perfectly, dear."

"It seems a queer sort of arrangement. It can't last forever, can it?"

"Forever is a long word."

"Do you think that you and I could ever be happy again, Lanny? I mean as lovers."

"No," he answered, promptly. "I don't."

"Why not?"

"It's like two comets flying about in space. We come near each other, and then fly a long, long way apart and stay for a long, long time."

"But I could stay with you, Lanny, if you wanted me very much."

"You're an actress, old dear. You know I like you, and I'll always be interested in what you're doing. Let's be friends."

She was leaning toward him, but he kept both hands on the steering-wheel, as good driving requires. She was going to a great city where there were plenty of men; perhaps she had one waiting there. Lanny's father had seen to it that he was well informed on the subject of venereal diseases, and Lanny didn't like the thought of Gracyn's men, and had no desire to take a chance on what they might or might not have had. He had made up his mind that one woman at a time was enough—and let it be some woman who wanted one man at a time!

The great steamer lay at the *quai,* and there were a couple of hours to spare. The actress had a comfortable cabin to herself, and there was a bolt on the inside of the door, so it would have been an easy matter for them to be alone for a while—such things have happened on transatlantic steamers, even in the *première classe.* But Lanny showed her the sights of the crowded *quais,* and took her to a little place where there was sawdust on the floor and *bouillabaisse* in bowls; he told her that Thackeray had praised this seafood mixture in a poem. When she revealed that she had never heard of that novelist, he told her about *Vanity Fair;* there had been people finding fault with fashionable society long before Rick was born!

When he took her back to the steamer he kissed her hand, French fashion, which she found delightful; he told her that he wished her all the luck there was, and promised to do his best to persuade Rick not to make that play too "radical." He quoted: "To go away is to die a little." She always took any quotation as a product of his own brilliance, so she said again: "What a darling you are!" Her last words were: "If ever you want me, Lanny, I'll come!"

23

And Both Were Young

THE Galeries Freycinet are strategically situated on the fashionable Rue de la Paix, and with money furnished by Lanny and his mother, Zoltan hired their two largest rooms for a month. This was a long time for a one-man show, but Zoltan was planning a campaign and was sure the public would keep coming. The first thing he did was to present a copy of one of Marcel's small seascapes to the art critic of one of the great Paris newspapers; so, a few days before the opening, this gentleman published a two-column article about a painter who was taking his place as a shining light in the galaxy of French genius. Without any advertising or promotion, Marcel Detaze was forging to the front of French representationalists; in spite of all the fads and follies of a frivolous time, it was possible for sound and solid work to find recognition in the art worlds of both Paris and London. This article was illustrated by the *Poilu*, the *Sister of Mercy*, and the aforementioned seascape; before the month was over, the seascape was placed on sale at one of the near-by galleries and sold for thirty-five thousand francs.

This one article started the ball rolling, and the other critics didn't have to be paid so much; there were even a few so important that they didn't have to be "sweetened" at all. Socially prominent persons had to be visited and told about the forthcoming event. For that purpose Lanny and his mother came to Paris a week in advance and told all their friends what they were there for. At such a time one reaps the reward of having such a person as Emily Chattersworth for a friend; she would spread the word among key people, and no one doubted her judgment in a matter of art.

The fact that Marcel's face had been burned off in the war, so that he had been forced to wear a mask, and that in spite of this handicap he had gone forward and developed a new style—this didn't make him a great painter, but it surely made him a great subject for conversation about painting; it made him popular with persons who had to fill newspaper space with gossip and comment. It caused his name to stand out, and gave people a reason for attending a one-man show instead of races at Longchamps, steeplechases at Auteuil, or polo at Bagatelle.

So the opening day was a real occasion. Zoltan acted as master of ceremonies; looking as if he had been "poured out of the egg," as the Germans say, precisely correct in his "morning," his striped gray trousers, large silk tie, and boutonnière. His slightly florid light-brown mustache lent the right touch of artiness. He had hired at a fancy price the best-trained doorman in Paris, who knew everybody who might by any possibility come to an exhibition; this man was provided with a telephone in a booth, and upstairs was a messenger who would bring word to the expert, so that he might be waiting at the head of the stairs. "Oh, how do you do, Lady Piddlington? Have you quite recovered, Your Grace?" Greeting each one in his or her own language—French, English, German, Spanish, Italian, Hungarian, even Swedish—he had a bit of them all. His manners were always French, they being international and romantic. He would stroll with the important ones and tell them what to see and they would see it.

Beauty Budd was, of course, an indispensable part of the show. You might say that she had been preparing for it ever since her arrival in Paris, a seventeen-year-old virgin. Meeting painters and posing for them, learning all the patter; meeting Robbie Budd and acquiring the manners of the *beau monde;* learning to dress, learning to be gracious, to exercise charm; meeting Marcel and loving him, so that he poured his genius into glorifying her. He had painted her when he had first met her, a piece of ripe fruit with the loveliest colors that nature can produce and that paint can imitate; a woman in a light summer dress, standing in the doorway of his cabin with a little straw hat and veil in her hand. He had painted her again in the days of his deepest tragedy, when she had stood by him and he adored her as the embodiment of womanly pity.

The picture, *Sister of Mercy*, was one of those things like Whistler's *Mother*, whose merit no critic can dispute, and which at the same time are so simple that the least-taught person can understand them and share their sentiment. There would always be some people standing in front of it; and when they saw Beauty, they would stare at her, and the blood would climb into her cheeks and stay there—in fact she wouldn't need any rouge at all for a month, though of course she would put it on for safety. She was forty-five, and no flower blooms, no fruit hangs on the tree, forever.

What she had to do for a whole glorious month was what she loved most of all things in the world: to dress up and meet swarms of the right people, and be admired by them, and tell them all they wanted to know about Detaze—who could tell them better than Madame Detaze, *veuve?* Zoltan had advised her to dress very simply, and with dignity, and she played to perfection the part of a woman who had been the saving influence in the life of a genius. The fact that she really had been that made the playing much easier.

II

Lanny also had his place in this more-than-one-man show. The stepson of the painter had shared the secrets of the last five years of his life; had traveled with him to Greece and Africa, watched his work of this period, and had something to do with its moods. This was also true of the war years—no doubt whatever that he had helped to bring some of these later works into being. He really understood Marcel's technique, and could talk to critics and experts about his development. Zoltan declared that many an art critic got his job because he was a relative of the newspaper proprietor or of his mistress, or because he owned the right clothes and would work for practically no salary. You saved the life of such a man when you tactfully gave him his cues and his technical terms.

Something even more important than being an art expert was being a social expert. Lanny knew how to talk to a duchess whose

title came down from the *ancien régime,* or to a Russian princess in
exile, or to a Hollywood movie star. He could guess that the
duchess had come because she loved paintings, but that she wasn't
likely to buy one; that the Russian lady was hoping to meet somebody to whom she could peddle her fur coat; that the movie star
wanted to be looked at and mentioned among those present. He
knew how to watch Zoltan and pick up his signals, whether he
should devote his time to this one or get rid of that one. He could
meet sudden emergencies—as when Zoltan introduced him to the
widow of a great department-store proprietor from St. Louis, and
this stout bejeweled lady somehow got things mixed up and proceeded to express to Lanny her wonder that one so young should
have painted all these lovely pictures. If he had dealt with that situation crudely and affronted a dowager queen of merchandising, he
might have deprived the people of the Mississippi valley of their
chance to have a great art collection brought among them.

To a show such as this came many sorts of people. Some really
appreciated the pictures, and followed Lanny about, drinking in
every word that he said. Some were persons of wealth, who might
have to pay in cold cash for their enthusiasm. Others bore upon
their persons evidence that they were poor—but Lanny would give
time to them, regardless of the high prices which he and his mother
were paying for these rooms. Old friends of Marcel, or young
painters and students from the Left Bank, word spread among
them—"*Il faut les voir!*"—and they came in clothes that had been
patched and collars that had been trimmed with scissors. Some
looked so ill-nourished that Lanny wondered how they could stand
up for long periods; their fingers were bloodless and wax-like as
they pointed out this or that feature of a canvas, and one couldn't
be sure whether the trembling was caused by excitement or ex-
haustion. But they were living the life of art which they loved,
and wine of the spirit was here poured out for them without price.

Great numbers of Americans were in Paris seeking culture, and
they always wanted the very latest thing. Some knew what they
were seeing, and others took it on faith. A couple of wizened little
old ladies whom Lanny guessed to be schoolteachers heard him

telling an English journalist about Marcel's life and work, and they attached themselves to his coat-tails and followed him from one painting to the next. They never made a sound, and in the end faded away as quietly as they had come; but for an hour or more they were his adoring pupils, drinking in culture like two topers who have knocked out the bung from a cask of wine.

Others did less honor to their native land. Two ladies of fashion, loaded with expensive decorations, gushing in unnecessarily loud voices—they too had read the papers, or perhaps somebody had told them, but they hadn't bothered to get it quite straight. They came up to a canvas and one said: "Who painted that?" The other drew closer and peered through her lorgnette. As it happened, if Lanny knew what a land- or seascape represented, he had given it a title as well as a number. The lady read and exclaimed: "Cap Ferrat! Oh, I adore his work!" Said the other: "Yes, it is grand. But I wonder why they call him 'Cap.'" The learning of the one with the lorgnette was equal to this test. "They say he was in the French army," she explained.

III

Two friends of the Murchisons from Pittsburgh showed up; elderly, quite plain-looking people, but you couldn't always tell by that. They said they liked the pictures, and spent a lot of time studying them and discussing them quietly. Finally they came to Zoltan and asked for the prices of three—one of the Riviera, one of Norway, and one of Africa. The prices were not posted on the pictures, but kept decorously on a typewritten list in the pocket of Zoltan and of an assistant. The cheapest of all the canvases was priced at fifty thousand francs, and the three which the old couple wanted came to a quarter of a million, or about ten thousand dollars. That didn't seem to worry them a bit; the man wrote out a check on a Paris bank and asked about arrangements to have the pictures shipped. Nothing was to be taken away until the exhibition was over.

Then an English couple, identifying themselves to Lanny as

friends of Rosemary, Countess of Sandhaven. This was a swanky young pair, dressed up to the last minute, the man with a monocle and the lady with a swagger-stick. She pointed it at a weather-beaten old Greek peasant, holding under his arm that little lamb which Mr. Hackabury had purchased and caused to be served for dinner on the yacht *Bluebird*. "How much is that one?" asked the Honorable "Babs" Blesingham, and when Zoltan said: "A hundred and seventy-five thousand francs," she exclaimed indignantly: "Oh, but that is cheek!"

Zoltan, who knew the manners of the British aristocracy, replied: "Your grandchildren may sell it for five thousand pounds, my lady."

She frowned as if she were doing mental arithmetic; then she said: "Well, anyhow, I like it. Send it around to my hotel when you're ready."

Zoltan, sure of himself and not awed either by smart costumes or by insolent manners, replied: "We are not reserving anything, my lady. If you wish to be sure of it, be so good as to make it definite."

"All right, Reggie, give him a check." Just as if she were tossing a five-sou piece to a beggar!

In the midst of all these excitements came the Robins. They had seen some of the paintings at Bienvenu, and now they saw them all, and were so excited that they wrote a long letter to Papa, enclosing some of the bought-and-paid-for newspaper clippings. The result was a telegram to Lanny, directing that the boys with Lanny's advice were to select a million francs' worth of the Detazes and have them shipped to him. Papa had just bought a palace in the suburbs of Berlin, it was revealed, and they were going to move into it, and Marcel's landscapes would hang on the marble walls of a very grand entrance hall where the proudest Prussian nobility had trod. Quite a step upward for a Jew who had been raised in a hut with a mud floor; also for a painter who had lived in a cabin on the Cap d'Antibes and dressed most of the time in a workman's blouse and a pair of corduroy trousers smeared with all the colors he had put on a hundred canvases!

Lanny couldn't give much time to the boys right then, but he had told Mrs. Emily about them, and they went out to Les Forêts

and played for her. She fell in love with them as Lanny knew she
must; she invited musicians to hear them, and made them happy
with her praise. She was one person who had no trace of prejudice
against the Jews; if they had better brains that was the hard luck of
the Gallic and Anglo-Saxon races! Lanny wasn't so sure about
Marie; but she knew how he admired this pair, and she couldn't
fail to invite them to her home and have them meet her two boys,
who were of nearly the same age and whose musical tastes she
wished to cultivate. Hansi was a good example for anybody's sons,
for all could see how hard he had worked and what a reward of
happiness he had won in his mastery of a great musical instrument. The boys made friends gladly and when the *Schieber* heard
how his dear ones had been received in two *châteaux*, he could consider that he had got double value for his million francs.

I V

The Budd family arrived on schedule. They had reservations at
the Crillon, Lanny's place of memories; he went there to see them
as soon as the boat-train arrived. Six years and a half had passed
since he had left their home; he had changed a lot, and wondered
how it would be with them.

It seemed to him that his stepmother hadn't changed at all. She
was one of those cool, quiet persons upon whom the years made
little impression; tall and still slender, with no wrinkles about her
eyes, no gray in her straight brown hair. She had parted from her
strange stepson on friendly terms, and greeted him as if it had been
last week. She had come to his world, where he would play the
host and she would accept his kindnesses as he had accepted hers;
she wouldn't approve of all that she saw, but she would be carefully polite, watch over her children, study the guide-books with
them, learn history and art—but not manners and surely not morals.

Robert, junior, was twenty and Percy a year younger. They
were handsome, upstanding fellows who had enjoyed the best possible upbringing, and had played football in prep school; both were
at Yale, the target which Lanny had been aimed at but had missed.

They were still repressed, and knew that it wasn't good form to show much excitement over being in a foreign country; but they had their own ideas about Paris, which they would reveal to Lanny before long. Their main desire was to get away from mother and Miss Sutton, the gray-haired lady who had been Bess's governess and had been as it were adopted; she traveled with the party as a combination of companion and secretary, doing the telephoning, buying the tickets, running the errands. No Budd would do anything so vulgar as to enlist among the "Cookies."

Bess was the one in whom Lanny had been interested in Newcastle. They had kept their promise not to forget each other, and had exchanged letters now and then, telling the news and enclosing snapshots. So Lanny knew that his half-sister had turned into a very proper young miss of seventeen; she was going to be tall, like her mother, and now she was what the English call "leggy." She had her mother's high round forehead and rather thin nose, but her brown hair was unruly like her father's; her upper lip was a little short, which made her smile rather quaint. She had candid brown eyes, and an expression of eagerness which mother and governess combined had been unable to subdue. Bess wanted to know, and not to have somebody tell her. She wanted to see Europe so eagerly that it hurt; she had kept her face pressed to the window of the train and of the taxicab. "Oh, Mummy, look!" Mummy would say: "Yes, dear." She had learned that it didn't do much good to say "Don't."

Now her wonderful half-brother was going to show her Paris: the Louvre, Notre Dame, Versailles, the Eiffel Tower— "Is that the Obelisk over there, Lanny? And is that really the Place de la Concorde? Have they taken away all the big guns? Is the picture exhibition still going? Mummy, can't we go over and see it right now?"

Esther wasn't ready to go out yet; she wanted time to prepare for the ordeal of meeting her husband's ex-mistress, who she had to pretend was an ex-wife; that was what Paris meant to a daughter of the Puritans, and no wonder she didn't like it in her heart. But she could think of no reason why Lanny shouldn't take the children to see his stepfather's paintings; the place was only five minutes' walk, he told them. So they set out, with the arrangement that they were to bring Beauty back for lunch.

Of course the three "children" had their curiosities about this mysterious mother of Lanny, about whom they had been told so little. Had the boys picked up any hint of the truth? If so, they were too well bred to reveal it. The Detaze show was the best of all places for them to meet the dubious charmer, with everybody paying court to her and two portraits presenting her in the best possible light—but not that naked one, which was safely locked in the storeroom at home!

Anybody who met Beauty could see that she was a kind soul. Naturally, she was in a flutter over meeting Esther's children, but then she was always in something of a flutter. She was still nearly as eager as Bess, interested in everybody and everything that came along. She wanted Robbie's children to approve of her, and she even had hopes that she might win their mother's regard.

The young people looked at the pictures, and Lanny told them the stories, and it was a most interesting lecture, something that couldn't have been had in Connecticut. It took them over the Mediterranean lands, and to the fiords of the Northland; it took them through the war, and taught them about French patriotism, as well as suffering and horror. The very elegant Hungarian art expert lent his aid, explaining the fine points about Marcel's technique. When the morning was over, the young Budds could never doubt that Lanny's mother had been married to a great painter. The prices asked for his work would have convinced them of that! Moreover, Mr. Kertezsi had told them that the French government had just purchased a Detaze for the Luxembourg. (He didn't tell them that he had let the government have it for a couple of thousand francs, so that he might have something with which to impress Americans.)

V

They went back to the hotel, where Beauty and Esther came face to face. The young people didn't realize that anything special was going on; they took divorces more as a matter of course than did their mother and, besides, young people are rarely interested in their elders' states of mind unless these are forced upon their attention. Assuredly that wouldn't be done by either of these disciplined ladies. It is one of women's duties to cover over and conceal the scars, the defacements, the wreckage caused by the sexual divagations of the male animal. Robbie Budd's two women kept smiling hard; Esther asked questions about the exhibition and Beauty answered them; both ordered something to eat and pretended to enjoy it. Meanwhile they measured each other, Beauty with tremulous concern, Esther with steady, businesslike glances which seemed to say: "You let me and mine alone and I'll let you and yours alone."

Really there wasn't any reason for their getting into each other's hair. Esther didn't begrudge the thousand dollars a month which Robbie paid to his former mistress, or the simple villa he had given her. In order to put his wife's mind at peace concerning his frequent visits to Bienvenu, Robbie had told her about Beauty's new lover. That, of course, seemed disgusting to a daughter of the Puritans; but so long as Esther didn't have to go there or to let the children go there, it wasn't her concern. She was prepared to believe that her husband's former mistress was no worse than most of the women who left their own country in order to enjoy the license of France. Esther knew how many had come in order to escape Prohibition, and she considered it a good riddance. Now when she saw this Madame Detaze, blooming so offensively, finding such pleasure in having paintings of herself hung in a gallery for the public to stare at, she was glad that the family program allowed only a week's stay in Paris, and none at all on that dreadful "Coast of Pleasure."

Knowing how her husband loved his first-born son and was determined to protect him, Esther said how greatly all her friends had been pleased with the Böcklins which Lanny had selected for her. It was her intention to visit the exhibition and perhaps acquire one or more Detazes for her home. Beauty said: "Frankly, we have put the prices very high because we don't want to sell too many. I'll tell Mr. Kertezsi to make them right for you." Esther replied: "Not at all! Please let me pay what anybody else would pay." That might be a way of making friends; or it might be a way of patronizing your husband's cast-off sweetheart. How difficult to be sure!

VI

Lanny said: "I hope you are free for tomorrow, for Mrs. Emily has asked me to bring you out to Les Forêts. Hansi and Freddi Robin are coming, and she has invited friends to hear Hansi play." Esther knew about Mrs. Chattersworth, and she had heard much about the Robin boys, their father being her husband's partner in so many profitable enterprises. She replied that they would enjoy visiting a great French château, and of course they must hear the young musician.

Lanny motored the family, Bess riding beside him and the mother and the boys in back. All the way it was history: the flight of King Louis and Marie Antoinette from Paris, and then the battle of the Marne, the first one, in which the Château Les Forêts had been so nearly wrecked, and the second one, in which Marcel Detaze had given his life to save Paris. Lanny told how the Germans had dumped the furniture of the château out of the windows, and how the old librarian had died of a broken heart. He told how Anatole France had talked on the lawn—the old gentleman had passed away just recently and had had a grand funeral in Paris. He told how Isadora had danced in the drawing-room—but not how she had tried to take her musician for a ride!

They arrived at the estate, and in the drawing-room where the best wits of modern France had exercised themselves the châtelaine received them graciously and introduced them to her guests—one of them the shepherd boy out of ancient Judea, the tall young David who had played the harp before the mad King Saul, the minstrel who had heard the voice of the Lord. At the luncheon table Hansi and Bess sat opposite, and each looked into the other's face and found something that neither had ever seen before. Bess saw fire in those large dark eyes; in the ascetic face she saw exquisite sensitiveness, as of someone who had come from a world where things were better.

Hansi saw what seemed to him the face of all his dreams, that would live in all the music he played from that hour forth. Each of them saw eager intelligence, asking a thousand questions of life and rarely satisfied with the answers it got.

In due course Hansi took his violin and stood by Mrs. Emily's grand piano, with Lanny sitting before it. On the rack was the piano part of Beethoven's violin concerto, a composition born of the master's deep stress. When Hansi sounded the opening theme it was as if the gates of heaven swung suddenly open before Bessie Budd; this strange-looking, tall young Jew took on the aspect of an archangel descending from the skies. She had never known that such sounds could be produced on earth. She needed nobody to explain this music, nobody to point out first and second themes, working out portions, modulations, harmonic intervals, or other technicalities; the music took her into its arms and carried her along through the many moods of which the human soul is capable. When Hansi came to the slow movement, the tears streamed down the maiden's cheeks; no use trying to stop them, she didn't even know they were there. Her mother, who never forgot the proprieties, not even for Beethoven, gazed at her in dismay. Bess's eyes were fixed as if she were in a trance; her jaw hung loose, as if she were trying to absorb the music through her mouth; she looked silly, and her mother wanted to nudge her—but unfortunately she was out of reach.

Esther was fond of music, or so she would have said; but she liked it to have dignity and restraint. She had been made uncomfortable by watching the seventeen-year-old Lanny in her home, pounding the piano as he did, losing himself so completely in it that he wouldn't know when his stepmother entered the room. Now here were two of them in that state, and no doubt it represented a lot of study and hard work, it was considered to be "classical," and all that; but the daughter of the Puritans disliked it, just as she would have disliked Beethoven if she had seen him composing it—roaming through the fields, waving his arms and shouting, or pacing up and down in his room, muttering to himself, rolling his eyeballs, carrying on like a crazy person.

VII

That stormy composition came to its end; and Esther was fully prepared to find that all the other persons in this drawing-room considered it a great work, or would pretend to. She was used to the idea that she was fighting against the current of her time, and wasn't succeeding in stopping it. Only the little bit around her, the members of her own family! Seeing her daughter sitting as if she thought the music was still being played, the mother arose and went to her and whispered: "Please, dear, try not to carry on so!" Bess started from her trance, and the mother went back to her seat and listened to excitable foreigners expressing their admiration for rare musical technique. Of course this dark-eyed Jewish youth loved his music, and maybe it was all right for him, it kept him busy and happy—but what did it do to people who let themselves get worked up to such frenzies?

They wanted him to play more, and the hostess said: "Some of your Jewish music." Her wish was a command, and Hansi, with his brother accompanying, played a new work called *Nigun,* from the *Baal Shem* suite of Ernest Bloch. This music of grief and despair Esther could understand better; she knew a great deal about the Jews, their ancient literature having been taught to her as Holy Writ. God in His dealings with His chosen people had of course been God, and you couldn't criticize Him; but the Jews in their dealings with God had been another matter, and Esther had got the feeling that they had been noisy, presumptuous, and disobedient, and had deserved most of the troubles that He had sent to them.

Their modern descendants in Newcastle, Connecticut, kept clothing-stores and drove shrewd bargains—to put it mildly. When Esther had learned from her husband that he had gone into business deals with one of them in Europe, mainly in order to please Lanny, she had been prepared for the worst, and when it didn't happen, she explained it by saying that of course a Jewish speculator had much to gain by keeping Robert Budd for a friend; he and his family aspired to rise in the world by attaching their fortunes to those of a prominent New England family. When Robbie came back and reported that the two sons of his partner were fine musicians and that one might be a genius, that was part of the same thing to Robbie's wife; now she saw the outcome—they had gained access to an elegant French château, and the musical genius was casting his net over Esther Budd's susceptible young daughter!

Esther couldn't find any fault with Hansi personally; she couldn't deny that he was of refined appearance and excellent manners; but that only made matters worse, it deprived the mother of any pretext for interfering with the operations of destiny. When she saw her daughter listening to Ravel's *Kaddisch* in that uncomfortable state of semi-hypnosis, she couldn't scold her publicly or drag her off privately. When Bess told Hansi how much she had enjoyed his playing, and when he told her that he would be delighted to come and play for her again, what could the mother do to break it up?

She learned to her dismay that the two Jewish youths were staying in Paris, and that Lanny was taking it for granted that they would be a part of the various sight-seeing expeditions. He had arranged for one to Versailles; he was telling now about the Île de la Cité and the sights to be seen there—Notre Dame, the Conciergerie where Marie Antoinette had been a prisoner, an old barracks occupied by the Sûreté Générale, where Lanny himself had been a prisoner on the day the treaty of Versailles was signed. He was telling the young people how he had been suspected of being a Red agent; he said it was a mistake of the police, but Esther knew about Lanny's Red uncle and wished very much that he wouldn't mention such unpleasant subjects to her carefully guarded children.

VIII

Whatever sins Esther Budd might have committed during her life she paid for during that unhappy week in Paris. She couldn't bring herself to break up their long-planned schedule. What excuse could she give for dragging the children away without seeing those sights about which they had been talking for months—yes, for years, ever since Lanny had brought his dubious glamour into their home? She couldn't say to her stepson: "We would rather see Paris by ourselves." Nor could she say: "We prefer not to have your young friends with us." Rack her brains as she might, she failed to find any reason why the Robin boys shouldn't stroll about the grounds and the palaces of Versailles with her children. Being Jews, they were bound to be on the lookout for slights, and Robbie had said: "If you meet those young Robins in Paris, be polite to them, because I've made a pile of money through their father." When Robbie used such a phrase, it meant a pile!

So there was nothing Esther could do but keep watch; and that didn't seem to do any good at all, for what was happening was like a river flood, it went on regardless of spectators. It was plainly a case of the distressing phenomenon known as "love at first sight," but it took forms to which the most exacting chaperon could make no objection. All that Bess wanted, apparently, was to listen to Hansi and her half-brother play duets. She wanted to hear everything they knew, and then hear it all over again, while she sat in her ridiculous pose, looking like St. Cecilia at the organ as painted by the German Naujok, a print of which Esther had hanging in her bedroom— never dreaming that it would come to life and plague her like this!

As for Hansi, he made matters more difficult by being so respectful that the mother couldn't find the slightest flaw in his conduct. Apparently he was so stricken with admiration for Bess that he couldn't bear so much as to touch her hand, hardly even to look at her continuously. Of course that was the right attitude for a Jewish lad of no family to take to a daughter of the Brahmin Budds, and if it hadn't been for Bess's temperament it might have been all right; but was Bess going to be content to sit on a throne the rest of her days and have this young genius kneel before her and bow his head in adoration? Not if Esther knew anything about her daughter—and she thought she did!

This torment went on during the excursion to Versailles and the one to Saint-Cloud. It went on amid the architectural glories of Notre Dame, the historial associations of the Hôtel de Ville, and even on top of the Eiffel Tower. It went on when Lanny purchased tickets and took them all to see Sacha Guitry. It went on in all the interims between excursions—for Lanny, in his role of young prince, had

had a piano brought up to the family suite, and lugged over a stack of music which he had in his rooms, and at Bess's suggestion Hansi kept his violin in the suite, so that every shining hour might be improved by the master-spirits of the past two centuries. Respect for "culture" required Esther to sit there and pretend to enjoy what was really an indecent spectacle, this open and public mating of two souls.

IX

The mother had had the fond idea that her little family of four, plus Miss Sutton, would "do" Europe as a group. But now it developed that the boys didn't want to sit in a hotel room, however elegant, and listen to violin sonatas, however well played. They wanted to see Paris. Lanny knew what this meant, for "Junior" had approached him rather timidly and asked for help in getting away from his mother and the rest, so that they might visit some of the "hot spots." These two youths had heard talk among the younger brothers of returned soldiers about the sights that were to be seen in such places; naked women dancing on the stage, and even more startling things. To come all the way across the ocean and miss them would mean being cheated badly.

Lanny didn't show surprise, for he had met other Americans in Paris, and not all of them young. He surprised his half-brothers by telling them that, though he had lived here most of his life, he hadn't ever been to those places. He said that they were run mostly for tourists, and that the French themselves didn't go. He talked with the pair frankly and learned that their father had done for them what he had done for Lanny in his time—that is, warned them about venereal diseases and the predatory nature of prostitutes, but he hadn't tried to teach them anything about idealism in sex. It was rather late now, because both boys had had experiences with girls in their factory town. Lanny told them that they really wouldn't find naked women so interesting; it was just a question of what one was used to—and why not try the Rubenses in the Louvre? It was cheaper and a lot safer.

Esther didn't know any of this, but she had her fears, and wasn't going to turn those boys loose on the streets of this most wicked of cities. She realized that it would seem rather absurd to send a gray-haired governess with them, so she found excuses to go herself. She thought that it was safe to leave Bess and Hansi together, so long as Lanny played accompaniments; but that was only because Esther didn't understand the many kinds of love-making which modern music has made possible. Hansi played Rubinstein's *Sphärenmusik* and Bess fell in love with him one way, and then he played Schumann's *Widmung* and she fell in love with him another way. He played the César Franck *Sonata*, which they had once played for Barbara; that set them to talking about an Italian syndicalist martyr —which caused Bess to fall in love in the most dangerous way of all!

She said she wanted to understand these ideas, but nobody would talk to her; either they didn't know or they didn't want her to know. Were the Socialists and Communists as bad as they were painted? What did Hansi believe about them and what did Lanny believe?— please tell her, and of course they did. Hansi expounded his beautiful dream of a world in which no man would exploit any other man's labor, but in which the great machines would be used to produce abundance, so that all might have a share; no child would know hunger, no old person would be homeless, no man would shed his brother's blood. It was an ancient Hebrew dream—Hansi quoted the prophet Isaiah: "And they shall build houses, and inhabit them; and they shall plant vineyards, and eat the fruit of them. They shall not build, and another inhabit; they shall not plant, and another eat; for as the days of a tree are the days of my people, and mine elect shall long enjoy the work of their hands."

A wonderful Hebrew dream, twenty-five centuries old, but it hadn't come true yet, and wasn't apt to during the lifetime of Bess's grandfather, the president of Budd Gunmakers, or of her other grandfather, the president of the First National Bank of Newcastle, Connecticut. The latter's daughter came in during this conversation, and it didn't stop when she appeared, for the reason that Bess had become kindled with the ancient Hebrew fire. Said she: "I always knew that it was wicked for some people to have so much and others to have nothing! . . . Oh, Mummy, you must hear what Hansi says about how machinery can make all the things we need now, so that nobody has to be poor!"

Lanny could understand everything that his half-sister felt, having been through it all when he was younger than she was. The sparks from the divine flame had leaped from Barbara's soul to his; they had leaped to the souls of the two Jewish lads, and so had been carried from Juan to Rotterdam and to Berlin; now apparently they were going to be carried from Paris to New England! What fuel would they find on that stern and rockbound coast? Lanny knew that the fire of social justice changes those whom it touches; it fills them with fervor and consecration, or else with irritation and rage. Impossible for Esther to conceal what was in her mind as she said: "Yes, dear. It is time for you to get ready for dinner."

X

At home in Bienvenu, before coming on this expedition, Lanny and his mother and Marie had discussed the entertainment of these guests from the land of the Pilgrims' pride. Lanny had thought of the Château de Bruyne as a delightful place for them to visit, for tea at least; and of Denis, *fils*, and Charlot, as French boys who would interest three young Americans. But Marie had said it was impossible; no woman could see her with Lanny and not become suspicious; Robbie's wife would think that he had committed an indecency in bringing her children to the scene of his offense against morality. "But how can she find out?" he argued; and his *amie* replied: "Women have a thousand ways of finding out. Suppose one of my boys makes a remark about your having stayed in our home, helped them with their piano lessons, gone fishing with them, played tennis—anything at all? Wouldn't your stepmother take notice?"

This discussion occurred in the intervals of a bridge game, and the fourth hand was M. Rochambeau, old friend of the family. A retired diplomat had time for reading, and he told Lanny about a novel by an American expatriate named Henry James; it was called *The Ambassadors*, and Lanny borrowed it. He was bewildered at first, but he put his mind upon the disentangling of those tremendous sentences, carrying a heavier burden of qualifications, reservations, modifications, stipulations, circumstantiations, elucidations, and other assorted subtleties than had ever before been crowded between two small black dots on a printed page. But finally he got into the story, and of course saw himself in that expatriate Bostonian, and watched the uncovering of his deadly sin in Paris. He finished the book before he left Juan, fully decided in his mind not to take the chance of bringing Marie's and Esther's progeny together.

What happened was that Marie chanced to visit the exposition at a time when Esther and her brood were there, and Lanny hardly dared speak a civil word to his *amie* in his stepmother's presence. After the ordeal was over and he met Marie at their rendezvous, she gave him proof of the strange intuitive powers of the experienced woman of society. Said she: "Your sister and Hansi have fallen in love."

"Oh, surely not!" exclaimed the stupid male creature.

"They are so much in love that their eyes cannot meet without a flutter."

"I thought she was moved by his music."

"Women aren't moved by music," declared Marie. "Women are moved by musicians."

XI

A day or two later Hansi came to Lanny and confessed. Bess was leaving in a couple of days, and he might never see her again. What should he do? He couldn't keep the tears from his eyes.

Lanny talked it out with him. He said that, so far as he personally was concerned, he thought it would be a grand match, and he would try to make it. Doubtless it would win him the everlasting enmity of his stepmother, who was bound to have some high state enterprise in mind—it would be the Empress Maria Theresa of Austria and her daughter Marie Antoinette.

"How will your father feel about it?" Hansi wanted to know.

"Robbie's a pretty good sport," replied Lanny. "He has some of the fashionable prejudices—we've got to face the facts, you know, Hansi."

"Of course. I know I'm a Jew."

"Robbie likes your father, and he admires you. He doesn't know much about music, but if you make a success he will hear about it."

"I *must* make a success, Lanny! I have waited too long!" Poor Hansi's proud aloofness had been knocked into a cocked hat.

"You're both young yet."

"Listen, Lanny—this is important. I have an old teacher who has moved to New York. He was in Berlin this spring and heard me play, and said he might get me a chance to make my debut with the New York Symphony there."

"Oh, grand! That would be a wallop!"

"You think Bess would come to hear me?"

"Of course she'd come. Maybe I could pull wires and arrange for you to give a concert in Newcastle. After the New York appearance, of course!"

Lanny advised Hansi to speak to Bess, but said he couldn't do it; his teeth chattered when he even thought of it. And, besides, what chance did he have? They wouldn't leave him alone with her for a minute. He could only speak with his music, and hope that she would get its meaning. Lanny replied that while program music was supposed to portray all sorts of natural phenomena, he didn't know any that would set a date for a wedding.

XII

They were going to the Louvre that afternoon. Lanny spent some time explaining the *Mona Lisa* to his half-sister, pointing out its qualities and telling her about Leonardo. When the others moved on he said: "Let's stroll the other way. I want to show you something."

They strolled; and perhaps Esther noticed it, but she couldn't very well object, for she had Hansi by her side, and it was of him that she was afraid. Lanny took Bess to a seat and got her firmly settled so that she wouldn't keel over; then he said: "Look here, kid; Hansi's in love with you."

She caught her hands together. "Oh, Lanny!" and then again: "Oh, Lanny!" Lovers are rarely original, and what seems eloquence

to them doesn't impress a third party, the sober man at the feast.
"Lanny, are you *sure?*"

"He has chills and fever whenever he speaks your name."

"Oh, dear, I'm so happy!"

"Did you think you weren't good enough for him?"

"I thought I didn't have anything he'd care for. I'm just a stupid child."

"Well, he assumes that you'll grow up."

"Will he wait for me?"

"I'm sure he will, if you ask him to."

"But he ought to ask *me*, Lanny!"

"He's too frightened of our god-awful family."

"But Hansi is a wonderful person! He has more than all of us put together."

"In his heart I dare say he knows it; but he doesn't think that we know it. It'll make the devil of a row, you know, for you to marry a Jew."

"Tell me, Lanny, do you think there's anything wrong with the Jews?"

"Bless your heart, old dear, there are so many things wrong with all of us—thee and me included."

"But I mean—so many people look down on them. What is the reason?"

"Well, Mrs. Emily thinks they have better brains than we have; or maybe they work them harder."

"Jesus was a Jew, Lanny!"

"I know; but the rest of them treated him badly, and they've been paying for it ever since."

"Lanny, I ought to tell Mummy, don't you think?"

"Indeed, I think it's the last thing on earth you should do!"

"But I want to be fair to her and Father!"

"If you tell her, you'll just keep her in misery, and she'll do the same for you. If you part friends with Hansi, she'll hope that you'll forget him, and you can go on with your school work without any fuss."

"But Hansi and I will have to write to each other."

"Write nice friendly letters—'All well, and hope to see you soon.' Tell him the news, and let your mother see his letters. Sign them all, 'yours truly'—that's enough."

"Are you sure it'll be enough for Hansi?"

"He'll be walking on the clouds until the day comes."

"And then what, Lanny?"

"Wait until you're eighteen; then, if you haven't changed your mind, tell your mother that you're going to get married."

"How will she take it?"

"Pretty hard, I imagine; you'll have to be ready for the worst. But have your mind made up, and don't give way. It's your affair; it means more to you than it can mean to anybody else." He thought for a space and then added: "Perhaps it might be wiser to go to Robbie first and get him on your side. You'll have a hold on him, because Grandfather broke up his love affair when he was young, and he knows how it feels. He told me all about it, and he took it terribly hard. Remind him of it, and that will break him down!"

24

To Madness Near Allied

I

THE new Tory government of England rejected the Geneva Protocol, which had been planned to bring peace to Europe by the method of boycotting aggressor states. The British gave several reasons, the most important being that the United States refused to pledge its support to the program. If the aggressor could buy all he needed from one great country, the other countries would be depriving their businessmen of profitable trade to no purpose. That statement set everybody in the States to debating; the Wilsonites, of whom there were many, insisted that their country was betraying the hopes of mankind. The crippled champion of internationalism had been in his grave more than a year, but his arguments lived on, and Lanny listened and as usual saw both sides of a complicated question.

Robbie Budd came over on some of his many affairs. He was the plumed knight of isolationism, riding at the head of the procession with a pennon on his lance. He said that both Britain and France were stumbling in the march of history, and might soon fall out. They were adhering to antiquated methods in industry and refusing to modernize their plants. America, on the other hand, renewed its machinery every decade, and could turn out goods faster and better than any other nation. All we had to do was to arm ourselves and be ready to meet all comers, but keep out of other people's quarrels. Let them destroy themselves if they wanted to; on that basis the world would be ours.

Robbie worshiped a deity known as *laissez faire*. Let manufacturers everywhere produce what goods they pleased and offer them in whatever market they could find; let government keep its hands off, and the intelligent men of the United States would make prosperity permanent. In the old days there had been crises and panics, but Robbie said that modern technology had solved that problem; mass production of goods at ever-cheapening prices was the answer to everything. Employers could afford to pay high wages, money would buy more and more, the workers would attain an ever-higher standard of living. The solution of this problem was America's; no other nation could approach her, and the one thing she had to fear was political demagogues throwing monkeywrenches into the machinery. Robbie said he didn't know why that name had been given to a useful tool, but it fitted the politicians who presumed to meddle with the production and distribution of goods.

Fortunately, the country had that most admirable of presidents, that strong silent statesman who never interfered with anything, but was happy to stroll through the power-plant and listen to the rich humming of the dynamos. Nobody was going to get Cautious Cal into any sort of foreign entanglement, no one was going to get him to stop any American oil man or munitions man from selling his products wherever in the world he could find a customer with the cash. The Vermont country storekeeper's son was going to sit tight in the comfortable mansion which the government provided him and save all he could of the $6125 per month which would fall due to him, up to and including the fourth day of March 1929. To Robbie Budd that was equivalent to saying that God was in His heaven and all was right with the world.

Robbie himself was "sitting pretty," but of course in a much more highly priced seat. He never told his son just how much his services to his country were bringing him, but from one sign and another Lanny knew that it was a very large sum. When Lanny said that he no longer needed the three hundred a month that his father was sending him, Robbie smiled and said it would be too much of an effort remembering to tell his secretary to stop it. When Bub Smith presented a bill for salary and expenses incurred in certain confidential work having to do with Standard Oil in the Near East, Robbie glanced at the account and read: "Eight thousand one hundred and seventy-five dollars and twenty-eight cents." He wrote a check for ten thousand, and remarked: "I couldn't manage to get all those figures straight."

II

A delightful thing to have such a father—and a temptation to agree with him on matters of business and finance. Very certainly the system of *laissez faire* was vindicating itself so far as it concerned Lanny Budd's own affairs. That system was pouring thousands of rich people into the playground of Europe, their pockets bulging with more money than they knew how to spend; quite literally bulging, for Lanny met men who thought nothing of carrying a hundred thousand-franc notes in a billfold, and when he asked one of them why he did it, the answer was: "Well, I might want to invite you to lunch." If these people had any culture at all—and many of them did—it was the easiest thing in the world to seduce them with the prestige of great paintings. Lanny's position became that of the fishermen on the rivers of Oregon during the latter part of the month of July; catching salmon becomes a labor, not a sport, and one never wants to see or smell or taste another fish.

People came every day and begged to look at Detazes, until that too became a nuisance; you had heard everything said that could be said, and you suspected the motives of people who posed as your friends and hoped to get a lower figure. "Boost the prices," Robbie said—that being the businessman's way of reducing an excessive demand. But it didn't seem to work in the case of art, for there was no way to determine the cost of a canvas; it was worth what you could get, and the more you asked, the more the customer seemed to value it. The dealers would come, and when you showed reluctance to sell they would assume that it was a business maneuver, and would go on making offers until it became fantastic. Lanny thought this couldn't last, but Zoltan was in command, and he said there might be a break in the case of work that was faddish, but not for solid merit like Marcel's. Ask a high price, pay some of the money as a tip to get the high price talked about in the papers—and then you could ask still higher prices!

Lanny had so much money that he didn't know what to do with it, and had to ask his father's advice. To Robbie that was a delightful experience; to have this playboy, of whose future on its practical side he had begun to despair, come of his own free will and ask how to invest a hundred thousand dollars that he had earned without a stroke of help from his father—well, that was something to go home and tell to the old man of the Budd tribe! Robbie sat down and made out a schedule of what he called a "portfolio," a list of gilt-edged stocks and bonds which his son was to acquire. Robbie took as much interest in it as if it had been one of those crossword puzzles which had become the rage. He wanted to explain it to Lanny item by item—A. & P., A. T. & T., A. T. & S. F.—as if Lanny could ever remember all those initials! The son wrote a check on his bank in Cannes, the father sent a cablegram, and, by the magic which American businessmen had contrived, all those valuable pieces of paper were in a vault in Lanny's name before he had gone to sleep that evening. Robbie estimated that his son would enjoy an income of more than seven hundred dollars a month for the rest of his days, and without ever doing anything but signing his name. How could anybody question the soundness of a world in which such a miracle could be wrought?

Yet Lanny couldn't keep himself from performing that unreasonable mental action. No longer an innocent child, he looked about him at the idlers of this Côte d'Azur and they had ceased to appear glamorous. He saw gambling and drinking and assorted vice, and what seemed to him an orgy of foolish and profitless activity. He saw swarms of parasites preying upon the rich, getting their money by a thousand devices, few of them so harmless as persuading them to purchase old masters. He saw, too, the signs of poverty and strain; when he went into the great cities he was made sick by the spectacle of human degradation, and he had too much brains to be able to salve his conscience by giving a coin to a beggar now and then, as some of his kind-hearted friends would do.

The spacious drawing-room of Bienvenu was cool on hot days, and a generous open fire kept it warm on cold nights. In it were courtesy, kindness, love, and every kind of beauty that the skills of men had been able to create: oriental rugs of rich harmonious colors on the floor, inspired paintings on the walls, long shelves full of masterpieces of literature old and new, the music of a piano, a phonograph, and the newly devised radio at command. But outside, waves of human misery beat against the foundations and winds of social rage howled about the eaves. The ladies of this house cried to Lanny: "Why have we worked so hard to make safety and comfort for you, only to see you go out into the midst of storm and danger? Is it because we haven't done our duty? Is it lack of devotion or of charm on our part that you wish to throw yourself into a chaos of clamoring greeds and hates?"

III

In Cannes lived a Spanish youth by the name of Raoul Palma. He was an ardent Socialist, and had brought a letter of introduction from Jean Longuet; "a faithful party worker," was the editor's phrase. Physically Raoul was a study for a painter; slender yet active, with delicately chiseled features and an expression of sweetness almost feminine—Lanny wished that Marcel had been there to immortalize him. The young man spoke all the languages of the Latin tribes, and had a good education, but worked in a shoe-store because that appeared to be the only employment available to one who wished to spend his evenings agitating for Socialism among the workers.

Cannes was thought of as a playground for the rich; a city of lovely villas and gardens, a paradise of fashionable elegance. Few stopped to realize what a mass of labor was required to maintain that cleanliness and charm: not merely the servants who dwelt on the estates, but porters and truckdrivers, scrubwomen and chambermaids, kitchen-workers, food-handlers, and scores of obscure occupations which the rich never heard about. These people were housed in slum warrens, that "cabbage patch" where Lanny's Red uncle had taken him to meet Barbara Pugliese. The ladies and gentlemen of fashion didn't know that such places existed; they could hardly believe you when you told them—and they wouldn't thank you for having told them.

If the slums of the Riviera were ever to be razed and decent housing provided, it could only be through the action of the workers themselves; the rich wouldn't make any move unless they were forced. The question was whether it was to be done by the method which the world had seen in Russia and didn't like so well, or whether it could be carried out by orderly democratic process, such as the workers of Vienna and other Socialist cities were proceeding to apply. Which way you chose determined whether you called yourself a Communist or a Socialist; whether your opponents named you Red or Pink. Raoul Palma, idealist and something of a saint, persisted in advocating the patient and peaceful way. His hobby was what he called "workers' education"; he wanted to get the tired laborers to come to school at night and learn the rudiments of modern economic theory: just how their labor was exploited and just what they could do about it. He wanted a Socialist Sunday school, to which the workers' children might come and learn those facts which were not taught in schools conducted by their masters.

Raoul had got a little group together, and they had raised a few francs from their earnings and bought pencils and paper and set to work, at first in an open shed in summer, then in an unused store-room. They needed more money; and how could Lanny, believing what he did, fail to help them? He rented a proper room with a stove to heat it when the mistral blew; when he saw how pathetically grateful they were, and how fast the enterprise expanded, he offered the young leader a pension of fifty francs a week, about two dollars, so that he might retire from the business of fitting shoes on ladies' feet and devote all his time to workers' education. Lanny would go now and then to the Sunday school, and thereby he acquired a number of what the ladies of his family considered undesirable acquaintances; he learned the names of a swarm of little brats who of course didn't know that they were brats, and would come running up to greet him when he was on his way into a fashionable hotel or restaurant, throwing their arms about him and calling him "Comrade Lanny"; which was hardly *en règle*, to say the least.

Lanny had entertained his little half-sister with Beethoven's *Country Dances:* delightful tunes with pronounced rhythms, to which she and Nina's children would caper about the room like incipient Isadoras. Why not have an entertainment for the children of the workers, and give them a chance to develop their latent talents? If Lanny could have had his way he would have brought the whole troop to Bienvenu and let them dance on the loggia, and Marceline with them; but the bare idea frightened Beauty out of a night's sleep. To her the very word "workers" spelt Red revolution and bloodshed; she had White Russian friends in Cannes and elsewhere who told her terrible stories of the outrages from which they had escaped. Out of the kindness of her heart, Beauty gave these people money, and a part of it went to maintain White Russian papers and propaganda in Paris. So Beauty's money worked against Lanny's money, and perhaps neutralized it. Lanny went and rented for one evening a sort of beer-garden in a workers' district, and there he had a party and played Beethoven's *Country Dances* for his little Red and Pink *gamins.*

IV

In October of that year 1925 the governing statesmen of the great
nations of Europe gathered for an important conference at Locarno,
a town on one of the Alpine lakes which are divided between Switzerland and Italy. Rick didn't attend this affair, because his new play
had been accepted by one of the little theaters, and he was rewriting
part of it, in spite of his literary *hauteur*. Lanny didn't go, because
Marie wouldn't keep him company and it wasn't so much fun alone.
He read accounts in the papers and magazines, some of them signed
by men he knew. Everybody considered it the most important conference since the war; Lanny, who had seen so many of them, tried
not to feel cynical about it.

Aristide Briand, the innkeeper's son, was Premier of France again,
and had taken up the job which he had been forced to abandon at
Cannes nearly four years earlier. This time he didn't need any fashionable ladies to get him together with the Germans; for now France
had the Ruhr and was getting so little out of it that peace and disarmament were the *mots d'ordre*. The German Chancellor was still
Stresemann, the pacifier, while the British Prime Minister was Sir
Austen Chamberlain, a proper Conservative with a monocle, so whatever he did would be ratified by Parliament. For the first time since
the war the great nations of Europe met as equals, and the word
Allies was not spoken at a conference.

Of course the diplomats had been working behind the scenes for
months, and had planned exactly what they were going to do. They
adopted a series of treaties, renouncing war as an instrument of foreign policy. Germany pledged herself to arbitrate all disputes with
her neighbors. All these proud nations abandoned a portion of their
sovereignty, and the glad tidings went out over the earth that a new
spirit had been born. Germany was to be admitted to the League of
Nations, and hopes were held out that before long France would
consent to withdraw from the Ruhr. The word Locarno became
one of magic, from which all good things were expected. Currencies
would become stable, trade and industry would revive, the unem-

ployed would be put to work. Even disarmament agreements were being discussed.

All this, of course, struck a sour note with Robbie Budd and Zaharoff. Robbie had promised his father and brothers fresh trouble in Europe and all over the world, and so his prestige was at stake. It was expecting too much of human nature that he should credit the fine promises of statesmen looking for votes. Robbie wrote to his son that the Germans were buying arms through Dutch and Italian agents, and doubtless some of these arms were going through Locarno while the statesmen were in session. He said also that there was another famine in Russia, and that when the inevitable collapse in that chaotic land occurred, all the bordering nations would grab what they could and the fat would be in the fire. "I have a chance to buy some Budd stock," wrote the father. "Shall I add it to your portfolio? It will give you weight with the family."

V

An Italian refugee by the name of Angelotti came to the gate of Bienvenu, having a letter of introduction to Lanny. A servant admitted him, saying that Lanny was expected, and the man sat on the front veranda for an hour or more. Beauty saw him and considered him a sinister-looking person—many Italians have dark hair and eyes, and are reputed to be vengeful, and to carry stilettos and the like. Beauty's distrust of the Reds was of long standing—she having a brother among them. This visitor wanted money, of course; it was a kind of polite blackmail to which Lanny exposed himself, and what would they do if he refused their requests? A thankless thing, for such people rarely repaid, even with gratitude; according to their theories, all your money ought to belong to them, and in giving them a part you were doing less than justice. Beauty would have liked to give orders that all such strangers should be sent packing, but she couldn't very well, for the prosperous Lanny was now paying half the expenses of the place so that his mother might be able to pay her dressmakers and hairdressers and the rest.

It happened that there was a murder committed in Paris shortly afterward, and the police were reported to consider it political and to be looking for an Italian anarchist by the name of Angelotti. It may not have been the same man, but Lanny said that even if it had been he would have refused to worry, because such cases often represented police frame-ups, or perhaps newspaper efforts to discredit what they chose to call "subversive movements." Naturally, this statement caused Beauty distress of mind, and they had an argument, and afterward the mother was uneasy, because Lanny might feel that his rights in the home were being denied him, and he might take up the notion to go off and get a place where he could see his friends when he pleased.

Beauty and Marie shared this problem, consulting each other and worrying together. And of course Lanny knew about it; people can't keep things from each other when they are living in the same house. He would go out and spend his time with alarming-looking strangers; then he would find his *amie* looking hurt; he would ask her about it, and all her tact would be needed to keep a controversy from getting started.

VI

Beauty had other worries, more and more of them, and all centering on Kurt. A sense of doom hung over her, knowing that she had had no business to take a lover so much younger than herself, and that some day fate would present the bill and she would pay with her happiness. Day and night she watched her German idealist and studied him, trying to please him, making herself a slave to this strange being. Kurt was a man of conscience, and she could hold him only by being good; but it must be his peculiar kind of goodness. She would lose favor with him whenever she revealed an excess of worldly vanity; he would let her have a fling now and then, just as if she were a drunkard going off on a spree, but it mustn't last too long or cost too much, and then he would expect her to come home and be a good German *Hausfrau*, managing her servants and taking care of her child according to his ideas of discipline.

With the passing of the years Beauty had grown more and more pro-German in her feeling. Not publicly, for she couldn't expect her friends to agree, and the best she could achieve would be to keep them away from the subject. She wasn't a political person, and couldn't understand all the forces and factors involved in the struggle for the mastery of Europe. What she wanted was peace in her time, and she would not haggle about the price. The news that came from Locarno rejoiced her soul; at last Germany was going to be allowed to take her place in the sisterhood of nations, and to build up her foreign trade and be able to import food for her hungry children. Germany did really feed her children, and care for her aged, and build decent homes for the workers, all of which practices Beauty praised ardently—never dreaming that they had anything to do with the dreaded Socialism. When her brother Jesse came along and uttered one of his familiar cynicisms, that all capitalist states must have things which they could get only by war, Beauty gave him a scolding so severe that it both startled and amused him.

During the period of Beauty's "spree" in Paris, Kurt had stayed at the villa, working on one of his compositions. When he wanted company he would play music for Marceline, and teach her German folk songs; she had already begun piano practice under his direction—and it wasn't going to be any haphazard, hit-or-miss technique such as Lanny had acquired. Then a cousin of Kurt's came with his young bride to Nice to spend a part of the summer, and Kurt would get on the tram and ride to visit them. When the cool weather came, his aunt, the Frau Doktor Hofrat von und zu Nebenaltenberg, returned to the apartment in Cannes from which she had been rudely removed during the war; she had vowed that she would never come back, but her health was troubling her, and now the Locarno settlement decided her to give the French another trial. She had told her nephew that Lanny Budd's mother was *unschicklich*, so she could hardly be deceived by the pretense that Kurt was Lanny's music-teacher; but men have been known to do worse things than succumb to the wiles of a fashionable widow, and any arrangement which survives over a period of six or seven years acquires a certain sort of respectability. Kurt came to visit his aunt and was not rebuked; he played his compositions for her and they were appreciated.

Thus in one way or another Kurt was meeting Germans. They had been coming back to the Riviera, and now with the new spirit of peace there arrived German steamers, brand-new and beautiful models of what a steamer should be, full of large and well-fed passengers desiring to put on bathing-suits and expose their fat ruddy necks and shaven bullet-heads to the semi-tropical sun. They brought with them rolls of money which had mysteriously become more stable and desirable than the franc; with it they could eat French food and drink French wines and put up at the best hotels; French waiters would serve them, and French *couturiers* would labor diligently but for the most part vainly to make their women *chic*.

Many of these Teutons were what Kurt in old days had described as "hottentots," crude persons without culture, and he had no more interest in them than in Americans or Argentinians of the same sort. But now and then he would meet some music lover or scholar, someone who had heard his music, or, hearing reports about it, wished to hear it. Beauty was always glad to have Kurt's friends come to the villa, any who were willing to keep up the polite fiction under which he lived with her. Once more the dream of the "good European" was spreading, and Bienvenu would become a center of international culture. This was the thing for which Lanny had been working and struggling ever since the happy days when the three musketeers of the arts had danced Gluck's *Orpheus* at Hellerau and had been certain that they were helping to tame the furies of greed and hatred. Lanny felt that the war was at last really over, and that Britain, France, and Germany were reconciled in his American home.

VII

At Christmas time the two friends made their customary journey north. This had now become for Lanny a business as well as a pleasure trip. He was learning more and more about the art world;

it happened almost automatically—a person from whom he bought a picture would tell his friends about an agreeable young American who had his suits of clothing made with a large pocket inside the vest, having a flap and a button, with a safety-pin as an extra precaution; from this secret hiding-place he would produce a flat packet containing an incredible number of immaculate new banknotes, and would count them out on the table and let them lie there until one could no longer withstand the temptation and would say: "All right, the picture is yours." Lanny and Zoltan between them had found so many persons who wanted to buy old masters that it was continually a problem with the playboy whether to do the things he wanted to do, such as listening to Hansi's music and to symphony concerts, or to go out and work up another deal.

Visiting Hansi was now quite a new experience. It appeared that the pressure upon a rich man to live according to his wealth was irresistible, and here were these Robins in this new and sumptuous nest, with servants in livery and everything perfectly appointed. Johannes was a man of action, and when he wanted something done he went and got experts and had it done right. In this palace he had been confronted by gaping rows of shelves in the library, and he had promptly had the shelves measured, and had summoned the manager of the oldest-established bookstore in Berlin and astounded that personage by saying that he wanted one hundred and seventeen meters of books. There they were, all sizes to fit the varying height of the shelves, and all subjects to fit the varying minds of readers. Johannes didn't have time for them just now, but his children and his children's children were going to enjoy culture.

The Detazes pleased the trader greatly, but they looked lonely on those vast walls, and he said that he wished to place an order for paintings by the square meter, or perhaps the square kilometer. Impossible to leave the place bare, because what was the use of having it if you didn't have it right? "Isn't it better to hang your money on the walls than to hide it in a bank vault?" asked Lanny's old friend. "Here I am getting twelve and fifteen percent for my money, and what am I going to do with so much?"

"You mean that's the interest rate?" asked the younger man, somewhat shocked.

"Our new rentenmarks are scarce," smiled Johannes. "They must be kept that way to be sure there's no more inflation!"

He went on to say that he knew one person whose taste in art he trusted wholly and that was the wonderful Lanny Budd. If he trusted Zoltan Kertezsi, it was because Lanny told him to. His idea was that Lanny and Zoltan should make a study of the palace and turn every room into a small art gallery—not too much, but the right number of pictures with the right atmosphere; they would go scouting over Europe with *carte blanche* to buy whatever they considered proper. Lanny was staggered, and said, well, really, he didn't feel equal to it, he hadn't intended to get so deeply into business as all that. "Take your time," insisted the money-master. "It'll be all right if I tell people that I'm looking for the best."

For a while the younger man wondered whether all this was part of the price of his half-sister, tactfully offered. But Hansi told him that he hadn't mentioned the love affair to either of his parents. Only Freddi knew—having been there and seen. They had decided that maybe they didn't have a right to speak of the matter; maybe nothing would come of it, and, furthermore, Papa might prefer not to know, because if he knew he might feel in honor bound to tell Lannys father. Lanny said they had been wise.

Hansi took him to his room, where he had devised a hiding-place to keep Bess's letters. They were written in that expansive handwriting which is taught to young ladies of fashion, perhaps because it uses a great deal of stationery without requiring them to have many thoughts. Hansi let Lanny read the letters, and they affected the brother deeply; they might have been written by a fourteen-year-old Juliet to her Romeo; they were naïve, genuine—and comforting to a heart-smitten musician not yet of age. The pair had devised a code for the reciprocation of their sentiments; when Hansi wrote about the weather it was to mean the state of his heart toward the granddaughter of the Puritans, and Hansi said he would declare that the weather was heavenly in Berlin, even when the iciest blizzard was raging.

While Lanny was there a cablegram arrived from New York with thrilling tidings: Hansi was engaged to make an appearance in Carnegie Hall during the month of April; they would pay him five hundred dollars, the first money he had ever earned in his life. When they were alone, Hansi looked at his friend with a frightened expression and said: "Bess will be eighteen!"

"All right," smiled the other; "why not?"

"What shall I do, Lanny?"

"Stand up to them. Get it clear in your head that they're just human beings like yourself; they're only great because they think they are."

"How I wish you'd come with me!" exclaimed the young virtuoso.

"Don't let them bluff you, Hansi. You'll find their bark is a lot worse than their bite!"

VIII

The morning before Christmas Lanny and Kurt arrived in Stubendorf. Emil couldn't come that year; it was some other officer's turn. Also the two Aryan widows were missing, Kurt's sister-in-law being with her parents and his sister with her husband's family. Thus it was a quiet Christmas, but happy, on account of the spirit of Locarno; Poland had signed those treaties, and the two peoples were doing what they could to get along with each other. Trade was picking up and life was becoming easier.

Lanny had serious talks with Herr Meissner. The old gentleman was beginning to show his age, but his mind was no less vigorous, and what he had to say about the problems of the Fatherland always interested Lanny; it troubled him also, for it seemed to reinforce the idea of his conservative father and his revolutionary uncle, that the basic demands of Germany and her neighbors were irreconcilable. Lanny still met no one in Stubendorf who had any other idea than to get back into the German fold, or who would think of the present arrangement as anything but a breathing-spell. But imagine saying that to a Pole or a Frenchman!

Heinrich Jung was there, and he was the lad that could tell you how the getting back into the fold was to be done. Adolf Hitler Schicklgruber, having had a whole year out of prison, had reorganized his movement and was carrying on his propaganda without rest. Had Lanny read that book which Heinrich had sent him? Yes, Lanny had read it. And what did he think of it? Lanny answered as politely as he could that it seemed to him to convey Herr Hitler's ideas successfully; it was unusual for a public man to outline in such detail a series of events which he intended to bring about. That satisfied the young forester, who couldn't imagine anybody's failing to honor the inspired leader of the coming new Germany. His sky-blue eyes shone as he informed Lanny that the great man was now in retirement, writing the second part of his masterwork. That too would be sent to Juan when it was published.

The truth was that Lanny had found the first portion of Adi's book extremely hard reading. It was called *Mein Kampf*—that is to say, *My Fight,* or if you wished to take it symbolically, *My Struggle.* But its author had no idea of taking it that way; his book was a declaration of implacable and unceasing war upon the world as at present organized and run. *Mein Hass* would have been a better title, it seemed to Lanny, or perhaps *Meine Hassen,* for Hitler had so many hates that if you read off the list of them it became a joke. Lanny saw him as Rick had explained him: the poor odd-jobs man, the artist *manqué,* the dweller in flophouses who craved ideas and read all sorts of stuff; it was jumbled up in his head, the true and the false hopelessly confused, but everything believed with a fury of passion that came close to the borderline of insanity. Lanny was no psychiatrist, but it seemed to him that here was an indivisible combination of genius and crackpot. Lanny had never before encountered such a mind, but he accepted Rick's statement that you could find them in every refuge for the derelict, or hear them by the dozens in Hyde Park, London, on any Sunday afternoon.

The author of *Mein Kampf* had a dream of a tall, long-headed, long-limbed, vigorous man with blond hair and blue eyes whom he called "the Aryan." This seemed funny, because Hitler himself was an average-sized dark man of the round-headed Alpine type. His dream Aryans didn't exist in Europe; for the Germans, like all the other tribes, were mixed as thoroughly as a broth which has been stewing on a hot fire for a thousand years. Hitler had got his emotions out of Wagner's Siegfried mythology, plus a bit of Nietzsche, who had gone insane, and of Houston Stewart Chamberlain, who didn't have to go. This provided him with reasons for hating all the other varieties of mankind. He hated the yellow ones as a kind of evil gnomes; he hated the Russians, calling them sub-human; he hated the French because they were lewd and decadent; he hated the British because they ruled the seas and blockaded Germany; he hated the Americans because they believed in democracy. Most of all he reviled the Jews, obscene caricatures of human beings who had crept into Germany and corrupted her heart and brain, and had got so much of her property away from her, and filled so large a share of the professions, crowding out the noble blond Aryans.

The Jews must be driven from the Fatherland and ultimately from the world. The Jews were the international bankers who had a stranglehold upon the poor; the Jews were Marxist revolutionists who wanted to destroy all Aryan institutions. That they could be both these things at the same time didn't surprise Adi because he himself could believe and be all sorts of opposite and incompatible things. He loathed the Marxists because they laughed at his Aryan myth and all others. He hated the people with money because he had never had any. He hated the department stores because they took the trade away from the little merchants, his kind of people. He hated the Catholics because they were internationalists and not German; he hated the Protestants because they taught the Christian ideals of brotherhood and mercy instead of the noble Aryan ideals of racial supremacy and world domination.

Lanny could picture this frustrated genius-psychopath, this great wit to madness near allied, shut up in a fortress because he had caused the deaths of sixteen of his noble Aryans in an effort to overthrow the republic which he hated because it had accepted the treaty of Versailles. His twenty comrades in confinement couldn't stand his oratory, so he had sat off in another room, dictating his frenzies to one patient and devoted disciple. Because he was a patriot in spite of being cracked, the prison authorities permitted him to keep a light until midnight, and there he sat, pouring out such venom as should have caused the pen to curl up and the paper to burst into flames. From April Fools' Day to a week before Christmas he spouted, and then he had a book, and one of his friends, a Catholic priest, straightened out the sentences and made what sense he could of them, after which an edition of five hundred copies was printed. Lanny Budd had honestly tried to read it, all the time thinking: "My God, what would the world be like if *this* fellow should break loose!"

IX

The strangest thing was the effect of *Mein Kampf* upon the person who for a matter of twelve years had stood in Lanny's mind as the representative of all that was best and noblest in Germany. Lanny had passed the book on to Kurt because Heinrich had asked him to, and because he thought that Kurt would be interested in it as a sample of mental aberration. But he found that the former artillery officer read the work with absorbed interest. While he agreed with many of Lanny's criticisms, he agreed only half-way and made so many qualifications that it amounted to a defense of both Hitler and his ideas. The man might be abnormal, but he was a German, and it appeared that German abnormality was only for Germans to understand. Kurt didn't say that, and Lanny didn't say it either, for he dreaded to wound his friend; but that was the impression he carried away from their discussions of the National Socialist movement and its newly printed bible.

Hitler hated the Poles, and Lanny could understand that Kurt should be especially aware of their defects, since they had taken his chunk of homeland and were governing it incompetently. Lanny could understand that Kurt should distrust the French, at whom he had shot many thousands of artillery shells, and against whom he had carried on a deadly secret intrigue. He could understand Kurt's being humiliated by the arrogance of the British ruling class —Lanny had learned that from his father in boyhood, and was now acquiring from his Socialist friends a new dislike of "brass hats" and "stuffed shirts" of whatever nation. But these feelings were internationalist, based upon a dream of a humanity to be helped and perfected. Adi, on the other hand, abhorred internationalism as a betrayal of the German spirit; he was for his Aryans and none others, and his words were incitements to all Germans to get together and compel the other races to submit to German domination.

This book provided a kind of litmus paper with which to test Germans and find out how German they were. "You can't deny that it is a forceful book," asserted Kurt, and Lanny answered: "Yes, but one can say that about a maniac who hurls half a dozen men about until they get him into a straitjacket. Force has to be combined with judgment if it's to be of any use in the world." That sounded reasonable, but Lanny saw that it hurt his friend, and they couldn't go on arguing in that manner. No use to quarrel with people; they were what they were, and would remain that; all you could do was to observe them, and understand what made them so.

Lanny retired into himself and faced some painful facts. Kurt hated Jews; no use trying to deny that any longer. Lanny had observed that Kurt always found some other reason for disapproving of Jews, but it was always about Jews that he gave these reasons. Year after year Kurt had refused to go to the home of a *Schieber* who was profiting out of the sufferings of the German people. All right, Lanny could understand that feeling; but what about this cousin of the Meissners who showed up for the *Weihnachtsfest* and mentioned casually in the course of the meal that he had had the forethought to sell marks all through the inflation? "Foreigners were losing money," he said, "and why shouldn't a German get some?" Kurt didn't leave the table or show any diminution of cordiality to this blond Nordic *Schieber*. Lanny said nothing; he was a guest and not a censor of Nordic morality.

X

Kurt talked about the new party and its affairs with the young forester, and Lanny sat by and absorbed information. Heinrich was the incarnation of the Aryan dream, and Lanny could understand his enthusiasm for a movement made to his order. Heinrich reported that the leader, the Führer, had been released from arrest upon a pledge to conduct his party as a legal one; the leader had adjusted himself to this idea, but it had greatly displeased some of his followers, for it meant going into democratic politics, which they had been taught to despise. There had been a lot of dissension, and some schisms, but all Adi had to do was to get them together and orate to them, and he could sweep all opposition before him; none of them could withstand the fervor of his eloquence, the contagion of his faith in the Fatherland.

Making all allowances for Heinrich's optimism, it was plain that this dangerous movement was growing, and that imprisonment had only served to increase the prestige of its founder. You could see this right here in Stubendorf, a German-owned estate governed by Polish officials and worked in large part by Polish peasants. The blond student of forestry had come home for vacations and distributed Nazi tracts among his German friends, especially the younger ones; he had invited them to his home and taught them the formulas, and now Stubendorf was a vigorous and active *Gau*, with Heinrich as proud and exultant *Gauleiter*, or district captain.

"Aren't you afraid of the government officials?" asked Lanny.

"What can they do?" challenged Heinrich. "We aren't breaking any laws."

"You're getting ready to break them, aren't you?"

The other smiled. "How are they going to prove that?"

"But it's all here in the book," argued Lanny, pointing to Heinrich's copy.

"They don't read books; and anyhow they wouldn't believe it."

"You expect the movement to grow, and if it does, people will certainly read the book. Does Hitler expect to convert the masses with a book in which he explains his contempt for them and shows how easy it is to fool them? He says it's all right to tell them a lie if it's a big enough one, for they will think you wouldn't have nerve enough for that. To me it just doesn't make sense."

"That's because you're intelligent," replied Heinrich. "You're an

Aryan, and you ought to join our movement and become one of our leaders."

Lanny said no more, for he had made up his mind that it would be poor taste for him to get into a dispute with Kurt or his friends while on a Christmas visit to his home. He would wait until they were in Lanny's home, and perhaps they would take a walk up to the heights of Notre-Dame-de-Bon-Port, which had so much meaning for them both, and then Lanny would ask his friend how he, a disciple of Beethoven and Goethe, could make excuses for a political movement which repudiated every notion of honor and fair dealing, both among individuals and among nations.

XI

Lanny had learned of some pictures in Dresden, and more in Munich, so they would take in these cities on their way home. Kurt was glad to do this, because it gave him a chance to become acquainted with the musical life of Germany. Zoltan met them in Dresden, and while Kurt went to a symphony concert, Lanny brought out the photos of the new Robins' nest, the plan of the rooms, and the ideas he had jotted down. Because Johannes had begun his career in Rotterdam and his children had been born there, Lanny had suggested that he put Dutch masters in the principal downstairs rooms, and Johannes had been pleased with this. He wanted no imitations of anything; he was prepared to invest several million marks in old masters, and then he would feel safe against any blows of fate. "Funny thing, how much it takes," commented Zoltan. "Doubtless he used to feel safe on his mud floor, and was glad if he had one ragged shirt."

They made purchases, and then went on to Munich. The distressed nobleman there had had time to incur new debts, and so they bought more paintings from him, and went scouting for others. Meanwhile Kurt went to the headquarters of the National Socialist party and talked with men whom he had met previously. Adi was scheduled to speak at a public meeting, and Kurt wanted to hear him: did Lanny care to come along? Lanny said he had too much work on hand; Kurt could tell him about it. Lanny had thought it over and realized that he was in a delicate position, for Kurt was not merely his friend, but his mother's lover, and if they got to disagreeing about politics it might have an effect on both relationships. Let Kurt believe what he pleased and let Lanny keep out of it!

The former officer came home late, with a moderate amount of good Munich beer in him and a large amount of bad Nazi eloquence. He said that he didn't like the type of men whom Hitler had got around him; they were adventurers, some of them no better than American gangsters. But the Führer himself was another matter; a complex and bewildering man. Almost impossible to resist him when he became inspired; he was simple and unaffected, but then something would rise up and take possession of him and he would become the very soul of the Fatherland. "At least that's the way it seems to a German," Kurt added, in an effort to be fair.

Lanny said: "Yes; but we're all trying to get peace right now, and surely Hitler isn't going to make it any easier."

"It's no good fooling ourselves," replied his friend. "If they really want peace with Germany, they'll have to make it possible for our people outside the Fatherland to get back in."

It made Lanny a little sick to hear that. He knew the answers, having heard every possible point of view threshed out during six months of the Peace Conference. If you returned Stubendorf to Germany, what about the Poles who lived in that district? For the most part these were poor, so they didn't count for very much, at least not in the estimation of the Germans. But if you made the transfer, then right away the Polish agitators would start working among them, and you would have the same old fight in reverse; it would be Hitler *versus* Korfanty to the end of time.

Lanny had definitely made up his mind not to argue. He said: "I don't know the solution, Kurt. But let's try to approach it in the spirit of open-mindedness, not of fanaticism." He wanted to add "like Adi," but he withheld the words.

In his heart Lanny was thinking: "Kurt is turning into a Nazi! And what is that going to mean?" The American remembered how vigorously his father had warned him, after their misadventure in Paris, that Kurt couldn't stay in Bienvenu and go on with his activities as a German agent. For years Kurt hadn't met any of his countrymen in France, but now he was beginning again, and would they be trying to use him as they had done before? Maybe it was snobbery on Lanny's part, but it seemed to him that agents of Hitler would be far worse than agents of the Kaiser! Lanny had seen enough troubles by now so that he was able to foresee them; and that has its advantages, yet also disadvantages, for one may take to seeing more troubles than ever eventuate. But Lanny couldn't help thinking: "Poor Beauty! What sort of Nazi is she going to make!"

25

Backward into Shadow

I

ANOTHER season on the Riviera. People piling in from all over the world, until the hotels and pensions were stuffed, and you couldn't get so much as a cot. It was fantastic, the prices which were offered for the rent of the tiniest cottage; some owners couldn't stand the temptation, they leased and went elsewhere. And still the trains and steamers came with fresh loads of passengers; they slept in the chairs in lobbies, or rented rooms in workingmen's quarters or the homes of peasants.

There was a building boom, and the soul of Beauty Budd was kept in torment by real estate agents who called and begged the privilege of seeing her; they had figured out a scheme whereby a little corner could be spared from her property without doing the slightest harm; they wanted to cut this up into *lotissements*, and

they offered such sums as made Beauty turn pale. When she said
no, they would come back with a doubled offer. For an acre they
would pay ten times what Robbie Budd had paid for the entire
estate twenty years ago! They argued that it was cruel to keep all
that land idle when it might be having a dozen cottages on it, filled
with happy people who would come to the village to shop and
thus build up prosperity for everybody. The agents put it before
Madame Detaze as a public duty.

To Madame it became a cause of distress to be so wealthy and
yet unable to touch the wealth. The villa and the lodge and the two
studios seemed to shrink to smaller proportions, and became unworthy of the immensely valuable tract which they occupied. Why,
it was almost as if you were living in a garage! But it made no
difference how many millions or tens of millions of francs were
offered, nobody could buy a square millimeter of this estate; Robbie had fixed it so, declaring that Bienvenu was Beauty's home, and
the home of her children and her grandchildren if and when. Accordingly Beauty had to get her happiness out of telling her friends
how rich she might become if she didn't love this old home so
greatly.

Rick and his family came for their customary sojourn. Nobody
mentioned to them the prices which had been offered for the rental
of the lodge, but they could guess, and were embarrassed to be taking so much from their friends. Rick's play had been produced in
London, and had done the same as the first one; that is, it had won
esteem but practically no money. And of course what a journalist
could earn by miscellaneous writing wasn't enough for a family
which had rich friends. Nina was game, and stuck by her husband
in his determination to write, but that didn't keep her from having
regrets. Beauty tried tactfully to help her without seeming to do so.
Whenever the Pomeroy-Nielsons had visitors who could be entertained, Beauty would beg to do it; if they needed a car, Lanny
would offer to drive them. "Friendship is more than money," he
would say, and of course it is, but the fashionable world isn't always run on that basis.

Kurt gave his annual recital at Sept Chênes, and played with three orchestras that season, with no little *éclat*. Lanny encouraged him and Beauty intrigued to push him to the fore. Lanny hadn't told his mother about his fear of the Nazis, for Beauty couldn't get political movements straight, and her son's antagonism to Hitler and Mussolini was to her merely an aspect of his friendship for the Reds. The Germans whom Kurt met seemed to be musical people, and all that Beauty wanted was for them to tell Kurt that he was a great *Komponist*, so as to keep him happy in his work. She would do any entertaining, pay any sums to that end; she would have been willing to pay orchestra directors to hire Kurt, if it had been possible to arrange this without its becoming known.

Lanny made trips to look at paintings, and Zoltan came to report on others. They had detailed plans of the Berlin palace, with red lines marking where pictures were to go and blue lines around them when the spaces had been filled. Gradually the blue was encompassing the red, and both men were making themselves multimillionaires—that is, of course, French multimillionaires, with the franc approaching forty to the dollar. The franc continued to decline incomprehensibly, regardless of Dawes Commission and Locarno treaties and all the rest. The cost of living kept rising, and in spite of the boom on the Riviera there were unemployment and very little increase in wages. A lovely world to be rich in, but not so good to be poor in.

II

There was a subdued but incessant strife going on between Lanny Budd and his mother over this issue of riches *versus* poverty, Whites *versus* Reds. From Beauty's point of view, everything was marvelous right now; everybody told her that it was "prosperity," and that it was spreading all over the world. Why couldn't they all be happy, after so many years of suffering? But Lanny had gone out and got himself mixed up with these malcontents, these agitators, people who were always in trouble, and kept coming to him with hard-luck stories and disturbing his peace of mind and that of his family. Really, Lanny couldn't get any pleasure out of his financial success because of the crazy notion he had adopted that this success was responsible for other people's failures; the profits he had made had been wrung out of the sweated labor of the poor.

Beauty couldn't keep from trying to set him straight about it; she would point out to him how, when she went to M. Claire and ordered a new party dress, several women were immediately set to work at good wages——

"How do you know they're good wages?" broke in the exasperating Pink. "Did you ever make inquiry?"

Beauty knew that a great establishment, the leading *couturier* of Nice, wouldn't have anything but the most skilled workers and pay them handsomely. Anything else was unthinkable. And couldn't you see how these employees would take the money and spend it in the stores, and it would keep circulating and make prosperity all over the Riviera? Some of Beauty's business friends had explained that to her and she had got it fixed in her mind. The people who came to Lanny with stories of unemployment and misery were moved by jealousy of the more fortunate classes, and naturally, if they spent their time agitating and making trouble, nobody would want to hire them. Lanny encouraged them in their notion that they had a grievance against society, and thus made them into permanent parasites who would never have any way to live except on his bounty.

"I suppose you're not doing anything to make parasites out of your White Russians!" the son would remark, not without irritation.

"But that's different, Lanny. Those people have been delicately reared and they've never learned how to work. What can they do?"

"No use to argue with a bourgeois mind!" Lanny would exclaim.

Beauty never got clear just what this meant, but she knew it was a term of reproach and it hurt her feelings. She was annoying her son, whom all his life she had tried to make happy. How could she help worrying about him and trying to keep him out of trouble? Twice he had been in grave danger and might have lost his life; but he wouldn't see it, he didn't care, he was willing to throw himself away on a sudden whim. How could his mother have any peace, knowing that every time he left the house he might be walking into some mishap of this sort? Oh, how Beauty hated those Reds! But she had to choke down her feelings and keep from exposing her "bourgeois mind" to the dialectical materialism of her too highly educated son.

III

Marie de Bruyne also was unhappy. She spent the winter in this lovely home, to which so many people would have paid highly to be invited; she smiled and played the social game according to the rules, but the verve, the *élan*, had gone out of her. Lanny assumed that it must be because of his misconduct: his interest in Socialist Sunday schools, his meeting with various Reds who came along, and giving them money for their propaganda. He didn't think it quite fair of Marie to take it so hard, and he tried to justify his ideas to her; she would listen politely and rarely argue, but he knew that she, too, believed in the property system of the world in which she lived. He felt that he was being punished rather heavily for having sought what seemed to him the truth; but he loved her, and wanted very much to see her happy as in the old days, so he made many concessions, gave up engagements and avoided expressing ideas which he knew were disturbing to the bourgeois mind.

But it didn't seem to do any good. He would see her sitting alone when she didn't know he was watching, and there would be an expression on her face of the *mater dolorosa*, the look which he had noticed the first time he had met her and had thought one of the saddest he had ever seen. He began to wonder if there wasn't something else upon her mind. Nearly two years had passed since the "scandal," and she had begun traveling about with him again; surely she couldn't still be brooding over that! Lanny had read that persons who had been brought up under the dark shadow of Catholicism rarely got over it entirely; they always had guilty feelings lurking in some part of their minds. Could it be that she was turning back to her husband and the family institutions of France?

He began to inquire, very gently, tactfully. Six full years since that luncheon at Sept Chênes, when it had been planned for him to fall in love with an heiress off a yacht, and he had chosen the wrong woman. Had he succeeded in making her happy? Or did she regret her choice? Smiles came back to her face. Now, as always, she responded to his advances of affection. He decided that his guess must be wrong.

Was it that she was troubled about her boys? They were good, sturdy fellows, both of them now doing their military service—something which Lanny had escaped because everybody took him for an American, and he hadn't ever had to show that he was born in Switzerland. Just what that made him he would never know to the end of his days, but it didn't bother him; he wanted to play the piano and he didn't want to shoot people. As for the young de Bruynes, they seemed to have a mechanical bent and were planning to study at the École Polytechnique; they weren't running wild so far as anybody knew, and there was no war in sight. Lanny asked casual questions about them, and made certain that they were not the cause of the mother's state of mind.

Could it be her deeply rooted idea that she ought to retire from his life? He redoubled his attentions to her, and his evidences of contentment; he became ostentatious in his lack of interest in the damsels who displayed their shapely limbs on the bathing-beaches and their virginal backs on the dancing-floors. But all in vain; Marie remained depressed whenever she was not playing a part. Her lover began to think of unlikely, even melodramatic reasons. Could there be some blackmailer preying upon her? That impecunious cousin who had come more than once to the Côte d'Azur and had shown a weakness for *boule*, the least expensive of the gambling-games?

He decided to force the issue. He brought her over to the studio alone, and sat by her and put his arms about her. "What is it, darling? You must tell me!"

"What do you mean, Lanny?"

"Something is troubling your mind. You are not yourself."

"No, dear, it isn't so."

"I have been watching you for months, a year. Something is seriously wrong."

"No, I assure you!" She fought hard and lied valiantly. It was nothing; she was the happiest of women. But he would not take no; she must tell. At last she broke down and began to weep. It was better for him not to know, not to ask—please, please!

But he didn't please, he wouldn't stop; he kept saying: "Whatever it is, I have a right to know it. I insist."

I V

In the end she had to give up. She revealed to him that for more than a year she had had a gnawing pain in the abdomen. At first it had been slight, and she had thought it was some digestive disturbance. But it had grown worse, and she was in terror of it.

"But, Marie!" he cried, amazed. "Why don't you have an examination?"

"I can't bear to hear about it. I am a coward. You see, my mother died—" She stopped. There was a word of dread which he could guess.

"And you've been keeping it from me all this time?"

"You have been happy, Lanny, and I wanted you to stay so."

"Darling!" he cried. "You have let it get worse, and it may be too late."

"Something told me it was too late from the beginning."

"That is nonsense!" he exclaimed. "Nobody can say that. I am going to take you to a surgeon."

"I knew you would insist. That is why I couldn't bring myself to tell you, or anyone."

A strange thing. Her resistance was gone. She couldn't bear to be examined, but she had known that he would make her go, and that she couldn't stand out against him. She was like a child in his hands. She didn't say yes, she didn't say no; she let him go ahead, as if she were on a train that she couldn't stop. She sat staring in front of her, her hands clasped, her face white, a picture of dread.

He rushed to his mother. He called up Emily Chattersworth,

who had lived in this part of the world so long, and knew every-body and everything. She gave him the name of the best surgeon in Cannes, and Lanny phoned and made an appointment. Marie had delayed a year, but Lanny couldn't bear to delay an hour.

He was ready to take her. Another strange thing, the fixed atti-tudes of women. She was numb with dread, facing the thought which had paralyzed her brain for a year—but she couldn't go to a surgeon's without being properly dressed. Lanny helped her, he took the part of a maid, of a nurse; from that time on he would be everything. All trace of their disharmony was gone, his irritation swept away in a moment. What a fool he had been, what a cruel, blind person, to be arguing with her about politics, to be finding fault with her in his heart, never guessing this dreadful secret!

To the doctor he said: *"C'est mon amie."* It was a recognized status, and no apologies called for; he went through the ordeal with her, stood by and held her hand while the surgeon asked her ques-tions and examined her. The man shook his head and said he would give no opinion until they had X-rays.

Poor Marie let herself be led like a lamb to the slaughter. Her lips trembled, and she pressed them together. Her hands trembled, and Lanny held them tightly. He would have liked to hold her soul, but there was no way to reach it. She awaited the word of doom, and it was delayed. The pictures had to be taken and de-veloped and studied. Somehow she would have to live through the night. She would take a sleeping-powder, something with which Lanny was to become familiar. Driving her home from Cannes he whispered consolation, or tried to. "I love you," was the only sen-tence that seemed to have any effect. She would answer: "Oh, Lanny, what will become of you?"

In those days the art of photographing the human interior was not so well developed as it has become. The surgeon pointed out shadows which were suspicious. He said that there was probably a growth, but there was no reason to assume that it was malignant. The fact that Marie's mother had died of cancer might mean some-thing, or might not—in short, there was no way to say except to perform an exploratory operation. There was certainly some pathological condition—the surgeon used long words which were not familiar to a youth whose reading had been mostly in the field of *belles-lettres*. The surgeon tried to comfort them both. If all the women who dreaded cancer died of it, the human race would be rapidly depleted.

Marie felt that it was her duty to write to Denis, and next day came a telegram from him, begging her to come to Paris, where he knew a surgeon in whom he had confidence. He telegraphed Lanny also, urging him to bring her to the château. It was an overture. In the presence of danger the members of any group get together; kindnesses are remembered, enmities forgotten. Marie said that might be better; she would be near the boys in case of emergency. Lanny said: "All right; let's start at once." He would take her by train if she didn't feel equal to motoring; he could have the car shipped to Paris, where he would need it if he were to be of use to her. She was shocked by the extravagance of shipping a car; she could stand the drive. "Then let's get going." That was his way, the American way.

V

In Paris there was the husband; anxious, kind, repenting of his sins, no doubt, and not reminding the truant pair of theirs. These two men, the old and the young, would walk together down a long road of sorrow which fate had paved for them. Hat in hand, they would wait in medical offices; they would walk through corridors of hospitals; they would go side by side to the bitter end. They had few things in common, but these they would talk about—for to sit without a word suggests hostility, and France is the land of *politesse*. The weather, political developments—facts, but never opinions; the international situation, the state of business, the decline of the franc; the pictures Lanny had seen or bought, the charms of a new actress, the voice of a new singer—with such matters they would seek to maintain sympathetic relations while they motored, waited in an office, dined in a restaurant—whatever circumstances compelled them to do.

The surgeon in Paris was no stranger to the customs of the land. It had happened before that two anxious gentlemen appeared, escorting one lady; it had even happened that two ladies brought one gentleman. That one of the men should be elderly and the other young was not incredible; that both should be rich, elegant in their manners, sorrowful in their souls—all that was nearly as familiar in medical offices as in *romans*. The surgeon made his "palpations," asked his questions, studied the X-ray photographs. His verdict was the same as the other's: an exploratory operation was called for, and ought not be delayed.

Marie let herself be handled as if she were a piece of merchandise; valuable merchandise, to be carefully packed and kept covered by insurance. Three men decided her fate; they fixed the time and the place; she had known that they would do it, and for that reason had kept the painful secret for so long, perhaps too long. The surgeon said nothing discouraging to her, but to the men he called it a great misfortune that she had waited so long. She knew he would say that; she seemed to know all things that were going to happen; it had been just so with her mother, and Marie had been old enough to watch it and remember it. Cancer is not hereditary, but the susceptibility to cancer is; she had that firmly fixed in her mind, and it was enough.

She was going to the hospital in the morning, and wanted to have a talk with each of her men separately; a sort of ceremony, a last will and testament orally delivered. What she said to Denis would never be known to her lover; what she said to her lover would never be forgotten by him—the words, the tones, the whole impress of a personality. No use trying to say that she wasn't going to die; she might not die on the morrow, but she would die soon, and the only way to help her was to assume it, and let her say her say.

She didn't know where human souls went when they died. Her childhood religion didn't return to life in this crisis. Denis wanted her to receive extreme unction according to the rites of their church, and she said that would be a small matter to make him happy, and perhaps the boys. Pascal had argued, with French common sense, that if it wasn't true it could do no harm, whereas if it was true it would be of great importance; so take your free chance of getting into heaven.

But Marie's thoughts were all on this earth; she was walking backward into the shadows. She wanted to know what was going to become of the two young soldiers whom she was contributing to the defense of *la patrie*. Lanny had been right, she should have told them the truth long ago; she wanted him to promise to talk to them, to be their friend, a *parrain* to them. Denis had consented to this; they were going to be tied together for the rest of their lives. No simple affair, *la vie à trois*, but a subtle and intricate product of an old, perhaps too old, civilization!

She wanted to talk to Lanny about marriage. She should have followed her better judgment and done it some time before. No one could appraise a woman but another woman; no one knew a man's needs but the woman who lived with him and loved him. "Look for a woman with a wise mind and an honest soul, Lanny. Pretty faces fade, as you can see by looking at me; but the best things endure longer." Tears came into her eyes; alas, the best things do not endure long enough! That, too, he could see by looking at her.

That was all she had to tell him; except to help poor Denis in case of need. He was a much better man than anybody guessed; perhaps that was true of all men. Her four men—husband, lover, and two sons—were going on in a cold and strange world; Marie herself was going into one perhaps colder and stranger, but she did not think about herself. Lanny must help the boys to choose their helpmates; that was a mother's duty in France, and they would miss her. Lanny would miss her, too; the tears were running down his cheeks as he promised to comply with her various requests. She said that if there were spirits, and if they could return, she would be present when he chose his bride. He tried to say that he would never marry, but she stopped his lips with her fingers. That was silly, that was no way to console her, and certainly was a poor compliment for the woman who for six years had sought so earnestly to make him happy.

VI

They took her to the operating-table, and the two men sat side by side in a waiting-room and tried to talk about other things, but found it difficult. She did not die, but perhaps it would have been better if she had. The surgeon reported that it was a cancer, and that it already involved the liver and was impossible to remove. Nothing to do but sew her up, and make life as easy as possible during the time that was left to her. It might be half a year, but probably less. She would have a great deal of pain, but they would ease her with opiates. The surgeon would leave it to them to tell her what they thought best.

The two men took their hats and walked down the corridor of the hospital. *Exeunt duo;* a melancholy stage direction. They had feared the worst and they had got something almost as bad. They got into Lanny's car, and he said: "We shall have to be friends, Denis. We must do the best we can for her sake." The other pressed his hand, and they sat for a while in silence before Lanny started the car.

When she was recovered enough, they brought her home and got a nurse to attend her. The two boys got leave and came to hear the tragic news, and to hear the messages of love and wisdom which she had for them. Each day was harder for her; the pain of the surgical .wound was replaced by the pain of the gnawing demon. The local doctor agreed that she should not be allowed to suffer; there was nothing to be gained by denying her drugs. The law did not permit them to put her out of her misery all at once, but it permitted them to accomplish the same result by stages.

Lanny was young and rebellious, and did not submit readily to these hammer-blows of fate. Once more he was in rebellion against a universe, a Creator, whatever one chose to call it, which decreed the snuffing out of his happiness. Even after having passed through the horrors of a world war and an abortive peace he could not become reconciled to the idea that Marie de Bruyne, a bubble on the surface of the stream of life, was about to break, and lose all her rainbow colors, and return to the substance of the stream. He wouldn't give her up; when he had worn himself out cursing the universe, he cursed the doctors who didn't know their business, who couldn't stop large wild carcinoma cells from eating up the normal, well-behaved cells in a female abdomen.

He went to an American surgeon, to see if he knew any more. This man called up the French surgeon and heard his account of the conditions in the interior of Madame de Bruyne, and then confirmed the diagnosis of doom. No, there was nothing new in the treatment of cancer; at least nothing that could affect such a case. Some day, perhaps, the world would know more; it might know it now if men had not expended so great a part of their energies upon the destruction of their fellows instead of upon the conquest of nature's hostile forces. The American surgeon had almost Pink tendencies, it appeared.

Still Lanny would not give up. He took to reading the medical books, and acquired a mass of information, most of it far from cheering; he went to the libraries and read the latest periodicals in French, English, and German which reported on the vast field of cancer research; he learned a great deal about the chemistry of cancer cells, their biology and habits, but he didn't find any hint as to how to stop their invasion of a woman's liver. There were left only the quacks, whose advertisements were prominent in the newspapers; also the various kinds of cultists, who were ready to tell him that cancer could be cured by a change of diet, the omission of meat, the use of whole grains, raw foods, or what not; also the faith healers, who would assure him that God could stop the growth of cancer cells, and would do it if the patient believed it. That mental changes in a human being might also change his body chemistry was a not altogether absurd idea, but Lanny had never heard of it, and if Marie had she did not mention it. The religion which she had been taught concentrated upon her sins and left her diseases to the doctors.

VII

Lanny went back to live at the château and devoted himself to nursing his beloved. When the sun shone he would help her into the garden by the south wall where the pear and apricot trees were trained like vines; there amid the colors and the scents of tulips and fleurs-de-lis, hyacinths and crocuses and narcissi, he would read her sad stories of the death of kings, and of the course of true love which never did run smooth. It had been springtime when he had first carried her away from this land of gentle streams and well-tended gardens; it would be springtime when an angel of mercy would come and perform the same service for her. When the weather was inclement, he would play music for her, gentle music which turned sorrow into beauty, gay dances to remind her of old days, brave marches to escort her into eternity. When her pains became too great for endurance, he would put her to bed and give her some of the sleeping-tablets which had been entrusted to him. Always he took pains to hide the bottle, lest she be tempted to take more than her due allowance.

He didn't want to do anything but stay with her. Business became a profanation, and meeting the Reds seemed like breaking faith with her. Pretty soon she would be gone, and then he would have no more of her time, so make the most of what was left. They talked long and deeply, probing the mysterious thing that is called life. They were in a state of ignorance very trying, but apparently not to be remedied in their time. If there was any plausible theory as to what life was, or why it was, that theory had not been brought to their attention. Marcel Detaze had speculated about these matters, but his ideas hadn't meant as much to a happy boy as they would have meant to an unhappy man. Apparently unhappiness had something to do with the teaching of wisdom, but that was another thing that didn't make sense to Lanny; he couldn't get up any interest in anything that he was learning or gaining just then. What he wanted was for Marie to get well; instead of which she was subjected to torture and destined to blind annihilation, and no philosophy or religion was anything but empty wind in the face of that cruelty.

They had been happy, and it pleased her to go back and remember the perfect days. Pain became endurable when they recalled the scenes of their honeymoon trip through northwestern France, and of their sojourn in Geneva; she saw with her mind's eye the cold blue waters of Lac Léman, the old city with the plane trees, the snow-capped mountains turning pink in the twilight. He recalled his later visit to that city, and told her about the American secretary who had fallen pathetically in love with him. She said: "That sounds like a very sweet woman, Lanny. Tell me more about her." When he did so, she said: "Why don't you go back there and meet her again?" When he said that no woman would ever be able to take the place of Marie de Bruyne, he brought down upon himself a gentle scolding.

"Dear," she said, "I cannot go and leave you to grief. I grieved for my mother, and then for my brother. It is the most futile of all emotions; it gets you nowhere, brings you no growth, no help. You have to promise me to put it out of your heart, and do something constructive, something that will be of help to other people."

She came back to this again and again, forcing it upon his attention; he must take it as a psychological exercise, to think of the good things he had got from her, and to lift himself out of grief. As a part of that, he must face the idea that he would fall in love again, and would marry; he must talk about it sensibly, and let her give him the advice which she would be unable to give later. She knew about women, and she knew about him; he would not be an easy person to mate. She voiced again the thought that she should have performed an act of renunciation some time ago. She saw herself going to some suitable damsel and saying: "I am growing too old for the man I love; will you consider taking my place?"

Lanny couldn't keep from smiling. He couldn't imagine any of the American misses he had met relishing that method of wooing. She answered: "You Americans leave engagements to chance, and you have many divorces."

"In America they have divorces, and in France they have *liaisons*."

"But there are *liaisons* in America, too." He couldn't answer that, statistics being difficult to obtain. He subdued himself to listen to her monitions, and promised to profit by them if ever the time came.

VIII

The pains increased, and the drugs she was taking reduced her strength; she could no longer walk alone and pretty soon she could not walk at all. It was evident that the final agony was approaching, and she didn't want him to see it. She begged him to go, so that his memories of her might not be defaced by these hideous things. But he wouldn't listen to her. He had loved her in happiness and would prove that he could love her in sorrow. He would drink the cup to the dregs.

Poor Denis didn't know what kind of friend he was, or what he could do. He loved pleasure and he hated pain; when she begged him to go she provided him with a good excuse; he could say that he was *de trop*, that she wanted to be with her lover. But his conscience tormented him; he would come back, and sit by her, and listen to her gasping out a few words, begging him not to grieve. She was determined to spare her sons this futile suffering. They had their military duties; let them stay and learn to serve their country.

Late one night she talked to Lanny with infinite tenderness, with all the yearning of her soul. There wasn't anything new she could say; there cannot be, when you have had so many years together. But she told him again of her devotion, and the bliss that he had given her; she left him her blessings, and then begged him to get some sleep. He counted out her tablets for her, a dose which increased almost daily; she told him to put them on her table; she wanted to write a letter to her boys before she took the drug. He went into the next room and lay down.

He slept deeply; he had made the discovery that painful emotions can be as exhausting as physical toil. When he opened his eyes, daylight had come, and he went to her room to see how she was, and found her lying still, her eyes closed. Something told him; he touched her and found her cold. On the table beside her was the bottle in which the tablets had been kept; she had got up in the night and crawled or dragged herself into his room, and slipped her hand under his pillow and found the bottle. It must have been an agony to her to get back into bed, but in the interest of decency she had achieved it; she had taken all the tablets, and her troubles were over. In past days she had said to him more than once: "Whatever may be the truth about the hereafter, I shall have got rid of the cancer, and you of the knowledge that I am suffering. Count that blessing—count it over and over."

So he obeyed her. He put the empty bottle into his pocket, and would take that secret to his grave. No need to shock a Catholic husband and sons. The surgeon who had opened her abdomen would have no difficulty in certifying that she had died of cancer.

She left a letter to the sons; and a little note for Denis: "*Je pardonne tout, et dieu le pardonnera.*" Another note, perhaps the last, very feebly written. "*Adieu, chéri.*" Underneath it, as if an afterthought: "*Ange de dieu.*" She meant that to apply to him, but he could take it as a signature; she had surely been an angel to him, and would accompany him wherever he might travel, here or hereafter. He put the note into his pocket, along with the bottle.

IX

The sons were summoned, also the relatives of Marie, and they had a proper French funeral in the village church which had been built five hundred years ago, and from which the husband's family had been buried. The elderly priest who had been their genial guest on occasions asked no questions about sleeping-tablets, and what he did not know could not hurt him with his heavenly powers. The neighbors came, in decorous black; they had gossiped about her in life, but in death they knew that she had been a good woman. The servants came, and tradespeople of the village who had known and esteemed her. In the family pew of the de Bruynes sat four men in mourning, and when they walked out two by two, the older pair leading, everybody bowed respectfully, and nobody considered it a scandal any more. These things happen, and it is well if there is only one extra mourner, male or female.

Marie was laid to rest in the family crypt, and the living members drove back to the château. Lanny had promised to talk to the boys, and he waited for a chance. He found that they had known the secret for years, and had no bitter feelings about it. They looked up to their mother's lover as a young man with many kinds of prestige; he was good-looking, he had traveled widely, he had conversation, and he made large sums of money; they would model themselves upon him as far as possible. He told them what their mother had requested him to do, and the kind of wives she had hoped that they would choose; he told them that, contrary to widespread belief, it was possible for a young man to wait until he had found a woman who was worthy of his love. He invited them to Bienvenu, and offered his mother's help with their matrimonial problems. Being French boys, they did not find anything strange in this offer.

Marie left a will. She had little property, but had bequeathed to Lanny a couple of paintings and some books that he loved, and smaller pieces of jewelry that would remind him of her. Denis told him to take these things without awaiting formalities. Lanny said his farewells to the weeping servants, and to Marie's relatives; he embraced the three de Bruynes in French fashion, and remembered once more the saying of their poet: "To go away is to die a little." He had lived in this château a great deal, and had died there still more. When he stepped into his car and drove out of its gates, it was the closing of a large and heavy volume of the life of Lanny Budd.

BOOK SIX

Some Sweet Oblivious Antidote

26

Pride and Prejudice

I

HANSI went to New York and made his debut at Carnegie Hall. This was shortly before Marie's death, and the news of it helped to divert her mind in the intervals of her pain. Since Lanny had attended a concert in that auditorium, he could picture the scene to her; since they had both heard Hansi play Tchaikowsky's concerto with Lanny's piano accompaniment, she could hear the music in their minds at the very hour it was being played. The concert was given on Friday afternoon, and then repeated on Saturday evening; the first performance, allowing for the difference in time, was at the dinner hour in the Château de Bruyne, and Lanny could hardly eat for his excitement. He wanted to hold his breath while he imagined Hansi playing the long and difficult *cadenza*. He felt better during the *canzonetta*, which every violinist tries to play, for he knew what lovely tones would come floating forth from Hansi's bow. He wanted to sit with his hands clenched tensely while he knew that his friend would be rushing through the frenzies of the *finale;* ecstasy alternating with depression, after the fashion of the old Russian soul. The Bolsheviks were laboring mightily to change that natural phenomenon, but whether they were succeeding was a subject for controversy.

Informed well in advance, Bess had extracted a promise from her parents to take her to this recital. How could they refuse, considering the nature of that institution known to Europe and America as "R and R"? Freddi was coming with his brother, and there was nothing that Esther could do but swallow her pride and prejudice and greet the sons of a man so important to her husband. The three

Budds sat well up in front, where they could watch the bowing of the young violinist and every expression of his face. Whatever these things meant to them, they couldn't fail to realize that he was making a success, for at the end of the stormy composition the audience rose to its feet and shouted approval, calling him back again and again; they wouldn't take the conductor's no, but forced Hansi to play an encore. He stood there alone, a tall, slender figure, and played the *andante* movement from one of Bach's solo sonatas, very dignified, austere, and reverent.

What happened after that Lanny learned in letters from Hansi and Bess, and later by word of mouth; also from Robbie—for it was an important story to them all, and had elements of both drama and comedy. Returning with her parents to their hotel suite, with the plaudits of the multitude still ringing in their ears, Bess revealed that she was going to marry that young Jew. As Robbie admitted to his son, neither he nor his wife was taken by surprise, for Esther had told about their daughter's extravagant behavior in Paris, and they had discussed the painful possibilities. Having watched the two Robin boys developing, the father admired them, and thought that Bess might go a long way and do worse; but out of consideration for his wife he had agreed to let her try to restrain the girl if it could be done.

To the mother it was a dreadful humiliation, and the more so because she dared not express all that she felt. Her prejudice against Jews was deep, but it was based upon the snobbery of the country club set, and she knew that this wouldn't get her very far in controversy with an idealistic child. "You will have children with kinky hair and short legs! They will be dumpy and fat when they are thirty!" Of course Bess didn't fail to point out that Hansi had long, thin legs, and hair that was only slightly wavy.

There wasn't a thing to be said against the young violinist, except that his father had been born in a hut with a dirt floor in a Russian ghetto; and you wouldn't have known that if he hadn't been honest enough to tell it. Mama Robin was said to be without equipment for a career in society—but then she lived in Berlin, and would probably never cross the ocean. When Esther protested against losing her daughter to a foreigner, Bess replied that Hansi would probably be coming on a concert tour every year; playing the violin was as international an occupation as selling munitions.

The one real objection was the youth of both lovers; they couldn't know their own minds at such an age. Hadn't it always been Bess's plan to go through college before she married? She answered that she was going to a different kind of college, one that she had learned about from Lanny; you could read books and teach yourself whatever you wanted to know. Bess was going to work at piano practice, so as to be able to accompany Hansi. She wasn't going to have any babies, whether long-legged or short—it was amazing what young women knew nowadays, and would talk about even in the presence of their fathers! Bess said that when Hansi went on tour she was going with him, to keep the other women away from him. Mummy had always said that travel was educational, and so were languages, and meeting distinguished people all over the world. Look at what Lanny had got during the Peace Conference in Paris; the girl had heard her father expatiate on this and had treasured it in her mind.

II

The most alarming fact was that Bessie Budd was of legal age and knew it; she had been making inquiries—in the Newcastle public library, of all places!—and had ascertained that she and her young genius could take a ferry-boat across the Hudson River and without any preliminaries whatever be married in a few minutes. That was what she proposed as a method of sparing her parents' feelings: to be united to her lover by some judge in a dirty police-court in Hoboken, or in the front parlor of a Weehawken preacher wearing a frayed frock coat and a greasy tie!

Bess was proposing to go back to Germany with Hansi, and the family need have no contact with the despised Jews. Newcastle would soon get over the shock—"Out of sight, out of mind," said the granddaughter of the Puritans. She had taken up the notion that fashionable weddings were "ostentatious," and much preferred to start her married career without any rice in her hair. With the self-confidence of extreme youth she never doubted that Hansi was going to make great sums of money; but they weren't going to spend it on themselves, they were going to use it to uplift the "workers." They used that Red word instead of saying "the poor," as Esther would have done. They were a couple of young Pinks, it appeared!

Amazing what had been going on in the mind of an eighteen-year-old girl; appalling to a mother to wake up and discover how little she knew her own daughter! The proud Esther couldn't keep the tears from her cheeks. "I don't see how you could do such a thing to me!"

The girl answered: "But you see, Mummy, you make it impossible for anybody to be frank."

"What do I do?"—for soul-searching, the conscientious examination of one's self, is a feature of life among the Puritans.

"You are so rigid," explained the girl. "You know exactly what is good for people, and it's no use trying to make you see that they don't want it. When I heard Hansi play the violin, I knew right away what I wanted; but I knew that if I told you about it, you would make yourself miserable and me too, because when I have made up my mind it's just as fixed as yours, and why should I make you suffer when it couldn't help either of us?" Bess rushed on, because she had a lot pent up in her.

"You don't even know the man!" exclaimed her mother.

"If you understood music, Mummy, you'd know that I know him very well indeed."

"But that is romantic nonsense!"

"Mummy, you're like a person on the witness stand who gives himself away without realizing what he's saying. You are telling me that you don't believe in music as a means of communicating. You might just as well refuse to believe that two people who are talking Chinese are communicating. Because you don't understand doesn't mean that they don't understand."

Said the daughter of the Puritans: "I suppose there were several hundred women in that audience who imagined they were in love with the violinist."

"Of course," replied the daughter of the daughter, "and they were. But only one of them is going to get him, and I'm the lucky one!"

III

It wasn't the first time in Robbie's life that he had sat by and watched members of the Budd family slug it out between them. He admired his daughter's suddenly developed sparring power, and made up his mind that she was coming out on top; but he wanted to keep out of it—for Bess was going to Europe, whereas he had to stay! When she appealed to him for his opinion, he said that he hoped she would find a way to avoid causing unnecessary unhappiness to her mother.

"It seems that one of us has to be unhappy," argued the girl. "And I surely think it means more to me who is my husband than it does to anybody else."

"It certainly makes some difference to me who my grandchildren are," replied the mother.

So they were back at the question of the Jews. Esther, who had been brought up to accept their ancient literature as the inspired word of God, couldn't plausibly deny that they were a great people. Somehow the opinions of the Newcastle Country Club shrank in importance when you quoted the Psalms of David or the Epistles of Paul; or even when you called the roll of the great musicians who had been Jews. Bess, who had been getting ready for this argument, named a list of names which Esther had heard all her life, but without knowing that they had been of the objectionable race. Hardly a fair debate, when one side has had time to prepare and the other has to speak extempore!

The outcome was a compromise. Esther would pay any price for delay; she would hope against hope that the child might change her mind. She begged her to agree to wait four years and go through college; then she whittled down her demand to one year. Finally she agreed to take six months—and she had to pay high for even that much.

Said Bess: "You complain that I don't know Hansi; but during our week in Paris you watched me as if I had done something wicked. Now if I give up my happiness for six months to oblige my mother, I surely have a right to be free to meet my fiancé as I would any other decent young man. If there's anything wrong with him, give me a chance to find it out! Here are these boys in a strange city, and Lanny accepted their parents' hospitality in Germany, and Father did it, too; but you seem to think you've done your full duty when you invite the boys to dinner in a hotel and take them to a show!"

Not easy to answer that argument. Obviously, it was Esther's social duty to invite the young Robins to Newcastle; Robbie wanted it, and had a right to ask it for business reasons. Yet, the moment Esther made this concession, other consequences would begin to follow. When a great lady of society invites anyone to her home, the guest becomes a person of importance, and her prestige requires her to insist upon it. Esther would have to take up the cause of the two strangers; she would have to remember that Hansi was a celebrity, with the glamour of a New York appearance. If the matter was handled properly, his newspaper notices would be reprinted in the Newcastle *Chronicle,* and the town would be on edge with curiosity. He would give a recital there, and the Budds would shine as patrons of culture. Make a virtue of necessity!

The young Robins were touchingly happy to visit the Budd home, but also a little scared; while they themselves lived in a very fine mansion, it wasn't real to them, and they wouldn't have been surprised to wake up some morning and find themselves back in the apartment with the steel door. But where Bess was, there was heaven, and to have her take you driving and show you the lovely New England country in early springtime was enough to inspire several new musical compositions.

Hansi consented gladly to give a recital for charity in the large reception hall of the Newcastle Country Club. The place was packed to the doors, and people paid to sit on campchairs outside, or just to stand and listen. It was the room in which Gracyn Phillipson, alias Pillwiggle, had first met Lanny Budd, and had danced with him with scandalous vivacity. Now it echoed the strains of Kreisler's *Caprice Viennois*, and Chopin's *E-flat Nocturne* as transcribed by Sarasate, and finally, as a compliment to New England, a transcription which Hansi had made of three of MacDowell's *Woodland Sketches*. He made his concert short and sweet, because Lanny had told him that that was what fashionable audiences appreciated—they would much rather talk about music than listen to it. Freddi played his brother's accompaniments—extraordinarily talented people, these Jews, and, gad, how they do work! All the Yiddishers of the Newcastle valley were there that night—a warm one, fortunately, so the windows were left open and everybody could hear, and according to Robbie's report the enthusiasm outside made one think of the "peanut gallery," sometimes known as "nigger heaven." The crowd applauded and wouldn't stop, and made Hansi play several encores. There had been no such triumph of the Hebraic race since the days of Solomon in all his glory!

IV

The outcome of that debut was highly amusing; Lanny collected the details from various sources and pieced them together. His stepmother fell victim to her own social campaign—or perhaps to the sovereign power of genius which she had set out to exploit. In the first place, just to have a genius in the house is a startling experience. Very timidly Hansi asked if it would be all right for him to practice; the most considerate of human creatures, he wouldn't dream of doing it if it would disturb the family—but Esther said no, not at all, go right ahead. It transpired that he was accustomed to practice six or eight hours every day, and he had no conception of vacations. He offered to retire to his room and shut the door; but obviously that was no way to treat a genius; Esther said to use the drawing-room, where Freddi or others could accompany him.

So there was that uproar and clamor, that banging, wailing, shrieking, grinding, going on all morning and most of the afternoon, setting the house a-tremble with clashing billows of sound. It was like living in a lighthouse on a rock over a stormy ocean; only it was an ocean which changed to a new kind of storm every few minutes—in other words, the human soul. Impossible not to be affected by it; impressed by the amount of labor, if nothing else—physical labor, mental labor, emotional labor! Impossible to resist the impact of it, to grow accustomed to it, to be dull in the presence of it—for at the moment when you had done so it devised a new method of attack upon your consciousness, it leaped at you, seized you, shook you. All the angels of heaven were in it—or the demons of hell, whichever way you chose to take it; but either way they wouldn't let you alone.

And then the social consequences of having a genius in the house; unforeseeable, and in many ways embarrassing to a person trained to reticence and decorum. The weather was warm and the windows stayed open, which meant that the billows of sound flooded the driveway, and people would stop and just stay there. Word spread that there was a free concert at the Robbie Budds' every day, and crowds gathered as if for a patent-medicine vendor or a puppet-show. They seemed to consider that the presence of genius rescinded the ordinary rules of privacy. Esther would find people on her front porch; not doing any harm, just standing or sitting: a boy who had delivered a package and forgotten to go away; an old friend who had come and hesitated to ring the bell. A schoolteacher of Bess's humbly sought permission to come and sit on the steps; she would steal up on tiptoe as if it were a shrine, sit with her head bowed, and steal away again without a sound. The servants forgot their work, and friends of the servants sat in the kitchen. The house was besieged—and every one of these persons administering a silent admonition to the daughter of the Puritans who considered herself the apex of culture; each one saying: "Do you appreciate the extraordinary honor which has come to you?"

All sorts of people wanted to meet the young genius; curiosity-seekers, lion-hunters, obviously not persons who had any right to enter the Budd home, and who had to be turned away. Others, more surprising to Esther, persons of her own circle who actually

considered that she was exalted to have a Jewish boy as her guest!
She was forced to give a reception in his honor, and let the socially
acceptable ones come and praise his playing and express the hope
to hear more of it.

V

Robbie Budd had a keen sense of humor, and knew the people of
his town and the members of his own tribe. Very funny to hear
him describe the social war that was waged over those two migra-
tory birds, those Russian Robins, those Semitic songbirds—so he
would call them according to his whim. The elders of the Budd
tribe coming to look them over, and to warn Esther and himself
about the alarming possibility of short-legged and kinky-haired
babies appearing in this old and proud New England family. Grandfather Samuel, now nearly eighty, sending for his son and having
to be mollified by the assurance that this shepherd boy out of ancient Judea was no upstart adventurer, but the son of one of the
richest men in Germany—far richer than any of the Budds!

Esther had fondly imagined that she could keep her daughter's
secret for six months; but in three days the whole town was talking
about it. Most distressing, but impossible to prevent! Anybody who
looked at the girl while she was with her young genius could see
the status of the affair; and there were Bess's girl friends, keen-eyed
as so many young hawks, and her boy friends, in whom she had
formerly been interested and to whom she was now indifferent.
Newcastle was quite a town, but its country club set was a small
village like any other, and Lanny knew from his own experience
how fast it could spread rumor and gossip by telephone.

Esther's friends began coming in to question her about this love
affair. By all the social conventions she had the right to lie brazenly
about it; also they had the right to know that she was lying, and to
say so, provided they used the polite word "fibbing." They told
her that if she didn't know what was happening she had better; then
they went away to take sides on the issue and fight it out all over
town. Robbie said it was what the diplomats call "sending up a trial
balloon"; they were able to ascertain Newcastle's reaction to the

proposed nuptials, without having to admit that any such proposal had been made. A staggering surprise for Esther Budd: there actually were some among the "best people" of her town who didn't think it would be a disgrace to the Budds to take a young Jewish genius into the fold! Members of the younger set mostly, the free-thinking, free-spending crowd, who sought their amusements in New York or Palm Beach, and were looked upon with silent disapproval by Robbie's strict wife; but there were more and more of them, and they made a lot of noise in the community.

It happened that Bess drove her friend to the country club for tea; and all the women came crowding around to pay their tributes to the "lion." Mrs. "Chris" Jessup, that maker of scandal—she who had got Lanny into the mess with the young actress—came up to Bess and exclaimed: "Congratulations, my dear!" Then, seeing the maidenly blushes, the flashy young matron had the nerve to add, in the presence of quite a crowd: "Newcastle needs a celebrity to put it on the map. The Chamber of Commerce ought to vote you a resolution of thanks!"

VI

Lanny knew his stepmother very well, and could put these episodes into their proper place in the story. She considered herself a person of wide interests, but in reality she was quite provincial. Hearing Hansi play in Paris had meant something to her, hearing him play in Carnegie Hall had meant more, but seeing the people on her front porch meant more than everything else. What broke her down was watching her own daughter; for now that the child didn't have to act a part, the state of her emotions was painfully apparent. While Hansi was practicing she couldn't be induced to go anywhere; all she wanted was to sit in a corner of the drawing-room and not miss a single note. She had promised to wait six months, and now she announced what she meant to do with those months—hire the best piano teacher she could find and spend all her time practicing. She had set herself the goal which Lanny had put into her head—to be able to pick up any music score and play it at sight. When she had perfected herself she would be her husband's accompanist and go with him on all his tours.

Impossible not to know that she meant it; and so for six months the mother would have to go on living in this lighthouse on a rock over a stormy ocean; either that, or have her eighteen-year-old daughter rent an office downtown and put a piano in it! The majestic and powerful Muses called to Bess like the Erlking to the child in Goethe's ballad. Said Robbie Budd to his wife: "It looks to me as if we're licked!"

The matter hung in the air until the night before the young Robins were scheduled to fly away to Germany. Bess came to her mother's room and sank on her knees before her and burst into tears. "Mummy, what right have you to steal my life from me?"

"Is that the way you feel about it, dear?"

"Don't you see what a responsibility you are taking? You lock me up, and send my lover away as if he were a criminal! Can't you realize that if anything should happen to Hansi, I could never forgive you? Never, never, so long as I lived!"

"Are you afraid that some other girl will get him?"

"Such an idea couldn't cross my mind. I think he might be ill, or hurt in an automobile wreck, or if the ship were to go down!"

"Your mind is really quite made up, my daughter?"

"The thought of changing it would seem like murder to me."

"Just what do you want to do?"

"You know what I want, Mummy—I want to marry Hansi to-morrow."

The mother sat for a while with her lips pressed tightly, her hands trembling on her daughter's shoulders. At last she said: "Would Hansi wait here for a week or two longer?"

"Oh, Mummy, of course—if you asked him."

"Very well, I'll ask him, and we'll arrange it in a decent way—not a church wedding, since you object, but here at home with a few friends and members of the family."

Bess dashed away her tears, and the music of the violin and piano which had been in the mood of *Il Penseroso*—"of Cerberus and blackest midnight born"—was changed as by magic to that of Milton's companion piece. A whole train of nymphs came dancing through the rooms and up and down the stairways of the Budd home, distributing freely their happy gifts—jest, and youthful jollity, quips and cranks and wanton wiles, nods and becks and wreathèd smiles, such as hang on Hebe's cheek and love to live in dimples sleek!

VII

A cablegram telling Lanny of this arrangement came just a couple of days before Marie died; he told her the news, and it brought a smile to her pain-haunted face. That was a lovely young couple, she said; life would renew itself, in spite of all suffering and defeat. After the funeral Lanny cabled that he was going back to Juan, and inviting Hansi and Bess to come there on their honeymoon travels. He didn't say anything about Marie; no use complicating the family relationships by letting Esther hear about her. He wrote the news about her death to his father, and also to Hansi in Berlin; Hansi could tell Bess about it in his own way.

The violinist had revealed the engagement to his parents prior to his leaving for the States, and Mama Robin had cried all over the palace. She had seen pictures of Bess, for these young people all had cameras, and whatever happened to them was preserved in innumerable little snapshots which became a nuisance in bureau drawers. A sweet-looking girl—but Mama would have liked it so much better if she had been Jewish. If it made Hansi happy, all right, but he was so young, and what would she do without him? She had thought of braving a sea voyage with him, but of course she would ruin his chances with those fashionable *goyim*. Mama had stopped wearing a wig and keeping the *shabbas*, but in her heart she was troubled, and was ready to fly back into the shelter of her ancient Judaism at the smallest sign of danger.

Papa Robin wanted to load his new daughter-in-law with more gifts than the Queen of Sheba had received from Solomon; but first he had to find out if she would take them. He began with a fancy sport-car made in Germany; surely that would be useful and sensible! Hansi would never drive, for a violin virtuoso does nothing with his hands that he can avoid. Cautious Mama wanted to wait and make sure that Bess knew how to drive, but Papa said: *"Gewiss, all those rich young goyim* have cars, in America they are driving all over the place." Indeed they were, and sometimes over bridges and embankments and things like that.

So this honeymoon couple showed up at Juan, radiating happiness like one of the new high-powered broadcasting-stations. It was the best of all possible things for Lanny, who was deeply depressed, and for a month had been playing the saddest music, such as the tone poem of Sibelius called *Kuomela,* which is *Death,* and the one called *The Swan of Tuonela,* which is *River of Death.* He had dug out a lot of old books from his great-great-uncle's library: books like Mackail's *Greek Anthology,* containing the sorrowful things which the ancients had carved on tombstones and mausoleums; also Amiel's *Journal,* full of discouraging reflections; a tome by a three-hundred-year-old Englishman, called *The Anatomy of Melancholy,* and another by an equally venerable scholar, entitled *Urn Burial.*

Beauty had been unable to get him to meet a single one of the many fair misses who would have been so glad to heal his broken heart. But now came Bess, his half-sister and the bride of his friend, and she was different from other young females. Marie had loved Hansi, and had put the seal of her approval upon these nuptials; so Lanny could enjoy vicarious happiness. Hansi knew what to do, and went right to it; he brought out his fiddle, and told Lanny how the Tchaikowsky concerto had been received in Carnegie Hall, and how differently the orchestra conductor had interpreted various passages; Lanny must try this and that, and he did, and naturally they could spend many hours getting that great work right. It would always be cherished by Lanny as his young friend's debut music.

And then those little MacDowell pieces which Lanny had transcribed, and which the audience at the country club had appeared to like. They were full of romantic feeling, and playing them and hearing about them carried Lanny back to his year and a half in Newcastle, now far enough away to appear glamorous. He was eager to hear the adventures of the young Jewish Lochinvarsky who had come out of the East. Hansi told his version, and later on, when Bess was alone with her brother, she added the intimate family details which Lanny had a right to know.

Beauty had never been to Newcastle, but she had been born in New England, and of course had had Robbie's family in her thoughts ever since she had met him; so Lanny couldn't withhold this delicious and exciting gossip from her. When you stopped to think of it, the story was not without elements of triumph for the mistress of Bienvenu; she the cast-off one, the almost *demimondaine*. Esther had raised a lovely young daughter, and tried her best to keep her, but now this pearl without price was in Beauty's hands! Beauty wasn't malicious, and didn't want to harm the woman who had supplanted her; but nobody could blame her if she was kind to Bess, and tried to gain and hold her affection.

At the first opportunity Lanny's mother would tell Lanny's half-sister the whole sad story of Marie de Bruyne; being now a wife and no prude, Bess would become familiar with the customs of France. Beauty would ask for her help in lifting Lanny out of his depression, and in finding some suitable wife for him. That would be among Bess's duties as a member of the family. There was a firm known as "R and R," and now let there be another known as "B and B."

Esther Budd's daughter was gaining her first knowledge of illicit love; also she was being initiated into the secret society of the matchmakers! A most noble, benevolent, and protective order—for how could Bess, drinking deep drafts of happiness herself, fail to wish the same for her adored Lanny, the center of her admiration since childhood? She would enter an alliance with this wise mother, and together they would search the Côte d'Azur, and pick the very likeliest among all the international damsels, and contrive plausible schemes to have her meet Lanny by pure chance. They would get the pair in a corner of the bowered summer house in the garden of Bienvenu, with the moon shining overhead, the scent of star jasmines loading the air, and Hansi on the loggia playing, say, the *Angel's Serenade*.

VIII

There was the empty lodge, Nina and Rick having returned to England in May. It would be at the disposal of the young Robins every summer, if they found Juan tolerable in the hot season. A great many people had discovered that they liked it, and more and more were coming. If you dressed lightly and followed the southern practice of the siesta, you would find it not so bad. Beauty urged Bess to think of this place as her home; for Lanny loved and admired her, and felt that her blissful marriage was partly of his making. There was a piano in the lodge, and Bess could practice as long as Hansi could stand it, and then she could come over to the villa and practice, for it made no difference to Beauty, who had lived in the lighthouse over a stormy ocean ever since Lanny had taken up the piano in earnest.

Of course Hansi wanted to pay rent for the lodge, but Beauty said that was nonsense; Lanny was making so much money out of Hansi's father that it was really embarrassing. He had those plans of the Robin palace with the red and blue marks on them; Bess had seen the paintings which were already installed, and now she and Hansi encouraged Lanny to show them the plans and explain what was to go here and what there. Prior to Marie's illness Lanny had "lined up" several paintings on the Riviera, and now came Zoltan, and Lanny had to take him to inspect these works. They took the bridal couple along, to continue their education in the graphic arts; this was a service to Zoltan, for in due course the sons and daughters of art collectors become collectors on their own. Incidentally it was another stage in the process of luring Lanny from his grief.

Kurt Meissner did his part, contributing dignity and prestige to the life at Bienvenu. Being a man of the world as well as a *Komponist,* he wouldn't fail to realize how important it was to Beauty to gain and keep the esteem of Robbie's daughter. Kurt's prejudice against Jewish *Schieber* could be modified to exclude their sons, especially one who was an artist. Since Hansi had been "finished" in Berlin, there was no basis for refusing to recognize him as a distinguished musician; Kurt, who aspired to compose for all instruments, could make good use of a violin virtuoso on the place. He brought out his orchestral works, both published and in process, and played them with Hansi, and discussed the technicalities of bowings and fingerings of the whole stringed choir; he was properly pleased by Hansi's praise of his work, and practiced piano accompaniments for the young artist's repertoire.

To cap the climax, Kurt said that if Bess really wanted to work at the piano, he would help her; but only if she meant it, and no nonsense. The granddaughter of the Puritans was in awe of this grave Prussian ex-officer, about whom she had been hearing ever since Lanny had read her his letters while he was serving a battery of heavy guns on the Russian front, and then lying in hospital with pieces torn out of his ribs. Bess was honored by his offer, and accepted it gladly, which meant that the young couple would stay at Bienvenu for a considerable time.

There was no use trying to hide from Bess the truth about Kurt and Lanny's mother, and Beauty told her the whole story, even the part about Kurt's having been a secret agent of the German government; seven years having passed, that could be classified with old, unhappy, far-off things. Bess was in a mood to believe in all love affairs; she felt that she was being initiated into *la vie intime* of Europe, and never stopped to realize how she was weakening the ties with her mother and her mother's world, and forming new ties with a world which had been a menace on the horizon of her mother's life for a quarter of a century. It was a sort of war; and it would go on and on, for it was not merely between two individuals, but between two civilizations.

IX

In this sheltered nest were all the makings of a happy family and a happy life; if only the outside world had been willing to let it alone! But in that world were misery and anguish, and they came knocking on the gates of the estate, and on the hearts and consciences of the persons who dwelt within. Impossible to build an ivory tower which was entirely soundproof; impossible to play music loudly enough to drown out the cries of one's suffering fellow-beings!

Less than forty miles from Juan was the Italian border, and within it a new form of society was being brought to birth. You might love it or you might hate it, but you couldn't be indifferent to it. Benito Mussolini, that Blessed Little Pouter Pigeon, had been proclaimed *il Duce di Fascismo,* and was making it necessary that you either adored him or wanted to overthrow him. His government was following in the path which all one-man governments are forced by their nature to tread. Having procured the murder of Matteotti, he was threatened by the vengeance of Matteotti's friends and followers, so he had to put these out of the way. He could not permit the agitation, the discussion of this notorious case in his realm, so he was driven to outlaw the opposition, and have its leaders slugged and shot, or seized and immured on barren sunbaked islands of the Mediterranean.

There was one continuous reign of terror, with thousands of people seeking safety in flight, trying to get into France by climbing through wild mountain passes or by rowing in little boats at night. They would arrive destitute, having had to flee with no more than the clothes they had on their backs, and sometimes these would have been torn to rags; many refugees had been beaten bloody, or mutilated, or wounded by bullets. They were pitiable objects, pleading for help in the name of that cause to which they had consecrated their lives: the cause of justice, of truth, of human decency. They appealed to Lanny Budd because he had been the friend of Barbara Pugliese and a public defender of Matteotti; they appealed to Raoul Palma as a leader of Socialist workers' groups, a conspicuous comrade; and of course Raoul would call up Lanny and tell him—for what could a few poverty-stricken toilers do in the face of such mass need? Lanny lived in a rich home, he was known to be making large sums of money, and how could he shut his ears to the cries of these heroes and martyrs, saints of the new religion of humanity? "For I was an hungered, and ye gave me no meat: I was thirsty, and ye gave me no drink: I was a stranger, and ye took me not in: naked, and ye clothed me not: sick, and in prison, and ye visited me not!"

The balance of opinion in Bienvenu had shifted on this issue; Marie, who had been Beauty's chief ally, was heard no more; instead there were Hansi and Bess, who were worse even than Lanny. Two sensitive, emotional young things, without any discretion whatever, without knowledge of the world, of the devices whereby charlatans and parasites prey upon the rich. If Hansi and Bess could have had their way they would have thrown open the gates of the villa and turned it into a refugee camp for the victims of Fascism; they would have had former Socialist editors and members of the Parlamento sleeping on cots in the drawing-room, and a continuous breadline at the kitchen door. Being guests, they couldn't do those things; but they gave away all their money, and wrote or telegraphed their parents for more, telling the most dreadful stories about the deeds of this black reaction. Such stories were hard for the parents to believe or understand, for the newspapers and magazines which they read were portraying Mussolini as a great modern statesman, builder of magnificent new morale in Italy, the man who was showing the whole world the way of deliverance from the dreadful Red Menace.

The worst of the matter was the moral support which the young idealists gave to the always pliable Lanny. They dinned their convictions into his ears, they swept him away with their fervor. To these exalted souls the thing called "social justice" was axiomatic, something beyond dispute; they took it for granted that all good people must agree with them about the wickedness of what was going on in Italy. Bess had come from a new land, where cruelty wasn't practiced; at any rate, if it was, nobody had ever let her know about it. Beauty saw that she had to step carefully in her opposition, lest she forfeit all that regard which she had been so happy to gain.

Nor could she expect much help from Kurt. To be sure, he disliked and distrusted the Reds and Pinks; the movement of National Socialism which he favored was pledged to exterminate them just as ruthlessly as Fascism was doing. But the Nazis were Germans, and Kurt was interested in German problems; he took no part in French politics, and concerning Italian politics he followed the advice of a distinguished personality by the name of Dante Alighieri —to do his work and let the people talk. Kurt and Lanny had an old understanding, that the Idea precedes the Thing, and now Kurt would remind his friend of it. He would say to Bess: "You remember that you weren't going to let anything interfere with your piano practice." He would say to Hansi: "The violin is an extremely complicated instrument, and if you expect to master it you will have to keep not merely your fingers but also your mind on it."

Quiet rebukes such as these would bring the young people to their senses for a time; but they did not diminish the disturbances in the world outside or the knocking at the gates of Bienvenu. Poor Beauty found herself back in the position of the early settlers of her New England homeland, with hordes of a new and more dangerous kind of Red Indian lurking outside her little fort and shooting arrows of poisoned propaganda into the minds and souls of her loved ones.

27

Neue Liebe, Neues Leben

I

IN OCTOBER Hansi and Bess motored to Berlin; Hansi was still a pupil—he said that the artist's path was without an end. It happened to be a time when the Red siege of Bienvenu was especially hot, and the worried mother thought that a change of scene might be of benefit to her too compliant son. She wrote a letter to Emily Chattersworth, explaining the situation, and by return mail came a letter to Lanny: wouldn't he come for a visit to Les Forêts, and visit the autumn *salon,* and perhaps take his hostess along and explain the new tendencies in painting?

Very flattering; and Lanny began to think of pleasant things in Paris at this pleasant time of the year. When you have stayed several months in one place, you develop an itch for adventure; distant fields begin to look green. Lanny reflected that Zoltan would be there, and they would have business deals to work out. He would meet painters, writers, journalists, and hear inside stories of events; he would pay a duty call upon the de Bruynes; he would see Blum and Longuet, and his Uncle Jesse, and, as usual, listen to conflicting views. Lanny had youth, he had health, he had a car, and he had all Europe for his entertainment. How pleasant it is to have money, heigh-ho!

He wired Emily, and packed up and set out with some eagerness; but he couldn't drive far without being assailed by melancholy. There was that empty seat beside him, and Marie would come and sit in it; he would comment on the scenery and remind her of the inns where they had stopped, the food they had eaten, the little incidents; he would tell her his plans for the future. A wave of grief would sweep over him, an ache of loneliness, and he would want to stop the car and put his head down on the steering-wheel and weep. Sentimental, and quite irrational, for France was full of lovely young women, her native product as well as visitors from hundreds of nations and tribes of the earth; how many of them would have been happy to fill that empty seat, and stop at the inns, and eat the delicious foods, and share in all the incidents! The number of young men in France had been abnormally reduced, and the same was true of most other countries of Europe.

Lanny knew that he could count upon the help of his hostess at Les Forêts. She would know the state of his heart without any explaining, and it would give her pleasure to assist him in finding a traveling-companion. The proprieties required you to wait a year after the death of a wife—but what was the rule regarding an *amie?* Lanny didn't know, yet he knew that he had waited longer than Marie would have wished, and that the empty seat was not of her making. Everything was pushing Lanny in one direction: his mother, Bess, Nina, Sophie, Mrs. Emily—every woman he knew, to say nothing of many who wanted to know him.

II

The day after his arrival at Les Forêts, Lanny drove the châtelaine into Paris and they wandered through the rooms of the *salon*, examining hundreds of pictures and discussing them. Then they had lunch; and because Emily wasn't as young as she had been, and tired easily, she went to a hotel room and lay down for a rest, while Lanny went back to the *salon*, to give more time to paintings which interested him especially. A matter of business as well as of pleasure; those paintings were for sale, and he had money in the bank. It was his form of gambling; he rarely went into the casinos and risked his cash on the turn of a wheel or a card, but he would risk it now and then on his judgment that this or that painter would some day win the prize of fame. Zoltan liked to play this game, and they would put their heads together, discussing details of technique and subject and feeling. It was one of the most fascinating speculations in the world; more so than the "woman game," which so many played with similar ardor.

Zoltan had many times as much knowledge and experience as his pupil; but Lanny was young, and bold, as becomes youth; many times he had bought paintings and put them away in the storeroom at home. Of course, having banked on a certain painter, he set out to make good on his guess; he would tell others about the man, and they would listen, because Lanny was getting a reputation as a connoisseur. He would mention him to critics and news-writers, and these would take his hints, for they were looking for things to write, and why bother to think for themselves when it was so much easier to pick up conversation? Of course Lanny wouldn't sound eager, or give any hint that he was backing So-and-so. It was a common practice to corner the work of some unknown painter and then have him boosted to sudden celebrity. The only trouble was that the painter might get busy and break your market; the ungrateful wretch would dig up his old works, or rush out new ones in a few days and sell them through some scoundrelly dealer!

Anyhow, the pictures were beautiful, and if you enjoyed looking at them, the rest didn't matter. What you lost on half a dozen bad guesses you would make up on one good one, and meanwhile you had the fun. You could have many kinds of fun in Paris, and if you chose wisely you could live to enjoy spring and autumn *salons* for many a year. It might have seemed strange that a young man who was to be twenty-seven next month, and who had grown a little brown mustache, English fashion, to make himself look more dignified, should choose to attend a *salon* with a white-haired lady who might be taken for his grandmother. To be sure, she was a very rich lady, and childless, and many a young man would have squired her about town on the chance that she would remember him in her will; but Lanny wasn't interested in that aspect of friendship, and Emily knew it, which was why she liked to be with him.

III

Reclining on a chaise-longue in her sitting-room in a very grand château, Emily listened to the tale of what had happened to him during a sorrowful year; also the story of Hansi and Bess, and an account of the great unhappiness in Italy and its repercussion upon the dwellers in Bienvenu. Emily didn't mention that Beauty had written about this; she heard Lanny's side of the story, and it was a means of checking on his mother, something which is just as well in dealing with fashionable ladies. They don't tell lies, but they frequently "fib," and if you wish to live wisely you watch people and understand their frailties—not blaming them too much, for we are none of us perfect, but knowing exactly how far you can trust each one.

"Do you want to marry, Lanny? Or do you want to go on drifting around?"

Lanny was prepared for that question and it didn't trouble him. He said that marrying seemed a serious matter, and maybe he expected too much, but he didn't want to tie himself until he had met a woman he really loved.

"Just what do you expect in a wife?"

He was prepared for that also; he had been forced to give thought to it by both his mother and Marie. He told her what his *amie* had said to him, the death-bed promises he had given her, and Emily knew that that had been real love, and wouldn't be easy to replace. Lanny said that he wanted a woman who was interested in the same things that he was, and when she opened her mouth he wanted her to say something. "Most of the time they're just trying to make conversation, and it gets to be a bore."

"If they're young," said the woman, "they don't know what they believe, or what to say; they're apt to be nervous, meeting an attractive young man, and they fall into a panic."

"What I find is, it's darned uncomfortable, because your emotions get in the way of your mind; everybody else is thinking, are you going to fall in love? The girl is thinking it, and you don't have any chance to find out what you really think about her or what she really thinks about anything."

"Sex is much too urgent," assented Emily; "but what can you do about it?"

"I often wonder if they've solved the problem in those co-educational colleges in the States. Do the young people get used to each other and go on with their work in a sensible way?"

"I hear a lot of talk about what they call 'petting-parties,'" replied the other. "When they are supposed to be reading Plato or Spinoza they are parked out somewhere in an automobile."

"I suppose so," he responded. There appeared to be more problems in the world than he or anyone could solve.

His friend mentioned a problem of her own. She had two nieces, one in New York and the other in the West; one the daughter of a sister and the other of a brother. They were both of marriageable age, and it was their aunt's obvious duty to invite them for a visit in Paris. "I haven't seen either since they were children," she said. "They have both been to finishing-schools and no doubt are perfect young ladies, and probably virtuous; their pictures are attractive, and their letters intelligent, but of course they can't say much because they don't know me at all. I can't recommend them beyond that, but it won't do any harm for you to meet them when they come."

"Of course, Mrs. Emily," he replied, "I'll be glad to meet relatives of yours; but it'll be a little awkward—" He stopped.

"I'll have them at different times," she smiled.

"I don't mean that; I was thinking—if it didn't happen——"

She began to laugh. "I absolve you in advance, Lanny. I have very little pride of family, and if neither of them happens to strike a spark in your soul, I won't have my feelings hurt."

"It's something you never can tell," continued the cautious young man. "They mightn't see anything in me; but if they did, and I didn't happen to—then I'd feel embarrassed."

"I could tease you," said his friend, banishing the twinkle from her eyes; "I won't, because I know you are kind. I have listened to women talking about you, and it appears that you are attractive to them. Do you know why it is?"

"I've guessed that it's because I have learned to do things by myself; I mean, I like to play music, and read, and look at pictures. I suppose that makes me seem aloof and mysterious to them."

"They are used to being pursued by men, and the men want only one thing, it seems. But they feel that you want more."

"I want love, of course," said Lanny.

"That's what the woman wants; but it's hard to find, and seems to be getting harder."

"They do appear more anxious," admitted the young philosopher. "It's getting so that it's dangerous to go about."

"I suppose it's the effect of the war."

"You show the least little bit of interest in one, even look at her a few seconds too long, and you see the color begin to mount in her throat—whatever places she hasn't taken to painting yet; you see her eyes get sort of misty, and you know you'd better cut the conversation off and get somewhere else. Don't even stop to shake hands, or you may find that you've got a girl in your arms, and you don't know what the devil to do with her."

The châtelaine of Les Forêts was laughing heartily. "I see I'll have to get busy and get you some protection," she said.

IV

Lanny called up Denis de Bruyne, and arranged to spend a night at the château. Charlot was still at his military camp, but Denis, *fils*, had finished his eighteen months' training, and he and his father would be at home. A widowed sister of Denis had taken charge of their household, and they all gave Lanny a warm welcome. A strange thing to return to that house where every object spoke of Marie; to sit in the chair where she had sat, to rest his head against a cushion which she had sewed, to touch the keys of a piano which she had played. He went into the garden, where the leaves that she had seen burgeoning had fallen and been swept up like herself; the flowers that would spring from her plants would never meet her eyes, and the fruits of her trees would never touch her lips.

They put Lanny in the room which had been his in the old days; there was a connecting door to her boudoir, in which she had died and which had not been used since her body had been carried from it. A clamoring multitude of memories, the intensest pleasures and pains that Lanny had experienced. On the table under his night-lamp lay the copy of *Eugénie Grandet* which he had been reading to her on the last day; a bookmark showed where he had stopped, and now, seeking to compose his mind, he lay reading the part which she would miss forever. Whatever they have in that land of shades, the *Comédie Humaine* of Honoré de Balzac would hardly be included.

In the library of Eli Budd the bereaved lover had found a two-volume work called *Phantasms of the Living*, a study bearing on that strange experience which he had had in his youth, when his English aviator friend had crashed and been near to death, and Lanny had seen, or had thought he saw, an image of him standing at the foot of the bed. That happening had been unique in his life, but from Gurney's volumes he learned that it was not uncommon, and that hundreds of persons had taken the trouble to write out detailed accounts of similar experiences.

More than once in her last days Marie had promised that if it was possible, she would come back to him; that was one of the

reasons why he had come to visit the Château de Bruyne, and why
he lay in this familiar bed in a room so haunted with memories.
Late at night, when the house was still, he turned the light out
and lay staring for a long time into the darkness; the door to her
room was open, and he watched it, and trembled at the thought of
what he might see, but he did not see it. Later he got up and lay on
her bed; he was there when the first trace of dawn began to outline the windows of the room. This was the hour when the image
of the wounded Rick had appeared to him in Connecticut, seeming
to gather all the coming dawn into an image of light. Lanny could
see an image of the wounded Marie in his imagination, but he knew
that it wasn't the real thing.

Perhaps she couldn't come; perhaps she had decided that it was
better not to; perhaps she just wasn't, and couldn't know or decide
anything. Lanny fell asleep at last, and when he opened his eyes it
was a bright and bracing autumn day, and he knew that he would
have only the memory of his beloved, and would have to make
some new love and new life for himself.

V

He came to Paris. That beautiful city was shining in bright sun-
light, and seething with an infinitude of activity. A delight to walk
its streets, so full of his own memories and those of the world for a
thousand years. Full also of promises of delight for a young man of
good health and inquiring mind. Gaily dressed and *chic* women and
girls tapped the pavements with their sharp little heels and smiled
their carmine-painted smiles at one who obviously had money in his
pockets. Lanny wished that he could have believed about them some
of the wonderful things which were necessary to his temperament.
He strolled up the slopes of Montmartre, through crooked old streets
which sometimes had only a couple of feet of sidewalk, and again
had sidewalks raised high above the street, with a railing. Queer
shops and odd sights—paintings for sale in many of the windows,
and out in the open, set up against railings, or hanging from lamp-

posts or trees. He would stop and look at them, but again he did not find the genius which his soul craved.

Isadora Duncan was dancing in Paris, and Lanny attended an exciting performance. Always now she included revolutionary themes and waved a long red scarf; when a part of the audience applauded, she came to the footlights and spoke in praise of Russia. After the performance, Lanny went behind the scenes and greeted her, lying on a couch with a heavy robe over her. She welcomed him cordially, and he told her that she was the world's wonder. She answered that Russia had conferred a great boon upon her by depriving her of twenty pounds of flesh; to a dancer it was a renewal of youth.

"Oh, Lanny, you should go!" she exclaimed, and he said it was one of the hopes he was cherishing. She told him of her adventures there, and in Berlin and New York, where she had made a tour—and many scandals. She had taken along the half-crazy and half-drunken Russian poet; a "divine child," this Essenin whom she had pitied and tried to help. "But evidently I wasn't the right person to do it," she remarked, sadly. "I had to divorce him, and now I'm desolate, as usual."

Isadora was as irresponsible as a child, and told with laughter things about herself which anybody else would have tried hard to conceal. In Berlin she had been stranded, unable to pay her hotel bills, and an American newspaperman had learned that she possessed a trunkful of letters from her old-time admirers, many of whom had admired extravagantly. The story had been cabled to America that she was writing the story of her love life, and meant to publish a selection of the letters. This had brought a cablegram from "Lohengrin," the American millionaire who had been the father of her second child. This gentleman's real name was almost as famous as the play-name which she gave him, for he had inherited a great company which made sewing-machines, and in remote villages of Paraguay and Iceland and Ceylon peasant women honored and blessed him. "Lohengrin" had come by the first steamer, and had provided for Isadora's needs so that she could discontinue writing and continue dancing.

But not even the wealth of a sewing-machine company could keep this daughter of the Muses in funds, for she spent everything as soon as she got it. She had found herself stranded in Paris, and her studio in Neuilly was sold for her debts, and she didn't even know about it because she had thrown the legal papers into the wastepaper basket. The news of her plight was published in the press, and the artists of Paris rushed to her assistance; funds were raised and the studio was saved, but unfortunately nobody thought to provide money for Isadora's food and lodgings, and she inquired sadly what good it would do to save her studio while she herself starved to death.

She asked what Lanny was doing, and he told her about his Socialist Sunday school. She had apparently not heard that his *amie* was dead; he refrained from mentioning it, out of fear that she might again propose to go motoring. He did promise to visit her studio and play for her when he had transacted certain business which he had in hand; but, thinking it over, he decided to stay busy for the present.

VI

He went to call on his Socialist friends and hear stories about the sufferings of the workers, the franc still going down and the cost of necessities rising. Great bitterness among the masses, and a plague of strikes. Paris was living by the tourists who came thronging to spend their money where it would buy the most; that was good for the merchants, but it took food out of the workers' mouths. When Lanny learned that they were printing a pamphlet to tell of the Fascist terror in Italy he gave them a thousand-franc note to help in the distribution. It was a fortune for them, but it represented only twenty dollars to him; less than a day's proceeds from the contents of his safe-deposit box in New York.

He went next to call on his Red uncle. Here, too, he heard about strikes and discontent; but here it seemed that the capitalists were less to blame than the yellow Socialists, who misled the workers into politics. It seemed to Lanny that the Communists were in politics also; but they called it revolutionary agitation, it was only for propaganda—using the institutions of the republic as a fulcrum by which to overthrow it. Lanny had described his uncle's discourse as a phonograph record, and now he put the record on and started it.

He found that the older man was informed as to what was going on in Italy, and hated the Fascists, but there was a subtle difference in his feeling—he had adopted the theory that *Fascismo* was a stage toward the social revolution; Mussolini was destroying the bourgeois state, and in due course the Communists would take it over. Lanny said: "When he gets through, there won't be enough of you left to take over a village." But the bald-headed and wrinkled old painter replied that hunger would make more; it was a process, like the grinding of a machine; capitalism put the workers through a hopper and ground the profits out of them, and the residue came out Red.

The nephew told about two young converts who hadn't had to be poor. A delightful story, even if it wasn't according to the Marxist-Leninist formula. Jesse's *amie* came in in the middle of it, with an armful of things which she planned to make into a supper; but she became interested in hearing about romance in a munitions town in far-off New England. With her was her younger sister, and the two of them, in spite of their revolutionary convictions, swallowed the details of life among the bloated rich as eagerly as any reader of a "confessions" magazine. Seeing how he had delayed their meal, Lanny said: "Let's go out and see what we can find."

He took them to a near-by café, full of tobacco smoke and a clatter of conversation about art, music, books, politics, and the events of the day. Artists with spike beards and flowing ties proclaimed the glories of surrealism, or pounded the tables and denounced it. A poet with a spade beard would be called upon by his followers and would stand up on a chair and recite. A singer with a von Tirpitz bifurcation would be shouted for, and he would chant a ballad denouncing the latest crimes of the government or praising the white limbs of the lady-love who sat by his side and did not blush. It was the *vrai ton* of Montmartre, but Jesse Blackless said that half the people in the place were tourists, and the old crowd was moving out and finding new haunts.

VII

Paris was a beautiful city, but, if you could believe a revolutionist and his companion, it was a city very near to collapsing of its own rottenness. Sitting at a crowded little table in this noisy room, being served a dinner which cost about fifteen cents per plate in United States money, *vin compris*, Lanny spent a couple of hours listening to a picture of corruption—moral, social, political, financial—that would have appalled him if he had not been taught from childhood that that was the way of all the world. The newspapers and every department of them were for sale to the highest bidder; and that went not merely for the scandal sheets, but for the most august and conservative, whose names were famous all over the world; they took British money, Turkish money, Polish money, even German money—as Lanny knew, because Kurt had been one of the pay-masters; they took the money of Zaharoff, and Deterding, and the Comité des Forges—the son of Robbie Budd didn't have to be told about that. The same thing was true of the politicians, the members of the Cabinet and of the Chamber—their campaign expenses were put up by special interests, and they faithfully served these until some more generous paymaster put in his appearance. From top to bottom this condition prevailed, so Jesse Blackless declared; the services of government were for sale to those who bid highest, and the laws were enforced sternly against the poor alone.

Paris was the world's center of fashion and luxury, and this in-cluded every form of vice that had been devised by mankind. No use to say that this was all for the tourists, for that didn't change the fact that it was Parisians, both men and women, who performed the services, and they were molded by the work they did. In the same block with the café where Lanny sat you could find a place where women dressed themselves as men and danced with women, and an-other place where men curled their hair, powdered and painted themselves, put on frills and flounces, and danced with other men. Upstairs were rooms where unnatural vices were practiced, and if you had a curiosity to witness them, the price would be within any means; benevolent *laissez faire* favored the customer in the field of depravity as in all others. For a few francs you could get a ticket to the Quatz-Arts ball, conducted by the art students, and there you could see naked orgies conducted on an open dance floor; you strolled about the great hall and observed raised platforms against the walls, with men and women giving demonstrations of every sort of abnormal procedure.

Such things had always been a part of the meaning of the word Paris, but they were far more open and more widespread since the war, so Jesse declared. This to him was a part of the breakdown of capitalism. As far back as one could peer into the mists of the past were civilizations arising, always based upon some form of slavery, the exploitation of man by his fellows; and always these great empires had been undermined by luxury at the top and misery at the bottom. To Lanny's Red uncle the spectacle of decadence was gratifying, because it proved his thesis that a parasitic society could not survive. Upon the walls of every splendid building of Paris he saw the handwriting of the ancient legend: Thou art weighed in the balance, and art found wanting!

VIII

Lanny had girls on his mind, and was thinking: "How would it be if I should find a Red one?" He looked at Françoise, the older of the sisters; she was somewhere between twenty-five and thirty-five, one couldn't be sure because she sacrificed her appearance for the cause. It had become the fashion for women to have their hair "shingled," but Françoise had done it for years, because it saved time and trouble. She wore cotton stockings, low-heeled shoes, and a brown dress with no aesthetic properties. She worked all day as a stenographer in the party office; she came home and prepared supper and cleaned up the rooms, and often they went out to a meeting, where she would sell "literature." Her talk was of party problems and personalities; Lanny knew that if he chose one like that he would have to follow the party line, and he couldn't depend upon himself.

Suzette was different; she was only twenty or so, her sister's *mignonne*. She had a thin, eager little face, decorated with purple rouge; the fashion of knee-length skirts suited her, both because it was economical and because she had shapely legs. She was a *midinette*, earning nine francs a day, which was little more than the price of the dinner to which the princely American was treating her. He asked questions about her life and that of her fellow-workers, collecting data which he could use the next time he got into an argument with his mother. He realized that Red doctrines wouldn't mean so much to this *petite;* she wanted a man, and her state of mind was such that it was the part of wisdom not to study her features or to smile at her with too great friendliness. He felt certain that if he crooked his elbow she would slip her little hand into it and go along with him to any place in Paris that he chose.

Parting from his three guests, Lanny set out to walk to his hotel. But it was difficult for a man to walk alone in Paris; he was favored with the companionship of a succession of brightly decorated ladies, each of whom would insist upon taking his arm. Lanny had been told that the easiest formula was: "*Je couche seulement avec des hommes.*" He couldn't bring himself to say that, but he would say: "I have *une amie*, and am on my way to her." He was always polite, because he had come to understand the economic basis of the oldest profession in the world. He knew that rich women deliberately starved themselves because they were commanded to be svelte; but these poor creatures of the *trottoirs* stayed in fashion whether they wished to or not.

There came one with a soft, murmuring voice which reminded him tragically of Marie's. He looked into her face, and saw anxiety and nothing worse, so he said: "*Vous avez faim?*" She answered promptly, and he took her into the first café and ordered a *plat du jour* and sat and watched her devour it; meanwhile he asked questions about her life and state of mind. So Jesus had done, and brought censure upon himself in ancient Judea, but it attracted no attention in modern France. When she had finished he gave her a ten-franc note, and the waiter a five-franc note, and went his way, leaving the two to speculate about him. "*Hélas*," exclaimed the woman, "it is always the best fish that gets away!"

IX

Mrs. Emily had been fishing also. Lanny found a telegram at his hotel summoning him to lunch next day. "I have a catch for you," it read, and Lanny replied that he would be on hand. At Christie's, and at the Vente Drouot in Paris, they set up pictures on an easel; at an auction of horses they trotted them out into the ring; while in the marriage market, the practice was that they came to lunch and you looked at them across the table and sampled their conversation. Always with decorum, pretending that it was a casual affair and that your mind was entirely absorbed in the conversation. Lanny was appreciative of the kindness of an old friend, and would do anything he could to oblige her—except marry some girl whom he didn't especially care about!

Emily had caught a whale this time; the young lady whose arrival was awaited bore the name of Hellstein, one of the most widely known Jewish banking-houses in Europe. Lanny didn't need to ask if it was the real thing, for the châtelaine of Les Forêts did not deal in imitation goods. He understood that she must have taken some trouble, for the daughters of such houses do not go out unguarded, and do not meet strange men except after careful inquiry.

Lanny had met not a few daughters of the rich, and had got the general impression that they needed only money, and so they had very little but money. But now from a limousine with a chauffeur and a footman in livery there descended a vision straight out of the Old Testament pages. What shall I liken to thee, O daughter of Jerusalem? What shall I equal to thee, that I may comfort thee, O virgin daughter of Zion? She had all those charms which had inspired the fervor of the Song of Songs. Turn away thine eyes from me, for they have overcome me! They were large dark eyes, very gentle, such as poets are wont to compare to a gazelle's; they were shaded by dusky lashes, which dropped modestly when a young man gazed. She was soft, tender, and well rounded, not more than eighteen, Lanny judged; the color which came and went in her cheeks and throat was not to be purchased in any cosmetic establishment.

Her mother, it transpired, was an old friend of Emily's, and her father had attended Emily's *salon* in years long past. He was a connoisseur of the arts, so his daughter had heard about them. Also, she possessed that which Byron describes as an excellent thing in woman, a soft voice. Had the hostess given her any hint that Lanny liked to talk? Anyhow, she listened, and interrupted rarely. She was greatly intrigued by the business of finding and purchasing old masters, and he told her enough, but not too much, for by no chance must it appear that he might be thinking of Olivie's family as possible customers. When they finished lunch they went into the drawing-room, and Lanny sat at the piano and made the discovery that she had a pleasing voice which she did not try to force beyond its capacity. In fact she seemed to be content to be what she was in all things.

Lanny found that he could think of her only in Old Testament language. How beautiful are thy feet with shoes, O prince's daughter! the joints of thy thighs are like jewels, the work of the hands of a cunning workman. Thy neck is a tower of ivory; thine eyes like the fishpools of Heshbon, by the gate of Bath-rabbim. How fair and how pleasant art thou, O love, for delights! Lanny remembered these phrases from the King James version, because he had been so amused by the efforts of the pious church scholars to interpret a torrent of sensuality into conformity with their doctrinal proprieties. They had put at the head of this chapter the heading: "A further description of the church's graces. The church professeth her faith and desire." Truly there was no way to keep men from believing that which they were determined to believe! Three hundred years ago the Anglicans had set out to prove that all sexuality was religion, and now came the Freudians to prove that all religion was sexuality!

"Well, how would it be if I chose this one?" he asked himself. Fate had given poor Beauty one Jewish near-relative, and if now it gave her a Jewish daughter-in-law she would be like the people of Jericho surrounded by armies of the Israelites. But the family was among the richest, and they would undoubtedly make a settlement that would smother any mother's objections. The girl would be devoted and submissive—or would she? That was the devil of it, you couldn't guess what any eighteen-year-old might turn into later on!

X

Lanny's destiny might have been on the way to being decided. He offered to call upon Olivie Hellstein, and she was pleased. He guessed that he would meet the great banking lady, her mother, and he would ask permission to escort the daughter of Zion to the *salon*, and there display the knowledge of the art of painting which he had acquired. Who could say what might have come of it? But chance was not planning for this playboy to chant the Song of Songs for the rest of his days; there came next morning a cablegram from his father, saying that he was sailing for London; also a letter forwarded from Juan, in a familiar square handwriting which he saw on the average about twice a year, and then not much of it.

"Dear Old Lannie," this missive began, and continued: "How are things with you these days? It is mean of you never to write"—not exactly to the point, since it was not Lanny who owed a letter. "There isn't much news here, I stay at home and am bored being domestic. Nina told me of your loss, and I meant to write, but you know how it is, every bally old thing has been said so many times. Cheerio! Come over and let me find a rich girl for you. We have brewers and South African diamond princesses and all sorts. I hear that you have got putrid rich selling old pictures. Do come and get rid of some of poor Bertie's, for the government are taxing us visciously." (She had never been quite sound on spelling.) "He is working hard for them and has to stay in town most of the time, but they don't remit our taxes for that. About the pictures, I am serious, because we have a lot of old things which people make a fuss about but to me are a ghastly bore. *Au revoir.* Yours as always, Rosemary."

It was a casual enough note, and the casual reader might have found nothing special in it; but Lanny was a different sort of reader, and knew what to look for between the lines. Rosemary, Countess of Sandhaven, was bored, and her thoughts had turned to that agreeable youth whom she had initiated into the arts of love more than ten years ago. All she had to do was to lift one finger and move it ever so slightly; if he was the same kind and understanding playmate, that would suffice. She conveyed the information that "poor Bertie" was in town; and when a woman precedes her husband's name with that adjective, and continues the practice after eight years of marriage, it tells everything necessary to a one-time lover. She provided a proper business excuse for his coming—was that in the interest of propriety, or because of some doubt in her heart as to his present attitude? If so, it was a new Rosemary! The casual "*au revoir*" was more like her; to Lanny it meant: "I told you that the wheel would make a full turn, and here it is."

The last time he had seen her was toward the close of the Peace Conference, after he had resigned in disgust. He had not offered to see her from then on, the reason being his preoccupation with Marie. Rosemary had known about the affair, for Rick's sister had been a schoolmate of hers—it was at The Reaches that Lanny had met her and sat in the moonlight holding her in his arms, listening to Rick playing Mozart's D-minor piano concerto. Lanny had been only fourteen then, and how wonderful she had seemed to him! Now he discovered that she hadn't changed; at least, not to his mind.

She had been not only his first love but his second mother; so kind, gentle, quiet—she had held him spellbound. She had always been a mystery to him, a combination of seemingly incompatible qualities; she was warm in love, but cool in the approach to love; cool in everything else, serene, matter-of-fact, sensible. He supposed it was the English temperament, which never loses self-control, never surrenders its integrity. "All right," it seemed to say, "I love you, and you may have me, but never forget that I am myself, and can withdraw into myself and stay there to the end of time."

Or was it the effect of the ideas of her age, that feminist move-

ment for which she stood to him? Now she and her suffragette
friends had got the vote they had fought so hard for; and what did
it mean to them, what had they done with it? Lanny wanted to hear
it from her own lips. He could think of a hundred things he would
like to ask her, and to tell her. What a good time they would have,
sitting in front of an open fire these chilly autumn days! He didn't
have to hesitate or debate with himself; he knew that he was going
to England to meet Rosemary Codwilliger, pronounced Culliver,
granddaughter of an English earl, wife of another, and mother of
one to be.

XI

What was he going to do about the daughter of Jerusalem? He
couldn't be rude to her, if only for Emily's sake. He must keep that
engagement, but of course his attitude would be different; he would
present himself as a candidate for friendship, not as a *parti*—at least
not right now! He drove to the town house of the famous banker on
the Parc Monceau; he passed Zaharoff's, not far away, and was reminded of the aging Greek trader. Poor old man—he had waited
thirty-four years for the thing he wanted most, and then had been
able to keep it only eighteen months! His duquesa had died that
spring, and left him without heart for anything, so people said; but
Robbie Budd had written to his son: "He still knows where his
money is kept!" Lanny, on his way to be inspected as a possible
son-in-law for another rich man, found his thoughts on the duquesa
of the many names and the two lovely daughters, either of whom
he might have had for a very small price—just selling out the American Commission to Negotiate Peace and becoming a spy for the
armament king of Europe!

What would he have to pay for the daughter of a banking-house
with branches in all the capitals? Doubtless he could have found out,
but he didn't want to; he was resolved to be as reserved as any member of the English nobility. He met the daughter of Jerusalem, and
her large-bosomed mama, wearing an Empire robe of purple velvet,
with pearls on her neck and diamonds on her fingers in the afternoon. His sense of humor was too much for him; he couldn't resist

the temptation to mention number 53 Avenue Hoche and his visits to that mansion so difficult of access. He told what a sweet and gentle person the duquesa had been, and how she had shown him her *bybloemen* and *bizarres;* also how she had been buried in a lonely funeral on the estate of the Château de Balincourt, favorite property of that embittered old man who had discovered too late the limitations of his money.

Madame Hellstein could not help being greatly impressed by these philosophic profundities. One must indeed have a great deal of money, and have had it for a long time, in order to regard it so patronizingly! Also, one must have lived among highly cultured people to be able to speak of all the arts with such intimacy as was revealed by this young man of fashion. He praised the voice of Mademoiselle Olivie, and hoped that he might be able some day to bring to her home his brother-in-law, who had recently made his debut with the New York Philharmonic; Hansi, a son of Johannes Robin, perhaps known to Madame. Yes, indeed, she knew about this active man of affairs, and was still more impressed.

Lanny said that, after all, Europe was a small continent, and they probably had many friends in common. Had Madame by any chance known Walther Rathenau? Oh, yes, they were old friends of that Jewish family; Madame told about the broken-hearted mother of a dutiful son who had never married. Lanny narrated how his mother and Mrs. Emily had hoped to solve the problems of Europe, and how Rathenau and Briand had been scheduled to meet in Bienvenu, but the Poincaré opposition in the Chamber had knocked the scheme on the head, and Europe had had to wait four years longer for Locarno. Lanny told the story with humor, and went on to mention funny things he had seen at the Peace Conference—Colonel House carrying his silk hat in a paper bag because he hated so to wear it, and so on, until the large lady with the pearls and diamonds found herself entertained in spite of herself.

Olivie Hellstein obliged her visitor with simple melodies such as a maiden will sing in the presence of her mother: Schubert's *Die Forelle* and *Hark, Hark, the Lark,* then *Florian's Song* in French. Lanny enjoyed these, and expressed regret that he couldn't call again

soon; his father was on the way to London and must be met, and
after that he had promised to visit the Robins in Berlin, and he always spent Christmas at Schloss Stubendorf—did Madame know the
place? It was in that part of Upper Silesia which had been turned
over to Poland, and so was not very happy. Lanny didn't know the
politics of his hostess, but assumed that international bankers would
have international sympathies, and this was a good guess. *Nie mehr
Krieg* struck a warm note in the soul of this mother of several sons,
and she invited the young man of brilliant conversation to repeat his
visit whenever his multifarious social duties brought him to Paris.

XII

Lanny reported to Mrs. Emily, and thanked her for her great
kindness. He had already shown her the cablegram from his father,
so he had a valid excuse for hastening away. Impatience possessed
him; "O that I had wings like a dove! for then would I fly away,
and be at rest." He might have taken a plane, but he would need his
car in England, so he faced a stiff crossing of the Channel and lost
his appetite for a few hours. The last time when he had gone to
meet Rosemary the submarines had been hunting him in those waters,
so now he counted seasickness as a small matter.

November is a raw and rainy month in this exposed island, and
the landscape is depressing; before Lanny's car the leaves dead were
driven like ghosts from an enchanter fleeing. But his thoughts were
on the problem of himself and his lady who awaited him. Ethical
problems, social problems, practical problems! Rosemary at the age
of eighteen had explained to him the marital customs of the British
ruling class. To oblige her family she would marry a man whom she
would possibly not love and who would possibly not love her; she
would bear this man two or three children, and when that duty
was done, she would be free. That was what "feminism" meant to
her; body, mind, and soul, she would belong to herself, and her
husband would belong to himself, and neither would ask questions
of the other.

This code had been presented to Lanny as something which the banded "wild women" of the suffrage movement had created and were willing to die for—and some of them did. Take it or leave us, they said, and Lanny took it, and so apparently had the young grandson and heir of the old Earl of Sandhaven. How had the program worked out? Rosemary's brief notes hadn't told Lanny, and he hadn't felt free to ask. But now he was going to learn!

Driving along the winding roads of England, he was saying to himself: "Take it easy, and don't lose your head. Maybe she just wants to talk to you. Maybe it's a business matter, as she says. Maybe she's getting along with her husband, and do you want to break them up?" That surely was not according to his code; he had never intentionally made unhappiness for any human soul.

But he would surely be making it for poor Beauty if he resumed this affair! After getting providentially free from one married woman, to go and tie himself to another! As he drove he had imaginary arguments with his mother. What was it that made it impossible for him to fall in love with some pure and innocent girl? Couldn't he manage to have his love and his conversation separate? Couldn't he be satisfied to talk with men? If he required a woman to know as much as himself, no wonder he had to choose old ones! Replying, Lanny pointed out that Rosemary was only a year older than himself, and really that didn't count at their age. "But I want you to have children!" cried the mother. "Not to go about adopting other men's children!"

Also he carried on one of his imaginary conversations with Marie. During her life he had told her all about Rosemary, and had said that he preferred not to see her again. But now that Marie was absent, it was all right. Rosemary was the sort of woman who would neither do him harm nor let him do harm to her. Receiving these assurances, Marie promised not to worry about it in the realm of the shades.

Thus Lanny Budd, completely surrounded by women; they traveled with him, talked to him, helped to decide his fate. It had always been that way, he had been a lady's man from childhood. Perhaps it was because he had had no father, except sporadically. Perhaps if he had been sent off to a boarding-school, English fashion, he might have learned to be a grand superior male, to shake the women off and go his lordly contemptuous way. But he had sat in his mother's boudoir and listened to the ladies discussing their clothes and parties and love affairs, using esoteric words which they imagined a little boy wouldn't understand—but he had worked it out after a fashion.

So here he was, no great shakes from the masculine point of view; he had never knocked anybody down with his fist, never fired a gun at anybody, didn't especially enjoy killing anything warmer than a fish. But he liked to be with women; he liked to listen to them and to tell them about himself; he set store by their opinions, and lived a good part of his life in and through them. Now he was on his way to one of the loveliest; and while his car sped past this chilly and very wet landscape, keeping carefully on the wrong side of the road, there raced through his head the glowing words of English poets and the tripping steps of Purcell's melodies, having so many notes to one syllable. A jewel is my lady fair, a queen of grace and beauty; and where she treads, each blossom rare bows down in humble duty!

XIII

Sandhaven Manor is a Georgian house of red brick, ample but not too much so; it has had bathrooms put in, but still requires maids to carry coalscuttles all day. When Lanny had visited it in the spring of 1919, Rosemary had been living in the "Lodge," but now she was the mistress of all she surveyed. He caught his breath when she came to greet him, for she was everything pleasant that he had remembered. She was the mother of three children, and had gained a little in weight, but that was becoming to her role of Minerva, goddess of wisdom. Feminist and rebel though she was, she still had her heavy straw-colored hair, and had made no attempt to "wave" it. She held out welcoming hands to him, and there was friendship in her hazel eyes and her serene, gentle smile—never anything to excess, everything exactly right for Lanny. Mother Nature had armored her against *malaise* of body, mind, and soul. Neurasthenia, restlessness, discontent—such modern ills were banished from her person and her presence.

"Oh, Lanny, this is the duckiest thing that has happened to me in a long time!" She took him into the library, where there was a great log fire, very welcome after a cold ride. She seated him in a massive ancestral chair, ordered him a whisky and soda, turned the beam of her smile upon him, and said: "Now, tell me about yourself!"

She had always been a tireless questioner, childlike in her curiosity about people. Her interest in affairs of the human heart made her sister under the skin to Uncle Jesse's Red Françoise and the little Suzette. "Tell me about Marie de Bruyne, Lanny! What a dreadful thing to happen to you! Is your poor heart entirely broken?"

She took him back over the happy years. Where had he met this French lady, and how had she behaved? Had she had to propose to him, as Rosemary had done? "Such a funny, shy little chap you were, Lanny! Do you remember how we sat on the bank of the Thames? Do you know what it was that Rick was playing up at the house? You must play it for me!"

He assured her that he had summoned his courage and fought hard for his right to Marie de Bruyne. He described their honeymoon trip—even to the too ancient inn with the built-in bed that had been a habitation of *Cimex lectularius*. He told her about the château, and the garden with the apricot trees that grew like vines, and about Denis who had to have virgins, and how well he had behaved. "Oh, the poor fellow!" exclaimed Rosemary. "I have an uncle like that, and nobody can do anything with him."

Then she wanted to know about Lanny's mother and that strange affair with a German. How was it turning out? What on earth did they talk about? These things were not gossip, they were psychology, the study of human nature, and it was the custom of all "advanced" people to tell everything about themselves and their friends, and the more painful the facts, the more credit you got for providing people with scientific data. Robbie Budd had said that the young people nowadays would talk about anything, and they wouldn't talk about anything else!

And then that story of Bess and Hansi, so delightfully romantic. Seven years ago Rosemary hadn't been much interested in Connecticut, she had thought of it as a remote provincial place; but now she wanted to know all about Robbie and Esther, and how they got along together, and every word they had said to their love-stricken daughter. Lanny said he was expecting his father in a couple of days, and Rosemary could ask him herself. She answered that he probably wouldn't tell her anything—these New England people seemed to be exactly like the English, only a generation or so behind. "I suppose they took everything over in those little ships, Bibles and bad manners and all."

"Even spinning-wheels and children's cradles," replied Lanny. "My stepmother has a cradle that was made in England before the Spanish Armada sailed."

XIV

Now Lanny had a right to know all about the life of an English countess. He had to draw it out of her, for she wasn't naturally prodigal of details. Was she happy? Oh, yes, of course; what was the use of being unhappy? She didn't mention this great house and the servants and tenants—all that was taken for granted, she being to the manner born. She mentioned her three lovely youngsters: the oldest the future earl, the second what Hollywood called a "stand-in," a precaution against accidents. Both were sturdy and sound, and then there was a girl, a quiet, gentle little soul; Lanny would see them soon and he would love them, they were darlings.

And Bertie? Oh, Bertie was in the Foreign Office, getting to be important, or so he thought; he was so-so.

"And do you get along?"

"Oh, well, you know how it is; we manage. He has a lot of friends, and I have mine."

"You know what I want to find out, Rosemary. Do you live together?"

"Oh, no. He has a woman in London, and they seem to be quite happy. I don't think so much of her, but then that's not necessary."

"And you, Rosemary?"

"Well, I get along. I don't have everything I want, of course."

"Have you a lover?"

"I did have, but they took him away from me."

"How do you mean?"

"A man has to marry. He was a dear fellow, but he was older than I, and his parents kept nagging him. No good telling you his name—it's rather important, and the family wants it carried on; they found him a wife, and of course I had to be a good sport."

"You don't see him any more?"

"We have an empire, darling, and it's rather hard on love. They've sent him to Singapore, no less."

"How long ago was that, Rosemary?"

"I've been a widow about as long as you've been a widower."

"And so you wrote me a note! It wasn't entirely on account of the pictures?"

"Lanny, don't be horrid! I wanted to see you after all these years."

"I'm not such a shy little chap now, dear. I know what I want, and I ask for it. Do you think you and I could be happy again?"

"I don't know, exactly. Do you want to try?"

"Indeed I do—the worst way."

"You still think I'm a good sort?"

"The best in the world!"

"You always were extravagant in your language, Lanny; but you were sweet and kind, and I don't suppose anything has spoiled you."

"If it had I wouldn't be the one to know it. But I know I still love you; I knew it the moment I read your note."

"You won't be thinking about Marie all the time? It's rather horrid, you know, to be making love to one person and thinking about another. That was the way it was with poor Bertie, so you see I didn't stand much chance as a wife."

"If there'd been anything like that, Rosemary, it would have been the other way around. You came first, you know."

"I suppose Marie didn't do you any harm."

"She taught me a lot, and it will all be of use to you."

"Probably that's the sensible way to look at it. I really think we might make a go of it, Lanny. Let's try."

Never had her smile seemed more lovely. He started to rise from the massive ancestral chair, but she stopped him with a little gesture of the hand. "Not here, darling. There are so many servants, and there'd be such a mess of gossip. You go up to town tonight and I'll come in the morning. Nobody pays any attention to you there."

He swallowed hard, and said: "All right."

"Before you go, do look at our horrid old paintings and see what you can do with them. I'm serious about that, too."

28

Fire Burn and Cauldron Bubble

I

ROBBIE BUDD arrived in London to find his son and the Countess of Sandhaven installed in adjoining suites in a second-class hotel where no questions were asked. Robbie was not disturbed by the information; he had thought that Rosemary was the right sort ten years ago and he found her even better now. He was not among those who were trying to get Lanny married in a hurry; let him have his fling, and he'd know better the sort of woman who suited him. It was the first time that father and son hadn't stayed together, but Robbie was very busy and had no time to miss him. He had lunch with the young couple, and, accepting Rosemary as a member of the family, he recounted news from home, including his observations of the Hansi-and-Bess adventure.

He spoke only in general terms about his many business affairs. When he was alone with his son he cautioned him that the less women knew about one's business the better for both sides; their heads were easily turned by the proximity of money, and they had as a rule no judgment where large affairs were concerned. Lanny replied that Rosemary had little interest in the subject, even where it concerned herself. In the manor they had some fine paintings which she disregarded just because they needed cleaning, and because she was tired of the sight of them. Lanny thought he could get at least fifty thousand pounds for them, and she would accept that as manna from the skies.

Robbie's purpose was to get information about the international situation. The domestic market for armaments had fallen off to almost nothing, owing to the spread of pacifist sentiment; even Robbie's ideal President, the strong silent statesman, was being influenced by it, and the State Department behind the scenes was mixing itself up with Geneva and taking part in silly schemes for disarmament. "All that is a snare for our feet," repeated the father— it was his theme-song. "The nations over here won't keep their promises, but we will, and get ourselves in a hell of a mess."

Lanny was pleased to serve as informant for this solid and vigorous father, reporting on the various capitals which he visited. What did Denis de Bruyne think about the prospects in France? Lanny reported that Denis was greatly distressed over the situation. Poincaré had been brought back, in an effort to save the franc, but Denis said that the prestige of the country was greatly impaired. Here too the ideas of disarmament had made inroads; they took the form of a line of defensive works all the way from the Swiss to the Belgian borders, in the hope of keeping the Germans out. That would be cheaper than a first-class army; but it wouldn't get France any coking coal for the Lorraine iron ore!

Then Robbie asked what Kurt's friends were saying. He didn't want Kurt using Bienvenu as a center of espionage, but he didn't mind if Lanny used it as a center of counter-espionage! Robbie reported that the Nazis were smuggling in more and more small arms to be used in their street-fighting against the Communists. The significant fact was that these fellows had so much money. Cash on the barrelhead! Bub Smith was directly in touch with their agents in Holland and had made several deals, which helped to keep up the courage of Budd's at home.

II

This gave the watchful father an opportunity for a little sermon, likely to be of use to a young man playing about with Reds and Pinks. Obviously, these National Socialists were taking somebody's money; and what did it mean? The situation was the same with each and every one of the demagogues and agitators: no matter what fancy labels they gave themselves, no matter how freely their hearts bled for the poor, the time arrived when they couldn't pay the rent for their headquarters, and they came cap in hand to some great industrialist, banker, or politician having access to the public till, and said: "I have some power; what's it worth to you?" They made a deal, and from that time on the movement became a trap for the millions of poor boobs who came to meetings, shouted and sang, put on uniforms and marched, and let themselves be used to bring a new set of rascals into power.

A discouraging view of modern society; but Lanny didn't want to get into any argument with his father. He had regretfully decided that Robbie was just another phonograph; or perhaps the same phonograph with a different record. The one labeled Jesse Blackless produced Red formulas, and the one labeled Robbie Budd produced anti-Red formulas; once you knew them, you wanted to leave them both on the shelf—or on different shelves, so they wouldn't scratch each other!

Robbie was to fly from London all the way to Aden below the Red Sea. He was going to have a look at that oil property which had been doing so well, but now wasn't. He and his associates suspected that some of his rivals might be interfering with production; no end to the tricks in this highly competitive game! He wanted to meet some of the desert sheiks who were the neighbors of his property, and make up his mind how best to deal with them; their prices for "protection" were going rather high. Robbie said it was like Chicago, where a fellow named Al Capone had to be seen if you wanted to do any sort of business.

All this promised to be interesting, and Lanny was invited to go along. Ten years ago he would have jumped at the chance; now he was tied up with Rosemary, and had engagements in Berlin and other places. He wasn't a playboy any more, but a man with affairs of his own, and Robbie was glad for that to be so, and didn't urge him. Lanny said he'd go if his father really needed him—but Robbie answered no, Bub Smith was going and he would be well protected. Lanny eased his conscience by promising to ask questions while in Germany, and report all he could learn about the Nazis.

Robbie said: "What I'd like to know is whose money they are spending for Budd automatics and daggers."

"Daggers?" echoed Lanny, much surprised.

"Yes," replied the other. "They tell us they are most useful in street-fighting."

III

Lanny and Rosemary were in love. Nothing had changed since a decade ago. Their passion was intense, yet peaceful and secure; it burned like the English soft coal in a grate, steadily and dependably, lending a glow to everything in the room. Magically they took it with them wherever they went or whatever they did: walking, talking, listening to music, meeting friends.

These friends came with eager curiosity. Rosemary, Countess of Sandhaven, had a new lover—what was he like?—*buzz, buzz!* An American, but half Frenchified, perhaps a bit of a bounder, good-looking and all that—but what a funny idea! Childhood playmates, and they thought they could pull it off again—*buzz, buzz!* Winnie and Patsy and Edie and Cissy, Creapy and Aggie and Jippy—all ultra-smart young men and matrons with nothing to do but play around all day and most of the night, and love was their most exciting form of play. When any pair of them tried a new combination, the rest came running like spectators outside the monkey-cage in a zoo, to watch and gossip and speculate. If one of them brought in a stranger, some welcomed a novelty, others resented it, but all chattered like the simians when a leopard appears under their trees. None of them took much stock in childhood sweethearts, but it was a chance to exercise one's wit, to show one's sophistication, ultra beyond all other ultras.

Rosemary and Lanny made a mystery of it and wouldn't give their address; it was a honeymoon. They went to theaters and picture exhibitions, they walked in Hyde Park, and when the fog was too thick to grope through they stayed in their rooms and he played for her—he always got a piano wherever he stayed for even a few days. Bringing it made exercise for four sturdy men who appeared glad to get the tips. Also he read to her. Nothing old, nothing foreign; she liked English scenes and people that she knew about. She found Galsworthy right, so he read *The Dark Flower*, and it caused her distress. A warning against letting passion run away with you! Keep your head, don't expect too much, or make extravagant promises! Sufficient to the day is the pleasure thereof, and tomorrow will be another day, and perhaps entirely different.

IV

Lanny telegraphed Zoltan, who was in Amsterdam, and he came at once. Lanny drove him and Rosemary out to the manor to inspect the paintings. Rosemary wasn't interested in the details; she went to play with her children and hear what had happened since Mumsy had gone up to town. Later, after the experts had finished their inspecting and discussing, she came to get the results. She was no trader, and made no effort to conceal her astonishment when this agreeable Hungarian gentleman confirmed Lanny's idea that they should be able to get at least fifty thousand pounds for those dingy and tiresome old family heirlooms. Absolutely incredible! Why, Bertie would be able to pay all his debts and be on easy street the rest of his life! The money-lenders had been riding him hard, and he couldn't sell any part of the estate because it was entailed. The Honorable Little Bertie, now seven, would have everything it might produce after his accession; but he needn't have any old paintings!

Rosemary said she would leave everything to Lanny. Make out a contract or authorization or whatever they needed, and she would take it to Bertie and have him sign it right away. She thought that Lanny ought to get more than five percent, but she waited until she was alone with him to say that. When he told her that they planned to put several of these English masters in the palace of the new German money-lord, Johannes Robin, and that they wouldn't charge her and Bertie a commission on these, because Johannes was paying them and they never took commissions from both parties, Rosemary had the bright idea that she would get that commission for pocket money! "I've done the work, haven't I?" she asked, and he assured her that he himself had received large sums for doing no more.

The three of them went to the shop of an expert in London who attended to the cleaning of old pictures. Rosemary was interested now, since she had learned how much money was at stake. She witnessed the excitement of the bespectacled old man who did this delicate work when Zoltan told him that they had an undoubtedly genuine Gainsborough of his best period, and two Richard Wilsons—"poor red-nosed Dick!" the man called him; also a full-length Raeburn, a Hoppner, and two characteristic portraits by Opie, that sarcastic and unpopular painter who had told a patron that he "mixed his paints with brains." Zoltan was minute in his instructions as to how each of these masterpieces was to be treated, and said that he would submit his orders in writing for safety. None of the "Joe Duveen monkey-shines" this time! Lanny listened attentively and learned how to handle such matters, what prices to pay and how to speak with authority, courteously and yet firmly. "This is what I want"—and if you knew what you wanted you could get it.

V

Rosemary went home for a week-end, and Lanny drove to The Reaches, home of the Pomeroy-Nielsons. Everybody so kind, and glad to see him, in the quiet, undemonstrative English way. Rick's sister, married for several years, gentle, refined young mother with two babies, had come for a visit. A sense of peace and security prevailed in this home; everybody did or said what he or she pleased, but no one did any harm, because they had lived that way for generations and learned to combine liberty with order. If only everybody, all over the world, would do the same! They set the example, and hoped others would follow.

Among the week-end guests was a member of Parliament; large sort of country-squire Englishman wearing a snuff-colored golf suit. His complexion worried you because you thought his blood vessels were breaking; but it didn't worry him. He smoked a pipe and listened to the others, and only when they got on the subject of "shootin' " did he have much to contribute. Later, after a game of billiards, he and Sir Alfred discussed foreign affairs and Lanny discovered that he was very well informed. They talked about France, which had done herself so much harm because she couldn't make up her mind whether to let Germany get up or not; she kept scolding at Britain like a bad-tempered woman, because Britain wanted to trade with everybody, including her former foes. There was trade enough to go round, and you could always make more. Why couldn't people do business instead of "fightin' "?

Mr. Cunnyngham learned that Lanny had come from France, and so took him into the conversation. What was the matter with those Nationalists? Lanny explained their neurosis on the subject of Germany. And did the plain people of France feel like that? Lanny said no, but they felt that they had been let down by the war. The average Frenchman had an urgent desire to re-establish the *foyer*. Also he wanted real disarmament—a peace that could be trusted. He was provoked by the idea that the English used the Germans as a counter-weight against the French. He felt contempt for the Americans, who had come into the war so late, yet thought that they had won it; who wanted their money back—as if it hadn't been America's war, too!

The talk moved on to Germany. Lanny told his new friend about the Nazis, but found that no member of the British governing class could be persuaded to concern himself with people of that sort. There would always be fanatics, and they would always be yellin' and makin' speeches; let the blighters blow their heads off. Mr. Cunnyngham told of troubles he had experienced in India. Cows were sacred, even though they blocked the streets and made them filthy; crocodiles were sacred, even though they ate the babies. The Hindu fanatics insisted on breakin' up the sacred processions of the Mohammedans, and vice versa—they were always havin' shindies in the streets, and the British had to bring up native soldiers armed with long sticks called lathis and beat them over the heads. In India these things were centuries old and you couldn't change them; but this fellow Hitler with his notions couldn't get anywhere in a country as enlightened as Germany. Let him fight the Reds—that was all to the good.

Lanny had expected to tell Nina and Rick about his new adventure in the garden of love, but he found that it had already reached them by the gossip grapevine which flourishes so luxuriantly in that garden. They thought the affair was "rippin'" and wished him happiness, and why hadn't he brought Rosemary with him? Rick had a new play, but hadn't been able to get it produced because it was too grim. People wanted to be happy, and tried so pathetically hard. Rick was writing articles in which he predicted new troubles for Europe, and nobody would publish them but the Labor papers. Rick didn't know whether they could afford to come south that winter, and Lanny had to argue with him; he stood to make more than half a million francs out of those pictures of Rosemary's, and what would be the good of it if he couldn't be allowed to buy a bunch of railroad tickets for his best friends?

They promised to come; and so did Rosemary. She hadn't had a holiday for many months, and this would be her time. She didn't care anything about Berlin, that cold, forbidding city, and, moreover, couldn't be away from the children at Christmas; but after that the youngsters would get along with a competent governess and maids, and Rosemary would come to the heights above Cannes, where one of her friends had a villa that stayed empty most of the time. If the friend came, Rosemary would be her guest, and otherwise the caretakers would take care of Rosemary, and in either case Lanny would visit her and everything would be "ducky." With Rosemary everything pleasant was that, and everything unpleasant was "horrid," and so one could get along with a comparatively small vocabulary.

But this was a minor defect in an otherwise almost perfect mistress. Lanny had everything that a man could crave; he would have said that he was completely happy—and yet always that worm within the bud, that doubt which gnawed in his soul: the spectacle of misery amid luxury in all the great capitals of Europe! The knowledge that you couldn't step a hundred yards off the main thoroughfares without finding yourself in some hideous and depressing slum! Here on one of the fashionable shopping-streets of this fabulously rich capital—on Regent Street, where the great ladies descended from their limousines to enter jewelers' and *couturiers'*—here you saw war veterans still grinding hand-organs or rattling collection boxes. England had just had a coal strike that had become a general strike and had looked desperately menacing; it had been starved out, and so bitterness and hate were in the faces of the people, and misery and depression could not be hid. All that a rich man needed to be happy was to have no heart. If he had one, then all the gifts which fortune showered upon him might turn to dust and ashes in his hands.

VI

In the middle of December Lanny set out for Berlin. He had a heating device in his car, and enjoyed seeing the German countryside in its winter garb, and watching the people at the places where he stopped. His mother was due to be waiting at the Robins', for she was coming with Kurt. She too had earned a holiday, and had found a reliable governess to take care of her child. An English maiden lady, very stiff and strict High Church, had been coming every day to give Marceline lessons, and twice a week took her to town for dancing-lessons. The proper soul must have been shocked by what she found going on in Bienvenu, but she wasn't asked to take part in it, and had become fond of her eager and lovely charge. Now she was staying at the villa while the mother was traveling. Beauty said that religious principles didn't make very good company, but were indispensable in the persons you employed to wait on you; she was always particular in her inquiries on the subject.

The blond Beauty was gorgeous in her autumnal blooming, and never more so than in this cold weather which seemed to bring a glow to her whole personality. The German palace provided just the sort of background she was made for; she was as completely in place in it as the owners seemed out of place, and they were aware of it, and proud and happy to have such elegant interior decoration. Beauty knew rich and important people in every part of Europe, and she brought some to tea and showed them the lovely paintings which her son had collected, and was as proud of them as she was of her son. It was the thing she had done through so many years for Robbie Budd, meeting the right people and making the right impression, so that they would buy machine guns and hand-grenades and automatic pistols; now she would cause them to buy Halses and Dürers, Marises and Israelses and Menzels—she could have drummed up enough business to keep Lanny occupied for a year, if the eccentric fellow hadn't preferred to sit and play piano accompaniments for Hansi and Freddi!

Only one fly in this Beauty cream—the painful news which Lanny imparted about his evil behavior in London. There wasn't anything the mother could do about it, of course; the tears ran down her cheeks and she said: "I am being punished for my sins!" Lanny wanted to know: "Am I such a bad sin? And are you really so sorry about me?" He petted her, and presently was able to get her to reflect that a genuine English countess wasn't such a heavy social handicap; she had only to look at the photos of Rosemary which Lanny had brought in order to see that she wouldn't really be embarrassed to present her son's lady-love in the drawing-room of her home. Beauty made a *moue* and exclaimed: "Oh, dear, what will poor Miss Addington say now?" Lanny burst out laughing and answered: "She'll say that Rosemary belongs to the aristocracy and that only God can deal with her."

VII

Hansi had made his first public appearance in Berlin with success, and Lanny thought he had never seen two human beings so happy as his half-sister and her bridegroom. Apparently Bess was never going to tire of listening to the music of the violin, clarinet, and piano, and had been working loyally at her own job—she had a teacher who came every day, and a study of her own in which to pound away to her heart's content. She wished that Kurt might see how much progress she had made. Lanny didn't tell her the true reason, but said that when Kurt came to Berlin he was occupied with his business affairs and with his brother and friends.

For how long would it be possible to keep hidden from a keen-eyed girl the painful facts about this Europe which she had adopted as her home? Not long, Lanny feared, for she was determined to know all about it; she read the incendiary pamphlets of which her husband had a supply, and Lanny saw Socialist and Communist magazines and newspapers in her study. It couldn't have escaped her attention that the Jews were the objects of bitter dislike among large sections of German people. Would she discover how the fashionable ones whom Beauty brought to the house despised the *Schieber,* their host, and resented the fact that he was able to live in a palace and to decorate it with masterpieces of art? Sooner or later Bess would have to learn that Lanny's friend and Beauty's lover tolerated Hansi only because he was a genius, and refused to tolerate Hansi's father on any terms.

Kurt's attitude was a source of increasing uneasiness to Lanny. He had difficulty in understanding it, and had started more than once to press inquiries, but had been forced to realize that they were not welcome. The Kurt Meissner who had come out of the trenches and entered France with forged passports and money to buy Paris newspaper publishers, was a different human being from the consecrated lad with whom Lanny had pledged everlasting friendship on the heights of Notre-Dame-de-Bon-Port. Kurt was a man who no longer told what he thought, at any rate not to foreigners. He had built a shell around him like a tortoise, and he drew into it and shut it tight when he was approached.

Kurt never said in so many words that he didn't like the Jews as Jews; but he must have known in his heart that it was so. Lanny asked, had any Jews ever done him any wrong, and Kurt replied that this was a ridiculous question; he didn't let himself be influenced by personal prejudices. His attitude to the Jewish race was a scientific one, he declared, based upon observation of the part they played in German society. Doubtless they had been a great race in their own Palestine, and it might be well if they went back there, as the British were endeavoring to arrange. But in Germany they were a source of many sorts of corruption. Perhaps they were too shrewd traders for the honest, straightforward, kind-hearted Aryan folk.

VIII

Lanny tried also to argue with Kurt about the National Socialists. They seemed to him terrible men; harsh and violent, their doctrine a kind of madness. Incomprehensible how a generous, idealistic philosopher could tolerate either their ideas or their company! Kurt would answer that Lanny didn't understand the position of Germany, a nation able to exist only upon the sufferance of Britain and France. Kurt would cite facts about the orders which the Reparations Commission was issuing to his country. They had even taken the national railways and turned them over to private foreign ownership! The Fatherland was to become a sort of serfdom, a nation of robots which toiled to produce wealth for their conquerors. The German people didn't think of themselves thus and wouldn't stay thus; they were a proud people, and had a future.

"All right," Lanny argued; "but can't we by orderly and peaceful methods——"

"We have tried them, and it's not that sort of world. It's a world in which you only get what you can take! We have to awaken the consciousness of the German people, inspire them with courage and hope, and that takes a leader, a prophet. If there's any other man in German life who can do it except Adolf Hitler he has not been shown to me."

"But look at the men he's got around him, Kurt!"

"He has to take what he can find. Our politicians are corrupt or cowardly, our intellectuals are infected with skepticism and dilettantism—this job calls for men of action, willing to go out and give their lives in the streets, fighting the Communists with their own weapons—and you can't get that sort of work done by saints and idealists."

Yes, Kurt Meissner was a different man! No longer rigid in his uprightness, but what the world called "practical," willing to compromise, to make concessions; he wanted to get something done so badly that he would seize whatever tools were at hand. He would excuse lying and cheating, and the smuggling in of Budd automatics and daggers! Nor was he any longer satisfied to live in an ivory tower and produce music which mankind might discover and appreciate after he was dead; he wanted to write something which would stir the German soul now—a rallying song for the people, a cantata which patriots could sing at meetings, and which would inspire masses of men to battle for the Fatherland. It was significant that Kurt didn't tell Lanny about this idea, which had been suggested to him by some of the leaders of the new movement. Lanny found out about it only from a chance remark of Kurt's brother.

So it was plain that Kurt was no longer trusting his friend. Here in Berlin he was going about with these Nazis, attending their meetings and conferences, not saying a word about it to either Lanny or Beauty. Kurt had chosen his way and didn't want any arguments about it. He was no longer interested in Lanny's opinions, because Lanny wasn't a German, and only Germans could understand German ways and German needs. Lanny realized that it would be better for him to follow this example and keep his thoughts to himself. For Kurt was not only his friend, he was Beauty's lover, and it would be a tragedy indeed if Lanny should force himself between them, and make Bienvenu a place where Kurt no longer felt at home.

IX

Lanny walked or drove about the streets of Berlin, another city with the double spectacle of wealth deliberately flaunted and poverty that could not be concealed. The number of undernourished and overpainted women roaming the streets was no less than in Paris; the males who strolled and bargained for them were larger and stouter, but their clothing had apparently been cut from the same cloth and by the same pattern. The night life of Berlin was said to be worse than that of any other city; it lacked the touch of *chic* which the French gave to everything, and was merely brutal and hideous. Germany was a republic, and had a constitution that was fine on paper, but it didn't seem to be living up to its language. The Social-Democrats, who had been preaching economic justice for half a century, appeared to be paralyzed by their notions of legality, and the bureaucrats were running the country in their ancient established way.

In the working-class districts, if you troubled to go there, you would see the swarming millions who existed just over the borderline of hunger. Better not pursue your researches in these streets at night, and better not wear jewels or fine raiment—some Communist might spit on them. Better not attend Communist meetings, because the Nazis made a practice of raiding them—the technique which had been known as "cutting out" during the war; an armed party would swoop down in motor-cars, seize several men and carry them off, beat them and throw them into one of the canals. You were safer at the Nazi meetings, because they had armed men on guard all the time; but don't express any disagreement with the speaker, and it would be safer to give the salute at the proper time.

The Hitler movement was a different thing from what it had been four years ago. Then it had been poor and rather pitiable, its followers wearing old war uniforms, often turned inside out for double use; an armband with a swastika on it and a home-made banner at the head of the troop were the only insignia they could afford. But now the storm troopers, as they were called, wore brown shirts, trousers with black stripes, and shiny leather boots; they had banners and standards, and, what was more important, side-arms in abundance. Where had they got the money for all this? If you asked them, they would say that the German people were contributing their pfennigs, out of devotion to the Fatherland and the Führer; but Johannes Robin said that it was well known in financial circles that Thyssen and his associates of the steel cartel had taken over the financing of the movement.

The attitude of the *Schieber* to this phenomenon was a singular one. He was a man of peace, and wanted to be let alone; he was afraid of the Communists, considering them wreckers and killers; he wanted them put down, and knew that the government then ruling Germany had put them down sternly, but he was afraid that it might

let them get up again, because they had four million votes, and politicians can hardly be indifferent to such power. These Nazis really
meant to finish the Communists once for all; they said also that they
were going to finish the Jews, but Johannes didn't think they meant
that, for some of their representatives had come to him privately and
told him so; they had asked him for money and he had given it, so he
felt that he had friends at court. His feelings as a Jew and his feelings as a rich man were in conflict, and he advanced contradictory
opinions. If you called his attention to this fact, he would smile
rather feebly and ask you, what could a man do in a world as crazy
as this one?

The pattern seemed even crazier when you considered the fact
that the two sons whom Johannes adored and the daughter-in-law
whom he had so eagerly embraced all declared themselves determined
Reds. Johannes didn't smile when you spoke of that; he said it was
because they were so young, and didn't really understand the world.
They took party platforms and doctrines at their face value—whereas
it was clear that such things were merely bait to draw young birds
into the snare. Johannes said you had only to look at Russia to see
the difference between Red profession and practice; the wonderful
fine language about brotherhood and solidarity of the toilers, and
the starvation and slavery which prevailed. Those things would become apparent to the young people in due course, and they would
be sadder but wiser. Johannes said that the remedy for poverty was
for people to stop fighting, and give trained executives like himself
a chance to show what modern machinery could do to produce
quantities of goods.

"Yes," said Lanny, "but what's the use of producing so much, if
the people haven't money to buy it?"

"They'll have money if we pay them higher wages, as we can all
afford to do in prosperous times."

"But suppose the manufacturers in other countries pay low wages
and undersell you, what then?"

The *Schieber* answered: "You know I never had much education, Lanny; I've just had to puzzle it out as I went along. I don't
pretend to know all the answers—maybe you smart people will have

to get the governments together and agree on a schedule of wages, and divide up the markets. Maybe those League people in Geneva are on the right track. All I'm sure of is that it won't do any good for either side to use force, because that doesn't convince anybody or run any machines."

X

Johannes Robin thought that he was putting money into circulation when he bought old masters; he thought also to win favor with the intelligentsia of Berlin by showing himself a man of taste. He was delighted with the pictures which Lanny and Zoltan had hung on his walls; many distinguished persons came to look at them, and the *Schieber* saw himself in the role of one of the old merchant princes, many of whom had been of his race. Being a person of expansive nature, happy to be seen and admired, Johannes turned his home into a sort of art gallery, to which any person with credentials would be welcome. He had engaged a man whom he called a "steward" to run his household, and one of his duties was to answer letters and make appointments, and then a footman in uniform would escort the visitors about.

In accordance with Lanny's suggestion of a collection of Dutch masters for the principal downstairs rooms of the house, a grave and impressive Rembrandt now confronted you in the entrance hall, while over the mantel of the dining-room was a fine van Huysum, and in the library a Bol, a Frans Hals, and a de Keyser. The great drawing-room was given over to various modern Dutchmen, Mauve, Israels, and Bosboom, Weissenbrun and the Maris brothers. A breakfast-room had been specially decorated according to Zoltan's idea, harmonizing with the moderns, Jongkind and van Gogh—in one painting the latter had put three suns in the sky to make it brighter! Johannes didn't own this particular work, but many people wanted to see anything by so original an artist.

The visitors might be taken even to the bedrooms when these were not in use; for there were French masters delightfully adapted to bedrooms: drawings by Watteau and Fragonard, Lancret and

Boucher. It had been hard for Johannes Robin to face the idea of paying forty thousand gold marks for a red-chalk drawing by the first-named of these painters; he had taken the precaution to bring in an independent expert and make certain that Lanny hadn't committed a folly in that case. The man offered him fifty thousand, and Johannes felt vastly relieved.

Visitors could stop in the hallway outside a door where Hansi was practicing furious arpeggios or difficult double stopping, or where Bess was running piano scales in octaves. Only one door was never opened, and that was where the Mama Robin had her nest; no pictures there, but all the old things from which she would never part, because they reminded her of the days when she and an ambitious young salesman had lived in one tenement room and had been lucky when they could have *gefüllte fisch* and *blintzes* for supper. Now they had dinner at eight in the evening, sat at opposite ends of a long mahogany table with silver service and hand-embroidered napery and two men servants to wait on them, and it wasn't comfortable because you couldn't talk about any of the intimate things you wanted to. You had to live that way because fashionable people like Mrs. Budd expected it; also the important business people whom Jascha—so she still called her husband—brought home with him. It was grand to know that her man had become so successful, but in her heart Mama would have been glad to take her little brood back to some poor street among the sort of people she could understand and be fond of.

Lanny told Johannes a lot about the English masters which he had been purchasing for him and which were in process of being cleaned. The *Schieber* said he would be proud to own heirlooms of the Earl of Sandhaven; it would be something to tell visitors about. Lanny didn't go into details about the countess, just said that she had been a girlhood friend, and that was how he had learned about the paintings. He knew that Johannes would be amused by the story of a noble English lady collecting a commission from her husband; incidentally this was a way of letting a man of business understand that Lanny and Zoltan meant what they said about never taking commissions from both parties. There was a lot of rascality in the world, and having elegant manners and even a title was no guarantee against it. Lanny took a haughty attitude about himself; he told his clients exactly what he would do, and then he did it, and if anyone so much as hinted at distrust of his word, he took up his hat and told that person that he would prefer to have him or her find some representative in whom he had confidence.

XI

Beauty of course couldn't go to Stubendorf, for the Meissners were people with fixed notions of propriety and, while they had doubtless guessed the truth about Kurt's stay on the Riviera, they couldn't be asked to receive the woman in their home. That didn't worry Beauty, because she had been used to such things all her mature life and was well content with her own world, somewhat more than *demi*. Kurt and Lanny would go to the Schloss, while Beauty continued to meet the smart set of Berlin and be made dizzy by the "social whirl." So many fascinating men—and she was still at an age where she might have made a brilliant match, if it had not been for her sense of loyalty to a penniless genius.

At Stubendorf life was quiet and happy. Locarno was having its effect; industry was reviving throughout Upper Silesia, both German and Polish, which meant that there was a ready market for country produce, and it was possible to get needles and thread and clothing and shoes as in old days. There was a member of the family whom Lanny had never met before—that shell-shocked brother whom Kurt had visited in the Polish town. A somber, sad-eyed man with prematurely gray hair, he was dealt with gently, a little fearfully, as if people weren't sure what he might do next. Lanny didn't know what to talk to him about, but found that he was fond of music, and after that it was easy.

Heinrich Jung was there, having completed his studies in forestry; but he wasn't going to work at it because he had become a party leader and gave all his time to that. He was the same ardent propagandist, but no longer naïve, and Lanny didn't like him so well. Was it just Lanny's distrust of the Nazis, or was it the fact that Heinrich had become harsher and more cynical? Lanny listened to the conversation of the two friends about the details of party affairs, which appeared to be intrigues and treacheries, gossip concerning personalities, their weaknesses and inadequacies, and the methods of driving them to do what you wanted. It appeared that two wings had developed in the Nazi movement: in the north the party was under the control of one Gregor Strasser, and was "radical," that is, it took seriously the party's promises of economic change; whereas Hitler and his Munich group were now "conservative," possibly because of the large sums they were getting from Thyssen and his steel cartel.

Would it have been the same if Lanny had been listening to the talk of Social-Democratic, or Centrist or Communist party organizers? He told himself that it was probably so, for human nature remained much the same, regardless of what theories or programs men adopted; those who acquired power in any field found themselves in conflict with others who coveted that power and who had to be held in subjection by fear or greed. Lanny wanted to go back to his ivory tower, but his heart was sore because he wouldn't be able to take his old friend with him. Kurt was going to compose music for the Hitler movement, and was to be paid for it out of party funds; so there would be people intriguing for and against him, and the lofty serenity of Johann Wolfgang von Goethe would no longer be his prized possession!

They had motored to Stubendorf, and as Heinrich wanted to attend some party affair in Berlin, Lanny brought them both back with him. Kurt and Heinrich sat in the back seat and talked all the way, and by the time they arrived there wasn't much that Lanny didn't know about the National Socialist movement. The Führer, it appeared, was an ascetic who neither smoked nor drank nor ate meat; but he had on his hands a group of men who were far from saintly, and he had to rave and storm at them; sometimes he had to overlook their abnormal conduct because of their great ability, with which he could not dispense. Lanny heard about an ace aviator by the name of Göring who had fled to Sweden because he would not live under a Socialist government; now he had come back to help put the Reds of all sorts out of the Fatherland. He heard about a little club-footed dwarf named Goebbels who was the most marvelous propagandist in all Germany. He heard about others who had been police agents and still might be; some who had been criminals, but had fallen under the spell of the leader's patriotic fervor. The war had deprived Germany of many things, but it had provided her with a super-abundance of ex-soldiers, especially officers, some eight or nine hundred thousand of them—from the Führer, who had been a corporal, up to the great General Ludendorff, commander of them all. From lowest to highest, all were discontented, and formed material from which this movement of patriotic resurgence had recruited both leaders and followers.

XII

Lanny delivered the pair safely at their destination, in spite of a snowstorm. He did not go to their party affair, saying that he had picture business to attend to. Later, Kurt told him that he wanted to go to Munich to make arrangements for the publication of the music he proposed to write; Beauty wanted to go with him, but didn't want Lanny to motor through the high mountains in winter, so she and Kurt would return to Juan by train, and Lanny would drive to Holland and so into France. At Flushing he would be met by Rose-mary; and what a blissful thing to be with an Englishwoman, after all the large beefy bodies, the loud guttural voices, the storm and stress and conflict of Germany! Lanny decided that except for Hansi and Bess and Freddi he didn't care for anybody in Germany any more, and wouldn't go there. He loved the English people, who were quiet and restrained and easy-going; practicing pacifists, safely tucked away on their foggy island; blundering and bungling, but managing to improve things little by little, and hating hatred and violence and unreason.

So when he saw his sweetheart coming off the packet-boat, with only a few of her blond hairs ruffled by the January gale, he behaved just like a proper Englishman; that is to say, he shook hands with her and inquired: "Passage too beastly?" When she said: "No, not bad," he knew that there would always be an England.

29

Let Joy Be Unconfined

I

A NEW stage began in Lanny Budd's career. Living with the
Countess of Sandhaven was a different thing from living with Marie
de Bruyne. The latter had been a mature woman of quiet tastes; she
had been content to stay at home and read or listen to Lanny's music.
But Rosemary was young and beautiful, popular and *très snob;* she
liked to go about, see the gay world, and meet other young people.
Be assured, if Lanny didn't take her, plenty of others were eager to
do so! Marie had been like a wife, upon whom he had claims; but
Rosemary was a sweetheart, having to be perpetually courted. She
didn't ever make him jealous, but just took it for granted that he
would look out for her, and, valuing his treasure highly, he did so.

Never had the Riviera been so gay. Each season surpassed the last.
By the beginning of 1927 prosperity had returned; industry was
booming to make up for wartime destruction, and everybody who
had money counted upon having more. Americans, escaping Prohibition, came pouring into France; with the franc at two cents, one-
tenth its pre-war value, champagne was practically free. In the cold
weather most Paris visitors came to Cannes or Nice, Menton or
"Monty," and the bands thumped, there was dancing all night, and
insane gambling in the casinos—it was done mostly with thousand-
franc notes, the highest the French government printed, and the
devotees of roulette, baccarat, and "chemmy" brought great wads of
the stuff into the gambling-rooms. Wild parties and every sort of
excess became familiar, and suicides were decorously hushed up.

In the daytime the outdoor sports flourished: golf and tennis tour-
naments, polo, and all sorts of water games, including the new device

of water-planing; a sort of sled was towed by a fast motor-boat and you stood on it and had a wild time keeping your balance. The young people with nothing else to do sought thrills of danger and found them. The bathing-suits they wore or failed to wear became scandals which lasted for a week or two, until people found something else to be shocked by. Novelty was craved above all things; love-making took exotic forms, and at the afternoon parties and *thés dansants* the ladies were not content to have shoes and stockings and jewels and handkerchiefs to match their costumes, they now sought rouge to match, and daubed their faces with green or purple, like realizations of those futurist and surrealist paintings which had seemed to be nightmares but turned out to be prophecies.

The granddaughter of an English earl and wife of another didn't take part in silliness like this, but she liked to watch the crazy ones and make amused comments; she and Lanny went about with the smart set, and many times it would be daylight before they returned to that villa in the hills where Rosemary was a guest. You slept by day if you slept at all, and it soon destroyed a woman's health and complexion. Lanny as a boy had seen Marcel protesting against it with his mother, and now he would protest to Rosemary, and she would promise to reform, and do so—until the telephone rang and it was another invitation.

Amusing to see the effect of all this upon Beauty Budd, that old war-horse, who would smell the battle afar off, the thunder of the captains and the shouting. She would start to run up bills at dress-makers' and *marchands de modes'*. The real estate men had convinced her that she was worth tens of millions of francs, so why not get some good out of them? Eat, drink, and be merry, for tomorrow you will be offered twice as much for your property! The ex-baroness Sophie, being an heiress, always had a superfluity of beaux, and she would tell one of these to take Beauty to a dinner-dance, or something that meant late hours, and brought the mother into conflict with Kurt's rigid notions. She too would have to promise to reform.

If she stayed at home she would play bridge, a game which had been something of a nuisance in Lanny's young life. It seemed forever needing a fourth hand—and how very unkind of anyone to want to go off by himself and read a book! It transpired that Rosemary liked to play, and also that she was used to having men be "attentive." What was the use of a title of nobility if you couldn't command the services of a commoner—a foreigner, too—upon whom you conferred your favors? Lanny played cards many times when he would have preferred to examine the contents of a weekly which had just arrived from England; he played and liked it, because his sweetheart said it was "ducky" of him—also his mother said it was "darling." Seeing him so obliging, Beauty became reconciled to the fact that he didn't interest himself in this or that heiress who was the toast of the Côte d'Azur and who might have been persuaded to furnish grandchildren. Very soon Beauty adopted Rosemary as a member of the family, and urged her to move to Bienvenu, which she did, and it was more convenient for all purposes.

II

Kurt Meissner looked upon these activities with thoughts which he kept to himself, but Lanny knew him well enough to hear the unspoken words. Lanny was a weakling; he had always been led around at women's apron-strings, and would never amount to anything because he couldn't choose and follow a consistent course. Kurt wasn't being led around by anybody—at least not by anybody in this land of wasters and parasites! Kurt solved the bridge problem by the simple method of refusing to know one card from another. He was working at his music, and produced a cantata for four voices and chorus, designed to inspire the youth of the Fatherland with new vision and resolve. Kurt showed his attitude to the playboys and girls of Bienvenu by not offering to perform this work for them, hardly even bothering to tell them about it. The culture of the Fatherland was becoming revolutionary and sublime, and was wholly beyond the grasp of slack and pleasure-loving foreigners.

Kurt sent the score to Munich, where the Nazis had a publishing-house and were pouring out a stream of literature. No delays, no inefficiency here; proofs came promptly, and Kurt read them, and

very soon had copies of his finished opus. Then it would have been
rude not to offer one to Lanny and Rick, and he did so. Lanny
played as much of it as could be played with two hands, and saw
that it was a glorification of young people as the builders of the
future, a call to them to take up the sacred duty of making themselves the torch-bearers of a new civilization. *Deutscher Jugend*,
naturally; *unser Jugend* meant National Socialist Party youth.

But why limit it that way? Lanny said that all the youth of the
world ought to help to build that future, and he felt sure that Kurt's
words could be translated and his opus published in Britain and the
United States, possibly also in France. He was saddened to find that
Kurt wasn't interested in this proposal; Kurt didn't think those nations could understand the spirit of his work, and didn't even care to
find out. Apparently he wanted the new German culture to be kept
a German secret!

Lanny knew that *Fascismo* had been devoting its attention to its
youth from the very outset; their song was called *Giovinezza*, and its
spirit was identical with that of Kurt's new work. But it would be
tactless to hint at this, for Kurt regarded the Italians as a thoroughly decadent race, and would be indignant at the idea that the
Führer had taken the smallest hint from the Duce. The fact that one
word was a translation of the other was not mentioned in Nazi circles. Truth was German, virtue was German, and power was going
to be German. *Kraft durch Freude* was a German phrase, and the
idea of cultivating youth, glorifying it, feeding it well so that it
would be sound and vigorous, teaching it to march and drill and
chant about solidarity and devotion to *lieb' Vaterland*—assuredly all
this had come not from Mussolini, but rather from Bismarck, if you
must go back of the present Nazi movement. It was a part of the
German system of social security. Call it paternalism if you wished
—it meant that the *Volk* was one, its sentiments one, and those who
had the gift of genius and the technique of art would inspire the rest
with hope and courage, a new ideal of service.

"Of course," assented Lanny; "that is what we have talked about
since we were boys. But what kind of service is it to be? For what

purpose are the young people marching? We used to dream that it was to help all mankind."

"The rest of the nations don't want any help from Germany," replied the ex-artillery officer; "neither do they want to give us help. We social outcasts have to do our own job."

III

Rick and Nina came, according to their promise. Nina was a devoted wife and mother, and didn't go about much. Rick was working hard, making a book out of his various magazine articles; weaving them into a picture of Europe during the eight years since the Armistice. He read, wrote, and studied most of the time, and was rather pallid and harassed looking. Nina tried her best to divert his mind and to get him out of doors. She and Rosemary, being English, understood each other and were good friends. Lanny would take them sailing, or drive them whenever Rick could be pried loose. The children played happily with Marceline, under the watchful eye of the most proper of governesses, who was glad to see one respectably married English couple installed on the estate.

Lanny took a great interest in Rick's output; read his manuscript day by day and discussed the different points with him. It was Rick's thesis that nature had intended Europe to be a unity; economics and geography made it necessary, and the splitting of the continent into a number of little warring states meant poverty for them all. Lanny considered that an unanswerable proposition, but when he took it to Kurt he got the reply that Europe would have been a unity half a century ago if it had not been for England, whose fixed policy it was never to permit one people to gain hegemony, but always to raise up a rival. Divide and rule, the ancient formula. What Rick wanted was a Socialist Europe; but when that proposal had passed through Kurt's mind it emerged as a Europe disciplined and organized by the genius of the blond and blue-eyed Aryans.

While the Englishman was in the midst of his work there arrived from Heinrich Jung the second volume of Hitler's *Mein Kampf*.

Kurt read it, but didn't offer to talk about it with either of his friends. However, to a visiting German professor he declared that with all its obvious faults it was the work of a genius, a revelation of the insurgent German *Geist;* all kinds of mystical things like that, and so Rick decided that perhaps the book had a place in what he was writing, and he borrowed and read it. He judged it important enough to write a review and offer it to newspapers and weeklies, but in vain —for nobody in civilized and rational England could be interested in such stuff. Rick's favorite editor wrote him that there were hundreds of eccentric movements all over Europe and thousands in America, and why single out an author who was so clearly pathological?

Rick didn't mention the subject to Kurt, or to any other German; but to Lanny he pointed out the passages in which the Nazi Führer proclaimed it the destiny of the German race to rule the world. That was what the blue-eyed young Aryans were being marched and drilled for, that was what the fair Aryan maidens were taught to have babies for! "It's nothing but old-style chauvinism, with a German label instead of French," said the Englishman, who knew his history. "Not a new feature in it from cover to cover."

"Isn't the anti-Jew business new?" asked the American.

"Have you forgotten the Dreyfus case? It's the same thing all over Europe. Demagogues who don't know how to solve the problems of their time find it cheap and easy to throw the blame on the Jews, who made use of the scapegoat and now have to play the role."

Lanny was sad over these developments. His private Locarno wasn't succeeding so well as he had hoped. Rick and Nina stayed more and more in the lodge, and Kurt stayed in his studio; both worked hard, and their products would go forth into the world to wage ideological war upon one another! How long would it be before that kind of war became a deadlier kind?

IV

Robbie Budd came back from his journey to the land of desert sheiks. Lanny and Rosemary drove to meet him at Marseille, and found him browned by the sun and fattened by the life on shipboard. With him was Bub Smith, ex-cowboy and handy man in all emergencies. Bub was taking the first train for Paris on important business, but the father was coming to Juan for a few days' visit with his ex-family, or whatever you chose to call it. Robbie was good company, as always; he had funny stories to tell about the primitive world into which he had plunged, and was proud of Lanny and the tiptop young female he had picked for himself. He showed it in just the right jolly way, and Rosemary, who didn't as a rule take to Americans, found this a pleasant breeze out of what was to her the Far West. Connecticut was an Indian name, wasn't it? Did they still have them there?

When Robbie and his son were alone in the sailboat, the father had a lot of news. He had found things very bad at the property of the New England-Arabian Oil Company. None of the various kinds of trouble had been accidental. Robbie had fired one man, and had cabled to New York for an engineer to meet him in Paris. Robbie had made friends with some of the desert sheiks, and Bub Smith had awed them by a demonstration of pistol-shooting the like of which had never before been seen in Arabia. Robbie had learned that the sheiks' increased demand for money hadn't originated in their own brown skulls, but had been suggested from outside—in short, money had been paid in this desert land to make trouble for Robbie Budd and his associates.

"Who's doing it?" Lanny asked, and Robbie said: "That's one of the things Bub and I have to find out. I've had a notion in the back of my head for quite a while that Zaharoff may have something to do with it."

"Oh, my God!" exclaimed the son.

"Don't put it beyond him. It's an old trick, and he knows them all."

"But why should he be sabotaging himself?"

"He owns many oil properties, and mightn't object to shutting one of them down and waiting. If he could get us well 'softened,' as the military men phrase it, he might buy us out at his own figure."

"He's supposed to be broken-hearted over the duquesa," remarked the unmilitary Lanny.

"Doubtless he misses her; but it only leaves him more time to think about his money."

"What do you expect to do about it?"

"I haven't made up my mind yet. I'm going to see him, and I'll be able to judge better when I note his attitude."

V

The old munitions king now spent his winters regularly at Monte Carlo, and was a familiar sight strolling on its wide parkway, or sitting in the sunshine alone, staring ahead into vacancy. If some stranger approached and ventured to disturb him he would bite, and the severity of his bite had become something of a legend. He stayed at that same hotel where the young Lanny had had his amusing adventure with him; thirteen years had passed, but the richest man in Europe had never forgotten it, and there was always a twinkle in his blue eyes whenever he saw the son of Budd's.

Lanny and his father came by appointment, and were ushered to the same drawing-room by the munitions king's secretary, a retired British army officer. They were struck by the change in their host. Both his face and figure seemed to have shrunk, with the result that there were wrinkles in his skin, and his green satin smoking-jacket was a size too big for him; it covered half his hands, and Lanny wondered if it was because of the fact that the duquesa wasn't there to get him properly fitted. The snow-white mustache and imperial which he wore seemed longer and more straggly, and perhaps he needed someone to remind him to have it trimmed. A forlorn old figure he seemed to the sensitive younger man.

He was glad to see this pair, because they had known the wife whom he so adored. He spoke of his bitter loss, and they talked for a while about her; Lanny would have talked the same way about Marie de Bruyne, and it seemed to him that the genuineness of the old trader's feeling was obvious. Was it possible that a man could speak such words of sorrow, and accept words of sympathy in return, and then go off and stab the speaker in the back? Robbie said that he could and would, and to Lanny it was a type to study and a problem to meditate upon. In spite of having lived in a very bad world, the younger man hadn't had much personal acquaintance with villains, and was inclined to think of them as sick men, objects of pity. Had this master of money spent so many years tricking people that he couldn't help doing it, even when he could no longer use his gains?

"Well, young man," said Zaharoff, "I hear that you have become a captain of industry since we last met." Lanny was struck by the remark, which seemed to suggest that the old spider was getting reports on him. Surely Lanny's doings weren't important enough to be a subject of investigation by the munitions king of Europe!

"It wouldn't seem much to you, Sir Basil," he replied politely. "But it's enough to keep me contented."

"In that case, you might take me into partnership," remarked the other. "You have a secret worth more than money."

"Well, if you have any pictures that bore you, I will help you to get rid of them."

"I have a great many, and they all bore me."

"Perhaps you have learned too much about your fellow-men, Sir Basil," suggested the young philosopher; and the other replied sadly that there was no way to unlearn such lessons.

He always talked like that to Lanny. Was it because of the odd set of circumstances which had begun their acquaintance? Or was it because he thought that was the way to please a young idealist? Robbie had remarked to his son that a rascal was the last thing in the world that a successful rascal would appear to be. If he wished to win your favor he would find out what you admired and then be that. So don't take any of Zaharoff's remarks too seriously; don't be surprised if he was a scholar and an art lover—or even a moralist and a pacifist!

VI

The two oil men got down to business. Robbie reported on his visit to the Gulf of Aden; he gave no hint of his suspicions of sabotage, but laid the blame upon the native turbulence of Arab sheiks. He reminded Zaharoff that his reason for taking British investors into this undertaking had been the hope that British power could be assured for their protection.

"Yes," agreed the other; "but you know that these are disturbed times, and governments are less willing to incur risk and expense for us investors than they used to be."

"It is an awkward position for Americans to be caught in, Sir Basil. We had every hope that your influence could be counted upon."

"My influence is not what it was, Mr. Budd; I am an old man, and have retired from all activities."

"But you have many friends in the government."

"Governments change rapidly, and so, I am sorry to say, do friendships. When you sever business ties, you find that you are left pretty much alone."

The old Greek talked along that line for quite a while; he was extremely pessimistic concerning both himself and his world. The Reds were hanging on in Russia, and this was having the worst possible effect in other countries; the propagandists of sedition were spending fortunes in all of them, including Britain and France, to undermine the morale of the workers. "That Zinoviev letter wasn't the only one, Mr. Budd."

Robbie knew about that document, which had been given out a few days before the general elections in Britain and had enabled the Tories to sweep the country. Lanny's Uncle Jesse was sure the letter was a forgery, but Lanny knew that this idea could have no place in the discussion of two masters of money. He listened in silence while his father felt out the old trader's position on the subject of oil markets, prices, prospects, and what might or might not be done to persuade the British government to give naval support in places under British mandate from the League of Nations. Robbie suggested that Zaharoff might go to London and see if he could not get the necessary assurances; but the reply was that he was seventy-six years of age and his physician would not permit him to take such a trip in winter.

Finally Robbie dropped a hint to the effect that certain of his associates were discouraged about the prospects for New England-Arabian Oil, and were inclined to dispose of their holdings. Both father and son watched with interest to see what would be the reaction. Zaharoff said that such persons would be ill-advised, because there were many signs of trouble in various parts of the world, and if war broke out, oil shares were sure to rise. Lanny decided then that Robbie must be mistaken as to Zaharoff's purposes; but later, when the pair were leaving, the old man put in a casual remark that if any of the Americans were determined to part with their holdings, he might be willing to consider making an offer. Lanny changed his mind hurriedly; and when they were out in the car the father said: "You see the old spider spinning his web!"

Zaharoff's last words had been addressed to Lanny: "Come to the Château de Balincourt some time during the summer and let me show you my paintings." So Lanny asked his father: "What does he mean by that?"

"He'll try to find out things from you, as usual. He'll ask you how I am and what I'm doing, and maybe he can get some hints—just as I got some from him. He guesses that we're in trouble; but you see how shrewd and cautious he is—he doesn't want to make any enemies, and if he takes our shares, it will be as a favor. But somebody has made more than one attempt to burn that oil field."

"But, Robbie, wouldn't that hurt Zaharoff, too?"

"The greater part of the wealth of an oil field is underground, where fire can't get at it. But if your derricks and your tanks burn, you have to raise a lot of new working capital, and that's where he figures he'd have us."

Lanny was silent for a while; then he said: "It's hard for me to look into a man's face and imagine him plotting devilish things like that!"

The father gave a little snort. "He has been doing things like that for fifty years. My guess is he has a dozen men in his employ, to any one of whom he can hand a hundred thousand francs and say: 'There'll be a million for you if that field should burn.' After that he can forget the matter and not let it worry him."

Lanny thought: "Thank God I didn't go into the oil game!" He didn't say it, of course; there wasn't a soul on earth to whom he could say it. He had been born in the crater of a volcano, and he still

played about its slopes, catching pretty butterflies and making gar-
lands out of flowers; but he heard the rumble and smelled the sul-
phur, and knew what was going on below.

VII

Kurt gave his annual recital at Sept Chênes. Each year he made a
deeper impression, and this year he was asked to conduct a program
of his symphonic works with an orchestra at Nice; it was the nearest thing to a *rapprochement* between France and Germany that
Lanny had been able to achieve, and he was happy about it, and
proud of the man whom he had encouraged and promoted. For
Beauty Budd it was a personal triumph, a vindication of her career.
The gossips might say what they pleased about her, but how many
women had helped two geniuses to flower? Whenever Zoltan came
with a dealer to buy a Detaze, or whenever a critic referred to the
classic dignity of Germany's newest *Komponist*, Beauty's sins were
turned to glories, and she went out and bought herself a new evening gown.

More Germans were coming to the Riviera, and Kurt was beginning to have some social life; he was more willing to meet people
since he had found a new hope for the Fatherland. He talked a great
deal about Adolf Hitler and his movement, and to Lanny it sounded
like propaganda, but nobody objected, because it was of a respectable kind. Lanny observed that whenever the Nazis talked among
themselves it was of the glorious destiny of the Aryan race to rule
Europe; but when they talked to foreigners it was of the Nazi purpose to put down the Reds. Practically all people of property and
social position wanted that done; they looked with favor upon Mussolini for that reason, and never got tired of hearing how all the
labor unions had been put down in Italy. Now they were glad to hear
that Germany had a capable and determined man who hated Marx-
ism and wasn't afraid to fight it with its own weapons. One and all
they said: "We need something like that here."

Lanny was amused to see how under Kurt's influence his own
darling mother was evolving into a Nazi. She tried not to show it to

her son, but she got the formulas in her head, and the emotional attitudes, and every once in a while something would pop out of her mouth. Lanny knew his mother pretty well and understood that she had to believe what her man believed; the son tried not to make it hard for her, and kept out of arguments with both of them. He didn't have much time for his Red friends these days, but he salved his conscience by giving them money to help them out of trouble. He learned to say: "Don't come to the house, please. You understand how it is with one's family."

He was interested to observe the attitude of his new sweetheart to his eccentricity. To Rosemary politics was a personal affair; that is, it meant that her friends got interesting assignments to do things for the Empire—in Africa, or India, or the South Seas, or whatever remote place. This was important for the younger sons of good families, who had to earn their livings; Rosemary knew a lot of them, and got word from one or about one every now and then, and would tell Lanny: "You remember that redheaded chap who danced so well at The Reaches? He's been made secretary to the Commandant of the Port of Halifax"—or it might be Hong Kong. The idea of worrying about anything that could happen in political affairs just didn't occur to the granddaughter of Lord Dewthorpe; she knew that there would always be a British ruling class and that she and her friends would belong to it. In her easy-going way she was amused by her lover's notion of knowing Red agitators, calling them by their Christian names, and helping to support a Socialist Sunday school; she looked upon it as rather a lark to go to such a place and let grimy little *gamins* adore her. *Noblesse oblige* was the formula; and so long as Lanny's hobby didn't interfere with his putting on the right clothes and taking her out to dance, she was willing to have him called a Pinko and to pass it off with a joke. Why shouldn't he be what he jolly well wanted to be?

VIII

Isadora Duncan came to the Riviera that season. In the outskirts of Nice she found a large studio, almost a cathedral, and hung her blue velvet curtains on the walls, laid a huge green carpet on the floor, and put couches around the walls, covered with old-rose velvet and great numbers of pillows made of the same stuff. Alabaster lamps in the ceiling shed their light upon immense vases filled with Easter lilies, producing a very gorgeous effect. The art lovers of the Coast of Pleasure were invited to pay a hundred francs to see Isadora dance, and as this was only a couple of dollars in American money they came in great numbers. She had grown heavy again, and didn't dance very actively, but made as it were motions symbolic of dancing, and, strange as it may seem, she conveyed her charm by this means.

Lanny and his countess were among the visitors. After the dancing there was a reception, and Isadora welcomed her old friend. She invited him to come and call on her, and he did so, taking his *amie* by way of precaution. The dancer talked about her adventures in Russia, and mentioned the sad fate of her ex-husband, the poet Essenin, who had sunk into the gutter and recently had hanged himself.

Isadora herself was unhappy because her tours in Germany and America had not been a financial success. The newspapers made a scandal of her dancing with red scarves and delivering Red speeches. Isadora mentioned this with plaintive bewilderment; she never could understand the bourgeois world, or why it wouldn't accept the love and kindness of her heart. She was childlike, and still charming, in spite of evidences of drink.

Here on the Côte d'Azur were many friends who had helped her, but they seemed to have grown tired of it. She told Lanny how she had gone to Sept Chênes, and the châtelaine had received her kindly, but had refused to give her any more money because she disapproved of her way of life. Such things threw a genius *égarée* into a state of melancholy which lasted for days. She always had some marvelous dream, and just now it was to send for the children she had trained in Russia and have them dance in Paris and London and New York. Or she might set up a school in Nice and train the children of the residents! Here was this lovely studio, a true temple of art—but unfortunately there was neither water nor gas in it, and where could she live? Didn't Lanny know some rich person who would help her? Couldn't Rosemary appeal to some of her English friends?

"Oh, Lanny darling, please, please!" she begged, and turned to the woman, saying: "Don't think that I'll try to seduce him again." (Lanny hadn't told Rosemary about the first time!) "I have a perfectly lovely Russian boy—he's a divine pianist, and stays by me and never gets drunk but plays for all my practice, and I couldn't get along without him. But you know that I can't make my art pay—" and so on. It was embarrassing, because Lanny had no such sums of money as Isadora would spend.

He gave her a little, so that she could eat if she would, but the empty champagne bottles scattered about the place suggested that she mightn't be hungry. He gave no more, because Beauty started making a fuss as soon as she heard about it. "The woman is crazy!" she declared, and begged Rosemary to keep him from going near her again. A day or two later the papers were full of a story about a drinking-party at the dancer's home, in which a young American girl painter refused to drink, so Isadora's feelings were wounded; she decided that her days of usefulness were over, and wrapped her green velvet mantle about her and stalked into the Mediterranean at midnight. She got in as far as her mouth when a one-legged British army officer came plunging after her and managed to drag her out unconscious. Assuredly a piteous story, and not a very good advertisement for a school for dancing children! Lanny was forced reluctantly to give up his idea of having Marceline sent to this school. The teacher went back to Paris, where she still had her empty house and her swarms of artists to appeal to.

IX

Robbie Budd had been to London to see what he could do with the British officials; he had got promises, he wrote, but the language of bureaucracy was vague. He was at home again, but might be returning soon; there was to be a conference on naval limitation at Geneva. America had let herself be drawn into it, and some of the armament people, the boatbuilders and armorplate manufacturers, were going to have representatives at this conference, so threatening to their common interests. "Let the rest of the world do the disarming," said the father. "They have nothing to fear from us if they let us alone, and they know it. So why should they concern themselves whether we are armed or not?"

In the month of April Herr Meissner was down with the flu, and Kurt was worried about him and wanted to visit him. It would be the first time in eight years that he had seen his family except for the Christmas week. Beauty would have been glad to go with him, but of course he couldn't ask her; Lanny couldn't go on account of Rosemary, and also Zoltan coming with an important customer. Sorrowfully Beauty saw her lover depart; the years were passing, and she couldn't hope to hold him forever. She tried hard to persuade herself that she had a right to try. He was producing worthwhile art, wasn't he? And wasn't that as important to the Fatherland as producing babies with blue eyes and straw-colored hair? If you argued that Kurt might produce both, Beauty was able to make out a good case, for he was earning very little money, certainly not enough to support a family, and if he had to earn it he would sacrifice that leisure to compose which he enjoyed at Bienvenu.

The mother talked about it with her son, and he said: "There's nothing you can do, old dear, but leave it to fate and take what comes. You know how much you wanted to get me away from Marie, and you can't blame Kurt's parents if they behave the same way. A grandbaby is bound to count for more with them than any number of musical compositions."

Lanny said this with bluntness, because he guessed what was in Kurt's mind. For how many years could a German live outside his own country and associate almost entirely with foreigners without losing touch with the soul of his own people? Great events were preparing in Germany, or at any rate so Kurt believed, and he wanted to be the interpreter of them, perhaps their spiritual guide. If the day came when he made up his mind that he had to live in the Fatherland, what would Beauty do? Apart from the question of Aryan babies, which she, alas, was no longer able to provide, would she be willing to break up the home in Bienvenu? Would she expect to take Marcel's daughter to Germany? Would she expect Lanny to come? Quite a complication of questions!

X

The son of Budd's had a problem of somewhat the same sort. Rosemary had been away from her children for four months, and that was long enough; also, springtime was coming, and "Oh, to be in England!" It was Lanny's turn to visit her, and it certainly would not be gallant of him to refuse. But he had invited Bess and Hansi to spend the summer at Bienvenu, and had been looking forward to that with joy. He kept quiet about the problem, because he didn't know the answer.

A solution presented itself, quite beyond guessing; a rising financier, Johannes Robin, appeared in the role of *deus ex machina*, cutter of Gordian knots, stander of eggs upon end, performer of all magical feats. It happened that during Lanny's pre-Christmas visit he had talked to his friend about the array of Detazes which he had acquired. It was supposed to be Lanny's duty to explain them. There being two of the Norwegian pictures, he had told about the cruise of the yacht *Bluebird* to those lovely fiords; there being a Greek picture and an African one, he had described the Mediterranean voyage, going into details of its delights: how Mr. Hackabury had bought a baby lamb for the larder; how his small boy guest had caught fish in the Channel of Atalante and the host had called them "lannies"; their visits to the hanging monasteries on Mount Athos; the music and dancing on the deck of the yacht—all sorts of goings-on which sounded leisurely, romantic, and *snob*.

"How does one get a yacht?" Johannes had inquired.

"One buys it."

"But where does one buy it? Do you go to a yacht shop?"

"I guess you go to a shipbuilding concern, if you want a new one; or else you find somebody who has one to sell. Mr. Hackabury found a man who was in financial difficulties, and he bought the *Bluebird*, crew, captain, and all, even to the groceries on the storeroom shelves."

"That sounds like fun to me," said the man of great affairs. "I haven't been sleeping well of late, and I know I've been worrying. If I got away on a yacht, I'd really have to rest, wouldn't I?"

"Surest thing in the world."

"Suppose I was to get one, and take Mama and the boys and Bess, and invite you and your friends, do you suppose they'd come?"

"Some of them would, I'm sure," said Lanny, using a bit of caution. "Those who didn't happen to have engagements."

Now came a letter from Freddi, telling the news that Papa had bought a yacht called the *Drachen*, but unless Lanny objected he was going to change the name to the *Bessie Budd*. It was in the Kiel basin and was being refitted. They were planning a cruise up the Norwegian coast during the months of July and August, and of course it wouldn't be any fun unless Lanny and his friends came along. Papa hoped that the whole family would come, even Marceline and the governess. Papa would leave it for Lanny and his mother to select the guests, so as to be sure they were all congenial.

Nothing could be handsomer than that, and it suggested a solution for more than one problem. Lanny would motor Rosemary to England and she would spend part of May and June with her children, after which she and Lanny would go on the cruise. Nina and Rick would join them. As for Beauty, she said yes, but then became uneasy about Kurt, who would certainly not join such a party. Kurt's father was getting better, and the son was talking of returning to Bienvenu for the summer; but if Beauty were not there, he would probably remain in Germany, and so she might lose him.

That settled the matter, and Beauty decided to stay at home and take care of Baby Marceline, which the stern Kurt considered her first duty. She would manage to entertain herself, for Sophie was staying at the Cap this summer, and she had a beau, a retired businessman of settled habits, among which was contract bridge; old M. Rochambeau could always be depended upon for a fourth. "You young people go and enjoy yourselves," said Beauty, wistfully. It was hard to give up the idea that she too was a young person!

There was only one difficulty, a question of morals. Lanny sat down and wrote a letter to Johannes Robin, imparting a family secret, the story of the Countess of Sandhaven, that lady to whose initiative Johannes owed his Gainsborough, his full-length Raeburn, his Hoppner, his two Richard Wilsons and two Opies. Lanny explained that this unhappily married noble lady was for all purposes his wife, but maybe Mama Robin wouldn't think so, and mightn't be happy on the yacht with such unconventional company; therefore he thought it best to decline the kind invitation. He put it thus, so that the Robin family might have an easy "out" if they wanted it; but straightway came a telegram reading: "*Das macht nichts aus. Wir sind nicht Kinder.* Please reconsider. R.S.V.P." This international message was signed jointly: Mama, Papa, Freddi, Hansi, Bess; so there was no more need for qualms, and Lanny, feeling gay over the solution of a difficult problem, telegraphed his Jewish friend a good-sized chunk out of Tennyson's *Ulysses,* writing it the way he had seen his newspaper friends do it:

QUOTE THE LIGHTS BEGIN TO TWINKLE FROM THE ROCKS PARAGRAPH THE LONG DAY WANES THE SLOW MOON CLIMBS THE DEEP PARAGRAPH MOANS ROUND WITH MANY VOICES COME MY FRIENDS PARAGRAPH TIS NOT TOO LATE TO SEEK A NEWER WORLD PARAGRAPH PUSH OFF AND SITTING WELL IN ORDER SMITE PARAGRAPH THE SOUNDING FURROWS FOR MY PURPOSE HOLDS PARAGRAPH TO SAIL BEYOND THE SUNSET AND THE BATHS PARAGRAPH OF ALL THE WESTERN STARS UNTIL I DIE PERIOD UNQUOTE SIGNED LANNY BUDD.

XI

The *Bessie Budd* came to rest in the basin of Ramsgate, near the mouth of the Thames. She wouldn't come up to London because her master told her owner that, on account of the traffic, that was the most dangerous stretch of water in the whole world.

The yacht was not so big as the *Bluebird,* but big enough; graceful, trim, and white as any swan, a product of the German effort to show how much better work they could do than the British. She had been built since the war and was Diesel-powered; the owner had died, and Johannes had stepped in with an offer—he didn't say how much, for he was playing the grand gentleman, showing these fashionable foreigners what a perfect host a Jew could be. Lanny and Rosemary, Rick and Nina, came on board with their belongings, and the proud owner was about to give the order to cast off when there came a telegram from Juan-les-Pins: "Will you wait for me if I fly? Beauty."

Of course he answered yes, and they waited. Lanny, who had just put his car in storage, hired one, and drove to the Croydon airport. He knew how carefully Beauty had thought out her plans, and he knew how she hated the idea of flying and had never done it; he guessed that this sudden change meant serious trouble. When she stepped out of the plane he saw her face was set grimly. "What is it, dear?" he asked, and she answered: "Kurt is going to be married."

He was so sorry for her, he caught her in his arms right there; but she said: "I've had it out with myself, and it's all over. Forget it."

There were passports and customs formalities to be arranged, and he knew she wouldn't want the officials to see tears in her eyes. "Business as usual," was the plucky English formula, so he squeezed her hand and went ahead helping her with the practical affairs. After they were in the car, and before he started it, she took a letter from her handbag and gave it to him. He sat and read:

DEAR BEAUTY:
This is the letter which you have so many times told me I would some day write to you. It is hard to do, but your kindness and common sense have made it possible.

I have been told by my father's physician that he is not likely to live many years longer, and so I have to consider his happiness, if ever. Hitherto he has made little objection to our relationship, but of course it is not what he has hoped for, and now he has put it up to me in a way which I have not felt able to refuse. In short, dear Beauty, I am planning to be married, so it will not be possible for me to return to Bienvenu.

Knowing your goodness, I am sure you will be glad to hear that the young woman whom my parents have chosen is one with whom I can be happy. She is nineteen, and while she has not your beauty, over which the world has raved, she is of the type which I admire; her family are old friends of ours, so my parents know her character and qualifications for wifehood. She is gentle and good, and I have made certain of her feelings toward me before writing you this news. I count upon your friendship, so many times manifested, to appreciate my position and understand that I could not refuse the duty which has been forced upon me here.

As you know, you have saved my life, and you must believe that my gratitude will never cease. I did what I could in my inadequate way to repay you. The happiness which you gave me for eight years I shall never forget, nor the wisdom and loyalty. If I possessed the magic to make you twenty years younger—and if you were not a rich woman—I would take you to my parents and they would love you also. But they feel about me as you feel about Lanny—they want me to have a family, and good sense as well as tradition is on their side. I write this with tears in my eyes and I know you will read it in the same way. Show this letter to Lanny and ask him to forgive me and permit me to think of him always as a dearly loved brother. Explain matters as you think best to little Marceline, and let her remain my adopted daughter as well as pupil. I hope that in the years to come we need not always be strangers, and I hope that you may find the happiness for which you were made and which you have deserved.

Adieu, dear Beauty. From now on, your half-brother and half-son,

KURT.

"Don't say anything about it to the others," Beauty commanded, with hands clenched tightly. "I don't want to be a wet blanket. I came because I felt I must have a change of scene."

"Of course!" he exclaimed. "I am glad, and the others will be, too."

"This thing has been hanging over me, and I suppose it's better to have it over with." She only half meant it, but it was good propaganda.

He started talking about the people he had met in London, the plays he had seen and the exhibition. The "season" had been a gay one; the country was recovering from the great strike, and everybody was making money again. Now and then he would see out of the corner of his eye that his mother was wiping away a tear, but he pretended not to notice. There were eight kind friends waiting for her, and the stimulus of companionship was what she lived by. "What shall I tell them, Lanny? I mean—why I came."

"Just say you couldn't miss the fun. That will please them all. But don't have your eyes red."

"Are they?" She got the little mirror out of her vanity bag; so he knew she was going to survive.

XII

The *Bessie Budd* put to sea, with her namesake and the other guests all determined to be happy, and succeeding as well as possible in an unhappy world. It was really too much to expect that Beauty wouldn't mention her secret; first she told Nina, who in turn told Rick; Lanny told Rosemary, and presently Beauty was tempted to unburden her soul to a kind Jewish mother who had no social pretensions and therefore made it unnecessary for other people to have any. These two female elders enjoyed exchanging wisdom, mostly in the form of personalities, as is the female way.

The marriage arrangements of this strictly brought-up mother of Jerusalem had been made by her parents through the agency of a *schadchen*, or marriage broker. To Beauty it seemed romantic to have been married in a tenement room, to have stuck to one poverty-burdened man and seen him become the owner of a palace and a private yacht, and seen your first-born make his debut in Carnegie Hall. Mama Robin didn't say that to her it seemed romantic to have run away from home, and to have been the adored of three remarkable men and the mother of a fourth; but she listened with eagerness to Beauty's tales about high life, and if she felt moral reprobation she kept it locked in her own bosom. She had known about Kurt Meissner for a long time, and had foreseen the grief that was coming; she was interested to be present at the *dénouement*, and to provide a receptacle for all the tears her fair but frail guest might desire to shed.

The little yacht slid over the still blue waters to Oslo. The munificent host hadn't been content with the piano which was fixed in the saloon; he had got an extra one on little rubber-tired wheels, so that it could be rolled onto the deck and made fast there. Hansi did his practicing in his cabin, but if you requested it he would bring his fiddle on deck, and Lanny or Freddi would play his accompaniments, and the cruise of the *Bessie Budd* resembled Rubinstein's *Ocean Symphony*. Johannes had been to his bookseller's again, and ordered eleven meters of books for the saloon of a gentleman's yacht, and there they were, safely shut up in glass cases to keep them from spilling. There was something for every taste, and their owner, who had never had time for reading, now proceeded to acquire culture with the same speed and efficiency he had displayed in acquiring ownership of industrial establishments throughout Germany.

He was interested in talking to all these people, who had come from social groups so far removed from his own; he was not frightened by any of their unusual ideas, not even those of a baronet's son. As for a countess, Johannes had the idea that she would prove not so very different from Mama Robin under the skin. They got along quite amiably; for Rosemary, Countess of Sandhaven, had that comfortable sense of superiority which is so very superior that it never has to assert itself, but takes it for granted. To her the owner of a yacht and the steward of a yacht each had his separate functions; the owner put everything on board at her disposal, while the steward performed the physical labor of bringing things to her, and each had his proper place and knew it. Lanny also had his duties, and performed them without too great reluctance; he was the only male on board who played bridge acceptably, and when Beauty, Nina, and Rosemary united their demands there was no escape for him.

XIII

The *Bessie Budd* followed in the long-vanished track of the *Bluebird* up the Norwegian coast. Beauty remembered the places, and noted the changes—there weren't many. She told about this place and that; she knew where the great waterfalls were, and the *saeters* to which you could be driven in a car. Up on that mountain slope was one of the very old farmhouses with a hole in the roof for a chimney; beyond that village was a house that had a tree growing in the roof to hold the turf—perhaps it had grown too heavy in fourteen years. Now and then Lanny would recognize a scene from one of Marcel's paintings; a great moment when Johannes cried: "Look, Mama, there is the place that is in our upstairs hall!"

Beautiful rocky shores, dark blue waters, towering mountains! The yacht went all the way north to the Arctic Circle, where there is no night in midsummer. Lanny had read in his anthology of English poetry about "the shore where loud Lofoden whirls to death the roaring whale," but he had never learned who or what Lofoden was. Now he learned that it was a group of islands much frequented by fishermen, but he couldn't seem to find any who had ever heard a whale roar.

The yacht put in to buy supplies at the little port of Narvik, where the Swedish iron ore was brought down in long trains of dump-cars, and day and night there echoed through the narrow fiord the sound of heavy minerals sliding down chutes into the ore-ships. The visitors were plain mortals with no gift of second sight, so they heard no other sounds: no shattering crash of shells, no airplane bombs bursting among the docks and loading machinery; no sheets of white flame, no shrieks of dying men, no rush of waters closing over vessels going down into the darkness. Wait a few more summers, O trim white *Bessie Budd*, and come back to loud Lofoden once again!

30

Birds of Passage

I

ON BOARD the *Bessie Budd,* Lanny and his lady were as happy as the prince and princess in a fairy-tale; but as the cruise approached its end a tiny rift began to develop between them. "Where do we go from here?" It appeared that the circumstances of their lives were in conflict; Rosemary had her splendid manor house and her children, while Lanny had his home, his mother and his half-sister, and these various possessions were hard to fit into one pattern.

On the Riviera Lanny had learned of some pictures that might be sold, and he had promised to inspect them in September; Rosemary had promised her children to be with them after the cruise, and also she had friends whom she wanted to see. All right, Lanny would go home and attend to his job, and then he would come back to England, and stay—how long? Rosemary wanted to be with the children until after Christmas; since Lanny hadn't been at home at that season for many years, he could surely afford to miss one more!

But it wasn't so pleasant for Lanny at Rosemary's home. He had to pretend to be a guest, and there had to be other guests, to serve as informal chaperons; and whatever he and Rosemary did that was not according to the code of Queen Victoria had to be clandestine. If they went up to London they traveled separately, and stayed at an obscure hotel, and Rosemary was not registered under her own name. All this was inconvenient for a businessman, and seemed rather futile, because if anyone had wished to employ detectives, these wouldn't have had any trouble in following Lanny.

What was the reason for all this? He could never be quite sure. Didn't Rosemary trust her husband entirely? She wouldn't admit it, and perhaps protected him even in her own thoughts. Impossible that an English earl might turn out to be a cad! Lanny knew the law— if Bertie proved one act of infidelity, he could divorce her, turn her out of her home, deprive her of her rights to her children. In that case it would be up to Lanny to marry her, and he would like nothing better; but apparently the Countess of Sandhaven wasn't satisfied with that solution of her problem.

So there were many difficulties. It was England, not Provence, and the proprieties must be observed. The servants must not be allowed to know that Lanny and Rosemary were lovers. They would know really, but not officially. Robbie Budd said that change in England was like the small hand of your watch; it moved, but so very slowly that no one had ever seen the motion. Lanny could comfort himself with the reflection that a century or two earlier Bertie would have challenged him to a duel, and a century or two earlier still Bertie's henchmen would have run him through with their swords.

The young art authority became more than ever a bird of passage, flitting back and forth between the Mediterranean and the English Channel, but having no regular seasons like other birds. When he could persuade his sweetheart to stay at Juan, he provided her with every comfort and some luxuries; but it appeared to be a matter of prestige with her to make him spend half his time in or about her haunts. In order to prove that he loved her he had to be damned uncomfortable: he had to miss his music, his books, and his regular habits, to say nothing of his mother and his half-sister. Marceline acquired the place of a stepchild in Rosemary's life, and her children became stepchildren to Lanny—and it is well known that this relationship is a perilous one. Little inconveniences produce larger jangles, and Cupid goes off in a corner by himself and sulks.

II

Marceline was ten years old, a slender, graceful child, full of eager gaiety. She was at about the same age as Bess when Lanny had first known her in Connecticut, and the difference between them made a study in heredity. Marceline was less intellectual than the daughter of Esther Budd; less concerned to know how the wheels went round, and rarely plaguing you with questions that you couldn't answer. Nor did she worry about whether what she was doing was right; she acted from the impulse of her heart, and if she was fond of you that was enough. She was the daughter of an artist, and would stand for a long time watching a gaily colored butterfly, drifting from flower to flower in the patio of her home; a sunset would cause her to lose herself as her father had done. When Lanny played the piano, she didn't want to sit and listen like Bess; every pulse of the music was a call to her feet.

Lanny had taught her all about her father. She had seen his paintings until they had become a part of her life. Lanny had related them to Marcel's life; so the child was conscious of being a daughter of France; she knew its recent tragic story, and the part her father had played in it. She was her mother's daughter also, and couldn't well forget it, with the mother right there to set her an example of beauty culture, to serve as a walking encyclopedia of fashion, of colors, of fabrics, methods of cutting and arranging them, and of displaying or concealing the feminine form divine. There was a dressing-table loaded with perfumes and cosmetics, all in the prettiest jars and bottles labeled with the most seductive names. There were Beauty's smart friends coming in at all hours to make use of these allurements, keeping up a chatter about them, their uses and effects. Marceline was a little primper, a little *modiste*, a little coquette.

Also there were the servants, who exercise great influence upon children everywhere, and nowhere more than in Provence, where they consider themselves members of the family, tell you about themselves and their families, give advice about yourself and yours. Leese, the cook, had gradually promoted herself to the position of housekeeper, with the power to hire and fire; so there were two families on the estate, that of the mistress and that of the servant, and neither could have got along without the other. Leese and her nieces and cousins all had their ideas and taught them to the child. When she was kind they adored her, when she was beautiful they raved over her; she ate their foods, spoke their dialect, danced their gay and lively steps.

Also a German musician, a former foe, had played his part in the shaping of the little one's character. Kurt had taught her discipline and obedience, and it was a serious matter for her when his influence was withdrawn. When Lanny came back in September he saw that she had already made note of the change; she could now have her way with the servants and presently she was having it with her mother. Lanny had the unpleasant duty of interfering; it wasn't according to his nature, but he, too, had learned a lot from Kurt, and would plead with Beauty to realize the importance of controlling a child's whims. Beauty would agree, and do her best—but she was part child herself, and needed someone to control her.

There was a gaping cavity in Bienvenu where Kurt had been: the deserted studio, the piano from which came no more rolling thunder; his room, his bed, the empty closets. Beauty had told the servants to pack up all his things and ship them to him, and this had been done: clothes, music, books, assortment of noise-making apparatus. The studio was locked up, and Beauty couldn't bear to go near it. But the place in her heart was not so easily shut, and Lanny saw her eyes red many a time.

What was she going to do about it? She swore that she was through with men forever, but Lanny didn't have to believe this; he took it for granted that she wouldn't spend the rest of her life alone, and the question was, what sort of man would it be? If only she would pick some settled retired businessman, like this Mr. Armitage with whom Sophie was getting along so well! But Beauty was flighty, and still had romantic notions buried somewhere inside. Of course, the man who won the love of Madame Detaze, *veuve*, would step into a warm and well-padded nest, and candidates presented themselves promptly. Lanny began to worry about the sort of men who came to this playground of Europe, and he took counsel with Sophie Timmons and Emily Chattersworth as to how to find a proper beau for his too charming widowed mother. The ladies found this delightful, and the story spread up and down the Coast of Pleasure.

III

Isadora Duncan came back to the Riviera. She put up at a little inn in Juan-les-Pins, and Beauty was quite indignant about it, saying that she would be expecting Lanny to pay the bills. The dancer had a woman friend with her, an American who was supposed to have money, but said that she had spent it all getting Isadora "out of hock." Beauty said that was the way they all did, they hid their money and said they were broke, trying to put the burden off on others. Well, Beauty was broke, too; she hadn't paid her dress bills for last season, and here was a new season almost upon them, and was she to go about naked—or to stay at home and die of loneliness and grief?

Isadora and her friend put on bathing-suits of the ultra-scanty sort and lay about on the white sand of the Juan beach. Lanny joined them and listened to an account of what had happened in France one night while Lanny had been on board the yacht in the North Sea— the night of August 22, 1927, when Sacco and Vanzetti had died. Lanny recalled the first time this case had been mentioned in his hearing, by Ambassador "Cradle" during the Genoa conference. Since then it had become an international scandal, and when the Italians were executed there had been mobs marching in all the cities of Europe, and many American embassies and consulates had had their windows smashed. To Isadora the two men were martyrs and heroes, and their death had been a personal bereavement; she was going to create a dance for them, and take it to New York—yes, and to Boston!

The daughter of the Muses was still a beautiful creature; she had been dieting and was getting herself into condition so that she could dance again. She was a completely reformed woman, so she assured Lanny; the rest of her life to be consecrated to that marvelous art which she alone could embody and express. She said it, and who could deny it? She was going to be a dancing nun from this time forth; except, of course, that she had to find a pianist, some devoted soul who would play her accompaniments. The young Russian had left her.

Always when Isadora was in a mood like this she had to have a school. Children became the incarnation of her thwarted dreams; children were the future, the repository of her art, the torch-bearers who would carry it to posterity. She had been to Les Forêts and persuaded Emily Chattersworth to give her another chance; now she wanted Lanny and his mother to persuade some of the fashionable residents to send her their children as pupils. That beautiful studio near Nice was to be consecrated to this noble service.

Lanny took the problem to his mother, who didn't want to have anything to do with it. He sought to persuade her that this might be the great chance of Marceline's life. Isadora was nearly fifty, and couldn't live forever. She had something that no other woman in the world had. Lanny reminded his mother of that cruel tragedy which had wrecked the dancer's personal life; thirteen years had passed since her adored little ones had been drowned in the river Seine, and everybody knew that she had never got over it, the horror haunted her dreams and poisoned her joys. And then her third baby, that had died in her arms a few hours after it was born—had Beauty forgotten how she and Emily had wept over the event, in those tragic hours while the troops were being mobilized in Paris and marched to the trains? Surely a woman who had suffered such griefs could be forgiven many errors!

Beauty said: "She will get drunk and the child will see her."

"All right," argued Lanny, "what of it? Marceline is not going to live in this part of the world without seeing somebody drunk. We'll just have to explain to her what it is. You managed to teach me not to get drunk, and surely you and I together can teach Marceline. If she sees an example it may give her a shock, but it will disgust her and warn her, too."

"All right," said the mother at last; "but it's your responsibility!"

IV

Lanny drove to tell the dancer that they would help to find pupils for her. But he found everything changed, the studio in a turmoil, Isadora raising a ruction because a second-hand dealer had offered her such small sums for the furniture of the place; she would give everything to a hospital, rather than sell at such prices. It appeared that she had changed her program a couple of days ago, and had been too busy or too excited to let Lanny know about it. She was taking a long motor-trip; she was going to be happy again; youth and joy had come back to her. She told Lanny about it in the extravagant language which she loved.

What had happened? She forgot to explain, but presently it came out—"Lohengrin" had returned! The sewing-machine man had promised her a large check, and all her problems were solved. "You know how I always adored him, Lanny." Yes, Lanny had met this tall, blond gentleman, who looked like a middled-aged Norse god, and poured out bounty like the purse of Fortunatus. He was going to take her on a tour, and they would sample the fresh new wines of all the vineyards of France. She would still have her school, of course, but it would have to wait. "Oh, Lanny darling," she exclaimed, "I am truly grateful to you—honestly, I'll prove it!" She gave him a great hug and kiss as earnest of her intentions. Rosemary was in England.

In the studio was a young Italian, who had been an ace aviator during the war, and Isadora adored men who had defied danger. He looked as if he didn't enjoy seeing Lanny kissed, so she kissed him also; she was so happy, she had enough for everybody. "This dark-eyed Adonis is going to take me to a concert tonight," she said. "Won't you come along?"

"No, thanks," replied Lanny. "I have an engagement at home."

"Oh, my dear, don't be provoked with me! If you knew the depth of misery I have been in, you would understand my need of happiness. Look, I will dance for you and change the world."

She had a marvelous red shawl made of Chinese silk crape, heavy, and with long fringes. It was a couple of yards in length, painted with an enormous yellow bird, and in the corners were blue Chinese asters and black Chinese characters; Isadora pretended to find meaning in the latter. She adored this treasure, and had used it in many of her dances. Now she caught it up from a chair, and tossing it about began a dance of the vineyards of France in the harvest season. "Play for me, Lanny!" she cried; and he, remembering the happy hours at Les Forêts, played the ballet music from *Samson and Delilah*. Again the magic of art; a lily blossoming from the mud, a miracle repeating itself, always astonishing, the last time as the first.

Lanny wished her luck and went home. Again he had no gift of second sight, and it wasn't until the next morning that he heard the dreadful tidings. The young Italian had come with his low racing-car to take Isadora to the concert, and she had come out from the studio with that marvelous long shawl about her neck. To those who came to see her off she said: "*Adieu, mes amis; je vais à la gloire.*" She stepped into the car, leaning her head against the side, and one end of the shawl hung down outside, and the wind blew it about. As the car began slowly to move, the fringes caught in the rear wheel and were twisted round and round. By the time the car had moved a few feet the tightening fabric had become a strong rope wound about Isadora's neck; it drew her lovely face against the side of the car and crushed it, broke her neck, and severed her jugular vein.

All the world of art was grief-stricken when that story reached it next morning. The ruined body was sealed in a zinc-lined coffin and taken in a funeral train to Paris. Lanny didn't go, for Lohengrin was in charge, the man she had chosen. At the Père-Lachaise cemetery there was such a throng that it was hard to get the funeral car in. Soldiers stood with heads bowed and art students sobbed aloud. At the crematory an orchestra played Bach's *Mass in D*, which was her favorite. Thousands stood and watched the pale gray smoke rising from the chimney of the crematory, and wondered to what heaven the soul of their adored one was bound.

V

Lanny came to London in the disagreeable autumn weather, and installed himself in a little flat to which Rosemary would come when the spirit moved her. Zoltan was there, and they attended the exhibitions and sales, and the Countess of Sandhaven helped to find members of the aristocracy who had old pictures and would prefer to have cash. There were theaters to visit, and concerts to hear;

dancing with the smart young people, and supper parties, all the "social whirl." One could have a very good time if one didn't think, didn't see the signs of poverty and suffering, didn't read the sort of papers in which such things were mentioned.

Robbie came for another visit. He had been in Geneva while Lanny was on the yacht, and had helped to set up a bureau to send news back to America, opposing the naval-limitation project which was being discussed. Robbie was aggressive and determined about it, and pleased because he had won. Britain and Japan had been unable to agree with the United States regarding the limitation of cruisers. Robbie said it was preposterous to imagine that Japan would keep such agreements; Japan would keep secrets.

This time Robbie was here because of his oil business. You couldn't make large sums of money without having troubles, it appeared; all sorts of people rose up to make them for you. One of the old sheiks had died, and his nephew had ousted the son—a sort of South American revolution in Arabia. There had been a raid on the oil field, just like the gang wars in Chicago; amazing how fast civilization had spread! Robbie had pulled wires through the State Department, and had got a British destroyer sent there, but the Arabs had fled on their horses and the destroyer didn't have any. Robbie wanted a British army post established on or near the concession of the New England-Arabian Oil Company, and when he failed to get it, he served notice that he was going to have his own private army, and cabled the New York detective agency which did the underground work for the Budd plant in Newcastle to go ahead and recruit some men. A rather amusing circumstance: Robbie Budd, head of the European sales department of Budd Gunmakers, was going to sell arms to Robbie Budd, president of New England-Arabian Oil—and get his commission on the deal!

Lanny and Rosemary would go to The Reaches for a week-end, and listen to Sir Alfred and his guests discussing the state of the world. The older men had now decided that Europe was in for a long period of peace, such as it had enjoyed before the World War; they would give figures regarding the revival of trade, and since the general strike had been put down, they expected prosperity at home.

Rick, the young firebrand, had written a book opposing this comforting faith; but nobody objected—in their easy-going way they all took it for granted that a young man should wave some sort of torch. Only when you were thirty-five or forty were you expected to settle down, and when you were seventy you were ready to become an unpaid magistrate.

Rick's book was out, and getting very good notices; he had a new lot of press cuttings whenever Lanny saw him. Because of Rick's knowledge of political movements in Europe a well-known theatrical producer had invited him to do some writing on a play; it might be an important connection, so Rick and his family wouldn't come to the Riviera that winter. As it happened, one of Rosemary's children had had a severe cold; and there was that lodge at Bienvenu standing vacant. Why wait for Christmas? Have Christmas there! The decision was taken; Lanny motored down to get things ready, and Rosemary came by train with the governess and maids and three children. Marceline would have a different set of playmates that winter, but Lanny would have the same one!

VI

The beautiful estate on the Cap d'Antibes had passed through a series of stages. It had been one sort of place when Lanny Budd had been a little boy and his mother had been alone. It had been another sort when Marcel was living there, and yet another under the regime of Kurt. Now, without Kurt and without Rick, the life was without its intellectual distinction. No more discussions of politics, literature, and art; no more music, except what Lanny made for himself, plus the phonograph and a new radio-set. Kurt's big piano had been brought over to Lanny's studio, and he would play it there; he found time for that and for reading, because the bridge problem had happily solved itself. Sophie Timmons had married her retired businessman, and was now Mrs. Rodney Armitage, and they made a contented four with Beauty and Rosemary.

Mr. Armitage was older than his wife, a widower with grown children in the States. It meant that Sophie had accepted middle age, and was sad about it, or pretended to be; though, with a comfortable villa and plenty of money, her fate might have been worse. The new husband was a vigorous man in spite of his gray hair; sensible and dependable, he knew several different bridge systems, and used the one his wife preferred, which, as everybody knows, is important to marital happiness. When they weren't playing cards he told stories about the strange parts of the world which he had visited as an engineer installing electrical equipment. Rosemary liked him, and got along with the flamboyant and free-spoken Sophie because they were so different that they amused each other.

Lanny's business kept on growing. Amazing, the way people were making money! Those who came to the Riviera seemed to have unlimited drawing-accounts, and those who laid claim to culture wanted to take home something distinguished to remind them of Europe. The Murchisons showed up, after nearly five years; Harry a little stouter, Adella more sure of herself. If she was shocked to discover Lanny with a married sweetheart, she was too well bred to speak of it; after all, an English countess was not to be sneezed at. Adella reported that the Goya and the alleged Velásquez had hit the bull's eye; also, those friends whom she had sent to Lanny were well pleased with what he had done for them.

Now they had more money than ever, for Harry was shipping plateglass all over the world. They wanted to be taken about and shown old châteaux, and meet distinguished people, and be told what was what by an elegant and fashionable guide, a super-cicerone. "Give us some of your time," said the lady from Pittsburgh, in her straightforward way, "and I'll see that it's made worth your while." It cost them a total of a hundred and seventy thousand dollars, but they carried home a couple of Gobelin tapestries and a magnificent Turner landscape which Lanny had discovered in the home of an English family, residents of Cannes for half a century. Lanny pocketed his ten percent and was satisfied with the value set upon his time.

Rosemary was more contented that winter, because she had the children with her, and didn't gad about so much or miss so much sleep. The children throve in the sunshine, and Lanny said: "Why not bring them every season?" Rosemary was pleased by this evidence of his honorable intentions, but she said: "What will Rick and Nina do?" The young prince of plutocracy replied: "I'll build another lodge for you."

Why not? Money was rolling in, and there was plenty of room on the estate; a house anywhere on the Cap would never be wasted, it could always be rented in case of need. Robbie approved of buildings, even more than of stocks and bonds, and Beauty, sociable soul, was glad to have more people around her. No sooner said than settled; they amused themselves planning the sort of house that Rosemary and her children and servants ought to have. The more nursery space the better it pleased Beauty, for she had a purpose hidden in her heart; that space wouldn't always be used by other men's children!

VII

Kurt was married, and sent a picture of his bride, sweet and gentle-looking, as he had said; a bit insipid, Beauty thought—but then you couldn't expect her to be enthusiastic. No doubt the girl was what Kurt needed, and Beauty hoped he would be happy, and not remember too vividly the raptures of illicit love. Kurt sent copies of his new compositions, and press items about them. He didn't send Nazi literature, for he knew that Lanny was never going to become a convert; but Heinrich Jung still clung to his hope—impossible for him to believe that anybody could resist the pull of a movement that was spreading so rapidly over Germany. Once in a while the papers he sent would have something cut out of them, and Lanny would smile to himself and wonder just what it was that Heinrich didn't consider proper for a foreigner to read. Some too crass announcement of Aryan purpose to rule the world? Some too crude abuse of that vile and poisonous race which was conspiring with both Bolsheviks and bankers at the same time?

Lanny still kept up his interest in the Reds and the Pinks, though he didn't work very hard at it. He took several of their papers and read them now and then, and his conscience was kept uneasy. In

Italy the labor movement was completely crushed; there were no more strikes, and those who might have any thought of opposing *Fascismo* were either dead or in exile. The latter group wanted support for their paper in Paris, and Lanny could help them generously, owing to the fortunate circumstance that what was a little money for him was a great deal for them. In France nobody was getting arrested or beaten, at least not that Beauty Budd heard about, so gradually she decided that being a Pink meant nothing worse than having lunch with a visiting journalist, or giving a thousand-franc note to some poor creature with ill-fitting clothes and hair untrimmed. Since the amount was no more than she would spend for a spring hat or an embroidered handkerchief, she put it down as a form of charity, to which we all have to make contributions for the good of our souls.

The only time when Bienvenu became really Red was when Hansi and Bess came for a visit. These two young people were really quite shocking; especially Bess, who now called herself an out-and-out Bolshevik. Silly to imagine that the propertied classes would ever give up their stranglehold upon society unless they were forced to! Silly to waste your time talking to them about brotherhood—who was ever brother to a slave but another slave? The daughter of Esther Budd had conceived the most intense antagonism to the social system which had given her so many privileges. She had decided that her education was a mass of falsehoods, and was ready to prove it by illustrations taken from personal experience.

That was the way the young folks were going, and there seemed to be nothing you could do about it. Hansi, gentle and sweet-natured, was careful not to say things to hurt people's feelings, but in his convictions he was at one with his wife. He was going back to Germany to begin a concert tour and in the autumn was going to make a tour of the United States. He was to be paid a percentage of the receipts, and if the tours were successful he would make large sums of money. Everything above their traveling-expenses he was going to turn over to organizations which gave relief to the refugees of Fascism and to workers persecuted for their labor activities. That meant for the most part Communists, and both Hansi and Bess were prepared to tell the newspaper reporters what they believed—and so perhaps ruin their tours, as poor Isadora had ruined hers.

Lanny saw in the attitude of his half-sister the impatience of the very rich, who were used to having their own way; also of the young, who had never suffered and therefore knew no fear. No stopping her, and no use to argue with her. To her mind Lanny had become one of those ineffectual dreamers who proposed to cut off the claws of the tiger of capitalism one by one—and always with the tiger's kind consent. It was all right to be a noble-souled idealist, but when you let your influence be used by Social-Democratic politicians who were misleading the workers, using them to get elected to office and then to dicker and betray—that was terrible! Lanny, for his part, thought that Bess was becoming one of Uncle Jesse's phonograph disks. As always, he lamented the tragic split among the workers, which made them impotent in the grip of their exploiters. In due course, he told himself, Bess would discover the flaws in the tightly welded formulas of the Communists; also, alas, the difference between the preaching and the practice of most humans. "Take it easy, kid," he would say. "A lot of things are going to happen, and you'll have plenty of time to think about them." So old and worldly-wise he had become!

VIII

Another old friend came visiting that season: Margy Petries, Dowager Countess Eversham-Watson. Poor old "Bumbles" had died in great pain of his gout, and his son by a previous marriage was the young lord. Margy wasn't as rich as she had been, for "Petries' Peerless" had been put clean out of business by Prohibition, the most wicked act of confiscation ever perpetrated, so Margy would declare; however, her family had seen it coming and had salted money away, so she didn't have to "go on the county," as the phrase was at home. She and Beauty were old cronies, and never were there two more sprightly widows; they would put on their best duds and amuse themselves breaking the hearts of all the suitors on the Riviera —but as for letting one trap them—never, never! Wealthy widows come to look upon themselves as grouse in the shooting-season; all the men on the moors are carrying guns and looking especially for them.

Margy solved the problem of Beauty's immediate future by inviting her to London for the fashionable doings. Margy still had her town house, her own property, and it was "a barn," and hard to fill; Beauty would come and help her to entertain. She could bring Marceline and the governess if she wished, and Marceline could have music- and dancing-lessons, or could stay out in the country, where Margy had the use of the lodge on her stepson's estate. Later on, the Robins were planning a cruise in the Baltic, and would visit—of all places on earth—the city which had once been called St. Petersburg and now had a name which one apologized for pronouncing. A special concession to the young Reds in the family, Beauty explained; but Margy said it required no apology, it sounded like a lark, and Beauty thereupon wrote to Johannes, who in turn wrote inviting the Dowager Countess Eversham-Watson to join the cruise. Lanny was delighted, for it meant, among other things, that he wouldn't have to play bridge on the new trip.

Thus everything was happily arranged for the rest of the year. Toward the end of April, Rosemary took her brood home by train and Lanny drove to Paris, where he met Zoltan; they discussed their many business affairs and attended the *salon* and some of the sales. Lanny paid his duty call at the Château de Bruyne and met the two young men, now students at the École Polytechnique; Denis, *fils*, had become affianced to a young lady of the neighborhood, the match having been arranged by his aunt. It seemed one of which Marie would have approved, and, anyhow, it would have been awkward for Lanny to meddle. He slept again in the room which had so many memories, but they were growing dimmer, or at any rate the emotions they brought were less intense. He saw no apparitions.

He went also to call upon his Socialist and his Communist friends, and gave them money which they promised not to use in fighting one another. They had their rival papers and rival political candidates. The Communists sang the glories of an epoch-making event now getting under way in the Soviet Union, the Five-Year Plan for the industrializing of what had been the most backward of great nations. The Socialists charged that their rivals were subordinating the interests of France to those of a foreign land. Uncle Jesse invited Lanny to a *réunion* of the Communists, and made a speech in which he denounced the rival party for betraying the international hopes of the workers in the interest of French nationalism.

Lanny refused to argue, but took the family to supper after the event. Little Suzette had got herself married to a party member who was one of those homicidal taxidrivers of Paris; he came along, and Lanny was amused to discover that he was much too far to the left for Uncle Jesse. Suzette was expecting a baby, and also expecting the social revolution in France, and didn't seem quite sure which would arrive first. Lanny thought he could tell her—and without being an authority on obstetrics.

Robbie sailed for France in his impromptu way, and Lanny waited to meet him. Always pleasant to hear the news from the family across the seas, and to tell Robbie about Bienvenu and its visitors, and about the beaux who were dancing attendance on Beauty, and about Robbie's Red daughter and son-in-law. But when those personal details were finished, Lanny didn't have much to talk to his father about. Robbie was a rich man, and growing richer, and this brought him satisfaction, but it didn't widen his interests. Such things as *salons* and concerts weren't real to him, and the details of his battles over oil and munitions brought Lanny no happiness.

Also, he had to work so hard to avoid provocative topics! Just now the father was in a state of exasperation over the so-called Kellogg pact for the outlawry of war, which had been the subject of negotiations between France and the United States for more than a year, and was now being broadened to take in all the nations. They were going to renounce war as an instrument of national policy, and forbid all wars except those of self-defense. As if any nation ever went to war without calling it self-defense! Robbie said that all these moves were just devices to keep the United States from arming as it could and should, and he took this Kellogg pact as a personal betrayal by the strong silent statesman whom he had helped to make President of the United States. Right now he and his associates were looking for a more trustworthy candidate!

IX

Lanny drove Zoltan to The Hague, where there was a friend of M. Rochambeau with some old Dutch masters for sale. From there they drove to Hanover, in Germany, where Hansi was giving one of his concerts. Bess was with him, also an accompanist—for Bess wasn't nearly good enough yet. All three were most conscientious about their work, and happy in its success; the audience was enthusiastic, and Hansi didn't wave any Red flags or make incendiary speeches. If he said anything about political questions to the interviewers they were considerate enough not to mention it in what they wrote. They reported that the German musical classics had a new and inspired interpreter; and Bess dutifully cut out the notices and mailed a set to Papa and another to Robbie.

Lanny and Zoltan took the Hook of Holland ferry to London and attended the sales and shows there. Another season, and everybody rolling in money—that word "everybody" being used in a special sense, for there were few streets so fashionable that you didn't see men peddling matches and women peddling their bodies. That remained a part of what was called civilization, and you had your choice of hardening your heart and refusing to think about it, or else tormenting yourself with problems which couldn't be solved. If you chose the former course, you became irritated with persons who threw spokes into the wheels of your forgetting machinery.

The play on which Rick had collaborated was produced, and Lanny and Rosemary, Zoltan and Beauty attended the opening. It was what the critics called a "problem play," and they praised it as conscientious and well informed, but didn't think it would appeal to the general public. Rick was choosing the hard road to success; he was interested in ideas, and refused to write down to his audience. His book had done fairly well, and he picked up a few pounds here and there, but couldn't have got along if he hadn't lived with his parents, and at Bienvenu.

Since Kurt Meissner had passed out of Beauty's life she had taken her position as a perfectly respectable Franco-American lady, widow of a painter whose work was winning the esteem of the most distinguished critics. There was no longer any blot upon her scutcheon; she could even be a chaperon! Rosemary invited her to visit at Sandhaven Manor, and she came for a week-end, arriving conspicuously with her son and her pretty little daughter, and being conspicuously driven away again. After that the most prudish Victorian could have cherished no doubts concerning the relationship between the mistress of the manor and the handsome young American who was conducting her education in the arts.

The season waned, and there came what was called the hot weather in London, though of course it never seemed that to visitors from the Riviera. The fashionable folk went away to the beaches, or to Switzerland, or to the Normandy coast. It was arranged that Marceline and her governess were to spend July with Rosemary's children at the seashore and August with Nina's at The Reaches. The yacht *Bessie Budd* made its second appearance at Ramsgate, bringing the Robin family and one new member, Freddi having got himself engaged, without the help of a *schadchen*, to a very intelligent Jewish girl, a fellow-student in the University of Berlin. She was an addition to any yachting party, for she had a lovely soprano voice and a boxful of music for which Lanny played accompaniments.

Also there were the ex-baroness and her new husband, and Margy with a visiting nephew who raised thoroughbred horses in the bluegrass region of Kentucky. Altogether a variegated party; a host who had sat and scratched fleas in a hut with a dirt floor in the ghetto of Lodz could figure that he had traveled a long distance in a very short time. Where had he acquired that cultivated, agreeable voice? By what model had he shaped his gracious manners? Who had taught him never to boast, never to make pretenses, never to talk about himself unless he was asked to, and then to say simply what he had been and how hard he had struggled to become better. A man can pattern himself on good models, but there has to be that in him which knows the good when he sees it. Jascha Rabinowich had learned something from every person of culture he had met in the forty years since his parents had brought him from Russian Poland to Rotterdam. And most of all he had learned from the Budd family.

X

The *Bessie Budd* sailed to Copenhagen and the party inspected that lovely city, not overlooking its art museums. Thence they proceeded across the Baltic, stopping in the harbors of those little states which had been set up by the League of Nations in the hope of keeping Germany and Russia apart. Nine years and a half had passed since Lanny had served as secretary to an expert on geography at the Peace Conference, and now another section of that geography came to life for him. He remembered the elaborate detail maps, tons of them; the filing clerks who had had to get them out and spread them on the floor, and the aged statesmen who had got down on hands and knees and crawled here and there making pencil marks to decide the destinies of millions. It had seemed rather haphazard and crazy at the time; but when Lanny told Johannes about it he said: "Was it any crazier than having armies fight battles and settle down on whatever they could take?"

The trim white yacht glided over the still blue waters, and they inspected the gracious capital city of Sweden. From there they crossed to the Gulf of Finland, and as they neared the head of it the owner and host told a story which he declared was true, he had it direct from the horse's mouth. There was, he said, a certain young graduate of the technical schools of the new Soviet Union who had been asked to fill out a questionnaire for the guidance of his superiors in placing him under the Five-Year Plan. He had received a mimeographed form and had studied the questions carefully and replied conscientiously, as follows: "Where were you born?" *Answer:* "St. Petersburg." "Where were you educated?" *Answer:* "Petrograd." "Where are you employed at present?" *Answer:* "Leningrad." "Where would you prefer to be employed?" *Answer:* "St. Petersburg."

This was a sample of the kind of anecdote which was going the rounds outside the Soviet Union. It amused all the guests on the yacht save the young ones: Hansi and Freddi and their two ladies. A curious situation, that Johannes should have toiled so hard to climb in the world, and should then discover his sons and the mothers of his future grandchildren looking with moral disapprobation upon his triumphs. He took it in a sporting spirit—too much so for some of his guests; Mr. Armitage, the retired engineer, remarked to his wife in the privacy of their cabin that it would have been better if Johannes had given the two young jackasses a good hiding.

A strange situation, and certainly not according to the alleged laws of economic determinism. If the formula had been working, you would have looked in the fo'c'sle for the Bolsheviks—and of course there may have been some there, though nobody tried to find out. The records of the Comintern contain cases of sons and daughters of the master class who have espoused the cause of the wage-slaves, but there has not yet been brought to light any case where the former have tried to incite the latter to mutiny on board their father's yacht!

The young people on the *Bessie Budd* were going to visit Leningrad with eager curiosity, while their elders were going to visit St. Petersburg if they could, and if not they were going to put flowers on its tomb. There were discussions, and when these became too animated, they had to be hastily dropped. The piano was wheeled onto the deck, the amateur orchestra struck up, and it was Flora's holiday, sacred to ease and happy love, to music, to dancing, and to poetry. Pipe and tabor gaily play, drive all sadness far away, and fitly crown with dance the day!

XI

The floating dance-hall came to rest in the harbor of the great city of palaces and churches built on a marsh. They had procured their visas at home, but discovered that there were many formalities to be gone through. Not many pleasure yachts came to "the Tsar's Window" in these days, and it was difficult for overworked and suspicious revolutionaries to realize that there were persons in the world with nothing to do but glide about from place to place on a vessel big enough for all the pupils of a school or the patients of a sanatorium. In the end the strangers were permitted to come ashore and spend their *valuta* in the new workers' state, but all baggage had to be gone through with care, and they might bring in without duty only precisely measured quantities of perfume, soap, cigars, and so on. They could not return at night to sleep on the yacht, or they would have to go through the same formalities each morning. They had to stay at the Hotel de l'Europe at twenty-five dollars a day per person, and be waited on by pathetic servitors left over from the old regime, men and women who had been born and trained in St. Petersburg and would have been glad to go back there.

The various members of the party saw what they had come to see. Several of the elders had visited this city in the days of the Tsars, and remembered the gaiety and splendor, the handsome guards, the elegant officers, the traffic, the busy shops, the scenes of luxury. Now they saw one vast slum, as drab and dull as it had been before Peter the Great had struck his staff into a marsh and said: "Build here." A tired, bedraggled population, wearing worn and patched clothing full of smells; execrable service, table linen unclean, toilets out of order, nothing in the shops, and in the markets the painful spectacle of former ladies and gentlemen peddling furtively their faded finery to peasants who brought in eggs and vegetables and stood on the embankments along the canals chewing and spitting sunflower seeds. It was enough and more, and the general cry was: "Let's get out of here!"

But to the young people there was a new world to be explored. Knowing few words of Russian, they employed the young women guides whom the regime supplied for tourists. These were ardent propagandists, inclined to patronize bourgeois visitors and, if antagonized, to argue in a manner most exasperating; but when you called them "tovarish" and convinced them of your good faith, their faces lighted up, and they would conduct you sixteen hours a day to look at nurseries and kindergartens, playgrounds and wholesale feeding establishments for factory workers, model creameries, clinics, laboratories—all the marvels of this new world which they were building with such pride and joy. It was "the future" to them, as it had been to Lincoln Steffens nine years ago, and it was still "working," as he had seen it with prophetic eyes. Huge new factories arising, former laborers learning to run them; rivers being dammed, power-houses constructed—and all these things public property in which everyone had the pride of ownership.

XII

A conflict of wills developed between the two groups of visitors. To the ladies of fashion it was as if someone had dumped them into the midst of the East End of London and left them there. The ex-baroness found a family of old friends, members of the former plutocracy, now turned out of their palace and living in one room in the utmost misery; the great slum became a jail to Sophie, a scene in a nightmare from which she struggled to escape. She and Margy and their escorts came back to the hotel for elaborate but tasteless meals, and exchanged new impressions of disgust. "Oh, let's go!" they cried, each day more loudly.

The plan had been for the yacht to visit the Finnish towns and sail up the Gulf of Bothnia. Now the young people said: "All right, but go without us! We want time to visit a co-operative farm and see all the things that interest us, and we'll rejoin you in Helsinki."

So the arrangement was made; and it suited Lanny, because Leningrad possessed one of the world's great treasure-houses of art, the Hermitage Museum, and he wanted to spend days wandering through its halls. Rosemary had no fine frenzies over paintings, but she elected to stay with him because she knew that otherwise she would have to help Beauty teach Mama Robin to play bridge.

When the reunion of the groups took place, the *Bessie Budd* had become a yacht divided against itself. There was no open warfare, for these were all polite people; but when the bourgeoisie spoke of the Soviet Union as a slum, the intelligentsia wanted to know how much time the contemptuous ones had spent in the slums of London and Berlin and Paris. When the bourgeoisie inquired what was gained by reducing everybody to the level of the lowest, the answer was that the slums of capitalist nations were a permanent part of their system, whereas the Soviet Union's prosperity, once achieved, would be shared by all. It was a debate that was going on in every part of the earth; "the future," as the Reds proposed to make it, by force if necessary, was a fighting topic wherever people talked, and on board a yacht the only solution was for the young to do their talking on one part of the deck while the middle-aged did their bridge-playing on another part.

It ruined the cruise, and made sorrow for the well-meaning host and hostess. Johannes took it without complaint, but he had to abandon his dream of using this trim white vessel as a means of cultivating the favor of the enviable classes. Otherwise he would have to leave his adored boys and their wives at home—and then, of course, it wouldn't be any fun for Mama, she would prefer to stay with her darlings, no matter what outrageous opinions they chose to voice. After all, there was something to be said for their side; it hadn't been so pleasant living in a slum, as Jascha himself ought to remember. Jascha talked about the problem with Lanny, strolling on the deck one windy night, and the best the young man could suggest was for the owner of the *Bessie Budd* to become a convert to the new cause, and use the trim white vessel for excursions of the proletariat in need of recuperation. A floating "Park of Culture and Rest"!

BOOK SEVEN

The Paths of Glory

31

God's Opportunity

I

Ex-TUTOR and ex-lieutenant Jerry Pendleton had set himself up, with Lanny's help, in a tourist bureau in Cannes and was doing well with it; in these times it would have been hard to do badly. His devoted French wife had three little ones, and the pension was thriving under the management of the hard-working mother and aunt; money was being put away, and some day it would come to Cerise and her children, so Jerry had every reason to feel content with the world as it was. He would visit Bienvenu now and then to go sailing or fishing with Lanny, or play tennis; once in a while Beauty out of the kindness of her heart would invite Cerise to a lawn party or other affair where there were many people and it wouldn't be necessary to devote much time to her. Cerise, although quiet and inoffensive, was an outsider because she couldn't talk about the fashionable people and what they were doing.

One of the steady boarders at the pension was a gentleman who had come from a small town in the American Middle West more than fifteen years ago, which was before the Budds had known Jerry or his wife. This boarder had been an insurance agent, and, having inherited a small income, had decided to see the world. He had discovered that his money would buy more in Cannes than anywhere at home, and so he had settled down in the Pension Flavin. He told a peculiar story about how he had come upon this respectable boarding-house; he had sat on a bench on the Boulevard de la Croisette and closed his eyes and asked God to send him to the proper sort of place; then he had got up and walked, and God had told him to turn off that fashionable and expensive avenue, and presently had told him to enter a certain house, and he had done so—and there he was.

The board had been forty francs per week, which in those days was eight dollars. With the rise in the cost of living the proprietors of the establishment had been forced to raise the price again and again, until now it was two hundred francs, which at the present rate of exchange was only five dollars; so the American considered that God had shown him partiality. He had occupied the same third-floor rear room all through the World War and the peace and what had come since. Having learned to speak French with a strong Iowa accent, he had won the esteem of everybody in the establishment.

This exemplary boarder went by the unusual name of Parsifal Dingle. The first half was due to the fact that an expectant mother in an unromantic small town on the prairies had seen a picture of an opera singer in shining armor. The French found nothing eccentric in either name; they pronounced the last one "Dang'," with their nasal sound. The visitor had long ago got used to this and other eccentricities. He told himself that God had made the French as well as the Iowans; God was in them all, and God no doubt had His purposes.

Mr. Dingle did not belong to any sect, or give himself any label, but followed along the lines of what was known at home as "New Thought." A surprisingly great number of people believed in it; people scattered all over the farms and villages of America, or living obscurely in the great cities, where they listened to lectures, formed hundreds of sects with odd names, and printed papers and magazines which often attained large circulation. Mr. Dingle subscribed to several, and after he had read them he would pass them on to others, and if these persons showed interest he would explain his ideas.

In brief, Mr. Dingle believed that there was a God, and that he, Mr. Dingle, was a part of Him. This God was alive and He was real, and He lived and worked in you; He would guide you if you asked Him, and especially if you believed that He would. The way of asking was to retire to some quiet place, as Jesus had directed, close your eyes and think about God and His goodness, and believe that He would do what you asked, if it was a good and proper thing. Mr. Dingle had never asked God to give him a mansion on the

Boulevard de la Croisette or a beautiful blond mistress, for he did not consider such things as proper objects of desire; he asked God to give him peace of soul, kindness to his fellow-men, and contentment with his lot in life, and God had granted these modest requests.

The effect of this credo was to produce a highly desirable inmate of a pension. He never tried to force his ideas upon anyone, and it was impossible to quarrel with him about anything; if you tried it, he would retire to his room and pray, and emerge with such a beatific countenance that you could only feel ashamed of your bad disposition. He was not stout, but comfortably eupeptic; his face was round and rosy, so that he looked like a mature, slightly graying cherub in a well-laundered white linen suit. Mr. Parsifal Dingle from the state which he called Ioway, at your service.

II

Ever since the year 1914, when a runaway college student boarding at the Pension Flavin had become Lanny Budd's tutor, the family at Bienvenu had been hearing about this unusual but worthy boarder. Jerry liked him because, their hometowns being close together, they understood each other's accents and taste in foods. As the years passed, Jerry began to talk about Mr. Dingle's peculiar ideas, first in a "kidding" way, later on more seriously. It appeared that Mr. Dingle had some sort of strange gift; he would put his hands on people and give them what he called a "treatment," and their pains would disappear. Neither Lanny nor his mother had ever met this boarder, but they had seen him coming out of the pension, and he had become in the course of the years something of a legendary figure to them.

A couple of years ago it had happened that Miss Addington, Marceline's governess, had suffered an unusually severe spell of her periodic headaches. Lanny had mentioned it to Jerry, and a little later Jerry had phoned; Mr. Dingle wanted to know if he might be permitted to call and try to help the lady; if so, Jerry would be glad to drive him over. The stiff and proper member of the Church of England was startled by the proposal; but she knew that the American gentleman operated in the name of God, and there was nothing in that special charter which God had granted to the Church of King Henry the Eighth which forbade other persons to call upon Him if they so desired; besides, the headache was really very bad. So Mr. Dingle came, and asked to be alone with her, which caused a maiden lady to feel uneasy; but he seemed to be a respectable person, and presumably one could think of him as a physician. He asked her to sit in a chair, and he stood behind her and put his hands across her forehead, and then just stayed there with his eyes closed.

The result astonished everybody, especially the governess. When he got through and took his hands away, he asked: "How do you feel?" and she blinked a couple of times and exclaimed: "Why, it's gone!" It was really quite preposterous, but it was so—and it was certainly convenient. After that, whenever Miss Addington had one of these spells, she would send in haste for Mr. Parsifal Dingle. She tried to pay him, but he didn't want money. Seeing that his cuffs showed signs of wear, she argued that at least she ought to pay his carfare, and in the end he permitted her to give him twenty francs, which varied somewhere between forty and sixty cents during this period.

Any prim and easily shocked maiden lady of forty was naturally a subject of humor among Beauty's fashionable friends. They anticipated a romance, and asked eagerly how it was developing. Sophie referred to the healer as Miss Addington's Knight of the Holy Grail, and said that the only barrier to a perfect match would be that dreadful name Dingle—why didn't he change it to Bell? Wasn't there a song: "Dingle bell, dingle bell, dingle all the day"? Margy, who had read poetry, said that a dingle was a dell or a dale, and the poor man ought to take one of those names. But Mr. Dingle had heard all these jokes when he was a schoolboy, and he stayed as he was.

III

Now came Rosemary with her brood and settled them in that comfortable, spick-and-span house which they were calling "the cottage," in order to have a name for it, though it was bigger than the lodge and nearly as big as the villa. The first thing that happened was that the youngest child, little Blanche, got hold of some green fruit and had a violent attack of colic. There was great excitement, and the English doctor whom they all patronized was not in his office. They gave the little one an emetic, but perhaps that wasn't enough; she lay in a semi-coma; her skin began to assume a greenish hue, her heart seemed weak, and Rosemary· was in a panic. Miss Addington, without a word to anyone, rushed to the phone and called Mr. Dingle, telling him to take a taxi at once.

The same thing happened again; Mr. Dingle asked to be alone with the child, and put his hands on her forehead, and in a very short while her heart had revived and her color returned and she fell peacefully asleep. Of course everybody knows that children have these attacks suddenly and get over them no less suddenly, and perhaps that was all it was; but it gave the ladies a great deal to talk about, and after this crisis was over, Beauty invited the gentleman with the strange gift to come over to the villa and tell her about his ideas and how he performed his miracles. He said very modestly that it was no miracle at all, but something which God did, and would do for anyone who believed in Him and who would take the trouble to follow the plain directions which Jesus had given us.

Now Beauty Budd had managed to live her adult life without any clerical assistance. She had been taught early in life that God forbade her to do all the pleasant things, and she had just gone ahead and done them, and decided that God was the creation of a domineering Baptist preacher by the name of John Eliphalet Blackless. Here on the Riviera were a number of well-trained professional gentlemen engaged in God's service, and she had met several of them, both Catholic and Protestant, and found them agreeable men of the world, good conversationalists and judges of food and wine. It had been tacitly understood that they kept God for those special occasions when they performed His rites in church, and you were free to attend if you cared to, but no priest or clergyman had ever been heard to mention the name of God on any social occasion; everyone whom Beauty knew would have considered it something in the nature of a *faux pas*.

So this idea of a God whom you carried around with you was something entirely new and decidedly startling. The idea that God was inside Beauty Budd, and had known all that she was thinking, and all that she had done—for God's sake, why hadn't He stopped her? Mr. Dingle insisted that it was a comfortable idea when you got used to it, because it took away all fear; God loved you, in spite of your faults, and all He asked was that you should try to improve yourself and let Him help you. It was what Mr. Dingle described as a "free" religion; you didn't have to have any priest to intercede for you, but God was here all the time, at the center of your consciousness, and you could appeal to Him, and get your answer in the state of your own heart. "No," said the healer, "you don't hear any voice, you just feel different. Try it; you may be astonished to see how it works."

Beauty knew how all her fashionable friends would laugh if they heard about this. But God wouldn't laugh, Mr. Dingle assured her, and it could be a strict secret between God and herself. But very soon, if Madame Detaze found that her prayers were being answered, she would gain courage, and would wish to tell others of her discovery, just as Mr. Dingle himself had been doing since the door of faith had been opened in his heart.

Of course it wasn't within Beauty's nature to keep any such secret. When Lanny came back from a swimming-party she told him what had happened to little Blanche, and all that Mr. Dingle had explained to her. Had Lanny ever heard of such an idea? The young scholar replied that he had indeed, many times; it was a very old idea, which had appeared everywhere among the tribes of men. Socrates had talked about his *daimon*, and Jesus about his heavenly Father. People of this way of thinking were known as "mystics," and Lanny had learned about them from his study of Emerson. He got the volume which Eli Budd had given him, inscribed by the philosopher's own hand, and told Beauty to read the essay called *The Oversoul*. But Beauty couldn't make anything out of this highbrow language, and much preferred the simple, A-B-C explanations which the healer gave her.

She invited him over to tea, and had only Lanny and Miss Addington and Rosemary—for of course the latter couldn't laugh, seeing how terrified she had been, and how kind the man had been, whether he had really healed the child or not. They all asked questions, and Mr. Dingle talked inspirationally. He had been thinking about these matters ever since he was a young man, and had absorbed the formulas of all the New Thought groups; but Beauty didn't know that, he seemed to her one of the most original and most exalted personalities she had ever encountered. No priest or clergyman she had ever heard in a church had more noble ideas, or voiced them in more beautiful phrases.

After that the gentleman with the odd name became an habitué of Bienvenu. No one could have been less intrusive; he never came unless he was asked, he rarely spoke unless he was spoken to, and if he had the slightest reason to think that he might be in the way he would go into the court and look at the flowers, or onto the loggia and watch the sun set over the *golfe* behind the Estérels, and you knew that he was praying. He was a very good influence for everybody, because they were ashamed to voice cynical or unworthy ideas in his presence. Also, it was comforting to know that if anything serious happened to you, he would be on hand and call God to your aid.

I V

There was never a more inveterate matchmaker than the lovely blond mistress of Bienvenu, and having this new male on the premises, she couldn't help thinking about Miss Addington. That badly inhibited English lady was surely in need of assistance; so Beauty would perform the kindly service of inviting Mr. Dingle to lunch, and then arranging that the governess should be excused from her duties for a while. This was easy, because there were two governesses, and the children wanted to be together all the time. Miss Addington became greatly interested in Mr. Dingle's views on religion, and he convinced her that there was nothing contrary to Anglican etiquette in what he did. Had not Jesus after his death returned to his disciples and given the explicit instruction: "In my name they shall lay hands on the sick, and they shall recover"? How could words be plainer?

But in spite of their being an obviously well-matched couple, that was as far as matters proceeded between them; and after several weeks of watching and waiting, Beauty began to find it rather provoking. What would become of the future of the human race if men and women did nothing together except to search the Scriptures and practice praying? If Beauty had been a selfish soul she would have remembered that she had a good governess and had better let well enough alone; but Beauty believed in love, and she thought: "I could arrange for them to live on the place, and Miss Addington could continue her duties until Marceline is grown." She had it all worked out in her head, and she tried to put it into Miss Addington's head. The maiden lady would blush, and the next time the visitor appeared she would have some old-fashioned ruching about her somewhat shrunken neck, also a bit of ribbon in her hair. But these hints didn't appear to be caught by Mr. Dingle.

Evidently he had lived alone for so long that he had become shy; or was there something in his religion which committed him to a celibate life, the attitude which Beauty had heard referred to as "platonic"? She felt that it was her duty to straighten the matter out; so one day when she was alone in the drawing-room with the healer she sprang the question: "What is your attitude toward love?"

Mr. Parsifal Dingle blushed slightly, and showed signs of being flustered. "I had," he explained, "a very sad experience, one which altered my whole life."

"Indeed?" said Beauty. She didn't say: "Would you mind telling me about it?" but there was that in her voice. She wished earnestly to understand this gentleman's ideas and everything that had helped to shape his personality.

"When I was a young man, Madame, I became deeply attached to a young lady of excellent character, and suffered a tragic bereavement. Somehow I have never been able to think about love since then—I suppose it is because I have looked for the qualities which I found in that young lady."

Beauty felt that such a love story would touch Miss Addington's

Victorian heart. She said: "I appreciate your delicacy of feeling; but is it wise to let one's whole life be dominated by an old grief?"

"I have never felt that it was a deprivation, Madame. I have submitted to God's guidance, and He has given me other kinds of happiness."

"Yes, Mr. Dingle; but have you never reflected that you might be denying happiness to some woman?"

"I must confess that I never gave a thought to that aspect of the matter. I haven't appeared to myself as an especially desirable suitor."

"Perhaps you are too modest. May I speak to you frankly?"

"Of course, Madame, I am honored."

"Well, you must know that I have come to have a very great esteem for Miss Addington, who has been with us for several years and has won the regard of everyone in our home. Has it never occurred to you that she might be interested in you?"

The blood began to climb into the cherubic cheeks of the man of miracles, and his bright blue eyes opened wider. "Oh, Madame!" he exclaimed; and there was no mistaking the tone of dismay.

"You haven't given any thought to her?"

"I have done everything in my power to assist Miss Addington, and to guide her in her religious researches when she herself requested it. I sincerely hope there has been nothing in my conduct which has caused her to think that I—that I harbor any other thoughts of her."

"You don't feel that you could be interested in her in that way?"

"Oh, Madame, not possibly."

"Why are you so positive?"

"It is difficult to explain without sounding offensive. Miss Addington is one of the most estimable of ladies, but she is not the type which could interest my—shall I say imagination?"

There was a pause; then Beauty was moved to ask: "Just what do you think would interest your imagination, Mr. Dingle?" She wished so much to understand the platonic philosophy.

"Would you really like me to tell you, Madame?"

"I want to be your friend, and to help you, as you have helped so many others."

"You do me great honor, and your kindness touches me deeply. I have never had anything in my life that has pleased me so much as your friendship, and I wish to preserve it as I would a precious jewel, and be sure never to do anything that would tarnish it."

"Of course not, Mr. Dingle—why should you?"

"You have asked me an intimate question, Madame, and it fills me with anxiety—because, through many weeks I have said to myself: oh, if only Madame were not a rich lady, so that I might be at liberty to tell her what is in my heart!"

It was the lovely blond Beauty's turn to blush, and be sure that she did not fail. The exclamation burst forth: "Oh, *mon dieu!*" The French do not spell it with a capital letter, which perhaps keeps it from seeming so violent as it does in English.

"Madame!" exclaimed the man of God with much anxiety. "You asked me a question, and it seemed to me that courtesy required me to give an answer."

"Yes, of course, and I am obliged to you; only——"

"I shall be deeply grieved if Madame is offended."

"No, surely not. Why should I be? You do me a great honor, Mr. Dingle."

"Please, please, do not let it make any difference in your regard for me. I know that it is utterly impossible, and I do not permit it to become anything but a beautiful dream, one which may perhaps be realized in heaven, where we do not take our title deeds to property. May I be assured of your forgiveness, and remain your humble and devoted admirer?"

"Yes, surely, Mr. Dingle. Yes, yes—let us talk about God for a while!"

V

Beauty had to tell someone about that most embarrassing episode, and she chose her son. First he said: "Well, I'll be damned!" Then he thought it over and added: "But, darling, you can't blame him; it's the price you pay for being irresistible."

"It's really most painful," complained the mother. "How am I going to meet the man after this?"

"Oh, you don't need to make so much out of it. You have had plenty of broken-hearted suitors around you."

"But, Lanny, a man of that class!"

"Class?" inquired the young Pink. "He's about the same class as my maternal grandfather, I'd imagine."

"But, I mean—a man of no culture."

"He's got a lot of culture, it seems to me; only it's different from ours; not so smart, but a lot cleaner, if I'm any judge."

"I didn't know you thought so highly of him, Lanny."

"Well, I think he's earned our respect. We don't have to agree with his ideas, but we can admit that he's honest and kind—and that's more than I can say for some of the men you have been stepping out with."

This was a subject on which the son had been expressing himself emphatically as occasions arose. In London there had appeared an elegant man of fashion and of no small means; he had been most attentive, but had omitted to mention that he had a wife somewhere in the background; Margy had found it out. Here on the Riviera had been il Conte di Pistacchio; a charming personality, only he disappeared now and then for a week and reappeared rather pale except for his painted cheeks—he had the habit of taking ether. On the last trip of the *Bessie Budd* Margy's nephew had attached himself to this richly blooming beauty, suggestive of the rose at its most complete unfoldment, just before the petals begin to drop; but he was even younger than Lanny, and surely Beauty didn't have to learn that lesson over again! In short, Lanny had a problem mother; and the more he thought about it, the less disposed he was to ridicule this conscientious if somewhat boresome man of God.

VI

Nothing more was said for a while; but Lanny watched closely, and suspected that nature was getting in her subtle work. Or perhaps it was God—it is a matter of words, for what do we really know about it after all? Mr. Dingle continued to visit at Bienvenu, and to instruct "Madame" in that New Thought which is so very ancient;

Beauty listened, with no apparent diminution of interest. The difference was that she no longer invited Miss Addington to share in the instruction. Did the man of God note this difference? And did he attribute it to the fact that he had disclaimed interest in the state of Miss Addington's heart? If so, what inference was he to draw from the fact that Madame continued as his pupil?

Whatever his thoughts may have been, he was invariably proper, even saintly in his attitude, and if his eyes happened to meet those of the lovely blond rose in full blooming, he would drop them quickly. His state of adoration was apparent, and could not be without its effect upon one who lived to be admired, as Mabel Blackless, alias Beauty Budd, alias Madame Detaze, had done since childhood.

Mr. Dingle began to come more frequently, and was told that he no longer needed to wait for a special invitation. Beauty's friends got used to finding him there, and after a while they got tired of teasing her about it; they didn't come so often, because the plain truth was, they began to find Beauty's conversation boring. That religious crank must have her hypnotized, for she talked about his ideas even without knowing it; things which had formerly been fashionable were now worldly, and those which had been delicious had become frivolous; it was really pathetic.

"Lanny," said the mother one day, "what do you honestly think about Mr. Dingle's ideas?"

"Why, I don't know," said Lanny; "they may be all right. A lot of great minds have accepted them. Very largely it's a matter of how you phrase things."

"Mr. Dingle seems to phrase them remarkably well. But I don't trust my own judgment—I'm so frightfully ignorant, you know."

"We're all ignorant," said Lanny. "If I were you, I wouldn't worry about that. If the ideas work with you, they're right for you."

"Why don't you try them, Lanny?"

"I suppose it's because I've never felt the need. People seem to take up with them when they get into some sort of trouble. What is it Mr. Dingle said: 'Man's extremity is God's opportunity'?"

"He was quoting Mrs. Eddy, I believe. Do you remember old Mrs. Sibley, Emily's mother? She was a Christian Scientist, and it seemed to work very well for her. She often tried to tell me about it, but I wouldn't pay any attention. I've been a very worldly woman, Lanny."

"I know," said the other; "but you've managed to get out alive." Then, with a wicked twinkle in his eye: "Would you like me to speak to Mr. Dingle and find out if his intentions are honorable?" The way Beauty blushed made the son realize that things were getting serious.

VII

Lanny wasn't surprised when a few days later his mother brought up the subject again. She had to talk about it with somebody, and there was no one so deeply concerned as Lanny. "Do you still have such a good opinion of Mr. Dingle?" she wanted to know.

"Better than ever," he replied. "It seems to me he has been behaving very well indeed."

"Do you really mean, Lanny, that you'd be willing for me to think of marrying that poor man!"

"What has being poor got to do with it? We have much more than we need."

"I don't mean poor in that sense."

"Then in what sense? If you mean that he isn't *chic*, we have enough of that quality also."

"Everybody would think that I'd made a misalliance!"

"Well, they thought that about you and Marcel; but you lived it down."

"Lanny, I believe you really *want* me to do it!"

"I've been thinking a lot about it. If you married him, you would know exactly what you are getting. He won't have his head turned by money, and he won't go chasing after younger women; he'll worship you as a goddess out of the skies."

"Oh, you want to get rid of me!" exclaimed the errant female.

"I'll stay right here," he promised, "and lend Mr. Dingle my Swedenborg and St. Theresa's *Way of Perfection*—Great-Great-Uncle Eli was strong on the mystics, you know."

"Lanny, I just couldn't face the idea of being known as Mrs. Dingle!"

"Let it be a sort of morganatic marriage; take him as a prince consort. Your friends will go on calling you Beauty Budd, and the servants and tradespeople calling you Madame Detaze. Why should anyone change?"

"Lanny, I think it's horrid of you to urge such a thing!"

"All right, old dear; it was you who brought up the subject. All I say is, if I had to choose among the beaux in sight at this moment, this miracle man would be my stepfather."

"Do you realize that if I married him here in France, he'd own— I don't know just what, but a large share of this property?"

"In the first place I doubt if he'd touch it."

"But he may have relatives who would feel differently."

"Well, go to your lawyer and fix up a property settlement. Marceline gets along with him all right; and you surely don't have to worry about me, for I can make what I need, and all I want for you is to be happy, and safe from the buzzards I see hovering over this Coast of Pleasure."

"Lanny, I think it's perfectly awful—it's humiliating!" There were tears in the mother's eyes.

"Bless your heart, I'll never mention it again. If you want to stay a fascinating widow, you have everything it takes."

VIII

Several days passed, and Beauty said no more. It chanced that Mr. Dingle came calling, and gave her an especially beautiful discourse on the love of God as an example to our frail mortality. Beauty was deeply moved, and when it was over, she began: "Do you remember what you said about your attitude to me, Mr. Dingle?"

"Of course, Madame. How could I forget?"

"Are you still of the same opinion?"

"I could never change."

Whereupon Beauty, blushing most becomingly, set out upon a long explanation, to the effect that she had two children, and that

Marcel had wished and Robbie required that her property should go to these children. If Mr. Dingle were to marry her it would be necessary for them to make a special legal arrangement.

"Oh, Madame!" exclaimed the man of God. "I wouldn't dream of touching a sou of your money! Never would the purity of my love for you be sullied by a question of property." He fell upon one knee before the loveliest of Franco-American widows and kissed her hand in the perfect tradition of the Victorian romancers.

Beauty might have said: "Rise, Sir Parsifal." But instead she sat with tears running down her cheeks, and when he looked at her and saw them, he also wept; it was an emotional betrothal, and very soon the pair were as completely dissolved in bliss as if they had been seventeen years old. If Beauty had not been restrained by fear of her fashionable friends, she would have got a complete trousseau and a dress with a train several yards long.

There is no such thing as getting married in a hurry in the staid land of France. For one thing, both parties had to have birth certificates especially obtained from their native land—the certificates had to be no more recent in date than three months. Also Beauty's lawyer had to prepare the documents concerning the property settlement; and lawyers work carefully and methodically in France. Then there had to be ten days for the publication of the banns. When all these formalities had been arranged, Sophie and her husband came over—two friends who could be counted upon not to laugh publicly; the party traveled to the *mairie*, where they were declared man and wife under the French civil code. They did not take a honeymoon journey, for Mr. Dingle said, what was the use of going elsewhere when God was here? Marceline and her governess went over to have a holiday with Rosemary's children, and the new bridegroom brought his few belongings and installed them in the room which had never been used since Kurt had moved out of it a year and a half ago. The miracle man moved also into the heart which Kurt had vacated, and he filled it full. An odd sort of ending to the adventures of Beauty Budd, but her son sighed with relief, and crossed off in his mind a string of painful incidents which weren't going to happen.

IX

Rosemary was not present at these nuptials because she had left hurriedly for London, there being some family trouble about which her brother had written her. She came to Lanny about it, but said that it was a matter of which she hadn't the right to talk; he understood that it was the well-known English reticence. He asked if there was anything he could do—go with her, drive her, run errands —but she answered that she would have to do it alone. She would write to him.

Rosemary's letters had never been what you could call inordinate; she used a lot of paper and ink, but gave only a sketch at best. This time, "A bally mess. Cheerio!" was the extent of her communication. However, Lanny had other ways of getting news. Rick was still in England, and he had played with Rosemary's smart friends in childhood—and what one of these young people knew, all the rest knew quickly. Moreover, this set went in for the intellectual life, and the smart press people circulated among them like busy bees, gathering tiny drops of the sweet honey of gossip. On the newsstands of every town on the Continent you could buy newspapers and magazines having columns from which you might learn that Lady T*tt*nh*mpt*n was seen frequently in the fashionable clubs nowanights, but she and her lawful spouse sat at different tables; her ladyship was oft observed in the company of a bachelor captain of the Hussars. A few paragraphs later you would read that Captain So-and-so of the Hussars had changed dancing partners recently, and was teaching the newest steps to a fair young matron in Burke's *Peerage.* If you couldn't put these twos together, you must indeed be ignorant concerning the ways of ladies and gentlemen in Mayfair.

From various sources Lanny was able to gather the story. Poor Bertie had had the bad judgment to stray from the couch of the lady with whom he had been happy, and she had left him in a fury, and from somewhere in the distant background a husband had appeared, making threats of a divorce suit and scandal. Being in the Foreign Office and hoping for a career, Bertie had paid the fellow money, but he, being a gambler, was never satisfied, and the two had got into a fight, and now it wasn't just a question of money, but a vicious grudge. After Rosemary arrived in London it broke into the papers. Bertie was considered to be "ruined," and was in that state where he might retire to his manor and shoot off his head. But the Earl of Sandhaven of course had influential friends, and Rosemary's family also had them, and they insisted that something had to be done to help the poor fellow. There were conferences with important officials, and presently came to Lanny the longest letter he had ever received from his *amie:*

DEAR LANNY:

I have had a hard decision to make, and can only count upon your kindness. Do forgive me and not take it too hard. Bertie has been offered a post which will give him a future. You know what I told you about the Empire and what it does to people's private lives. The condition of this appointment is that I shall go with him to the Argentine, and that he promises to settle down and work very hard. I assume you have been told about some of the unpleasant events here, and will not expect me to put the details on paper. Believe me that life has jolly well got to be real and earnest for us; the law has been laid down. It is a question of my children's future, and the situation is such that I am morally bound. It is just one of those things that come, like the war, you know. Your many kindnesses to my family will never be forgotten, and I hope you will do one more and tell me that you understand and forgive. I have told Nina about it, and she will tell you.

Bertie and I are leaving for our new post in a few days. I am writing the governess to bring the children home at once, as we are taking them. Give my best love to your darling mother, and thank her for her hospitality. I will write her a note before I leave. You can understand that I am frightfully crowded. Everything has to be arranged in a few days. Good-by, and believe that your friendship will be one of my very best memories; nothing will take it from me.

ROSEMARY.

So there it was. When you had to cut off a love affair, you just took a pair of scissors and—snip!—there it wasn't. Lanny couldn't complain, for Rosemary had made it clear to him that that was the way with life among the governing classes of an empire. Britannia, who ruled the waves, had put an end to Rosemary's previous affair, and now had put an end to Lanny's. How many times he had heard his sweetheart say: "We mustn't fall too much in love, dear. We can't count upon it." Now he learned the lesson of how to write a letter that could never be used by any blackmailer. One can never tell into what hands a letter may fall, and when you belong to the governing classes, you are careful what you set down on any piece of paper!

X

Lanny hadn't taken Rosemary's advice, and neither had she; they had fallen too much in love, and would suffer, in spite of all resolves. There was nothing he could do about it; she preferred her social position, and the future of her children in the Empire, to what she got from him, and so she had taken herself out of his life. He didn't want to make it harder for her, so he telegraphed that he understood her position and wished her and Bertie all good luck in their new career. Everything would be done to help the governess and children get off promptly, and Beauty and Marceline joined in sending regards. A message that could do no harm in the hands of any blackmailer.

Man's extremity being God's opportunity, this might have been a time for Lanny to turn to his mother and her new husband, who was now available at all hours. But it happened that Lanny had just been reading an article about Chopin, who had been proud and passionate, and had been spurned in love and brought to despair. Lanny went down to his studio and played all the eighteen Chopin nocturnes, one after another, and imagined that Rosemary was in the room and sorrowing with him. He played other Chopin pieces, not forgetting the very somber funeral march. In the course of days and nights he played ballades and polonaises and mazurkas, fiery and tempestuous, yet freighted with a burden of bitter pain; he played études which were studies in emotionality even more than in piano technique. Before he got through he had played some two hundred compositions and got a fine lot of exercise, a workout both physical and spiritual. After it he was ready for some new kind of life.

There came a telephone call from that patient, hard-working young Socialist Raoul Palma, who was in need of help, and Lanny decided on the spur of the moment that this was the fellow who understood what was wrong with the world and what to do about it. While Lanny had been playing around, tied to the apron-strings of a shining lady of fashion, his friends the workers had been having a devil's own time with the rising cost of living, wages lagging behind, and no certainty and very little hope in their lives. Lanny decided that he had been an idler, a parasite, deserving the worst that any rabid agitator could charge against him. To the young Spaniard's delight he announced that he was ready to teach a class in the night school, and one in the Sunday school. He would tell the workers of the Riviera and their children about the great war which was already growing dim in the world's memory; he would try to explain to them the forces which had caused it, and what they could do by their collective efforts to prevent another such calamity from breaking in upon their lives.

Naturally, this interfered somewhat with Beauty Budd's honeymoon and her initiation into the contemplative life. She was greatly upset about it, but knew better than to make a frontal assault upon her son. In his *distrait* state of mind he might go off to Paris and get mixed up with Jesse and his dreadful crowd—for Beauty had managed to get into her head the distinction between Red and Pink, and which was worse. It was just before Christmas, and she wrote to Nina, begging her and Rick to come immediately after New Year's, so that Lanny might have somebody to tell his troubles to. Also she wrote to Emily, telling her what had happened, and asking about her plans. Now was the time to put an end to this business of Lanny's living with other men's wives and raising other men's children! Out of the kindness of her heart Emily had forgiven the playboy's rejection of her last effort; she wrote that she was coming, and that Irma Barnes also was coming, and what would Beauty say to her as a possible daughter-in-law?

What Beauty would say would have taken a whole mail-pouch to

carry it. She started saying it *viva voce*, first to Sophie and then to
Margy, who arrived to occupy the "cottage" as soon as Rosemary's
children had been sent to England. These three knew that they
had to move with caution, owing to Lanny's peculiar Pink attitude;
the moment he heard that anyone had a great deal of money he began finding fault with that person and shying away from him or
her. So there must not be the faintest hint that anybody was thinking
that he might fall in love with Irma Barnes, or even that he might
meet her; he must just begin hearing about her charms, about the
sensation she had made in New York, about her interest in intellectual things—in short, everything except that she was the legally established possessor of twenty-three million dollars in her own right!

XI

J. Paramount Barnes had been a public utilities magnate, or, as
they were now being called, a "tycoon," and had had a dizzying
career in the "pyramiding" of companies. Robbie had explained this
process to his son in his half-cynical, half-respectful way. There
were men who controlled the investing of insurance company funds,
and of industrial concerns which kept hundreds of millions of dollars in "reserves." Those who handled such funds were, of course,
favorites of the big banks, and could borrow unlimited amounts of
money which nowadays came pouring into Wall Street from all the
rest of the banks of the United States. Using such borrowing power,
these men would get options upon the stocks of utility concerns controlling the light and power of cities and states, and would organize
a great "holding company" to own these enterprises. The top concern would be controlled by three "voting shares," having a par
value of one dollar each; which meant that the colossal enterprise
would rest permanently in the capable hands of J. Paramount Barnes,
his personal secretary, and one of his office clerks. The concern
would proceed to issue several hundred million dollars in common
shares, give part of them to Mr. J. Paramount Barnes for his services,
and sell the rest to the public. In their present mood millions of the
plain people all over the country would rush to buy the shares of

any concern about which they read in the papers, and they would start bidding up the price on the exchange so that everybody would be rich and continuing to grow richer every day.

Such was the Wall Street game, with which Robbie had been in conflict over a long period of years. Robbie himself was really producing things, and when he issued stock it represented real value in equipment, land, and so on; he sold the shares to people in Newcastle and elsewhere who trusted his name, and when the Wall Street slickers came and wanted to work their rackets with his company, Robbie would tell them to go to the devil. What they would do was to go to the stockholders and buy some of them out, and then the crooks would show up at a stockholders' meeting of the company and try to get control. They would prepare an elaborate campaign, hiring shrewd lawyers and publicity men, and framing a set of false charges to bewilder and confuse investors, most of whom didn't know about the business and were ready to run and sell their shares at the least rumor of something wrong.

J. Paramount Barnes had begun life as a broker's messenger boy, and had learned all the tricks and invented many new ones. He had organized a utilities holding company, and had been so successful that he had repeated the stunt again and again, until he had a holding company for holding companies, a colossal pyramid with himself sitting on the top, and so many subsidiaries and investment trusts and stock-issuing and dividend-receiving devices that it was to be doubted if any human brain knew the whole of that tangle of complications.

And then one day J. Paramount Barnes suffered a heart attack and dropped dead in his office. It was discovered that he had left a comfortable income to his wife, a small one to his son who lived in Hawaii and was rumored to be "no good," and had left the bulk of his fortune in trust for his only daughter Irma. How much it amounted to made a guessing contest for the newspapers of the metropolis; the conservative ones said fifty million dollars and the yellow ones said two hundred million or more. It transpired that the "tycoon" had got rid of his holdings in his own companies and had put most of his money into bank stocks and other gilt-edged securities. After the lawyers had been paid, and the commissions, and the state and federal inheritance taxes, and the back income taxes which were in dispute with the government, Irma Barnes, just about to emerge from finishing-school, had a net fortune of twenty-three millions, and, at the rate which the investments were earning, would have something over two million dollars to spend or invest each year.

This favorite of fortune was good to look at, and had been taught how to dress and to walk and to talk; so she became a headliner in the newspapers, and what the gossip columnists called "the toast of New York." It meant that a train of suitors attended her; whenever she entered a restaurant everybody turned to stare at her, in the night clubs the spotlight was turned upon her and the band played a song which had been composed in her honor. Pictures made her features familiar to the great public, and what she wore set the styles for shop-girls as well as debutantes from Portland, Maine, to Portland, Oregon.

And now Irma Barnes was coming to spend the winter on the Riviera! Forthwith the promotion agencies of half a dozen towns began cabling to New York and pulling wires to get her. Her social secretary, her publicity man, her business manager were besieged by representatives of noblemen who had palaces to rent, of hotels which wished to lodge her in the royal suite, of automobile manufacturers offering to put a fleet of cars at her disposal. The French newspapers took up her story, so typically American, and the smart people of the Coast of Pleasure speculated about her for hours on end.

XII

In her letter Emily Chattersworth explained, among other details, that the maternal grandmother of this matrimonial prize had belonged to one of the old New York families, and had been at school with Emily; she had been a guest at Les Forêts on various occasions. So now it had been arranged that Irma was to visit Sept Chênes for a week or two, until she had a chance to look about and judge where and how she wished to live. If during that period a fastidious young art expert saw fit to call and pay his respects, he would have the inside track over the other suitors. If his sense of dignity forbade him to do so, perhaps he might condescend to be at home when Emily brought the young lady to call upon his mother.

Having read all this more than once, Beauty retired to her boudoir to pray, in the fashion which her new husband had taught her. "O Lord, grant that Irma Barnes may fall in love with Lanny!" But then a sudden fear smote her, a doubt whether this might be considered a proper subject for a petition to the Most High; whether, in fact, the desire might not be an unworthy one, what Mr. Dingle had taught her to think of as "worldly." She began to argue, saying: "No, no, God! I want Lanny to have children! I want him to have the happiness of true love, as you have given it to me!"

"Couldn't he just as well marry a poor girl?" inquired the voice inside.

Bewilderment seized the soul of the lovely blond mother. Was that really the voice of God, or was it just her own frail mortality, or the notions which Lanny had helped to fix in her head? She cried: "Please God, don't be unreasonable! This girl is all right, and the fact that she has money surely ought not to bar her from having a good husband such as Lanny would make. Think what sort of man she might get here on the Riviera! Young as she is, and ignorant of the world!"

The voice said: "My daughter, it is the money you are thinking about, not the girl."

So then Beauty became rebellious—just as had happened in the case of Lucifer, aeons ago. She exclaimed: "My God, that is ridiculous! I never agreed to give up everything. If Lanny has money, he can help people in all sorts of ways, and Lanny would know how to do it much better than any of these idlers."

The voice replied, sternly: "Be careful, Mrs. Dingle!" It had taken to calling her that when it wanted to humiliate her. Now the tears came into her eyes, and she was in a state of confusion. The "Way of Perfection" was far less simple for a worldling like Beauty Budd than it had been for the naturally pure St. Theresa in medieval Spain.

Beauty felt the need of counsel, but was determined not to take the problem to her husband. Was she afraid of what he might tell her? After all, he had had little experience in the *grand monde*, and one might be justified in distrusting his judgment. Beauty knew that, whatever she did, he would not interfere, for he never tried to impose himself, even morally; he was content to go on living his inner life, trusting that it would have its effect upon others in time. Let your light so shine before men that they may see your good works and glorify your Father which is in heaven!

32

In That Fierce Light

I

RICK and Nina showed up in due course, very curious to see what sort of man it was who had managed to crash the gates of Beauty's heart. Lanny in his letters had put the best possible face upon the affair, and Rick and Nina, as guests, would do the same. In the privacy of their chamber Rick said there was one thing you could say for Mr. Dingle, he didn't try to force his ideas upon you; too bad the same couldn't be said for his wife! It was going to be a bit trying, but of course they would have to be polite. Nina said she hoped none of the children would fall sick, because Beauty was obviously hoping for a chance for Mr. Dingle to display his powers.

The young couple told Lanny the details of the Rosemary affair, and Nina delivered the messages which had been entrusted to her. Poor Bertie had got himself into a frightful mess; he had paid the blackmailer a good part of the money he had got out of his family art treasures. He wasn't a bad fellow, but weak, and a woman could twist him around her finger. An odd aspect of life in the diplomatic service—the head of the Foreign Office had come to the manor and had put it up to Rosemary: a scandal in London could be pardoned, but the prestige of the Empire couldn't stand one abroad, therefore Bertie's future depended upon his wife's willingness to go with him and stick by him. It amounted to getting married all over again; "forsaking all others, cleave to him only." But this time it wasn't a formula that you said in church, it was a gentleman's agreement, and you had to mean it!

Rick was now thirty-one, and was recognized as one of the younger writers with a future. He was working on a new book, not just a compilation of articles, but a carefully thought-out discussion of the world as it stood at the beginning of the year 1929. It was his thesis that the improvement of communications, especially the airplane, had reduced the size of the world so that there was no longer room for separate nations with their separate sovereignties. When airplanes loaded with high explosives could appear over the capital of a nation without warning, that nation wasn't safe; since it had to arm against the same sort of attack, the other nations were no safer. Agreements such as the Kellogg pact, which had just been signed with a great fanfare, meant nothing; each nation was an agency for its big-scale businessmen, competing for markets and resources, and the coming of war didn't depend upon signatures and gold seals on pieces of vellum, it depended upon some dissatisfied group of exploiters wanting more than they had, and seeing a chance to strike and get it.

Lanny had decided that Rick was the sanest thinker he knew, and he longed for the completion of this book so that he might give copies to various persons with whom he had arguments. Lanny couldn't pretend to foresee what was coming, but he had got fixed in his mind the proposition that there would never be peace in the world so long as the sources of wealth were left to be scrambled for and seized by the biggest and strongest. Lanny's young life had been dominated by one great war, and now he saw another in preparation, and who was going to stop it? Surely not those futile old gentlemen whom he had followed about Europe and watched in action at one conference after another. Ten years had passed, and they hadn't yet succeeded in fixing the amount of German reparations!

Young people in each nation were making up their minds that the only force in modern society that might avert another catastrophe was the exploited workers, organizing themselves for resistance to the ever-increasing pressure of capitalist greed. Rick was calling for an international government based on a Socialist economic system. That had to come, he insisted, and the only question was how was it to come? There were only two ways; revolution on the Russian model, or action by democratic consent to abolish autocracy from industry, as the British and Americans had long ago abolished it from their political affairs. The trouble was that you put off gradual changes until there was a crisis, and then it was too late. Rick said it was later now than anybody realized.

The two young men would discuss those questions in abstract, theoretical terms, and then Lanny would go to his class in the workers' school and be confronted with them in concrete, personal terms: Socialists *versus* Communists! There was hardly a question of strategy or tactics in the workers' struggle that didn't end up in that. If you urged obedience to law, the Communists would point out the lawlessness of the capitalists. If you talked about acquiring possession of the means of production by democratic methods, the Communists would say: "By electing politicians?" They would point to the career of one statesman after another; Briand, for example, had been chosen as a Socialist, and after he got power the railway workers struck, and he mobilized the troops and made them run the railways. Now he was a "radical," French style, which meant that he signed peace pacts, but took no step to interfere with the stranglehold of big business and finance on the people's means of life.

II

Emily Chattersworth came and opened Sept Chênes, and naturally one of the first things she wanted to do was to come over and inspect Beauty Budd's newest acquisition. Beauty was a friend, but also she was a phenomenon of nature, and the idea of her having got religion was nearly as entertaining as her having been shut up in a hotel suite with a German secret agent. Emily had done considerable reading in her life, and she knew that the idea of the immanence of God hadn't been invented in the state of Iowa; but it was undoubtedly "new thought" so far as Beauty was concerned, and what had it done to her? Lanny, who had learned to talk to this old friend with frankness, assured her that she would be disappointed in the result; like many other kinds of respectability, it was rather humdrum.

He told Emily the news about the pictures that Zoltan was selling, and the prospects for one that she wished to get rid of; about Hansi and Bess and their tour in the United States, the fine notices they were getting, and how Esther Budd had apparently reconciled herself to having a genius in the family; about his own latest bereavement and the state of his heart. "Do you miss her very much?" asked Emily.

"To be perfectly honest, not so much as I did Marie. She never wanted love as Marie did, wouldn't accept it from any man. I knew it was bound to end sooner or later; I was up against the British Empire."

"Did you get along well with her?"

"It was like being married. I had to go a lot of places when I'd much rather have stayed at home and read a book."

"You really want a studious woman, don't you, Lanny?"

"One that wears glasses," he smiled.

"Most of them would rather go blind nowadays," replied this white-haired *grande dame*—who used a lorgnette except when she was reading. Presently she remarked, *à propos de bottes:* "Irma Barnes is coming next week."

"I know; the ladies are all ganging up on me. Even Nina has joined."

"Don't be foolish, Lanny. I have every reason to think she's a fine young woman. I haven't seen her since she was a girl, but then she was bright and intelligent. Her mother is one of the Vandringhams—an excellent family, old New Yorkers, not the flashy ones."

"Quite a change in one generation, wouldn't you say?"

"You can't blame a girl because her father grows rich. It's to be doubted if she put him up to it."

"I know, Mrs. Emily; but the fact remains that when people have so much money, it does something to them; it seems to be stronger than they are."

"That is true; I've felt it myself, even though I never had any such sums as the Barneses. But remember, she's a girl like any other, and she wants some man to love her for herself."

"She'll have the devil of a time finding him, I'm guessing."

"If so, that's a reason to be sorry for her."

"Oh, I'll do that," he laughed; "but I doubt if she'll thank me!"

"What I mean is, give her a chance, like anybody else. See what she's really like, and don't make up your mind in advance."

Lanny told her about Tennyson's *Northern Farmer: New Style*, with which he had teased his mother. "Doänt thou marry for munny, but goä wheer munny is."

"You come to lunch and meet Irma and her mother, and I'll let them know that you're one caller who isn't interested in her fortune."

"I wonder," said the young man, promptly. "I have been quite entertained, thinking what I'd do if I had a fortune like that. I've decided that I'd set up a foundation to study the effects of stock-market speculation upon wages and the cost of living!"

III

Kurt Meissner wrote now and then. He was glad to hear the news about Beauty's marriage, and sent his best wishes for her happiness. He enclosed a picture of his young wife and their first baby, a boy; also of the very modest cottage in which they were living on the Stubendorf estate, the Graf having given them the use of it for the glory of German music. Kurt told about the composition on which he was working, and about a trip he had made to Munich, where his work was being taken up by the National Socialists with ardor. Heinrich Jung had become an active party leader, and they had won successes at the last elections. They were a legal party now, but they were still carrying on street wars with the Communists.

Rick looked at the photo of the bald little Aryan, and said: "I suppose they'll be having one every year for the glory of the Fatherland." He added: "Birth control is an important discovery, but it may prove a trap for the more progressive nations if the backward ones refuse to adopt it."

"Is Germany a backward nation?" inquired Lanny, with a grin.

"It'll be one very soon if those Nazis have their way. Women become brood-mares, and babies become soldiers to march out and conquer those decadent peoples who dream of being let alone."

Rick was worried about what was going on in Germany. He insisted that the republic was growing weaker, and failing completely to deal with the nation's internal problems. Britain and France couldn't agree on any consistent policy; they wouldn't help Germany to get on her feet and they wouldn't pay the cost of holding her down. They had just lifted the arms control of the country, and Germany was busily arming—Rick agreed with Robbie Budd about the facts, and what they meant. The next war was going to be fought with airplanes, and Germany hadn't been permitted to have military planes, but had been getting a great fleet of commercial planes, and how long would it take to convert them? Moreover, what was important was not so much the planes, but the factories and the skilled workers. Given these, a fleet of war-planes could be turned out in a year or two.

Rick had been to Geneva in September and had written up the situation confronting the Ninth Assembly of the League of Nations. Germany had been admitted, and had been fighting the admission of Poland to the League Council. Anyone could see that Poles and Germans were ready to fly at each other's throats. "That's where the next war will start," said Rick; "right at Stubendorf, or perhaps in the Corridor. It would take a permanent army there to prevent it —and who's going to pay the bill?"

Rick brought another item from Geneva; greetings to Lanny from Mrs. Sidney Armstrong, wife of that young American functionary who had introduced them to the insides of the League. "You remember her? She used to be his secretary. Janet Somebody."

"Sloane," said Lanny. "A jolly girl. We had the idea of falling in love with each other, and I was thinking I might go back and ask her to marry me."

"You waited too long, old top. They have a baby."

When Lanny told his mother about this, she said, with a touch of acidity: "There, now! Another one for you to adopt!"

IV

Lanny kept thinking: "Do I want to give my time to that Barnes girl?" He knew he had to give it to some girl before long; but a girl with twenty-three million dollars—even supposing that she would look at a poor man, and that he married her—what a nuisance to be carrying a load like that, having the world make a fuss over you, everybody trying to get something out of you, nobody ever telling you the truth, newspaper reporters besieging you for interviews! What could you say? Lanny had been with Hansi Robin when newspapermen had called, and that had seemed all right, because Hansi had done things and was going to do more; he had talked about music, and it had been worth while. But to talk because you had inherited more money than any other girl! Or because you had married such a girl! Lanny felt cheap even to think about it.

He discussed the problem with Rick, who looked quizzical, and said: "You really haven't the least bit of curiosity about her?"

"Maybe a little; enough to last through one luncheon."

"Well, I'll tell you what: be interested for me. Go and find out all you can about her. Ask her straight questions: What does it feel like to be a glamour girl? Are you excited, or are you bored, or are you scared, or exactly what? And whatever you get, bring it home."

"What for?"

"Copy, you imbecile. Don't you know that's what the public would rather read about than anything else in the world? You and I will collaborate on a play called *The Glamour Girl*, and make such a hit that we'll be the glamour boys of Broadway."

Lanny grinned, but then he reflected: "I'm afraid that would be giving her a rotten sort of deal."

Said the baronet's son: "If you find that she has a noble soul and that you are falling in love with her, I won't use the stuff."

V

Irma Barnes arrived at Sept Chênes, and the reporters came hurrying, and the photographers, and they put her on the front page of the Riviera papers. Emily telephoned that Lanny was to come to lunch next day. Beauty wasn't invited, because she might talk too much; Emily didn't say that, but explained that she wanted Lanny to have the field to himself, and Beauty understood. She had managed to get matters straightened out with God, and He had agreed to allow Lanny to treat Irma Barnes as he would any other young woman, not denying her happiness just because she was rich.

The mother had worked herself into a state of excitement, and came to Lanny's room to see if his tropical worsted was without a spot or wrinkle, and that the shades of his brightly striped tie harmonized with his tan-colored shirt.

"You know, old girl," he said, "your high-up Englishman is a trifle careless in his dress."

"He has some details that look careless," responded the fashionable mother, "but they are studied."

"Which details of mine are supposed to be careless?" inquired Lanny.

"You're not English," said Beauty, and passed on to another problem. "What are you going to talk about?"

"I rather thought I'd leave it to the inspiration of the moment."

"If I were you I wouldn't talk about politics, because you don't want her to find out that you are radical."

"All right, dear."

"And I wouldn't say anything about Marcel's work, because they might think you were hinting for them to buy it."

"I'll leave all business out, I promise."

"You understand that any sums of money you have made would seem just small change to her."

"I understand."

"And better not mention Budd's, because you don't want her to think that you're bragging. Emily will have told her all that sort of thing."

"I get you," said Lanny. "I'll tell her that the sun is shining brightly outside, and that we have many such days on the Riviera, even in January."

"You used to let me give you advice," complained Beauty; "but now I've become just an old shoe."

He gave her a hug and a large fat kiss, and said: "I never did that to any of my shoes."

The mother exclaimed: "Wait! You have pushed your tie all crooked."

VI

The elaborate carvings on Emily's white stone villa in French Renaissance style were shining brilliantly in the aforementioned January sunshine when Lanny came up the broad drive. Half a dozen cars were parked there, and he wondered if there were other guests after all; but they were cars of the members of the Barnes entourage who were staying at a hotel in Cannes, also of persons who were trying to see the heiress but were seeing the secretary instead. Lanny went into the drawing-room, and, having been at home here since childhood, he seated himself at the piano. He tried to think what might appeal to a girl who had just come from the hurlyburly of the Great White Way, and he chose the very lovely andante movement of Kurt Meissner's *Spanish Suite;* a serenade having all the seductiveness that anyone had ever imagined about Valencian nights. "Come out," it seemed to say, "for the scent of the orange blossoms is heavy in the air, and my heart aches with a longing which I strive to express—it is something beautiful which torments the soul—which cannot be explained."

Lanny thought: "I will find out if she knows what music is."

The three ladies appeared in the doorway, and he stopped. The hostess entered first: kind Mrs. Emily, her white hair worn long in defiance of the fashion of the hour; her finely chiseled, intellectual face lined with wrinkles which could no longer be concealed. She had had a surgical operation last summer, and was now supposed to be getting stronger. She had spent a lifetime entertaining other people, trying to give them pleasure, and at the same time a little more wisdom than they had or seemed to want.

Next, Mother Barnes, who had been born a Vandringham, and had acquired weight and majesty through the years; she had an ample bosom, and layers of *embonpoint* which the dressmaker's best arts were powerless to suppress; her gray silk chiffon might have been a maternity dress. She had dark hair, and dark eyes set under heavy brows, looking at you through a lorgnette. She was not a talkative person—it seemed that it might be an effort to bring that deep contralto voice into action; but when she did speak it was with authority. She listened and watched attentively, and Lanny could be certain that every detail concerning himself was being noted—perhaps even things which he himself didn't know. After the meal was over, and they lighted cigarettes, he saw the butler bring Mrs. Barnes a silver tray containing a long torpedo wrapped in gold foil. She unwrapped a dark brown cigar, bit off the end like a man, and proceeded to light up and puff vigorously.

And then Irma. A brunette like her mother, and no sylph according to the modern style, rather a young Juno. Her dark hair was shingled in the current style and waved about her ears; she wore a cream-colored frock of a simple cut, with a necklace of pearls. Her features were regular and her expression rather placid; she smiled easily, but quietly. Lanny saw at once that she was not a talkative person, which was rather a relief from his home life. She didn't say: "Oh, what was that lovely music you were playing?" She wasn't going to gush about anything, but wait for the world to bring her gifts; she would examine them carefully, and if there was anything wrong with them, her mother would tell her about it afterward.

All right; Lanny could talk for a whole tableful of people. He asked the young visitor how she liked the Riviera at first glance, and she replied that it reminded her of parts of the California coast, and also of Bermuda. Lanny hadn't been to either of those places, but he said that he had lived here since he could remember, and it had been pleasanter in the old days, before the place was so much advertised and such mobs came in. He told how it was when the beach of Juan-les-Pins had been used by fishermen, and he had played with their children, and helped to haul the seine. He had seen many strange creatures come out of that water—the strangest of all a submarine. Then Lanny told about the monument inscribed to the little "Septentrion child" who had "danced and pleased in the theater" some two thousand years ago. He told about the ruins and relics which various tribes of mankind had left on this Côte d'Azur, and how it was still the custom of some of the peasants to pray against the coming of the Saracens.

VII

In short, Lanny did what he could to entertain the minds and stimulate the imaginations of two ladies whom he didn't know at all. He brought his gifts of myrrh and frankincense, and the queen mother and the royal princess accepted them graciously, but did not indicate that they found them superior to the many other gifts which had been laid before their throne. Presently Lanny told about M. Pinjon, the gigolo, who had come when Lanny was a little boy and played the piccolo flute and showed him the steps of Provençal dances; afterward the poor fellow had lost one leg in the war, and had retired to his father's farm, and every Christmas he sent Lanny a little carved dancing-man of olive tree wood. "How pathetic!" said Miss Barnes, and Lanny replied: "The Duquesa de Villafranca, who was Zaharoff's wife, was so touched by the story that she sent him a very fine flute, and I suppose he plays it every night while the flocks come in. Some day, if you and your mother would enjoy a trip into the mountains, I would take you to call on him."

It appeared that the girl was about to say yes, but she stole a glance at her mother, and then said: "Thank you. Perhaps we can arrange it some time."

Well, Lanny had done his part. He let the stately Mrs. Emily talk about the fashionable people who were on hand this season, and the interesting events which were scheduled. After the meal they strolled out to the loggia in the rear, overlooking the gardens. The best view was from the front, but they couldn't go onto the portico because of strangers coming and going. However, on the second story there was a balcony, and Lanny asked if Miss Barnes had observed it. He offered to point out the landmarks to her, and she assented.

To the west lay the Estérel mountains, of blood-red porphyry, and to the east Monaco on its rock. The city of Nice was white sprinkled on green. In front lay the blue Golfe Juan, with several gray French warships at anchor; beyond were islands, one of them Sainte-Marguerite, where you could sail and have tea; the Germans of the Riviera had been interned there during the war. Over to the left were the heights of Notre-Dame-de-Bon-Port, where the sailors came once a year, walking with bare feet and carrying the image of the Virgin down to the sea so that she might bless the waters and protect them from storms. Apparently Miss Barnes found all this interesting, and Lanny said that he would be happy to come and take her and her mother to see the sights of the coast. She thanked him, and he wondered, was she more human than her mother? Did she perchance consider that she had enough money, so that she might feel free to chat with a poor man now and then? A plausible theory, but it required more evidence.

They went downstairs and he didn't offer to play the piano, because she knew that he could do it, and it was up to her to ask the favor if she wished it. After some miscellaneous conversation he excused himself, and made no suggestion of a second meeting. If they felt any urge to see him again, they could reveal it to Mrs. Emily. He had done his duty, and at home Rick would have some pages of new manuscript ready—not a play about a glamour girl, but a book supporting the program of the Socialist International!

VIII

"Well, how did it go? What is she like? What did you talk about? What did she say?" Such are the questions which every mother asks; and every mother knows that her son makes unsatisfactory answers, and has to be cross-examined—but not crossly! It all sounded rather enigmatic as Lanny told it, and Beauty could hardly wait until she had a chance to ask Emily. They could only talk guardedly over the telephone, but Emily said that Lanny had been his usual friendly self and nobody could help but like him when they knew him. The last clause gave a dubious turn to the statement; but apparently it was all right, for the next day Emily called Lanny and asked if he would come and take them for a drive—she had assured the ladies that he could tell them more interesting things about this Coast of Pleasure than any other person she knew. "Good old scout!" said Lanny—and that was hardly being guarded!

Doubtless there had been some conversation between mother and daughter, and it must have contained an element favorable to the young art expert, for in spite of the fact that they had a chauffeur with them, and that Mrs. Emily also had one, they permitted Lanny to drive them about. Miss Barnes sat in the seat beside him, and he pointed out the places of interest and told her about the life, not all of it favorable; it would be well for her to know that the coast abounded in swindlers and pretenders, many of them highly ingenious. He mentioned the Rumanian countess, genuine, who had sold him a vase that wasn't.

They came to Monte Carlo, and had lunch at Ciro's, and strolled about, looking at the sights. Lanny said it was time for Zaharoff to be taking his constitutional, and Irma asked: "Who is he?" He told her, and thought it was interesting, but discovered that for the young the aged are but dim shadows. His offer, half playful, to take them for a call upon the munitions king did not interest a glamour girl; what she wanted was to see the gambling which people talked about all over the world. Followed by the two elders as chaperons, he escorted her into the sumptuous rococo palace; they wandered through the white and gilt rooms, overdecorated and very ill-ventilated, and explained that they no longer belonged to Zaharoff; the old trader had sold the place for three times what he paid—trust him for that!

They watched the players at the various tables, and finally Irma wanted to try roulette. Did Lanny have any idea which number was likely to win? He said that he had not the slightest idea; his father had insisted that he must never harbor any such thought, never let anyone persuade him that it was possible to know or to guess, for that was the shortest road to ruin in the whole world. Irma said she had a hunch for the number eleven, having somewhere heard somebody say "Come eleven," so she took out a ten-franc note and laid it on that number; if her hunch should prove correct, she would be paid thirty-five times the amount of her stake.

The *croupier* spun the wheel, and presently said his formula: "*Rien ne va plus.*" The little ball dropped into number twenty-eight, so the *croupier* raked in Irma's ten francs. She moved on, saying: "Perhaps it's just as well, or I might have got interested."

"It doesn't always work that way," commented the escort. "Many people try to win their money back, and that's where their troubles begin."

The party had been recognized in the restaurant, and people had turned to stare at them; several had followed at a discreet distance. Now they were known in the casino, and next day stories appeared in the papers; the American heiress had visited "Monty" and risked and lost ten francs. This seemed to amuse the newspapermen; they figured that it was the one hundred-millionth part of Irma Barnes's fortune, and telegraphed this calculation all over the world. One of the gossip writers in New York compared it with the practice of another very wealthy American, old "John D.," who gave a shiny new dime to every person rich or poor whom he met. Mrs. Barnes received a cable from her brother in New York, saying that this wasn't very good publicity; he didn't make clear whether he meant gambling in general, or gambling for such a puny stake. He himself was a Wall Street operator.

The incident had its effect upon Lanny's affairs. He was named as the escort of the glamour girl, and it gave him a taste of publicity not so disagreeable to his mother and her friends as the occasion of his escape from the Fascists. Many persons called up Bienvenu asking to meet the American heiress; persons whom Beauty had well-nigh forgotten presented themselves suddenly as old friends. They had houses to rent to Irma Barnes, family heirlooms to sell to her, sons to marry to her—or they just wanted to meet her on general principles, they were moths who flew to the spotlight, hoping to have their names in the papers as Lanny had succeeded in doing. Beauty informed these persons that Miss Barnes's business manager was staying at such and such a hotel in Cannes; but of course that wasn't what they wanted.

There was a very grand reception to the heiress at Sept Chênes, and the *crème de la crème* attended; more titles than you could shake a stick at, or could keep in your memory no matter how hard you might try—and Irma didn't. To an American girl the difference between a marquess and a marqués and a marquis and a marchese was not readily apparent, and a dark brown skin meant just one thing to her, even when the bearer was an East Indian potentate. Some of these gentlemen were bachelors, and others willing to become so if Irma Barnes would smile upon them; since she smiled upon all impartially, they gathered around her like bees at swarming time. Lanny, having no title and no fortune to speak of, realized what a silly enterprise the women of his circle had pushed him into, and sat out in the sunshine with M. Rochambeau and a French diplomat of the latter's acquaintance, discussing the probable life-span of the Kellogg pact and which nation would be the first to breach it.

IX

Irma Barnes had inspected the Riviera, and had learned that Nice was "common," while Cannes was "right." She had visited and approved the château of an American copper-mining heiress up on the heights not far from Sept Chênes. There she and her entourage were installed: a business manager, or steward, his secretary and a bookkeeper, Irma's social secretary, her maid and her mother's maid and a chauffeur; that was the staff with which she traveled, and the manager would engage servants for the château locally. She herself would never have to move a finger, or use her mind longer than it took to learn the names of the butler and the housekeeper. Her function was to have beautiful clothes draped upon her, and go forth to give the world the pleasure of gazing at her. In due course she would be named as one of the best-dressed women of the Continent, an honor which one attained by purchasing the most clothes from the fashionable *couturiers* of Paris—or from their Riviera branch establishments—and permitting them to design everything and charge double or triple prices.

The story which the papers told was that the great American heiress had come to Europe in search of "culture," but of course that didn't go down with the *beau monde*. It was taken for granted that she was looking for a husband, and it would have to be a title, one of the greatest. Every mother of an eligible son was on the *qui vive*, and some came to the Riviera especially on Irma's account; who would begrudge the price of a ticket in a lottery such as this? The smart people were agog, and the smart newspapermen amused themselves and their readers by listing the eligibles, as they would have done for a race at Longchamps: the name of the entry, what stable it was from, what prizes it had won, the names of the sire and the dam. This was a convenience for both Irma and her mother, for they could cut out the list and learn the titles: Prinz zu Pumpernickel of the royal house of a German state, the Duc de Choufleur of the old French *noblesse*, the dashing young Baron Snuffsky from Poland, the fabulously wealthy Maharaja of Gavardior.

The proper procedure was for Mrs. Barnes to have a lawyer to whom these candidates might send their lawyer, presenting their photographs and credentials, a list of their titles, castles and other possessions, and a statement of the dowry which the bride would be expected to bring. Mrs. Barnes's lawyer would convey these various proposals to her, and if the family was interested, arrangements would be made for a meeting between the bride and the prospective bridegroom. That was the dignified way to handle it, but of course with crude Americans one must be prepared for almost anything. Did they expect the business manager who hired their house and paid their servants to handle their marriage arrangements? Or did Mrs. Barnes expect to discuss such matters herself? The social secretary was asked this question, Mrs. Chattersworth was asked it, and discreet inquiries came to Mrs. Barnes by mail: "Will you kindly designate in what manner, etc."

Lanny had retired to his studio and was reading Marx's *Capital*, in order to try to understand the theory of surplus value to which Rick and others were so frequently referring. Emily came to Bienvenu, and she and Beauty had a pow-wow, after which the châtelaine of Sept Chênes strolled over to the studio and walked in on the young social scientist. "See here," she said, "do you want to or don't you?"

"Don't I what?"

"Don't waste my time. Do you or don't you?"

"Well, honestly, Mrs. Emily, I don't think that I do and I do think that I don't. It's awfully good of you, and I'd do most anything in the world to oblige you; but I just feel silly. The girl hasn't any interest in me, and I don't want anything she has, and why should I sacrifice my self-respect and make her think that I do?"

"Are you quite sure she hasn't any interest in you?"

"Well, my God, she had every chance to show it, but I might as well have been a hired guide."

"Do you expect the woman to do the wooing?"

"You're darn well right I do—when she has as much money as this one. A man feels like a cad if he so much as looks at her."

"Are you sure you're not the one who's making too much out of her money, Lanny?"

"Well, I know a little about the world; and if that mother of hers isn't thinking about her money, then I'm a hard-boiled cynic."

"Let me tell you about them. Irma loves her mother, and respects her, but all the same there's a struggle going on between them, and it's hard on both. Fanny Barnes has had a very unhappy life; her husband kept women all over town, and she loathed him; it's affected her attitude to pretty nearly all men. She doesn't like to see them come around Irma; she can't help knowing what they want, and not liking it."

"Does she want the girl to grow up an old maid?"

"What she would like is for her to marry some mature business-man, who can handle her fortune; she has a man in mind in New York, but Irma won't have him, so here they are."

"Well, I'm no businessman, Mrs. Emily, and I wouldn't have the least idea what to do with her fortune."

"What Irma wants, Lanny, is to fall in love."

"Has she told you that?"

"Not in so many words, but it's written all over her."

"Well, if she wants to fall in love with me, the first thing would be to know something about me. She can't very well judge with her mother sitting by and making me feel that she'd like to call the police."

"No doubt she would," laughed the woman. "But she won't."

"Irma has got swarms of men around her and she's on the go all the time. I don't think she's missing me."

"Maybe she's missing something that might be of advantage to her if she knew about it."

"You were always too kind, Mrs. Emily. The way I feel is this: whether she likes it or not, she's in the position of a queen, and if she wants a man she has to say so. He can't ask her."

"That's really making it too hard for any girl."

"Well, if she wants a man who doesn't want her for her money, how else will she get him?"

The woman thought that over; then she inquired: "Is there anything you would suggest?"

"I'd suggest meeting her like any other young woman. I'd invite her for a drive, or a sail, or something, and she could see if she likes me, and I'd see if I like her."

"All right," was the reply. "It may mean a fight with Fanny, but I'll see if it can be arranged."

X

Rick said: "I'm not rotting, there's an idea in that play. If you'll get the stuff, I'll write it."

Lanny, amused, inquired: "Shall I tell her that you want to write it?"

"Tell her that you want to write it yourself."

"That would make me another kind of fortune-hunter. And a cheap one, I fear."

"Well, don't fear too much. Go right after her."

Lanny said: "I'll see." He was amused by the advice, so exactly the opposite of Rick's own manner of approach to anything or anybody. An Englishman's idea of an American man dealing with an American woman!

One bright and pleasant day right after lunch Lanny drove up to the château on the heights, and the new English butler received him and said: "I will notify Miss Barnes, sir." Lanny sat in a large reception hall which had portraits, and he used such occasions for testing his professional skill. Without looking at the signature, he would ask himself: "Who painted that? What is the period? And what would I offer for it?" He would find out how near he had come on the first two points, and Zoltan would tell him about the last.

The daughter of Midas appeared, wearing what was called a sports ensemble, white with gold trim, very gay. "Take a warm wrap," he said. "You can never tell when you go sailing." They rolled gently down the slope, over the boulevards of the city of Cannes, and out to the Cap, where Lanny had his boat. On the way he asked what she had been doing, whom she had met and what she thought of them—the easiest kind of conversation. She was reserved in her comments on people, and he thought: "Is she being kind to them? Or is she not very perceptive?" A few matters he had become certain about; she would never "rave" over anything, and, on the other hand, she was not malicious, she didn't say contemptuous things. Maybe she was just slow in her mental processes. It was hard for Lanny to imagine that, for his own mind was usually behaving like fireworks inside.

He assisted her into the boat. Just enough breeze for pleasant sailing; but one couldn't count upon permanence in January. Emily Chattersworth had assured Mrs. Barnes that Lanny had sailed the Golfe Juan since he was a boy, and never had been upset. He would take her around the Lérin islands, and perhaps stop on Sainte-Marguerite and have tea under the soughing pine trees.

He said: "Over there close to shore is where the submarine came up. It was always my favorite spot for torch-fishing." He told her about Captain Bragescu, the Rumanian officer who had painted and powdered his face, but, even so, had speared and landed the biggest green moray that Lanny had ever seen. He told about goggle-fishing, and how for months he had watched and stalked a big *mérou*. He mentioned that his father had used this boat as a place of retreat in which to impart the weightiest secrets about munitions deals. "I'm not sure they were really so weighty," he said, "but he wanted to impress me with the importance of not letting people fish things out of me. You can see that a sailboat is a fine place for private conferences."

"I wish my father had thought of it," said Irma Barnes. Evidently she had some incident in mind, but didn't tell it.

Lanny said: "Do you find it interesting to watch people and try to understand them—what they're thinking about and what makes them tick? They don't always want you to know."

"I've been told that is sometimes the case," admitted the heiress with a smile.

"My life has been a queer one," the young man went on to explain. "I've never been great or important, and never wanted to be; but accident has thrown me among people of that sort—at least, they considered themselves that, and were able to get the world to accept them. My father being in munitions, I can't recall the time when I wasn't meeting generals and cabinet members and bigwigs like that. Then for six months I was on the American staff at the Peace Conference, and I didn't really have any influence, but a lot of people thought I might have it. So, one way or another, I'd meet this or that headliner, and I'd think: 'What is he really like? What's he thinking about right now? What does he want to get from me, or from my father, or from my chief?' It gets to be a habit—maybe a bad one."

"It sounds rather alarming," commented the girl in the sailboat. There were a few others on the *golfe*, but some distance away.

"Oh, I never did any of them any harm," said Lanny. "I just thought about them, and often I never had any chance to check up and find out if I was right."

"Are you trying to check up on me?" she smiled. It was certainly a "lead," but Lanny judged it best not to follow it too eagerly.

"I told you about Zaharoff," he said. "I saw a great deal of him during the Peace Conference in Paris. He wanted something from me—I'm not at liberty to say what it was, but it was a matter of state, and the old gentleman gave quite a fascinating demonstration of how a Levantine trader sets about getting what he's after. You understand, he was at that time the richest man in Europe; my father said he was the richest man in the world. He has two daughters who are going to be his heirs. He invited me to meet those young ladies —he was using them as bait. I was supposed to keep on coming, so that he could win me over. They were lovely girls, and their mother was a Spanish duquesa, a relative of King Alfonso. They probably had no idea what they were being used for; they met a young American connected with the Peace Commission, who told them amusing stories about what was going on; they were modest and reserved, quite romantic-looking—I was only nineteen at the time, so I was susceptible. I had read fairy stories when I was a child, and I thought: 'Here are two princesses, and I wonder what princesses really think about, and are they as interesting as the stories make them seem.'"

"What happened?" asked Irma.

"It's too bad. It's like a serial story when you miss the next issue of the magazine. My position was such that I couldn't honorably go back again."

"You were just getting to the interesting place," remarked the glamour girl.

XI

The breeze was from the west, and the little boat was close-hauled; Lanny, holding the tiller, had to keep watch ahead, so the girl, seated farther forward, was in his line of vision. She, for her part, might have been interested in the view, in which case she would have turned her back to Lanny; but she didn't. Looking into the mainsail of a boat gets rather monotonous, so now and then she would direct her glance toward the young man at her side. It was a time for confidences, if ever. "Go after her hard!" Rick had said.

"Now I meet another princess," Lanny remarked, "and I am wondering what she is really like."

"Oh, dear!" exclaimed the girl. She shot a quick look at him, and then, meeting his eyes, looked back into the mainsail. He saw the color mount in her cheeks.

"I have been thinking a lot about a princess," he said. "It is not just a title, you know; it's a state of affairs. Few kings of old days had as much power as your father wielded, and few kings' daughters have as much passed on to them as you."

"I suppose so," she admitted, in a low voice. She did not look at him again for quite a while.

"A princess is born to power; she doesn't have to do anything to get it, and, on the other hand, she has no way to escape it. She is a prisoner of her destiny. People behave to her in a certain way, and expect her to behave to them according to her station; there is a code of etiquette which has grown out of the circumstances, much the same all over the world, and it quickly becomes fixed. The courtiers and ladies-in-waiting are shocked if the princess doesn't do what they expect, and the princess, knowing this, finds it hard to break out of her role. Isn't that true?"

"That's about the way it is."

"But all the time the princess knows that she's a woman, like any other. She becomes a double personality, leading a double life. So when someone comes to me and says: 'Would you like to meet the Princess So-and-so?' I usually answer: 'Not especially.' I have learned that meeting one is usually a bore; you don't meet the real person, you only meet the role, so to speak, the figurehead. Of course if you believe in royalty, and like to stand about a throne—or if you're looking to get something by royal favor—that's another matter. But not wanting anything, I find myself thinking: 'What is Her Royal Highness really like? What is she thinking at this moment? Is she bored by her role, or does she enjoy it? Is she perhaps frightened —afraid not to play it right, because people will laugh at her if she does it wrong? Is she flattered by their praise, or is she afraid of their malice?' That malice can be a terrible thing, Miss Barnes; for the world is far from being kind."

"I know," said the young woman, her voice still low.

"Maybe I'm imagining most of this, and maybe you haven't ever thought of it, except vaguely. Maybe you've just been raised a certain way, and you go on living from day to day. Maybe you don't like to question your own soul, or to have some impertinent young upstart begin doing it!"

His companion had turned her head away, and he saw her reach hurriedly for her handkerchief and put it to her eyes. He exclaimed, in concern: "Have I offended you?"

"No," she answered, hastily. "Wait." He did so, and presently she turned her face half-way toward him, and explained: "You see, Mr. Budd, my father killed himself getting all that money; and I'd ever so much rather have had him."

XII

There was the answer to the riddle, and there was Rick's play if he cared to write it. Irma Barnes had loved her father. Had she known that he "kept women all over town"? Maybe so, maybe not —Lanny wasn't going to inquire about that. Anyhow, she had loved him, and admired him, a capable, hard-driving master of men, a gay companion when he was at home. She had known him as a little girl knows a playmate and friend, and when she learned that he had dropped dead in the middle of a hard Wall Street battle, she didn't feel compensated by his possessions. She didn't mention her mother, but that too was significant, and, with the hint that he had got from Emily, Lanny could guess that she thought her mother had set more store by the money than by the man.

Anyhow, there was the soul of a princess. After a while she smiled and said that Lanny wouldn't miss the next installment this time. He decided then that her mind wasn't slow; she just stayed withdrawn into herself, watching the world go by and doing what people asked her to do. Was it out of kindness, or lack of initiative? She was only twenty, and hadn't thought much.

What had they taught her in school? Apparently nothing very useful: good manners and deportment, some French, and a smattering of the arts. She knew how to read, but she didn't know how to enjoy reading. When you have so much money, and so many persons to attend you, it becomes your duty to let them do it; having things done to you and for you is in accord with your station in life, your social importance; but to go off into a corner by yourself and bury your nose in a book is a waste of opportunity, to say nothing of seeming churlish to all the dressmakers and hairdressers and manicurists and masseuses and dancing- and music-masters and maids and secretaries and other humble persons who get their living by serving you, and are so pathetic in their efforts to please you. "You've no idea how many people I had to disappoint in order to get this sail with you!" confessed the princess of public utilities. "But I'm glad I did."

The ice was broken, and she told him about her life, which seemed like one in a high-class jail to Lanny, who had been accustomed to do so much for himself and to spend so large a share of his time alone, dreaming his dreams, trying to express them on the piano, or to find them in books or works of art. Irma Barnes had hardly ever been alone in her life, despite the fact that she had been an only child. She had hardly ever been able to do anything for herself; there was always somebody ready to leap to do it ahead of her, and to have his or her feelings hurt if the young mistress didn't wait and submit. That she was physically vigorous was due to the fact that she had played tennis with a tennis instructor, ridden horseback with a riding master, swum with a swimming expert—and so on, one thing after another all day long. Irma Barnes had never hauled a seine with fisherboys and -girls on any beach; to her a fish was something the butler brought in steaming hot on a large dish of chased silver, and showed to the master with a flourish, and then proceeded to cut into slices on a side table.

XIII

The weather continued to favor them, and they sat at a little outdoor table by a teahouse and ate tiny biscuits with butter and honey, discussing the fact that riches accumulated automatically, and what caused them to behave in that way. Someone had told the mother and daughter about Lanny's strange eccentricity of teaching in a Red Sunday school. He was quite sure it wasn't Emily who had done this; more likely some lady with an eligible son of her own. The facts were notorious, and, despite his mother's anxious warnings, Lanny had no idea of trying to slur them over. What he believed meant much more to him than it did to Beauty, and it would have been silly to let the girl take an interest in him without knowing the pink tinge of his mind.

He told her about the children of the workers who came there; what they looked like, how they behaved, what he taught them. She imagined unruly little ragamuffins, but he assured her that they came with clothes carefully mended and that they had been washed for the occasion, at least everything that showed. They were, he said, the élite of the children of the poor; alert, eager-eyed, taking their class-consciousness as a religion; their parents had been acquainted with suffering and they knew that life was no playground. To all this a glamour girl listened as to something from another planet; things strange, rather thrilling, but also alarming.

What was it all for? What did these people expect to do? He explained in words of one syllable the idea of social ownership: the means of producing what all had to use were to be public property, publicly administered for the public benefit; something like the post-office, the army, the trams. He forgot for the moment that Irma came from a country where the trams and the railroads were privately owned, and that her father had owned some. She listened to his picture of a co-operative society, out of Bellamy, and she brought up the stock objections. Who would do the dirty work? Would people work if they didn't have to? And would you pay everybody the same?

She wanted to know how he came upon these unusual ideas. He told her about his Red uncle, not trying to prettify him. This dangerous person, so greatly disliked by Lanny's father, had taken him, half by accident, to a slum in Cannes. "Oh, do they have slums in Cannes?" exclaimed the girl, and Lanny replied: "Would you like to see them?" He told her about Barbara Pugliese and her tragic fate. He told about the Blessed Little Pouter Pigeon, and the regime of despotism which he had set up in Italy. "Oh, but they tell me the country is much better managed!" exclaimed Irma. "The trains all run on time!"

Lanny perceived that he would have a job of educating to do. He talked about the Peace Conference and what he had seen and learned there. He mentioned Lincoln Steffens, and found that she had never heard the name; in fact, her mind was pretty much a blank about current events. She knew the names of the leading screen stars, of the singers she had heard at the opera, the leaders of jazz bands who were announced over the ever more popular radio; but literary names, except for a few best-sellers, were unknown to her. The names of statesmen also were vague in her mind; she had no idea what they stood for, except that her father had approved of certain ones at home and disapproved violently of certain others. Lanny could guess that the former were men with whom the father had been able to do business.

It wasn't at all the sort of conversation that he had planned, or that Beauty would have approved; but the heiress asked questions, and he answered, and told her stories which he thought were within the range of her understanding. Perhaps he did not allow enough for the immaturity of her mind; perhaps he talked too long and wearied her; but certainly she saw that he was kind, and perfectly respectful, possibly even grandfatherly. If she was looking for a man who wasn't after her money, she had reason to believe that this was the one. She said: "I don't think my mother would approve of these ideas."

He replied: "Probably not. You don't have to tell them to her unless you wish." That was the nearest he came to sedition, or seduction, or whatever the mother would have considered it.

They went back to the boat, and it was turning chilly, so she was glad to have her wrap. The breeze held, and they sailed before it merrily. They saw the sun go down behind the open sea, and before dark they reached the little pier. Driving to her home he was smitten by doubts, and said: "I do hope I haven't been boring you with all this political stuff."

"Not at all," she answered. "I was truly interested. I hope you will come again."

"I'll be delighted to. I know that you have many engagements, and I don't want to intrude; but this is my home, you know, and I am at your service."

"Call me up," she said; and they left it there.

Driving back to his home, Lanny was thinking: "Well, she'd be all right, if I could get her out of that environment." But then he thought: "Her environment is her money, and she won't get out of it till she dies."

He found that his mother was out, so he strolled to the lodge. "Well?" asked Rick, quizzically. "Did you get me that story?"

"I got one," Lanny replied. "But I'm afraid I can't let you use it."

The lame Englishman sat up in his chair and looked at his friend. His wife was in the next room and he called: "Ho, Nina, come in here! Lanny is going to marry Irma Barnes!"

33

Uneasy Lies the Head

I

IRMA BARNES was going about with Lanny Budd. All the Riviera took note of the fact, and the million tongues of gossip were busy. He was the lucky one; favored over all the millionaires, the princes and the dukes and the marquesses. In various ways it was made apparent to him that he had become a person of importance. The spotlight swung onto Bienvenu and stayed there. Peace and privacy were gone; there were visitors calling, motor-cars in the drive, the telephone ringing; people urging Lanny and his beautiful mother to come here and there. "And bring Irma," they would add, casually.

He had the time to give to her, and she took it for granted that he would give it. She enjoyed his company; he knew everybody and everything, or so it seemed to her; he made clever remarks, and while she wasn't clever herself, she smiled appreciatively when he was. Moreover, he was kind; and while nobody was unkind to her, she had been put on guard against insincerity. It wasn't long before they were calling each other by their first names, and he had the run of the château. Irma had had it out with her mother; the older woman wasn't pleased by it, but she would be polite, because the young generation was running wild and you had to give them their head.

Lanny played tennis with Irma and beat her regularly. It was a novel experience for her; not one of her suitors had had that much originality. He escorted her to a cocktail party, *très snob,* and when she had had two drinks he told her that was one too many, she showed the effects. He wasn't sure if she'd take it from him, but she did; moreover, she told others about it, and rumor spread, he had her completely under his thumb; he was posing as a young Puritan, a moralist. Imagine, after the way they lived in Bienvenu! She'd soon find out, if the million tongues had their way. One proper English lady told Mrs. Fanny that the place had "a faintly incestuous atmosphere!"

Lanny didn't leave it for the gossips to tell about himself. He took Irma for a long drive in the mountains, to that village of Charaze where the one-legged gigolo resided. On the way they talked about love, and he told her the story of Rosemary, beginning on the banks of the river Thames when he was sixteen and she was seventeen, and ending two or three months ago, when she left for the Argentine. No use keeping back the names, for "everybody" knew about it, "everybody" knew that he had built a "cottage" for her and her children. Just now the Dowager Countess Eversham-Watson had it for the season. "You know," said the million tongues, "that whisky woman from Kentucky. Is she his latest flame? Nobody seems to be quite sure about it."

There was snow up in those mountains, and one had to drive carefully. The retired gigolo hopped up on his peg-leg and embraced Lanny; he was so happy that the tears stood in his eyes. He had a wife and several brown little ones; they sat in his stone cabin and listened while he played the marvelous silver-embossed flute which the duquesa had presented to him. The wife spread a red-and-white-checked cloth on the table, and brought a long loaf of bread, fresh butter and cheese, dried figs and new wine; before they left, Irma purchased the whole row of little dancing men which M. Pinjon was carving for the next Christmas trade.

Then, driving down in the late afternoon, Lanny told the story of Marie de Bruyne. Again no use hiding names, for it had been in the newspapers; it was a "scandal," and there were those who cherished that sort of history and would remember it till they died—and perhaps later, if they were consigned to the same place as Marie. Lanny had no shame about the story, and if it was going to shock a strictly brought-up American girl, the sooner he knew it the better. He was in his thirtieth year, and had had only three women in his life; he hadn't bought any of them, or betrayed any, and all had been happy. If Irma were to investigate the records of her many suitors, both in New York and on the Riviera, she would hardly find a better one.

II

Irma Barnes liked love stories, it appeared; especially when they were autobiographical. She asked questions, not bold or improper, but questions of a stranger in a strange land, trying to understand its customs. This very old continent of Europe had its long-established institutions, and *la vie à trois* was one of them; doubtless the practice existed also across the seas, but more carefully hidden, at least from young girls. It was a daring adventure to have a man tell her such things; a tribute to her maturity, and one more proof that he wasn't after her money—or if he was, he was taking a bold line!

He didn't say: "I tell you these things because I am thinking about asking you to marry me." But it was understood between them. Silly to pretend otherwise, when it was in the thoughts and conversation of everyone who knew them. They were feeling each other out, trying experiments, making little tentative approaches and then retreating. Lanny would go off and think: "Well, what would it be like with her?" or "What did she mean by that remark?" Irma would step out of his car, asking herself the same questions. She would go into the house, and there would be an Austrian baron or the son of a South African gold magnate waiting to take her to dinner. She would think: "Would this be better?"

Everywhere she went people were attentive to her; every man bowed, clicked heels, kissed her hand in the romantic European way. Each studied her tastes, her whims, and sought to please her by every gesture and word. The European men were ardent; with hardly an exception, they made love to her all the time. Never for a moment did they let her forget that they were men, and she an adored woman; their manners, their phrases, their tones, had all been created for that purpose. It was called "gallantry." She found it exciting; she lived in a pleasant state of surprise, for there was always a new type of man, a new sort of elegance, a new distinction of appearance, costume, gesture, intonation; a new foreign accent, with perhaps a hint of mystery, of power, something to be awed by, perhaps even to be afraid of. Hard to be sure, when you were so young, and didn't entirely trust anybody, not even your own mother. How often she missed the strong, capable father, who knew men and could have told her what she needed to know.

Lanny was different from all the others. He was casual, sometimes irritatingly so; he seemed to take too much for granted. Or was it that he thought too well of himself? Was he a bit conceited? She asked him, and he said it wasn't that he valued himself so highly, he valued some of the other men so little, and didn't care to mix up with them. Was it the remark of an honest man, or of a jealous one? She asked him about some of the other men. He answered that he didn't know these individuals, but he knew a lot about European men in general; watch their attitude toward women—other women!

Lanny was younger than many of the suitors, but he talked the oldest. Many of the things he said were over her head; she told him so, and he explained what he meant. He didn't make love to her; hadn't even tried to take her hand. She wondered why. He had made love to other women. Didn't he care for her that way? Was it because of her money? Hang the money!—so she would think, but not for long. It was pleasant having money, and if anyone failed to treat her with the deference due to her money rank, she would re-sent it quickly. Her mother kept her attention firmly fixed on the fact that she was the greatest "catch" on the Riviera, perhaps in Europe.

The ladies at Bienvenu and its vicinity did the same thing for Lanny. With them it was the way it had been during both battles of the Marne; everybody wanted bulletins every hour! They were, as the phrase had it, "dying with curiosity." Nina and Margy would come over to the villa to hear what Beauty had to report, and Emily and Sophie would telephone and ask questions—not going into detail, because telephone wires have leaks. Each of the ladies would give Lanny advice; Sophie, the henna blond with the henna laugh, quite differently from the gentle, reticent Nina. But even Nina prodded him. "You know, Lanny, girls don't propose to men, except in Bernard Shaw's dramas." Rick added: "Not even in *The Glamour Girl* by Pomeroy-Nielson!"

The drama of Lanny and the heiress was being produced and directed by the wise and tactful Emily Chattersworth. She would carry messages back and forth; she would investigate the wavering young hearts and report upon their condition. Irma found it amusing that a white-haired *grande dame*—everybody considered her that —should be carrying on a proud young man's romance for him; she didn't mind being questioned, though she knew that every word she said was going back to Lanny. She liked him very much, but she liked other men too; she liked the excitement of keeping them on a string and watching them dance, such very elegant and graceful dancers. In return for this confession she received the latest cardiographic reports from Bienvenu. Lanny liked her, but didn't know if she liked him enough, or if he could make her happy, or whether a poor man had a right to try. He was afraid he bored her, and also afraid she wanted to "gad" too much. The tactful ambassadress took the liberty of putting this last in more diplomatic language.

III

This went on all through the Riviera season; they had a pleasant time, and nobody was hurt, unless possibly it was Beauty, who de-

clared that she was living "on pins and needles," a distressing state of
affairs even for one so well padded as she was getting to be. She had
got it fixed up with God so that He didn't object to Lanny's marrying Irma, and didn't even object to petitions ascending to His Throne
soliciting aid in the matter. Beauty had even been able to make some
impression upon her spiritual-minded husband, by persistently calling his attention to the many worthy works which he and she might
be able to do—not with Irma's money, but with Beauty's and Lanny's,
which might be released for the service of Divine Truth if Lanny
were to marry a fortune. The devil is a subtle worm, and it is known
that he assumes many disguises to gain access to the hearts of his
victims.

Lanny, being a human ego, operating in connection with flesh and
blood, was likewise exposed to these satanic wiles. It occurred to his
mind that a Socialist Sunday school which was helping the workers
of Cannes might be extended to bring similar benefits to the workers
of Nice and Toulon and Marseille. There might arise somewhere on
the Riviera a so-called People's House, an institution such as Lanny
had inspected in Brussels to his great satisfaction. Also, if an Englishman of brilliant parts were to write a wise and useful book, it might
be possible to have it printed in a cheap edition and made available
to the sort of persons who needed it. Such thoughts, haunting the
mind of Lanny Budd, were proof that the mental powers of Satan
have remained unweakened during the course of nineteen hundred
years.

"Lanny, for God's sake, why don't you ask her?" clamored
Beauty.

"I really think that the time has come," declared Mrs. Emily. It
was a special council of war, called at Sept Chênes.

"I simply can't do it," declared the scrupulous suitor. "She has too
much money."

"You just don't care for her enough!"

"I care for her enough so that I would ask her if she didn't have
so much money."

"Then can't you say: 'Irma, if you didn't have so much money, I
would ask you to marry me'?"

"No, because she has the money. I simply won't put myself in the class with those fortune-hunters."

So there they were. Beauty said: "Lanny, you are provoking!"

Emily said: "Just what do you want to happen? Does she have to say: 'Lanny, will you marry me?'"

"I don't care what words she uses. She can say: 'Lanny, I know you're not a fortune-hunter.' That's what I want her to know, and I want to know that she knows it. She ought to understand my feelings. If she expects to be happy with me, she must never have the thought that I was after her fortune. It's a question of her self-respect as well as of mine."

Beauty broke in: "Suppose she should ask you to kiss her?"

Lanny grinned. "Oh, I'd kiss her," he said. "But that wouldn't be asking her to marry me."

"I think you're acting horrid," said that exemplar of the proprieties.

IV

Such was the point at which matters stood when the telephone rang in Emily's Renaissance villa, and it was Mrs. Fanny Barnes saying: "Emily, I want to talk with you about something urgent."

"All right," said the châtelaine. "Come on over."

So the mother of Irma had her two hundred and forty-five pounds of dignity transported down from one Riviera height and up to another, and came stalking into Emily's boudoir, holding in her hand a small rectangular piece of paper having on it the imprint of a transatlantic cable company. "Please read that," she said, holding it out. "From my brother."

Emily took it and read: "Definite reliable information party illegitimate no marriage occurred advise immediate breaking connection greatly concerned please acknowledge receipt. Horace."

"Well?" demanded the mother of Irma, frowning under her dark, heavy brows.

"Of course," replied the older woman, quietly. "You didn't have to cable inquiries. I could have told you if I had thought it would interest you."

"Interest me? Good God! You mean you knew all along that this fellow was a bastard?"

"We're in the twentieth century, Fanny, not the eighteenth. Lanny's father has acknowledged him as his son. The boy lived in his father's home in Connecticut during all the time that America was in the war."

"Emily, you introduced this man and let him make love to my daughter!"

"My dear, you're just working up an excitement. You know of many cases—I'll name names, if you want me to."

"Not among the Vandringhams."

"Maybe not—I admit that I lack the data. But let's not be childish. Robbie Budd and Beauty were for all practical purposes man and wife. He told me the story and asked me to befriend her, and I did. The only reason they never had a ceremony was that Beauty had had her portrait painted in the near nude—a very lovely painting which Lanny now has in his storeroom, and which he'll show you some day. The old grandfather is some sort of hardshell fundamentalist, a religious crank, and he threatened to disinherit Robbie if he married, and Beauty wouldn't marry him, which was something very much to her credit. I've known Lanny since he was a tiny little fellow, and right now I've been having rather amusing negotiations, because he has old-fashioned notions of honor that won't permit him to ask for a rich girl's hand."

"You don't think his old-fashioned notions of honor ought to have caused him to tell the girl that he's a bastard?"

"I'm quite sure he gave no thought to it, Fanny. He's managed to get along quite cheerfully in spite of that handicap."

"He knows about it?"

"Beauty told him when he was a small boy. He can't see that it's done him any harm, and neither can I; nor can I see how it would do Irma any."

"I must say that I am surprised by the extent to which you have adopted European attitudes toward moral questions."

"Well, my dear, there's an old saying over here: 'When you are among wolves you must howl with them.' When you talk about

moral codes you raise a large issue, and I think it better to deal with
the practical question. Robbie Budd told me that Lanny is to share in
his estate."

"Thank you, Emily, but I don't think Irma will be much concerned about that aspect of the matter."

"Are you quite sure she will be concerned about the bad name you
give her young friend?"

"I don't know, but I certainly hope so. I may be eighteenth-
century, as you say, but I still have the idea that a mother ought to
have something to say about her daughter's love affairs, and that she
ought to be a party to whatever negotiations are being carried on."
And without another word the outraged Mrs. J. Paramount Barnes
lifted her two hundred and forty-five pounds of majesty out of her
chair and bore them swiftly out of the room and down the stairs to
her limousine.

V

Fate arranged it that this was the moment when Ettore, Duca
d'Elida, showed up on the polo fields of the Riviera. He was twenty-
four years of age, a cousin of the Italian royal family; handsome as a
movie idol, tall, dark, romantic-looking, with regular white teeth
and shiny smooth black hair. He was hard as nails and rode like the
devil, and when the polo game was over he put on a brilliant uniform, being a captain in the Italian air force. He knew all about Irma
Barnes, and when he was introduced to her he displayed none of the
inhibitions of Lanny Budd. He didn't mind asking for the hand of a
rich girl, and the presence of spectators did not deter him from being
stunned by her beauty, ravished by her charm, completely carried
away by her *tout ensemble* of dignity, grace, and general irresisti-
bility. He told her all that in very nearly perfect English, and a thrill
went through the spectators of the scene.

There ensued a whirlwind courtship. He followed her everywhere, and never left her side if he could help it. He said that she
was a treasure—and then, minding his metaphors, he said that she was
a vision out of heaven, and that he desired only to dwell in the light

of her presence and never depart therefrom. He seemed to know all the beautiful phrases that had ever been written or sung in praise of woman; to Irma it was all the things she had seen portrayed on the stage, sometimes lifted to glory by operatic music. This was love, this was passion, this was romance.

Lanny Budd's nose was put completely out of joint. He was no longer invited to the château on the height, and he did not attempt to go. He gave up without a struggle; if that was what she wanted, all right, the quicker she found it out the better. The ladies of his entourage all but went into mourning; his mother scolded—but he wouldn't budge. No, indeed, she had a free choice, and if she wanted to be an Italian duchessa, that was one way to invest her money. The smart set might get what pleasure they could out of his humiliation; he would go back to his Sunday school and his music, and manage to have a very good time, as before.

"But, Lanny," cried his mother, "she doesn't know what it will mean to marry an Italian! Somebody ought to tell her what their attitude toward women is, and their marriage laws."

"Somebody else will be the one to tell her," said the haughty young intellectual.

"Oh, I was so happy in the thought that you were going to get settled down!"

"Well, don't give up, old dear. There are as good fish in the sea as in any man's net—even a duca's."

The season was drawing to its close on the Riviera; the season at Rome was just beginning, and abruptly it was announced that the Barnes family was leaving for the Eternal City. That settled it, of course; she was going straight into his arms! The business manager hired an airplane and flew to Rome, rented a suitable palace and engaged servants, and a couple of days later everything was in readiness for the queen mother and the princess. They would be taken up in aristocratic circles, received by the king and queen, surrounded by pomp and glory; Lanny Budd, notorious young anti-Fascist agitator, wouldn't even be permitted to attend her nuptials!

What he did was to stroll over to the lodge and say to Rick: "Well, old sport, you can write that play!"

VI

Robbie Budd came to London. He was having more trouble with his oil wells in Arabia; also he was in a state of exasperation because the Geneva politicians—Robbie's name for the League of Nations— were threatening to interfere with the international shipment of arms. They had been talking about it for years, and now they seemed to be at the point of taking action. If you studied the list of portions of the earth's surface to which they proposed to forbid such shipments, you would observe that they were those inhabited by dark-skinned peoples; but some of these peoples had gold that was no darker than any other gold, and Budd's could see no reason for not doing business with them.

Beauty wrote Robbie the news about Irma Barnes, and of course that touched the father deeply. He telegraphed, offering to come to the Riviera and interview Mrs. Barnes and try to straighten matters out; a day or two later, when he learned that the ladies had fled to Rome, he offered to travel there. Lanny and his mother had quite an argument about it, and settled it by agreeing that each should wire what he and she had to say. Beauty said: "Beg you to come. Your action might be decisive." Lanny said: "Always glad to see you but don't want intervention in personal matter." Receiving those conflicting messages, Robbie decided that it would be pleasant to have a swim and a sail in the Golfe Juan; also to see Beauty's new husband. He stepped into a plane for Paris, and next morning stepped out of the night express at Cannes.

After having heard all sides of the story, Robbie found it hard to decide whether his son was being quixotic or whether he didn't really care enough about the girl. Anyhow, it seemed certain that the "wop" was going to get her. There were Rome newspapers to be bought in Cannes, and Lanny had some of them, and translated for his father accounts of the "to-do" that was being made over the American heiress. "That's what they both enjoy," said Lanny, "and I'm just not equipped to play that game."

"It's possible that I might be able to make some impression on the old lady," said the father.

"You don't know her," replied the son. "She'd light up one of her cigars and blow the smoke into your face and read you a lecture on your loose ways of life. She hates men, and she'd be sure you were just another fortune-hunter."

"I used to know J. Paramount," commented Robbie, "so I can understand her distrust of men."

He decided to forget the matter and enjoy a few days' rest, which Lanny said he appeared to need. He didn't feel right until he had had a drink in the morning, and his hand trembled as he lifted the glass. "To hell with all this money!" exclaimed the son. "You're doing what J. Paramount did—killing yourself for what your heirs won't know how to make use of."

Lanny got his father out in the sailboat, but it wasn't very restful, because Robbie had a long story to tell of troubles with his oil business; he was an outsider and a little fellow, and it appeared that the big fellows resented intrusion, and were even more unscrupulous in the oil game than in munitions. Robbie was more than ever convinced that Zaharoff was maneuvering him into a position where he would have to sell out; but Robbie wouldn't give up, because it was a matter of pride with him—he had got his friends into this thing, and he didn't want to have to take a licking. He had hopes of getting his way now, because he and his friends had got a new President of the United States. This was an oil man, like Robbie himself, one who had made a fortune in the game, and so knew what it took. Hoover was his name, and he was known to his admirers as "the Great Engineer." To Robbie his inauguration meant the coming of a new era of efficiency and prosperity to his country, and perhaps to the whole world, which would learn from America how to manage large-scale business.

Yes, Robbie said, the British would have to give protection to American investors in Arabia and elsewhere under British mandate, or else the Americans would find ways to do it themselves. Robbie meant to visit Monte Carlo and tell Zaharoff about this change in the world situation; but when he phoned he learned that the old spider was up in Paris, or perhaps at the Château de Balincourt, his estate in Seine-et-Oise. Robbie went north, saying that he would call on him there.

VII

Lanny didn't realize how fond he had become of Irma Barnes until it was too late. He tried Chopin's nocturnes again, but they didn't work. She had been such pleasant company, and it would have been so easy to make love to her; he had just got himself to the point where he was ready to begin, and to have her whisked away was most disconcerting. He told himself that for her own good he ought to have taken her. She was a child, and had no idea of the trap she had walked into. Fascism represented the lowest degradation of women that had been on the continent of Europe since the days of old Turkey. What sort of brood-mare would she make, that high-spirited American girl? If she tried to kick over the traces, they would take her money away from her, and her children—they would break her heart. When he imagined what might happen, he had an impulse to fly to Rome and save her. But no, they wouldn't even let him in; to say nothing of letting him out again!

Zoltan Kertezsi showed up with news and proposals about pictures; and that was a good thing. Even thinking about being engaged to a glamour girl put the "kibosh" on Lanny's little private industry; what were the few thousands which he could earn compared with the millions he would have if he became Mr. Irma Barnes? Mere chicken-feed, beneath his dignity to think about! But now Zoltan said that the time had come to have an exhibition of Marcel's work in London; he proposed to rent a gallery for the last two weeks in June, and then in the autumn to take the pictures to New York for a showing. As before, he said that the thing to do was to sell a few works at very high prices, and thus confer honor upon the rest; he said that, with business booming as it was in both the great cities, people simply didn't know what to do with their money; they wanted to be asked fancy prices, because that was the only way to be sure that what they got was excellent.

The Pomeroy-Nielsons were about to leave for England, and so was Margy; also Hansi and Bess were sailing for London after their

American tour. Lanny said: "All right, let's have a holiday." He had always had a good time in England. But right away the thought of Rosemary smote him. Wouldn't he miss her there? Would London ever seem the same again? Lanny had become like a sailor with a girl in every port—only these were ghosts of girls: Irma on the Riviera, Marie in Paris, Rosemary in England, Gracyn in Connecticut and New York. Would he find one with a spell powerful enough to exorcise four such delightful ghosts?

Everybody agreed that he must go where the girls were: the lovely young creatures, the debutantes, fresh and virginal, each so carefully groomed, like a thoroughbred for a cup race; each quivering with excitement, sniffing the air, hearing the shouting of the vast throng. One by one they would be trotted out, each representing a fortune in time, thought, and money; each in the pink of condition, at the top of her form. The marriage market! Mayfair! The London "season"! Lanny was excited by the thought of it, and would enjoy it with one half of him, the social half, that of his mother and her friends. The other half would analyze it and reduce it to economic formulas; that half would say: "What am I doing here? Is this what I really want?"

Lanny's new stepfather was going along, his first journey since before the war. He told the stepson he thought it was his duty to go because he was able to moderate Beauty's extravagant tendencies; she had expanded her requirements on the basis of Lanny's supposed conquest, and hadn't yet adjusted herself to the fact that he had been unhorsed in the fray. The travelers made a big party, almost a migration: Lady Eversham-Watson and her maid; Beauty and hers; Marceline and Miss Addington; Nina and her three children, and their governess. The Riviera was used to seeing families going out wholesale in that fashion in April and the beginning of May: English and Americans especially.

Lanny motored Rick, who wanted to stop in Paris and meet political people and journalists. Lanny always liked to have lunch with his Socialist friends, and then spend an evening with his Red uncle and family and hear their caustic comments on the Socialists. Lanny had the idea of being broad-minded, but what actually happened was that he became confused, and found human society more bewildering, more painful to contemplate. He had dreamed a Utopia in which people might be happy; but here they didn't seem to know what was good for them or how to get it, and intellectual life degenerated into wrangling and scolding. It was that way in politics, both domestic and international; it was that way even in the arts, where beauty, order, and serenity should have reigned. Every old master had its price, and became the object of barter, intrigue, and "bluff."

VIII

Robbie had written about Zaharoff; he had seen him in Paris, and the old man had taken up the role of the sphinx of Egypt; all that he would say was that he had laid down the burden of business forever. Lanny, knowing that a heavy part of this burden had been laid on Robbie, gave some thought to the matter, and recollected Zaharoff's invitation to call. The young man had a sudden impulse to try to help his father. It would be the second time he had made such an attempt in connection with Zaharoff, and the first had not been conspicuously successful; however, he had the entrée this time, and wouldn't have to break any laws.

He telephoned to the Avenue Hoche, and learned that Sir Basil was at home and would be pleased to receive him. Approaching the familiar mansion, he noticed that smoke was coming from one of its chimneys in front; it might have struck him as peculiar for anybody to be having a fire in his drawing-room on this particularly warm spring afternoon; but Lanny's thoughts were on his father's affairs, and what he was going to say to an old Greek trader. His imaginative mind was living a series of detective stories, in which one of the shrewdest and most devious intriguers of Europe was continually betraying himself to a very young Franco-American idealist.

Lanny might have worked his imagination for many a day without inventing anything as odd as what he actually ran into when the tottery old butler escorted him into the drawing-room. Everything stood exactly as the duquesa had arranged it, Lanny didn't know how many years ago; the only difference was that on the oriental rug in front of the large fireplace were several metal boxes and wooden chests, and in the middle of them, seated on the floor in oriental fashion with his legs crossed and drawn under him, was the Grand Officer of the Légion d'Honneur of France and Knight Commander of the Bath of Great Britain. Only he wasn't in the regalia of either of these high offices; on the contrary, he had taken off his smoking-jacket and tossed it onto a chair, and then, becoming still hotter, he had taken off his shirt, and now sat in his undershirt, facing a hot fire made of logs augmented by quantities of paper which he was tossing in.

"Well, young man," he said, with that strange smile in which his eyes never took part, "you have arrived at what the future may recognize as a historic moment." He did not offer to rise, but said: "Seat yourself over there," pointing to a chair at one side, where the heat from the fireplace would not strike directly. "Take off your coat," he added, and Lanny did so because it was surely warm in the tightly shut room.

What strange whim was it which had moved Sir Basil to receive a visitor at such a time? He had always treated Lanny differently from any other person, so far as Lanny had been able to learn from those who knew him. The son of Budd's had made his appearance as a little thief of conscience; he came now at rare intervals, an itinerant idealist, a roving philosopher, transported as it were from another planet, playing the game of life according to an odd set of rules of his own invention.

"You have perhaps read about the burning of the library of Alexandria by the Arabs?" inquired the aged trader. When his visitor answered in the affirmative, he added: "You are witnessing an event of similar import."

"I understand that historians deplore the loss, Sir Basil."

"Only blackmailers will deplore this. I am saving the reputations of most of the great personages of my time."

"I have been told that you were a fireman in your early days," ventured the younger man.

"In those days I put out fires; now I make one—a beneficial fire, a fire of hope and salvation for my enemies as well as my friends. Many tons of dynamite would not do so much damage as the contents of one of these little books." The pale blue eyes turned from Lanny to the metal boxes, and the white imperial waggled with laughter as its wearer lifted up a notebook bound in worn red leather. There was apparently a whole box of them. "These are my diaries; a history of world business and diplomacy for more than fifty years. You heard perhaps that these volumes had been stolen?"

"I read something about it in the papers."

"A scoundrelly valet sneaked off with them. Fortunately the police recovered them, and so far as I can learn nothing is missing. But I was forced to give thought to the future of European civilization, and whether it is worth saving. What would you think?"

Lanny never could be sure how much this strange old man was teasing him. He replied: "I should say, Sir Basil, it would depend upon what one had to put in its place."

"Quite so; but unfortunately I have nothing better. Perhaps some day the Ice Age will return, and a vast glacier will spread over Europe and grind our cities to powder. Or perhaps bombs will have done it already."

Lanny made no reply. He knew from before the World War that the old man's imagination was haunted by images of destruction to be made by the weapons which he himself had been producing most of his life.

"Many people think that I am not a kind man, Lanny; but you can tell them what trouble I have taken on their behalf. I would not trust any person alive to perform this labor; I am doing it with my own hands, and at a cost of considerable discomfort, as you can see. There are a thousand eminent persons who will sleep more peacefully when they learn what I have done."

"Do you intend to notify them, Sir Basil?" It occurred to Lanny that this might make a first-rate story for Rick; but the fireman turned stoker merely smiled, and took some more of the leatherbound books and tossed them skillfully into the flames, causing them to fall on edge, and no two on top of each other, so that the fire would get a good chance at them quickly.

IX

This went on for quite a while. The flames mounted merrily, and the spacious drawing-room grew hotter and hotter. Lanny watched the yellow tongues creeping round one mass of paper after another, and he felt sorry about it, for he knew that the world was losing many a good story, and he himself some personal enlightenment. What would there be among those papers concerning Budd's and its European representative? What about the New England-Arabian Oil Company?

The last scrap of paper was in, and the flames were roaring up the chimney. Lanny was about to decide that a Greek born in Turkey could stand more heat than an American born in Switzerland, when there came a banging on the front door. The aged butler came in haste, and then ran to the drawing-room door. "Master, the people say the chimney is afire!"

"Indeed," said Sir Basil, placidly. "Let it burn. This is an important cremation."

"But, master, it will set fire to the house!"

"The fire is more important than the house!"

The old servant stood, staring helplessly. "You do not wish me to summon the fire department?"

"Under no circumstances; at any rate, not until the papers are consumed. Go close the door and let no one in."

The munitions king did not move from his seat. Was he playing a role before his visitor? Or did he count upon it that some busybody outside would turn in an alarm? It seemed a safe gamble; and, sure enough, after a while the sound of the engines was heard outside. The old gentleman got up, with the servant's help and some grumbling about the state of his bones. He put on his shirt, in the interest of propriety, and, knowing the ways of firemen, he told the butler to go and open the door for them. Then he began poking up the fire, so as to observe the condition of the papers, and promote the process of incineration. When the firemen rushed in, they halted before this venerable presence, and listened in confusion of mind while the master of the house explained what he had been doing, and why he did not wish his fire disturbed.

It transpired that in a modern city a man may not let his house burn even if he wishes to. The best that he can do is to start an argument, and gain several minutes during which the flames may continue their work. Out of the technical knowledge gained in his youth Sir Basil undertook to maintain that a fire in a chimney would burn only the soot which had accumulated in the chimney; but the chief of the Paris fire company, from his more up-to-date experience, insisted that there might be cracks in the chimney; also that when it was heated up it might set fire to the joists or rafters of the mansion. Lanny stood listening with amusement to this novel debate.

The great man had made his identity known, and his wishes were difficult to disregard; the chief finally agreed not to attack the fire in the hearth, but to go after that in the chimney with extinguishers from the roof. The firemen were escorted upstairs; and presently came jets of liquid dropping down into the fireplace, splashing black soot upon a beautiful and costly rug. There stood the retired munitions king of Europe with a long-handled poker, trying to keep the sacrificial flames alive, and grumbling because of the lack of consideration of modern fire departments. Said he: "When I belonged to the *tulumbadschi*, those capable firemen of Constantinople, if someone wanted his house to burn down he could arrange it."

Lanny was tempted to add: "For a consideration?" But he decided to let the Grand Officer make his own jokes on this delicate subject.

X

Lanny did not find out anything about the affairs of the New England-Arabian Oil Company. Instead, he went for a stroll, and stopped in the famous Café de la Rotonde, and there met an English journalist, a big handsome fellow with florid blond hair and mustaches which had been conspicuous at all conferences from San Remo to Locarno. They compared notes, and found themselves in agreement as to the state of Europe. Germany wouldn't go on paying indemnities many years longer; there was a new generation, which felt that it was not to blame for the war. The Allies had gained little by their colossal effort; it was a saying that men had fought for freedom of the seas and women had got freedom of the knees. The two men now watched the women tripping by in their abbreviated skirts. "I suppose the new generation will be used to legs," remarked the journalist.

"I'm not sure," responded the grandson of the Puritans. "When they've seen all there is to see, they get bored, and want something *outré*."

They talked about the public balls of Paris, which grew more scandalous every year. They talked about the Negress from America, whose stage performances had become "the rage." Paris had formerly been celebrated as a home of elegant conversation, and now it was the home of tough dancing. It was the "cocktail era," and you ordered drinks with fantastic names—*Quetsche de la Forêt Noire, Arquebuse des Frères Maristes*. People ran from one sensation to another, until really it seemed that they were going crazy. A man gave a concert with sixteen pianos played by machinery, also a loudspeaker and a noisy fan. The audience stood up and shrieked either approval or disapproval. That was the way to fame; the surrealists had achieved it by creating riots, and now it was Dada, something even more loony. A painter had hoaxed the Salon des Indépendants by tying a paint-brush to a donkey's tail and letting him do the art work; the result was entitled *Sunset on the Adriatic*, and it was hung. When the story was told it caused a good laugh, but didn't stop the crazy art.

"Too much easy money," was the Englishman's diagnosis of the trouble; but what could you do about it? Lanny said that the wrong people got the money, and his friend agreed; but again, what could you do? Lanny said he didn't believe the workers would stand it indefinitely; which led them to Moscow—all talk about economic affairs ended up in the Red capital nowadays. Conflicting reports came out—the Five-Year Plan was a great success—the Five-Year Plan was a fiasco. You believed what you wanted to. Lanny's companion had recently been in Germany, and said that the Communists were still very strong, and apparently gaining; the republic found it hard to avoid dealing with them. The Stahlhelm, militant organization of the reactionaries, had a new *Hymn of Hate* against the republic, based on that charge.

They talked about Italy for a while. The Englishman said that *Fascismo* might be the next stage through which the aged and unhappy continent had to pass. He agreed that Mussolini had learned from Lenin, and Hitler had learned from Mussolini. Lanny found that the journalist knew about Herr Schicklgruber; the Nazi movement had forced its way into the headlines. Any movement started by reactionaries was hated and feared by the masses, and could never get the votes. But here was one that appeared to come from the left, it was of the people, and promised them the peace and plenty which they craved. "Votes from the left and cash from the right"—such was the formula for victory at the polls.

X I

Lanny and Rick went on to London. The baronet's son had finished his book and the manuscript was in the hands of a publisher. He went to get the verdict and came back disappointed. The publisher, a friend of his father, had sought to persuade him to modify his too leftish views. It was a mistake to put a label on himself. Socialism? Yes, we were all Socialists now, more or less; but to espouse a party cause was to weaken your influence, to limit yourself to an audience of the already converted, who didn't need you. To plump for outright socialization of basic industry—well, it sounded impressive, but it discouraged people who might be willing to consider useful reforms; it played into the hands of the Communists, whether one meant to or not. It seemed plain that capitalism had reached a stage of stabilization in which prosperity was spreading its benefits among wider and wider groups of the community; mass production would come in England as it had come in America, and mass distribution would follow as a matter of course.

In short, the publisher didn't want the book, and he didn't think any other commercial firm would want it. If Rick wasn't willing to modify it, he would have to go to some out-and-out Socialist or labor group, and injure his career by getting himself set down as that kind of writer. Said Rick to Lanny: "When I pointed out our million and a half unemployed, he said that I mustn't lose faith in Britain!"

Lanny and his mother and stepfather were staying with Margy. You might think that Mr. Dingle wouldn't have fitted very well into a Mayfair mansion, but that would be because you were out of touch with God, who is the same in marble halls as in a cotter's hut. Beauty had already taken her man to a tailor and had him made presentable, and now he was a quiet elderly cherub who addressed the servants in the same benevolent tone as he addressed their mistress, and if anything troubled him, he retired to his chamber, where his Heavenly Father comforted him with melodious words: "Well I know thy trouble, O my servant true!"

When Beauty went out to garden parties and *thés dansants*, Parsifal Dingle would wander about the streets of the smoke-stained old city, seeking his own in his own way. Presently in a poor neighborhood he came upon a chapel of some "quietist" movement, and there he learned that God was working in England much the same as in Iowa. There were all sorts of spiritual cults; American New Thought magazines were to be bought, and there were many groups of religious healers. Mr. Dingle carried home literature, and began attending meetings, and then he prayed that Divine Power would persuade his wife to accompany him, which it did. He escorted her to a Christian Science church, and to a Swedenborgian church; then, to his own great surprise, he made the discovery that the august Anglican establishment was making timid efforts along the lines of healing by prayer. "We are really quite respectable here!" exclaimed Beauty Budd's new husband.

XII

But the greatest experience of Parsifal Dingle in England's green and pleasant land took place in the rear parlor of an obscure lodging-house in Bloomsbury, to which Divine Guidance had seen fit to lead him. It wasn't the first time he had attended a spiritualist séance, but it was the first time that the gates of the future life had swung open for him personally. A few lower middles, small tradesmen and such, sat in a circle, holding one another's hands in the dark, while a stoutish lady medium went into a trance, and an illuminated trumpet flew about over their heads, and various voices came from it—those of William Ewart Gladstone, Napoleon Bonaparte, and Pocahontas, each in turn describing the state of bliss in which they lived on the other side. That they all spoke with a Cockney accent troubled nobody, because the medium had explained that the spirits of the departed would be using her vocal cords, and naturally would speak as she spoke.

Missouri wasn't far away from Mr. Dingle's place of origin, and he remained in a dubious state of mind—until suddenly the trumpet stopped close to his ear, and the same Cockney voice said: "This is your brother Josephus." The gentleman from Iowa could not help giving a start, because Josephus was certainly an unlikely name for a lady medium in Bloomsbury to think of—just as it had been an unlikely name for Parsifal's mother to think of when her second son was born. She had assumed that it was a Bible name, and had learned her mistake too late. The bearer of this odd name had "passed over" in youth, and now claimed to be hovering over his older brother, and for identification he mentioned the pump with the broken handle which had stood on the back porch of their home. This caused perspiration to stand out on the visitor's forehead; and when the spirit declared that Aunt Jane and Cousin Roger were by his side, Lanny's stepfather decided that a new stage in his mental progress had begun.

He went and told Beauty about it, and prayed that she might be well disposed toward his words; and again the prayer could not be resisted. Beauty went, and was troubled because the place was so "common," also the people; but her husband explained that it was people of much the same class whom Jesus had picked out for his disciples, and to whom he had appeared at Emmaus. So Beauty listened submissively; and when the trumpet stopped over her head and the voice said: "This is Marcel," and called her "*Chérie*" half a dozen times, she felt a stirring as if every hair of her body was moving. When the voice said: "You have put my little blue cap away on a shelf in the closet," Beauty began to sob audibly, and came near to breaking up the show.

She went out from that séance in a state of great confusion. For right away treasonable doubts began to stir within her. She was well known as the former wife of Marcel Detaze, whose forthcoming one-man exhibition was being discussed in the newspapers. That a French painter should have an old blue cap, and that his widow, getting married again, should have put it away on a closet shelf—well, it was at least conceivable that somebody might have made such guesses. She had been warned that there was a widespread circle of fraudulent mediums who gathered data and assisted one another. Such are the problems which a lady of fashion prepares for her mind when she starts investigating occult phenomena!

Beauty told her friends about it, and learned that she and her husband were not alone in carrying on such researches. The great city was full of mediums of all sorts—and not all in cheap lodging-houses, but many established in the most fashionable places. It was one of the striking results of the great war; so many wanted to hear the voices of their lost loved ones. There were hordes of soothsayers, clairvoyants, and psychometrists, seers of crystal balls, readers of palms and cards and teacups. They would tell you that you were about to receive a letter, and that a dark man was coming into your life; sometimes these things happened and sometimes they didn't, but the former cases made the greater impression on your mind. As for Mr. Dingle, how could anybody ever persuade him that a medium could have found out that there had been a pump with a broken handle on the back porch of his boyhood home in far-off Iowa?

34

To Him Who Hath

I

PARIS was called a city of women, while London was a city of men; not *chic*, but always in need of housecleaning. It made no fuss over you, but let you go your own way; it was dignified, even austere, and if you wanted anything improper, you had to know where to look for it. In this moral man's town you didn't pay the art critics to tell the public about what you had for sale; you managed it in the respectable way, which was to pay for large but conservatively worded advertisements in the papers. Seeing these, the critics would know that the work of Detaze was significant.

Zoltan understood such matters; he knew the writers, the editors, the dealers, and, more important yet, the buyers. He knew how to place the interesting facts about Detaze where they would get publicity; he knew who would be impressed by the prices which had been paid at Christie's, and who by the fact that there was a work by this painter in the Luxembourg. Beauty pulled wires shamelessly, and Margy helped, and likewise Sophie, who came with her new husband for the season. Very elegant show rooms were engaged, and Jerry Pendleton saw to the packing of the paintings at Bienvenu and drove the truck himself; it was off season for the tourist trade, and his little wife could attend to the office.

Hansi and Bess arrived from New York, with stories about the success of a concert tour, including a recital in Newcastle and a reception at Esther Budd's home. Genius had won out over Jewishness; Hansi was a lion, and his roars had shaken the town, and Mumsy had been all smiles over her daughter's happiness. Bess was really sticking to her piano, and Hansi thought that with a couple of years more she might be able to serve as his accompanist. "But, dear, aren't you going to have any babies?" Esther had asked. The daughter had wanted to say: "I am afraid they might have short legs!"—but that would have been mean.

Robbie had told the family about the Irma Barnes fiasco, and Bess thought it was a tragedy that Lanny couldn't find a proper wife. Wouldn't he let her take up the matter? "Where would you look for one?" he inquired, and she answered: "Not among the smart people of this town, or on the Riviera." That was the trouble— Lanny didn't go where there were decent, hard-working girls who would appreciate what he had to offer. These ultra ladies who drank like whales and smoked like volcanoes in eruption were just looking for new thrills, and when they were tired of Lanny it would be off again, gone again. A young Red was telling him!

Hansi had a bright idea, not for a wife, but for a holiday, to divert Lanny's mind. Hansi was always scheming to get his father away from business for the summer months. If they stayed at their summer place on the Wannsee there were always telephone calls and telegrams, putting problems and cares on Johannes's mind; but when he got off on the *Bessie Budd*, his subordinates had to do the worrying, and in the end everything came out just as well. The family had been planning a short cruise by themselves—since it was so plain that the fashionable folk didn't like the young Robin Redbreasts. But why wouldn't Lanny come, and just Beauty and her husband? If there was to be a Detaze show in New York in October, why not cruise by the northern route and down the coast of Labrador and Nova Scotia? Freddi was going to be married, and it would be a honeymoon for him. Maybe Bess could think of some nice girl to bring along, and Lanny could play duets with her even if he didn't want to make love to her. Lanny consulted Beauty, and said they would go with pleasure; but leave out the girl, he'd play the duets with Bess. Hansi sent a telegram to his father, telling this good news; then he and Bess left for Amsterdam, where Hansi was to give a recital.

II

When Lanny had been in London as a little boy, before the World War, watching his young mother dressing for parties and going off with fashionable gentlemen such as Harry Murchison, he had thought that the acme of all delights would be to grow up and put on a white tie and tails and take that lovely creature to dances. Now he had the opportunity, and used it. Margy gave a grand ball at the Savoy, and the blond Beauty, who would never cease to think that she was a debutante, went with her son in just as much excitement as if he had been her first beau; she really looked as lovely as ever, for she had been dieting and dancing off her *embonpoint*, and the real debutantes were using so much makeup that they made it easier for matrons and grandmothers.

Also Lanny took her to the sporting events: to Epsom Downs to see the great race, which was called the "Mystery Derby" that year, because nobody could· guess the winner; also to Ranelagh for polo, and to the opera at Covent Garden, where Rosa Ponselle was singing. Nothing could have been more chaste and proper, and society was amused at these evidences of reform on the part of a pair who hadn't been exactly conventional in the past. There was a husband in the background, who retired to his chamber and communed with God. Was it his prayers that accounted for the transformation? Or was it that the American heiress had put Lanny's nose out of joint, by running off and getting engaged to an Italian duca? By the way, did you· see the report that their engagement was shortly to be announced? Poor Lanny, what a come-down, to have to take to selling pictures again! But they say that fellow Detaze is bringing tremendous prices. Is he dead, or what?

Lanny played his part acceptably in this world of gaiety and gossip. When the bright young debs asked him sly questions about heiresses he told them that his heart was broken and would they help to heal it? "Is this a proposal, sir?" they would ask, and he would say: "Would you like it to be?" So they would spar and play, like a couple of kittens exercising their clawing apparatus. The kittens might grow up to be tigers, or fairly useful domestic cats—it took an expert to tell them apart. Lanny was something of an expert; but perhaps he was fastidious, he wanted more than nature provided in one female organism. Or was it that his imagination had been dazzled by Irma Barnes? He thought of her a great deal, and it seems to be one of the weaknesses of our humanity that we appreciate something only after we have lost it.

He didn't find the "society" game as delightful as he had imagined it fifteen years ago. For one thing, his conscience was continually troubled. Rick came to town, and talked about his rejected manuscript, so full of distressing facts about unemployment; about conditions in Wales and the Tyneside, where whole communities were without a single man who had steady employment. Ships were burning oil, so it appeared that Britain's coal trade was slowly dying. Steel was depressed, because the Americans had new "straightline" processes, and British employers couldn't be induced to reorganize the industry. Here in London, amid all the display of pomp and luxury, one saw the old sights of misery and despair, and knew that for every case exhibited in public there were a thousand hidden behind the dingy walls of Britain's ancient slums.

How could anyone be happy putting on fancy clothes and playing about like children in such a world? But they did; it was the "season," and the rout had never been so noisy. There really seemed to be some law that the more poverty there was for the poor, the more riches for the rich; and how they did spend it, what fantasticalities they contrived! Just now the ladies were wearing knee-length skirts on the street, but in the drawing-rooms they had long tails and streamers and what-not touching the floor. Margy, Dowager Countess Eversham-Watson, made her appearance in a teagown of blue-and-gold georgette with a long spreading train having bold futurist designs and completely bordered with ostrich feathers. Sophie, former Baroness de la Tourette, went to the races wearing a coat trimmed with mink-tails: three mink-tails around each cuff, a wide band of mink-tails dangling from either side of her waist, and an extraordinary collar made by laying thirty mink-tails not end to end, but side by side, as a baker might place ladyfingers in a tray. In all, sixty minks had died to make an Ascot holiday for this hardware lady from Cincinnati.

Naturally, in order to move in company such as this, Lanny Budd had to put some tailors at work in a hurry. The old things that he had brought in his car were out of the question. Gentlemen's morning coats had only one button this season, and if you had two or three, you declassed yourself at once. Gentlemen's coats had huge lapels, and they wore wide, bulgy ties, and rather voluminous trousers. Their top-hats were slightly less tall and more flaring. What would become of the tailoring trades if gentlemen failed to do themselves properly?

III

Lanny did as the ladies urged, because they insisted that somewhere in this rout he was going to find the girl of his dreams. Would he catch a glimpse of some gentle, shy young thing hovering on the outskirts and recognize her as a kindred spirit, wishing to escape? "Somewhere there must be one made for this soul to move it!" With the poet's lines in his ears he went from place to place, wherever his mother asked to be escorted. He watched and she watched; she saw some that pleased her, but he found faults.

Beauty heard a rumor about a costume party that was to take place on board a ship at one of the docks, very mysterious and *recherché*. It was called "A Voyage to the Island of Cythera," and as this island had been devoted to the worship of Aphrodite, the name was suggestive to say the least. The engraved invitations didn't say who was giving the party, but it was observed that only the most exclusive members of society had received them; therefore it must be important, and the newspapers were full of speculation. On the back of the invitations was a figure in an elaborate Watteau costume, telling you what to wear and informing you that you would be admitted only upon presentation of the card. Since you didn't know who was giving the party, you couldn't wangle permission to bring your friends. People found it provoking, and curiosity mounted to a high pitch.

Margy managed to solve the mystery, but only under solemn pledge of secrecy. She got a card for Lanny Budd and lady—and of course that lady would be his darling mother. He had himself fitted in the garb of a lute-player, while Beauty appeared as one of Marie Antoinette's dairymaids—the one who had the shortest skirt and the lowest-cut corsage. At ten in the evening Margy's limousine delivered them at Charing Cross Pier on the river Thames. The dark-eyed little whisky lady from Kentucky was a charming Columbine, and the widower gentleman from South Africa who was wooing her at the moment was appropriate as Pierrot. The four of them went on board an elaborately decorated brig, and found themselves among a troop of eighteenth-century ladies with powdered hair and gentlemen with perukes and swords, wandering about gazing at decorations which included Gobelin tapestries, and divans and chaises-longues covered with magnificent silks from China and Japan. The deck of the vessel had been turned into a series of bowers and nooks, all discreetly dark; while below was a great compartment with a bar at one end, having the contents of a champagne warehouse on top and behind and under it. At the other end was a jazz band with players in eighteenth-century costumes; this was certainly a novelty, and would have been a greater one if it could have been presented at the court of Louis le Bien-Aimé!

The Voyage to the Island of Cythera proved to be an imaginary one. The vessel stayed moored to the pier, and the guests danced, drank the free champagne, rested in the quiet nooks. As night turned into morning, they became hilarious, and the sights were not so different from those of Paris; except that nowhere else had Lanny ever seen half-drunken gentlemen climbing the masts of a ship and diving into the water from the yard-arms! The tide carried them swiftly, but they landed at other piers, walked back, and came in dripping to dance some more. In the small hours two in succession tried to lure Marie Antoinette's dairymaid to one of the divans, and judging by the way they handled her they must have thought she was the real thing. Rather than risk a fight, Lanny took his too attractive mother home. Later they learned from Margy that this affair, attended by the most prominent folk of London, had been an advertising stunt devised by an interior-decorating concern. Seeing that they had all the divans, the Gobelins and silks and satins, it had cost them only a thousand pounds, and they had had all London talking about it for two or three weeks.

I V

The Detaze exhibition opened, and the fashionable crowds came, just as they had come in Paris. Zoltan was on hand, elegant and affable as always. Lanny was there to help him, and Beauty to play the queen. The papers said all the kind things which Marcel's work deserved, and the high prices did not alarm the wealthy art patrons. A new assistant at this show was Marceline, now eleven; growing fast, and rather "leggy," but with sweet features and perfect manners, a miniature little *charmeuse*. It was her debut as her father's daughter, and she was bursting with happy pride at the attention given to his work. She had no memory of him, but his sad story was a part of her being, and she could talk about any one of the paintings with as much sophistication as Zoltan himself—in fact, his very phrases.

Nina brought her children up to town to see this show. They, too, had heard all the talk and knew the phrases—Detaze was a family affair. Little Alfy, two months older than Marceline, with dark eyes and dark wavy hair like his father's, talked with his father's sophistication about "representational art" and "symphonic color effects." These children, destined for each other by family arrangement, maintained a tension which was practice for matrimony. Alfy was the haughty, impervious male; Marceline was learning how to tease him, and this one-man show was her great opportunity. It was her father, not his, who was being glorified; and had not Rick been heard many times to say that the critic must hold himself subordinate to the creator? This controversy would be continued all summer, for Marceline was going to be a guest at The Reaches while her mother was visiting among the Eskimos.

Johannes Robin wrote that he had some business to transact in

London prior to the sailing of the *Bessie Budd;* so the yacht would arrive at Ramsgate, with the family on board, and they would come up to town and have a look at the exhibition. Maybe Johannes might decide that he wanted some more of those paintings in his home. Lanny said to his mother that he would drive down and meet them and bring some of them to town; he would rent another car for the rest of the party. Johannes had stated the day they were due to arrive, and Lanny looked up the tides.

V

On the morning of the day when the yacht was due, Beauty awakened first, and lying in bed she looked at the morning paper; then with a cry she started up, and slipping on her *peignoir*, ran into her son's room. "Lanny! Wake up! Look at this! Irma Barnes is in town!"

Lanny, having been to a dance and having had some champagne early that morning, had to rub his eyes and shake his mind to make sure that he wasn't still dancing. He looked at the London *Daily Mail*, which had made a conspicuous story out of the fact that the great international catch, having twenty-three million dollars in her own right, had arrived unannounced with her mother and had put up at one of the fashionable hotels. There was her picture to prove it—Irma, his playmate of a Riviera season, looking a bit careworn, less blooming than when a young Puritan had had charge of her drink and her dancing hours. The reporter had asked her about the Duca d'Elida, and she had replied, casually: "Oh, that was just newspaper talk."

"You are not engaged to him, Miss Barnes?"

"He's a very charming man, and we are the best of friends, but that is all." So ran the interview.

"Lanny, they've had a quarrel!" exclaimed the mother.

"It sounds like it, for a fact."

"You must call her right away!"

"Do you think I should?" A rather superfluous question—but Lanny, taken by surprise, was thinking out loud.

"Oh, my God!" exclaimed the mother. "If you don't call her I surely will!"

"We don't even know where she's staying." After the custom of newspapers in dealing with the great, the name of the hotel wasn't given. It was a favor which the press did to important persons, to spare them the importunities of the needy and the cranks.

However, there were only half a dozen places grand enough for the Barnes family to stay at, and Beauty guessed them in order of importance, and made Lanny inquire. It wasn't long before he had the social secretary on the phone, and only a few seconds more before he had the heiress herself. Beauty, waiting with bated breath, could hear only one side of that conversation: "Well, darling! What a surprise! What brings you to town? . . . Well, how nice of you! . . . Of course I want to see you, right away. . . . How about lunch? . . . All right. One o'clock? . . . It's a date. How are you? . . . Only so-so? Well, see you soon. Lots of news. Cheerio!"

And then, of course: "What did she say, Lanny?"

"She said she came to town on purpose to see me."

"Oh, thank God!" The phrase carried a different significance since Parsifal Dingle had come into Beauty's frivolous life. "Lanny, she's broken with that fellow and come to look for you!"

"It really sounds like it, doesn't it?"

"She found out about the Italians for herself!"

"About the Fascists, let us say."

"Anyhow, you have your chance. Oh, Lanny, you *must* ask her now!"

"I will unless she forbids me."

"You must do it anyway. Don't let anything stop you!"

"Take it easy," chuckled the son. "Remember, the duca tried to rush her off her feet, and apparently he didn't get away with it!"

VI

"Take me to some place where they won't know me," said Irma, in the lobby of her hotel.

"That's not so easy, with your picture in all the papers this morning."

"Couldn't we go a long way out into the country?"

"This is England, not France. You'd have a choice of cold mutton with pickles, or veal-and-ham pie, and you wouldn't like either."

"I'm not thinking about the food, Lanny. I want to have a talk with you."

"Well, we'll drive, and see what we see."

He took her to his car. She looked very lovely in another sports ensemble of a light worsted, brown trimmed with white at the neck and sleeves, and a little brown cap to match. She seemed to be saying: "This is simplicity, the way you prefer." Her manner was humble; she had had some unhappiness, and it had chastened her; she seemed more mature and, as her picture indicated, she had lost weight.

As soon as they had started, he said: "You have left that fellow?"

"Yes, Lanny."

"For good?"

"Forever and ever. Oh, why didn't you tell me the sort of man he was?"

"I didn't have much chance to tell you anything, Irma."

"You didn't try very hard."

"I had told you about the Fascists, and what I thought of their code. I told you what they did to Matteotti, and the experience I had with them in Rome. I thought: 'Well, if that doesn't mean anything to her——'"

"It did mean a lot in the end. It was what saved me. You remember you told me about the newspaperman, Mr. Corsatti? He was one of the first persons I met there—he and several other reporters came to interview me. The Americans always come, you know."

"Certainly."

"Well, he said: 'I know a friend of yours, Lanny Budd. I saw a lot of him here five years ago.' I said: 'Oh, yes, he told me about you.' So we were friendly; and when the trouble came, it seemed to me he was the one person in Rome I could trust."

"What was the trouble?"

"It's something horrid, I feel ashamed to talk about it."

"I'm no spring chicken, Irma. And, anyhow, I can guess it if you want me to. You found out that Ettore had a girl? Or was it a boy?"

"Oh, such a nasty thing, and it came in such a nasty way: an anonymous letter. At first I thought it was some vile slander, and I would be noble, and tear it up, and tell him that I had done so. But I'd heard things about European men, and I thought: 'Suppose it is true?'"

"What did it say?"

"It said he was living with the *première danseuse* of the ballet, and had told her that his marriage wouldn't make any difference. I thought: 'Ettore has some enemy, somebody who is jealous of him and wants to ruin him.' There was another man paying me attention, or trying to, and I thought: 'Maybe he has sent this, or caused it to be sent.' I took the letter to my mother, but she wasn't of much help, because she said that all men were like that, and there was no way to tell, and one shouldn't break one's heart over it. I said: 'I don't believe they are all like that.' Are you, Lanny?"

"I have my faults, but that is not one of them."

"I thought: 'I've got to know the truth.' So I called Mr. Corsatti and asked him to come to see me, and showed him the letter. He was worried at first and said: 'Miss Barnes, if I talk to you about this and it becomes known, it will be the end of my job here in Italy.' I gave my word of honor never to mention it to a soul, not even my mother. Later on he said I might tell you, because he was sure you would understand and keep it quiet."

"Of course. What did he advise you?"

"He said if I was looking for a husband who would respect me or be faithful to me, I had come to the wrong part of the world. He said that what the letter told me was true, that all the newspapermen knew it, and wondered if I knew it. He said there were decent men in Italy as everywhere else, but they weren't in power, and I would have no way to meet them. He said that when you met a Fascist you met a man without honor, one who laughed at it. He said: 'I've been here for ten years, and I've watched them from the beginning. If you take my advice you won't say a word to anybody, but take a plane and get out of Italy.' He really thought that Ettore might have me kidnaped."

"They've done much worse," said Lanny; "but not to foreigners, so far as I know."

"Well, anyhow, I was through. I told mother I was going alone unless she would go with me. We hired a plane to fly us to Cannes, and then I phoned to your home and learned that you were in London. So here I am. Are you glad to see me?"

"More glad than I can trust myself to tell you."

"Why not trust yourself just for once?"

"Well, you know how it is, Irma——"

"I didn't tell you all my conversation with Mr. Corsatti. Shall I finish? He said: 'Why the hell didn't you marry Lanny Budd?'"

Lanny couldn't help laughing. "How did he come to say that?"

"We had got to be pretty good friends. I had done some bawling in his presence—because I felt so cheap and humiliated."

"What did you answer?"

"Do you really want to hear?"

"The worst way in the world."

"I said: 'Lanny Budd didn't ask me.' He said: 'That proves he's a gentleman.' 'Maybe so,' I said; 'but it doesn't help me. Can I ask a gentleman to marry me?' He said: 'Sure you can. You'll have to. With all that money you've got, what can a fellow do?' So we talked about you. I told him that you had told me about Marie de Bruyne— he knew about her, of course."

"It was all in the papers," assented Lanny.

"Well, he said: 'That's a different sort of story. A man has a woman that he loves, and he sticks by her, and that's all anybody has a right to ask.' Then he said: 'If you really care for Lanny Budd, take my advice and go and have a straight talk with him. Tell him I told you to say: "I know I've got too much money, and it's silly, but it isn't my fault and it oughtn't to be allowed to mess up my life."' So I said: 'All right, I'll go and do it.' Now I've done it, and you can tell me whether he was right."

VII

So there it was. Driving on the Euston Road and watching out for the traffic, Lanny found time for a quick glance at his companion and saw that a mantle of blood had climbed to her throat and cheeks. He realized that she was doing something which she considered desperately bold. He managed to spare one hand from the steering-wheel long enough to lay it on hers. "It's all right, dear," he said. "It's very kind of you and I'm deeply grateful."

"Are you going to be sorry for me?"

"I'm going to do just what Pietro Corsatti said, have a straight talk with you. In the first place, there's that embarrassing fact that my father never married my mother."

"I don't care a thing about that, Lanny. The point is that you got here somehow."

"It's going to worry your mother a lot; and you saw that it worried her brother in New York."

"Well, I'd like to make them happy, but it will have to be in some way that doesn't make me so unhappy."

"I want you to face the facts about us," persisted the amiable young bastard. "I wouldn't be honest if I didn't point them out. If you marry me, the newspapers will probably be moved to dig up the painful secret. I doubt if they'll say it in plain words, because it's hard to prove a negative, and there'd always be the possibility that Robbie might have had a secret marriage, and that I might come down on them for a million dollars. But they'll have deft little touches, to the effect that your family has been making genealogical researches as to the bridegroom. All the smart people will know what they mean."

"I don't care what they know or what they say, Lanny. I'm sick of publicity and gossip, and all I want is to get away from reporters."

"You feel that way at the moment; but you have to live in the world, and your family and your money are both things that are going to stay with you."

"What I want to know is just one thing, and that is what you really feel about me."

"I'll tell you as honestly as I can: I think you're a grand girl, and if you'd come along with just a reasonable amount of money, I'd have kissed you sure and certain, and the rest would have depended on what you wanted. But you know how it is, you came like the Queen of Sheba—rings on your fingers and bells on your toes. I saw all that crowd of suitors. I knew some of them, and what was in their minds, and I just had too much respect for myself to breathe the same air with them."

"I know, it's all been hateful. But can't you manage to forget my money and think about me for a while?"

"You asked me to talk straight, and I'm doing it. We'll be fooling ourselves if we forget your money, for the world won't let you forget it, and you don't really want to forget it yourself. You've got to own it, and manage it, and spend it, and you've got to know that pretty nearly everybody you meet is thinking about it. You've got to shape your life accordingly, and if it isn't to get you down and ruin your happiness, you'll have to be a wise and careful person."

"You make it sound rather awful, Lanny!"

"Well, I want you to know that I've been thinking about your money, and just what I've been thinking. Everybody I know has been urging me to ask you to marry me. My mother has her ambitions for her son, just as your mother has for her daughter. So I had to put my mind on the problem, what would it be like to be married to a very rich woman? What would I do, and how would I keep it from getting me down? I said: 'First of all, she'll have to know that I don't want her money. It's got to be so that never as long as she lives will that thought cross her mind.' "

"So you took the chance of letting me go off and marry a Fascist!"

"I let you do what you wanted, Irma, because that is your right. It'll still be your right if you marry me. You'll do what makes you happy, and if you love me, it'll be because you want to."

"Are you sure that a woman wants so very much freedom?"

"When she's very much in love, she thinks she doesn't; but it won't do any harm for her to have it."

"What a woman wants is for a man to want her very much."

"She wants that; but she must remember that there are long years ahead, and she needs a lot of other qualities and virtues in the man who loves her. She wants him to be able to think straight, and to control himself."

"You talk like an old gentleman."

"I'm a lot older than you, and I have had experience, and made a lot of mistakes which you won't have to suffer for. I want you to understand me, and not expect any more than I can give."

"What could I expect that you haven't got, Lanny?"

"It all comes back to the problem of your money. I don't mean merely that I'm not much of a businessman; I mean that I don't have a proper respect for large sums of money. I don't believe in them. I've watched people getting them and spending them, and neither job appeals to me. I think that money does things to people, and when it gets through, I don't like them any more. I'd rather be able to sit down at the piano and play a Beethoven sonata than be able to make all the money in the Barnes fortune; and when you see me doing what I like, will you get provoked and think I'm an idler?"

"I don't know that I ever heard a Beethoven sonata," said Irma Barnes. "But if I promise to let you be happy in your own way and never, never ask you to have anything to do with my money, will that satisfy you?"

"Suppose you find that I am voicing ideas which imperil your fortune? I don't mean your particular fortune, but all great wealth, as something that oughtn't to be allowed. Suppose people tell you that I'm a dangerous Red, and keeping bad company, and being watched by the police?"

"They've already told me that. But you see I came and asked for you."

"Suppose I answer yes, just what would you want to do?"

"I think I should want to go to some place a long way off, where there wouldn't be any horrid gossips and reporters."

"That would be a long way, indeed!" But then an idea occurred to him, and he added: "You remember my telling you about my brother-in-law, Hansi Robin, who is such a fine violinist? Well, his father has a yacht, and they're begging me to go for a cruise with them. They're Jews. Does that bother you?"

"Not if they're friends of yours."

"There's Hansi and Bess, and there's his younger brother Freddi and his bride. They're all musical, and it'll be pretty noisy; but you can go off in a corner and read, or Mama Robin will teach you to knit sweaters for the poor."

"It sounds very homey and nice. Where would they go?"

"Iceland and Labrador, and all the way to New York. I doubt if we'll meet any reporters until we get to America; only whales and icebergs. The only difficulty I can see is how to get married without too much fuss, and having Ettore brought into it, and my bastardy."

"Oh, Lanny, don't use that horrid word!"

"You'll hear it a lot—no good fooling yourself. Would you be satisfied with a quiet wedding, or will your mother require a dozen bridesmaids and six flower girls and a cathedral?"

"Lanny, I'll go off and marry you before a justice of the peace, or however they do it here."

"You really mean that?"

"I've thought it all over. I'm throwing myself at your head."

"When?"

"Right now, if you say so."

"Before lunch?"

"Hang the lunch!"

So Lanny drew up by the left-hand curb of the street, and performed a little ceremony of his own devising. He took her two hands in his and said: "I will be gentle and kind. I will study your wishes, and try to oblige you. I will be your friend as well as your husband. I will try my best to see that you do not regret this step. Is that what you want to hear from me?"

"Yes, dear," she responded, and her eyes were misty. "Only one thing you forgot. You didn't say: 'I love you.'"

"I admit that was an oversight. I love you." He kissed her again, regardless of the spectators on the street. He had seen the English poor doing this on Hampstead Heath on bank holidays; and if the rich could see the poor doing it, why shouldn't the poor see the rich?

35

Whom God Hath Joined

I

So NOW began the adventure of trying to get married in England. Lanny had only the vaguest notions about it. Was it done by a clergyman, or by some public functionary, or both? Was the consent of parents necessary? And up to what age? "Perhaps you had better say you are twenty-one," he suggested. Irma answered with a straight face that she had become twenty-one the week before.

The first idea that occurred to him was a "chapel." His new stepfather went to meetings in little buildings called by that name. It must be that the minister, or preacher, or whatever he was called, could marry members of his own flock, and maybe he could oblige two visiting strangers. Lanny turned his car off the main road and began wandering through little streets. Presently he stopped a small boy and inquired, in the best English he could muster: "Eh, laddie, where's the chapel?"

"Wot chapel?" demanded the boy.

"Any chapel."

"Don't know no chapel."

So the car rolled on. It was a peculiarity of this tight little island that its own inhabitants rarely knew where anything was if it was more than a quarter of a mile away. They must have had a difficult time with their geography lessons, because every villa had its individual name, and so did most every field, large tree, stile, pump, or other creation of nature or man. Few streets could pass more than three intersections without acquiring a new direction and a new name, and from there on you were in a foreign country.

At last they found a man who attended a chapel, and gave them directions in language which Lanny was able to interpret. In the living quarters adjoining the building they found a gray-bearded gentleman who said that he was the pastor, and when Lanny asked: "Can you marry people?" he declared with dignity: "This is a place of worship duly registered for the solemnizing of marriage under the Marriage Act of 1836, and I am a person duly authorized by the governing body of the place of worship in question."

"Then.we should like to be married," remarked the visitor, humbly.

"I shall be happy to accommodate you," said the man of God. "Are you a resident of this parish?"

"I don't know. What are the boundaries of it?"

The minister outlined them, and they were not big enough to include either Irma's hotel or Margy's town-house. "However, that is easily arranged," said the pastor. Apparently he had noted the fashionable costumes of the strangers, and now he noted their fashionable addresses, and desired to retain them as customers. "All that is necessary for you to do is to rent a room and leave a bag in it, and that constitutes it your legal residence."

"For how long do we have to do that?"

"The banns are published in this chapel next Sunday and for two Sundays thereafter, and then you can be married at any time."

"Oh, but we wish to be married at once."

"Unfortunately that is not possible, sir."

"You mean that nobody can marry us at once?"

"You can obtain a special license from the Archbishop of Canterbury—but that will cost you something like sixty pounds."

"And then we can be married today?"

"Then you can be married after twenty-four hours."

"But that is extremely inconvenient. We wish to travel."

"I'm sorry, sir, but that is our English law." So Lanny and the old gentleman expressed their mutual regrets, and Lanny and his lady went out to their car and drove away.

II

"Maybe he wanted the fee," suggested Irma; "so he wouldn't tell us any other way."

"My father has a firm of solicitors in London," replied the would-be bridegroom. "I will consult one of them."

He found a telephone, and presently was in conversation with Mr. Harold Stafforth, of the firm of Stafforth and Worthingham. Lanny and his father had had lunch more than once with this gentleman, and now as Lanny talked he had before him the image of a tall, lean-faced person of dry temperament, precise ideas, and extraordinarily few words. Lanny knew that he couldn't fool him, and that the first duty was to satisfy him. He said:

"Mr. Stafforth, I wish to get married. The young lady in question is a great American heiress, and her mother is not entirely cordial to me. My father knows all about the match and approves it; he offered to travel to Italy in order to try to arrange matters with the young lady's mother. I know you will wish to be sure of this, and I pledge you my word. Now the young lady has come to London, and has made up her own mind, and in order to avoid discussion and publicity we decided to have a secret wedding, and have it today if possible. Is that possible?"

"Not in England," said the solicitor. Having answered the question, he waited for the next one.

"I have read somewhere about people going to Scotland to be married, and I have a car and could drive there. Can that be done?"

"You can be married in Scotland at once, by taking each other's hands and saying that you are man and wife."

"And will that be valid?"

"It will be valid in Scotland."

"But will it be valid elsewhere?"

"It will not be valid in England."

"Then that wouldn't do. How about the possibility of traveling to Belgium or Holland or some other country?"

"I do not happen to know the laws in those countries, but I shall be happy to look the matter up for you if you wish."

"Can you suggest any way in which we could be married without delay?"

"If you are prepared to take a sea voyage, you can be married on the high seas by the licensed master of any merchant or passenger vessel."

"And will that be valid anywhere?"

"Provided that you are ten miles from the English coast, it will be valid under English law, and so far as I know it will be valid under the laws of all countries."

Lanny thought quickly. "I have a friend who has a yacht. Would the master of such a vessel be in position to marry us?"

"Is the yacht of British registry?"

"German."

"I cannot tell you about the German law without looking it up; but if such a master is authorized by the German law, the marriage would be valid under our Maritime Act of 1894."

"The German master would probably know what he was empowered to do, I suppose?"

"I should say that he would be required to have a copy of the laws in which his own powers and duties are defined."

"I will make inquiries of the master. Thank you very much, Mr. Stafforth."

"You are quite welcome," said the solicitor. "I wish you success in your efforts and happiness in your marriage."

"Thank you again," replied the young man. "Kindly charge this service to my father's account." All the proprieties having thus been conformed to, he hung up.

III

As it happened, Lanny had already consulted the newspapers and made note as to the state of the tides; he believed that the *Bessie Budd* could not yet be in the basin of Ramsgate, but he took the precaution to telephone and make sure. In this little harbor the vessels lie against an embankment, so that they are right in the street, or alongside it, and the first thing which happens is that a telephone cable is run aboard; on the *Bessie Budd* they had had a telephone not merely in the saloon, but in every cabin, in the steward's office, and on the bridge. Lanny now called the town, and learned that the yacht had not yet put in appearance.

He went out and told Irma what he had learned. He proposed that they should drive to Ramsgate, and as soon as the yacht arrived it would turn around and start another voyage.

"Oh, how romantic!" exclaimed the girl. She was charmed by the idea of being taken out to sea in order to escape from the clutches of the Archbishop of Canterbury. "Do you suppose Mr. Robin will really do that for us?"

"Of course he will. If he's too busy himself he can go on to London and let Captain Moeller oblige us. The whole family will be delighted. They already have one bride and groom on board, you know."

"Let's get going!" said the girl—who came from New York.

They set out down the valley of that not very large river which is so crowded with shipping from every part of the earth, and with tugs and lighters and pleasure craft and everything that floats. The tide rushes in very fast and rushes out even faster, owing to embankments which keep it from spreading out over the marshes. Where nature had put marshes men had made great basins with piers and sheds, and behind them gigantic slums for the workers. Lanny told his bride-to-be-soon how he had got lost in those slums when he was a small boy. He told her about Charing Cross Pier and the Island of Cythera—not failing to mention what lady had shared these revels with him.

They discussed the problems of their honeymoon, and agreed that they would tell their mothers, but that nobody else was to share the secret until after the *Bessie Budd* had sailed. Irma made note of the name of the yacht. Was she the least bit inclined toward jealousy of it? "Lanny," she asked, "are you sure it wouldn't be better if we got one of our own?"

It gave him a start. He could have a yacht if he wanted it! The biggest yacht in the world—enough to carry a dozen Red Sunday schools! But he said: "Let Johannes have the troubles. He has asked for them."

"Will I like those people, do you think?"

"You'll find them the easiest in the world to get along with; and, moreover, you won't be under any obligations. Johannes considers that my father has paid him for life."

In after years Lanny would look back on a remark like that, and marvel anew at the strange fate of men, who can see when they turn their eyes toward the past, but are totally blind confronting the future. Bacon has said that he who marries and begets children gives hostages to fortune; and the saying surely applies to him who acquires friendships—especially if the year is 1929, and the place is Germany, and the friends are "non-Aryan"!

The eloping pair talked about themselves, a subject of interest and importance to young people. "Oh, Lanny, I have been so unhappy!" the girl exclaimed. "I want somebody I can trust."

"You have him, dear."

"I am so ashamed of what happened in Italy!"

"That's ancient history—leave it to the bookstores."

"I'll have to have time to get over the humiliation."

"Tell yourself that Ettore was a well-practiced lover, and carried you off your feet."

"That wasn't all. I wanted to be something great and important. But I didn't like those people. I didn't like the place."

"What place do you think you would like?"

"I think I'd like Juan the best of any I've ever been to."

"Well, that's fine, because that's the way I feel. There's a lovely house there, waiting for us. Only you'll have to get used to hearing people say that I built it for Rosemary."

"Lanny, I promise I'll never be jealous of her."

"There's nothing to worry about, because they're going to keep her in the Argentine, I'm pretty sure!"

IV

They were driving along the Kentish coast, through a succession of small watering-places looking out over the sea. Chance brought them to a country inn which had some outdoor tables, and they sat under an arbor of vines and had cold mutton and beer—something of a come-down from the caviar and champagne in which Lanny had indulged himself in the wee hours of that morning. They drove again, and were on the Strait of Dover, where it was all one town with different names, and presently the name was Ramsgate, a popular "watering place." In its little harbor, perhaps a quarter of a mile each way, the trim *Bessie Budd*, gleaming with several coats of new white paint, was in process of being laid against the side of the street.

There were all six of the Robin family, standing by the rail as in a line-up. How delightful to see Lanny come along and park his car right beside the berth of the yacht! But who was that lovely brunette Juno, wearing a sports ensemble of brown worsted trimmed with white, and a little brown cap to match? Had he at last found himself a girl whom he liked enough to take about on his drives? When the yacht was close enough so that they could chat comfortably, Lanny said: "Let me introduce Irma Barnes. Irma, meet Mama and Papa Robin, and, reading from left to right, Hansi and Bess and Freddi and Rahel." They all bowed and smiled, and politely covered their excitement at the magic name of the brunette Juno. They had a right to feel pleasure in meeting any friend of their darling Lanny. Of course, Hansi and Bess hadn't failed to tell the story of the famous heiress, and how Lanny had been too haughty and had wooed her with too little ardor. By what magic was she now at his side?

Obviously it was a story! Lanny took them into the saloon and closed the doors, and said: "Irma and I are trying to get married, and the English laws won't let us. We don't want a lot of fuss and newspaper talk, so will you let Captain Moeller take us out and marry us on the high seas?"

Well, you could have knocked that family over with a feather—so the saying runs, but Lanny didn't have any feather. Anglo-Saxon reticence was forgotten by all; Bess hugged and kissed her half-brother, she hugged and kissed Irma, and Mama began to sob with whatever it is that moves motherly souls at weddings. The young Jewish people all wrung the hands of the happy pair. Hansi was the first who had a wonderful thought, and exclaimed to the bride: "Oh, you will come with us on the cruise!" There followed a clamor of acclamation which left no doubt in the soul of an heiress that she was welcomed—and not entirely for her money, for, after all, Mr. Robin had his own, as this yacht proved.

Johannes said: "I will see Moeller." Captain Fritz Moeller was a gray-bearded officer who had commanded a great passenger liner before the war, and now was thankful for a chance to manage a pleasure yacht for a Jewish *Schieber*. Johannes had a talk with him and came back looking sorrowful. "*Ach! Er kann es nicht. Verboten!*"

"What is the matter?" asked Lanny.

"When he commanded a passenger vessel, yes. And before that, when he was captain of a merchant vessel. But for a private yacht, *nein*."

"He is sure?"

"He says that you would not be married, and he would be deprived of his license."

Grief appeared on the faces of all the company. How very provoking, to ruin their delightful adventure! "Well, it looks as if we have to go back to the Archbishop!" said Lanny.

"And all that publicity!" added Irma.

"Is that what is troubling you?" inquired the owner of the *Bessie Budd*.

"This kind of thing," said Lanny, and took from his pocket the clipping from that morning's *Daily Mail*. "There was a duca in Italy who thought that he was engaged to Irma; and now the papers bring it up, and write a lot of gossip."

"And my mother makes a fuss," added the girl. "We thought that we could get it over with, and then she would make the best of it."

"Couldn't we go to France?" inquired Bess.

"It is no better there," said Lanny. "They have the banns, and it takes ten days. Moreover, you have to have birth certificates. My mother and Mr. Dingle had to cable for them."

"How would it be in Holland?" persisted Bess.

"Worse yet," said Johannes. "It takes four weeks. Nowhere in Europe do they take getting married so lightly as in the States."

"It is very silly," opined Irma. "If it suits us, why should anybody else be concerned?"

Johannes looked at her. A very fine-looking girl, and he knew about her twenty-three million dollars. Lanny was too well bred to show it, but it seemed to Johannes that anybody who had a chance to marry her would be in a hurry. He could be sure that Lanny's father would take it as a favor if he went to some trouble to bring off this match. "Well, if you are game, I'll get you married tonight."

"How?" It was a chorus.

"There are plenty of passenger and merchant vessels out there in the Strait of Dover. The sea is smooth, and it should be an easy matter to get one to stop if we pay them enough."

Young hearts leaped and young faces lighted up. "Oh, how charming!" exclaimed the would-be bride.

"Are you game?"

"Indeed I am!"

"But," objected Lanny, "would the master have a right to marry two people who aren't passengers?"

"You can be passengers. We'll leave you on board."

"Where would we go?"

"We'll flag a vessel that is inward bound. You can be married before it enters the ten-mile zone, and the Archbishop of Canterbury can go hang."

They were young, they were rich and accustomed to having their own way; they were not too much burdened with a sense of their own dignity, or with respect for the laws and institutions of any nation. Mama Robin was the only one who was shocked by all this; the others were in a state of hilarity, so she held her peace. The bridegroom said: "Let me have a few minutes to get my car parked and send a couple of telegrams."

V

Lanny darted onto shore. He had agreed with Irma upon two identical telegrams, one signed by her to her mother, and one signed by him to his: "Everything settled have gone to visit friends will write"—something which these ladies would understand, but no one else. That attended to, and the car placed in a garage, Lanny hurried back to the yacht, and it crept through the opening in the breakwater and headed eastward into the Strait of Dover.

They stood in the stern and watched the sun set behind them, and Lanny talked about the exhibition and how it was going; the pair had collected themselves, and were Anglo-Saxon again. If they were to express their feelings, it could only be by the means of art. Presently the piano on rubber wheels was rolled onto the deck, and Hansi got his fiddle, and they listened to Scriabin's *Prelude*, gently solemn, with very beautiful double-stopping—a performance for which an audience would have paid a large sum of money. Bess played the accompaniment, and Lanny saw that she was improving all the time, and told her so; he was proud of her, and of the match which he had helped to make. Now they were repaying him!

Somewhere in that vague region where the Strait of Dover merges with the North Sea, so that you cannot tell which is which, appeared the lights of a dumpy old freighter. By her course they judged her to be London bound, and they waited for her, and when she was near laid their course alongside. There was just enough light so that the two masters could vaguely see each other's form. The sea was so smooth that they could talk without the need of a megaphone and a conversation ensued:

"Ahoy there! This is the motor yacht *Bessie Budd*, German registry, out of Bremen. Who are you?"

"British passenger freighter *Plymouth Girl*, Copenhagen to London."

"I've a couple of passengers who want to go ashore at London."

"All passenger accommodations full, I can't afford to stop."

"What do you want to heave to?"

"Ten pounds."

"We'll pay you twenty pounds. The young couple want to get married on the high seas. Will you oblige them?"

"Are they British?"

"Both Americans, of legal age. They want to avoid the delays of getting married on shore."

"Will they pay cash?"

"As soon as they come aboard."

"I'll take them."

The dark shape came to a stop and the yacht slowed up accordingly; when they lay still they weren't more than a cable's length apart. A dinghy was lowered from the *Bessie Budd*, also the gangway, and Irma and Lanny went down; when they reached the old vessel they were helped up a rope ladder, not so clean, and welcomed by a burly son of the sea whose job was transporting butter and eggs from a land of dairies to one of factories. Several members of the crew and a couple of passengers stood staring by the dim light of lanterns. What they thought of the adventure was not revealed.

·Lanny presented two indubitable ten-pound notes and, after examining them, the captain said: "I never done this before, but I'll chance it. Can you tell me what I have to say?"

"Sure," said Lanny, who had attended many fashionable ceremonies. "You ask me if I take this woman for my lawful wedded wife, and you ask this woman if she takes me for her lawful wedded husband. We answer yes, and then you say that by the authority vested in you under the Maritime Act of 1894 you pronounce us man and wife. You give us a certificate that you have married us, and you enter it in the ship's log, and maybe you have to report it to the Registrar ashore—I don't know about that, but you can find out."

"Well, I hope there's nothing bogus about this that would get me into trouble."

"Not at all," said Lanny, promptly. "We are of legal age, and we wish to be properly married. We're yachting, and it seems that it takes a lot of time to get married ashore." He said nothing about the publicity, because that might have meant risking some.

VI

The freighter had started her engines, and so had the *Bessie Budd*, and they were running side by side, a safe distance apart, but not so far that you couldn't hear the music distinctly. Hansi and Bess were playing the Mendelssohn *Wedding March*, to which irreverent persons chant: "Here comes the bride; get onto her stride." But there was nowhere to march to. After clearing his throat several times, and repeating the names to make sure that he had them right, Captain Rugby of the *Plymouth Girl* asked the crucial questions and said the crucial formula. Then he took them to his cabin, and wrote out a certificate. He offered them the use of his cabin, for it was a long time before they would dock in London, but Lanny said no, they would sit on deck that pleasant summer evening and listen to the music.

The *Bessie Budd* was still alongside, and Hansi and Bess were playing the Queen Titania music. When it was over they had a gay long-distance chat, and Lanny introduced the new Mrs. Budd, and the crews of both vessels listened and acquired information as to the ways of the idle rich. There was more music, and presently refreshments were brought up on the yacht. They offered to send some over, but Captain Rugby wasn't willing to stop again; he produced some sherry and biscuits, which they ate with a good young appetite. The celebration went on until the freighter was at the Nore lightship, when the passengers of both vessels stood by the rail and sang: "Goodnight, ladies, we're going to leave you now."

So the two vessels parted company and faded out of hearing. It made them feel lonely, and Irma said: "Do you think we're really married?"

"Don't worry about it too much," he replied. "When we get to the States we can have it done again. I'm told they don't make so much fuss about it over there."

At the mouth of the Thames great numbers of vessels lay waiting for the tide. When it was right, a pilot came aboard, and a ghostly procession started: every kind and size of steamer that could be imagined on the high seas, great passenger liners down to tugs with barges. It resembled what you saw when a school bell rang and the children came trooping in from all the homes in the village; a few hours later another bell rang, and they came rushing out—only in the case of the Port of London it would be a different lot each time. They glided up the river under their own power, and in the dim moonlight Irma and Lanny could see great mud-flats, and then, standing up bare and stark, factories, many of them brightly lighted, working at night, and piers with ships being loaded or unloaded by arclights. Presently the river narrowed, and there were entrances to great basins, and the fleet of vessels began to dissolve to right or left, the big ones first and the smaller ones higher up the river.

When the *Plymouth Girl* came to her berth, there was a sleepy official to inspect her papers and interview her passengers. Going off on a friend's yacht and coming back on a dingy old freighter was a sufficiently unusual procedure to attract attention; but money can do a lot at any port in the world, and it quickly brought a couple of messenger boys, one to go to Lanny's hotel and one to Irma's, to fetch their passports. These being in order, the delay was brief and they stepped ashore. By the same magic of the Bank of England's notes Lanny arranged at a garage for a car to be driven to Ramsgate, and a man in the back seat to take the car back.

They found the *Bessie Budd* safely reposing against the street, but all the passengers had already left for London. Lanny got his own car, and he and his bride set out to explore England in the lovely month of brides and roses. "Mr. and Mrs. L. P. Budd" attracted no attention on the registers of country inns, so they had a quiet time. Up in London the Robin family kept the secret, and so did the mothers. The formula "gone to visit friends" left the newspapers baffled. Beauty, being so much the poorer woman, took it as her duty to call on the haughty Mrs. Fanny Barnes. Fate had thrown them together, and they would have to make friends; fortunately they both played a good game of bridge. Lanny had been anxious as to the possibility that his new mother-in-law might expect to be taken on the yachting trip, but Irma said she was an especially poor sailor and was planning to go to Deauville with friends.

So everything was "jake," as they said in America. The bride made the discovery that she had found an ardent lover; it was easier to forget Italy and the Fascists than she had expected. Also it seemed possible just then to get away from her money with all its claims and obligations. She hadn't brought much with her, and Lanny was paying the bills and making jokes about keeping her in the style to which she was accustomed. He pointed out the features of English landscapes and told stories out of English history; delightful indeed to have a combination of husband and tutor! In the parlor of an establishment called the Duck and Turtle he seated himself at a not too badly cracked piano and played Schumann's *Widmung. Ich liebe dich in Zeit und Ewigkeit!* It would have been a "give-away" if anybody in the place had known German music, but no one did.

VII

In short, they had a jolly time, and the only reason they returned to London was the exhibition. If Lanny stayed away from this event, some clever person like Sophie or Margy might connect him with the missing heiress. They came back and amused themselves playing a game of hide-and-seek with the smart world. Lanny resumed receiving guests at the show, and among them were Mrs. J. Paramount Barnes and her daughter. He greeted them casually, and introduced them to Zoltan, who, knowing how rich they were, produced his best "spiel" about a French painter who was forging so rapidly to the front. Word spread that this was the famed heiress, and people watched her discreetly, and it surely did no harm to the reputation of Detaze that she expressed lively admiration for his work.

It pleased her to return and continue her art studies, and to bring other Americans whom she knew. She introduced these friends to the charming Hungarian gentleman who presided over the show, and left it for him to present them to the widow of the painter and his gay and eager little daughter. If now and then the painter's stepson was included in the introductions, that amiable young man would give intelligent answers to questions about the paintings. Irma showed no special interest in his remarks, but told the alert Mr. Kertezsi that she had decided to have several of these paintings in her Long Island home. He helped her to make a selection, received her check with many bows, and made note of her address and shipping instructions. Once more Zoltan was vindicated in his theory that it was better to price works of art too high than too low!

Then, when the show closed for the night, Lanny would drive his car to an appointed place, and Irma would arrive in a taxicab and transfer herself, and they would do a little winding about the winding old streets to make sure they were not being followed. Irma would be "visiting friends" again, and Lanny amused her by taking her to that second-class hotel where he had kept two rendezvous with Rosemary Codwilliger, pronounced Culliver, some twelve years previously. The building was still there—all buildings always stayed in London, they were permanent as the pyramids, he declared. He told her how a shrapnel splinter had crashed through the window of their room in the night, and Irma exclaimed: "Oh, how exciting! Do you suppose that will ever happen again?"

VIII

The *Bessie Budd* set sail with her five honeymoon couples; at least, Johannes said that he and Mama had been on a honeymoon ever since their wedding day, and the same was true of Mr. and Mrs. Dingle and of Mr. and Mrs. Hansi. Nobody needed to say anything about Mr. and Mrs. Lanny, or Mr. and Mrs. Freddi; their state of bliss was written all over them, and made them very pretty to watch.

The yacht sailed north, past the Faeroe Islands, and toward the land of the midnight sun. They saw some whales, but no icebergs in July and August. They came to a great island set in a lonely sea; they nosed into fiords much like those of Norway, and found a lovely little city scattered over the hills of a good harbor. The name Iceland sounded forbidding, and they were surprised to encounter a cultivated people who managed to have books and newspapers in their strange tongue, yet to escape most of the evils from which the *Bessie Budd* had fled. Surprising too to see hot springs and geysers bursting out of ground which was frozen most of the year; to see active volcanoes surrounded by glaciers. Beauty, who had grown soft in the warmth of Provence, shuddered at the thought of winter on these barren, storm-swept hills; but Lanny thought the people fared better than the dwellers in the slums of Riviera "old towns."

They went on toward the west. The glowing sun went down into the water while they slept, and soon afterward it came up out of a near-by place in the water, and it was broad daylight most of the time; apparently the globe on which they lived had got tipped out of place and didn't behave as they were used to seeing it. Unexpectedly, when the sun shone in an unclouded sky it became quite hot on deck, and you might imagine you were off the coast of Africa. You had to learn to sleep in the light, or tie a bandage over your eyes.

Great lonely wastes of water—Beauty said, what on earth had it all been made for! Only the seabirds and the porpoises for company. The birds could sleep on the water, but you never saw them doing it, nor did the porpoises ever seem to rest. When fogs settled down, the yacht barely crept along; when storms came, she headed into them, with just enough speed for steerage way. The voyagers were in no hurry; they had an abundance of food and water and fuel, and had left all cares in Berlin and London, places which had so many that a few extra would hardly count. They did not dress for dinner, as they had done on the previous cruise, the fashionable one. They wore yachting togs and sports clothes, and were comfortable and free; they agreed with the one-eyed calender in *The Arabian Nights:* "This indeed is life; pity 'tis, 'tis fleeting!"

There were five musicians on board, not including Mr. Dingle, who could play the mouth-organ, or Beauty and Irma, who had learned a few pieces after the fashion of society ladies. They had great quantities of scores, so many that the handling of them was a problem, and Freddi's wife constituted herself librarian. Hansi, who would never stop improving while he lived, practiced every day. Following a custom which they had inaugurated on their first cruise, Hansi and Freddi went frequently into the forecastle and played for such of the crew as were not on duty. On this trip, having no snobbish folk on board, they went farther, and every Sunday evening invited the crew into the saloon and gave them a regular concert.

This, of course, in the name of the brotherhood of man. Mr. Dingle, exponent of the fatherhood of God, made an even wider breach in the class lines, which are nowhere stronger than on board ship. When one of the men fell ill he went and prayed for him; and thereafter he would go frequently into the forecastle and explain his ideas, and also play the mouth-organ with members of the crew who had mastered that humble instrument.

Mr. Dingle said that it made no difference what instrument you played, any more than it mattered where you traveled; God was with you on the loneliest ocean, the rockiest, fog-bound shore. He was the same God in whatever aspect you found Him. In His guise as Orpheus, maker of melodious sounds, He brought to the *Bessie Budd* all climes of the earth and all ages of history; He peopled her deck with mythological creatures born in the fancy of the various tribes of mankind; He made her guests acquainted with the moods which had possessed the souls of men since first they opened their eyes and discovered themselves struggling and aspiring, loving and hating, fighting and dying, on a great ball of matter whirling at unthinkable speeds through an incomprehensible universe. All that men had felt and suffered had been recorded and preserved in musical sound, a heritage for those who had ears to hear and minds to understand.

IX

Through long, peaceful days and too abbreviated nights Lanny Budd studied that private and special gift which his complicated fates had awarded him. After no end of uncertainty and many mischances, he had got himself a wife; in a hurry, and half by accident, as happens to many two-legged creatures, as to those which have four, six, eight, or a hundred legs! Now that all barriers were down and all veils dropped, what was this woman who was his?

For one thing, she had a naturally cheerful disposition, an excellent thing in crowded quarters. She had a normal enjoyment of her food, and of being made love to. It wasn't necessary to her happiness to talk all the time; she would give him a chance to think, even when she was in the same cabin with him. She liked to walk on deck, and enjoyed any sort of game; she was still very young, and seemed in no special hurry to grow up. She had married him in a fit of pique, but she was loyal, and expected to make the best of her bargain. He couldn't guess how they'd get along in the midst of that crazy world of money and fashion which sooner or later would come clamoring after her; but in this floating playground, with only a few kind friends, and little reason for dressing up—he had persuaded her to ship her maid back to New York with the rest of her staff—here things were peaceful and pleasant enough.

He investigated her mind. Ideas didn't mean much to her; she saw no special reason for getting excited about them. Perhaps she might later on, when she discovered that they affected herself and her life and fortune; meanwhile, it was all right, because Lanny had enough ideas for two. He discovered that she didn't understand music; its structure meant nothing to her, but she liked to listen to harmonious sounds, they threw her into a pleasantly excited state. Perhaps her subconscious forces were being stimulated to their task, the miracle that was beginning within her. Irma wasn't going to master the piano like Bess; she was content to be a wife and let nature have its way. That suited Lanny, and still more it suited Beauty, who was in the seventh heaven of mothers-in-law; she lavished her affection upon the girl, watching for the symptoms, telling her own varied experiences. Women, who have to nurse babies and change their wrappings, learn to employ explicit language, and the things that Irma said to Beauty about Lanny would have caused embarrassment even to that son of the warm south if he had heard them.

The other young wife was in the same state of mind and body, and she too had a future grandmother in a state of rapture not to be repressed. Presently the four of them got together, Beauty Budd and Mama Robin, Irma and Rahel, and after that a section of the yacht might have been called the maternity ward. Four females whispering to one another, and Johannes, proprietor of the vessel, fain to listen in but not allowed to! And aft on the deck, under a gay-striped awning, four musicians pounding and thumping, tootling and tinkling and scraping, trying in vain to create or imagine anything more strange and romantic, more terrifying and delightful than the possibility of having a baby!

BOOK EIGHT

Lead But to the Grave

36

Prince Consort

I

EARLY in the month of September the *Bessie Budd* appeared off the mouth of the Newcastle River. Lanny had telephoned from Boston, and Robbie had a pilot waiting for them in a launch; he blew on a little tin horn, and the two draw-bridges swung open, first the road bridge and then the railroad bridge, and the trim white yacht glided slowly through and was brought neatly alongside one of the wharves of the Budd plant. Robbie was there with three cars, and all ten passengers stepped ashore: the family of his former wife—so called in the interest of public decency—and the family of his business associate, including Robbie's daughter. Also, there was his new daughter-in-law, whom he had never met, so it was an important occasion for him.

In fact, it was to be doubted if ever since the days of the slave trade such a package of excitement had arrived by sea in the little harbor of Newcastle, Connecticut. The news of Lanny's marriage to America's newest heiress had been released by Mrs. Barnes as soon as the yacht had left London, and it hadn't taken many hours to reach the home of Budd Gunmakers Corporation. Soon it had become known that the yacht was coming here, and fashionable society was sitting up in watchtowers. Several of the smartest set had met Irma Barnes in New York, and these distributed their information and helped to keep curiosity alive.

Irma was the brightest star in the constellation, but by no means the only one of the first magnitude. For more than thirty years the tongues of gossip had been busy with the personality of Beauty Budd. She had never been to Newcastle; in fact she had never visited her native land in all those years. Now she was coming, and was to be received in the Budd home—the fiction of a marriage and divorce being maintained. This had to be done, if only on account of Irma; impossible for the family to admit that there was anything wrong with the mother-in-law of their new fairy princess!

Also in this constellation was Beauty's son, whom you might call a variable star; a dark one when he had passed below Newcastle's horizon, he was now shining brightly, even though by reflected light. There is a phenomenon of the heavens known as a double star: a dark one and a bright one revolve about each other, and thousands of eyes are kept glued upon them in the hope of gleaning new items of information concerning the nature and behavior of celestial bodies.

And then the Robin family. Hansi might be likened to a shining meteor which sweeps through the night sky and sweeps away again. No one could be certain how long he would last, but meanwhile he was a portent, and Newcastle would not forget the explosion he had caused by picking up and dragging off in his train one of the brightest planets of the Newcastle Country Club system. Hansi's father also was a sun in his own right, and marked on the map of many Newcastle stargazers. To drop an overworked simile, Johannes was an important financier, and many of the town's leading businessmen held stock in his enterprises; these solid citizens didn't go in for society flubdub, but were glad to meet and converse with a man of ability and experience.

II

The party was taken to the Robbie Budd home for tea, and members of the family were on hand to welcome them. Not old Samuel, for he rarely went out now, and not even after thirty years could he be persuaded to meet the woman who had seduced his son. But others of the tribe were less stiff-necked, and the younger generation was possessed by curiosity. From this tea party the news spread quite literally with the speed of lightning, for in every home except the very poorest in Newcastle this force had been harnessed and taught to serve the public welfare. "What hath God wrought?" the inventor of the process had piously inquired, and the answer was that

God had wrought a means whereby gossip might be distributed over a small city with astonishing celerity. "What does she look like?" and "What was she wearing?" and "What did she say?" and "How did Esther greet her?" and "Is she going to keep them in her house?"

The press had fair warning, and it was a red-letter day for local correspondents; the stories they sent over the wire would not stop until they had reached Key West and San Diego and Walla Walla. Lanny Budd, who had had such a blissful time for two months in the haunts of the whale and the eider duck, now discovered suddenly what this marriage was going to mean. On the wharf were several men with square black boxes which made snapping noises when a button was pressed; already they had snapped the yacht, and now it was necessary for Irma and her husband to line up, and then Hansi and Bess with them. The local photographers wanted the whole party. Meanwhile the reporters were plying Irma and Lanny with questions: where had they been, what sort of weather had they had, what had they done, where were they going to live, what did they think about Europe and America, and which did they prefer?

You had to be polite to them, for they represented the most powerful force in the land, and could make you or break you. If you were wise you would employ a skilled publicity man to tell you what to say, and to be present at interviews and smooth over the rough places. Irma's mother had engaged one in New York, but now Irma was taken by surprise, and Lanny couldn't help her very much, his experience having been slight. Robbie had arranged for a collective interview at his home, but deadlines know no decorum, so Lanny had to try to think in a hurry what the great public might like to read about a bride with twenty-three million dollars, and also about the lucky young "socialite" who had got her. What would have pleased the public most was a bulletin to the effect that she was pregnant; but that being barred, Lanny said that they had played music on the deck most of the time, they had a piano on rubber wheels, also a violin, a clarinet, and a soprano voice. He didn't mention the mouth-organ; but, as it happened, one of the reporters dug that out of the crew, and made an amusing item about life on a German millionaire's yacht.

Somehow the word got about that the sons and daughters-in-law of Johannes Robin were Reds, and that the spouse of Irma Budd was decidedly tinged with pink. Wasn't there a story about his having been kicked out of Italy five years ago? The ordinary press associations didn't refer to this, for it was not their practice to mention dangerous thoughts unless the carriers of them had got arrested or something like that; but there were "tabs" in New York which would publish anything "spicy," and there were men who specialized in collecting personal details about celebrities and broadcasting them over the radio. Lanny found that he had become almost overnight a shining mark for these gentry. They didn't intend to be mean to him; he was just an amiable playboy who had been catapulted suddenly into the spotlight and had, at a conservative estimate, thirty million pairs of eyes fixed upon his daily and nightly doings.

III

Esther Budd considered it her duty to invite the entire party to her home, which had plenty of room. But the guests had talked the matter over in advance and decided otherwise. The young people would come, but the middle-aged, the mothers and fathers, would stay on board the yacht, where they were comfortable and wouldn't be in danger of spoiling the good times. Mama Robin didn't care for fashionable society; she knew perfectly well that these smart people would be laughing at her stumbling English, and she preferred her own little nook where she had everything the way she wanted it. As for Beauty, she knew that she was being forced upon Esther, and desired to make the strain as light as possible. Also there was the obstacle of Beauty's husband, whose private wire to heaven would please the daughter of the Puritans no more than that of Roger Williams had pleased her forefathers of three centuries earlier.

The Robbie Budds gave a reception in their home the second evening after the yacht's arrival, and all the members of the party came to that, and met the social élite of Newcastle valley. The doors of the country club were opened to the visitors, and there were dinners and festive events. Irma had telegraphed for her staff, and her chauffeur was on hand with her car, her social secretary, and her maid; her wardrobe trunks were brought out of the hold of the yacht, and without a moment's delay she fell into the routine which had been dropped when she fled from Rome. Everything was done to make smooth her path, and she would emerge from her boudoir ready for the world to gaze at her, and certain that it would. Lanny, too, might enjoy the same assurance; he had nothing to do but display himself as the winner and keeper of the most precious prize in the lottery of high life.

As usual, one half of him liked it, and the other half was skeptical. He had not forgotten how all these people had received him when he had come among them as a lad; not unkindly, but with watchful caution, and then with amusement or indignation, according to their temperaments, when they saw him following the footsteps of his mother in the primrose path of dalliance. Now he returned in glory, and his sins which had been scarlet became white as snow. Now he was the glass of fashion and the mold of form, the observed of all observers, the model for youth to follow—in short, he had "made good," and young and old hastened to lay their tributes at his feet. The girls of Newcastle who had been sub-debs during the war now had new names and were the "young matrons" of the country club; they recalled themselves to him, and noting his elegant manners and brilliant conversation, compared him sadly with the rather dull young businessmen whom fate had assigned to them. If only they had been clever enough to realize how an ugly duckling can grow into a swan!

The same thing happened to Mabel Blackless, alias Beauty Budd, alias Madame Detaze, alias Mrs. Parsifal Dingle. Shining in the re-flected glory of her son and daughter-in-law, she was really phe-nomenal. Her years were almost fifty, but she had devoted a great part of them to keeping herself beautiful, and had acquired no little skill. Had she set out to punish Esther by making a conquest of the town? She treated Robbie as an old friend, and in fact treated all Newcastle that way; her manner seemed to say: "Yes, we have lived together in our thoughts for a long time, and I know that you have not appreciated me, but I don't hold it against you, for there were three thousand miles of ocean between us and you couldn't be expected to understand me and my ways. But I have always known about yours, and you are being so kind to me and my darling boy and his lovely young bride, and we all hope you will love us and see that the evil gossip about us was not true." It was a symptom of the change in the times that Beauty Budd could "get away with" all that, and that a town with so many Protestant churches presented her with the keys of its country club.

<h1 style="text-align:center">IV</h1>

One of Lanny's first duties was to take his bride to call upon his grandfather. The president of Budd Gunmakers was now eighty-two, and failing; his cheeks hung in pouches, and there were folds of loose skin under his chin; his hand trembled so that he had a hard time drinking a glass of water. But he still hung onto his power; those shaking hands held a great business, and no important decision was made without his knowledge. His sons tried to spare him, but he wouldn't let them. His old home was unchanged, and his old servants; his Sunday morning Bible class for men was now conducted by an assistant, but the old gentleman came and listened to make sure that there was no departure from the principles set forth in that *Brief Digest of the Boston Confession of Faith* which he had handed to his grandson at their first encounter.

The old man lifted himself carefully from his chair in honor of the lovely young woman who was escorted into his study. He had heard all about her, looked her over carefully, and made sure that she was well formed and healthy. "Welcome, my dear," he said; and then to Lanny: "You waited quite a while, young man!"

"I only just met her at the beginning of this year," said Lanny, with a grin. "She was worth waiting for."

The head of the Budd tribe couldn't dispute that statement. His vast plant had to work several years to gain the profits this young whippersnapper had picked up by walking off with a girl. It seemed preposterous, but it was a fact and had to be faced. "We are happy to welcome you into the Budd tribe," said the old Puritan; it was a condescension, and the new granddaughter expressed her gratitude and said that everybody was being very kind to her. He was looking at her steadily, but that didn't worry her, for she knew that he couldn't be displeased with what he saw.

"Well, my boy, I hear that you have turned into quite a business-man of late."

"It wouldn't seem very much to you, sir, but it has been con-venient for me. It's partly due to the fact that my late stepfather's work has been winning so much attention. It really looks as if the paintings which he left would bring more than a million dollars."

"You don't say so! Make people pay for them—they will think a lot more of them."

"Yes, sir. That appears to be the way. It is too bad that some way can't be found so that painters may reap some of that benefit during their lifetimes."

"Unfortunately, paintings are out of my line," said the aged Puri-tan. ("Thou shalt not make unto thee any graven image, or any like-ness of anything that is in heaven above, or that is in the earth beneath, or that is in the water under the earth.")

"Have you seen any of the pictures which I have purchased for clients in Newcastle, sir?"

"I haven't seen them, but they have told me that they are pleased; and a satisfied customer comes back for more business."

"So I have observed."

"Well, Irma?" The old gentleman turned again to the bride. "You have come into the Budd family, and I hope that you will not re-gret it."

"I am sure I never will, Grandfather."

"And I hope you will do your duty. Remember the injunction of Holy Writ, to be fruitful and multiply, and replenish the earth, and subdue it. In my time, and in the days of my forefathers, large fami-lies were the rule, and the modern practice of birth control was unknown."

"Yes, Grandfather."

"May I hope that you will not interfere with God's will in that respect?"

"Yes, Grandfather; I have no intention of doing so."

"You are *not* doing so?" The president of Budd Family looked from one to the other. He wanted an explicit answer; Irma was blushing.

"We are not doing so," declared Lanny. "As a matter of fact we have reason to think that the desired event has already happened."

"Indeed!" said the old gentleman, with the widest smile that Lanny remembered to have seen on his rather forbidding countenance. "That is very good news, and I will see that your child has a place in my will. Not that he will have any need of it," he added, to Irma; "but every little helps."

Many years had passed since Lanny had sat in the Bible class of the old munitions manufacturer; but the teacher knew what he had taught, even if the pupil had forgotten what he had learned. Said Samuel Budd to his grandson: "Do you remember the words which the aged Saul spoke to young David?"

"I remember some of them, Grandfather."

" 'Swear now therefore unto me by the Lord, that thou wilt not cut off my seed after me, and that thou wilt not destroy my name out of my father's house.' That is the voice of the Lord speaking to you both."

V

The great plant of Budd's was pouring out smoke from many chimneys. Business was booming as it hadn't boomed since the war. Under the watchful eyes of the Lord's deputy one department after another had been reorganized and retooled, and now they were making everything from thimbles to elevators. And they were finding markets for them all over the world; American money was being lent to all nations and the money was being spent for American products. Lanny had listened to his father talking to Johannes about it; the Bolivian government had borrowed a total of some forty million dollars in Wall Street, and Johannes didn't think much of Bolivian credit; but it didn't seem to make any difference, the public absorbed one issue of bonds after another, the money was being spent for American products, and Budd's was getting its share. It meant new office buildings going up in Bolivian cities, it meant Bolivian citizens ascending in Budd elevators, and when these got out of order they would be repaired with Budd wrenches.

More than that, if the Bolivians got to fighting with the Paraguayans, both sides would come to Budd's; for the munitions part of the business hadn't been abolished. They kept it going on faith, or perhaps lack of faith in human nature, which couldn't go on indefinitely without wars. It was a patriotic service to make the jigs and dies for a new and better machine gun which might be needed by the American government; the public didn't appreciate that service now, but it would when the time came. Lanny remembered a remark of Bub Smith, the ex-cowboy, that a gun was like a certain toilet necessity, you didn't need it often but when you did you needed it bad. Lanny didn't pass this Texas humor on to his wife, but he told her in a general way about the patriotic principles of the Budd tribe which had been taught to him all his life.

The old gentleman had suggested that Irma should see the plant; he wanted her to know that there were real things in the world, and how they were made. So Lanny took her through and showed her the sights which had so thrilled him as a youth. The girls who sat by the assembly lines were putting different gadgets together, and probably they were different girls, but their behavior was the same. Somehow or other they knew that the elegant pair strolling down the aisle and staring at them were the young lord and lady about whom they had read in the papers; but their job gave them little chance to observe costumes and manners. They would sit for hour after hour, day after day, year after year, making precisely ordained motions; millions of products would slide off the lines, and Lanny's and Irma's "seed" had just been promised a share of the profits in the name of the Lord. If there was anything wrong with all that, what could Lanny do about it? How could he even explain it to his wife?

She was immensely impressed by what she saw. The business of forming holding companies was purely a paper one, so all that Irma had seen at her father's office was rows of clerks sitting at typewriters and adding-machines and cardfiles. But here was something tangible, and it made the Budd family important and aristocratic, and made Lanny much less of a "come-down." She had seen him adopted into this old family, and she too had been adopted, and her seed had been blessed; it had been embarrassing, but she knew that it was out of the Bible and therefore respectable. Irma was happy in the thought of telling her uncles and aunts about it, and they would realize that this was no misalliance. After all, J. Paramount Barnes had begun life as an errand boy, but Lanny's forefathers had been building this great plant for generations. To be sure, they didn't make so much money as her father had done, but money wasn't everything, no matter what you might say.

VI

The firm of "R and R" hadn't had a consultation for some time, and they took this occasion to go into details about all their affairs and to plan what they would do in the future. Some of the concerns which Johannes had purchased in Germany were turning out the same sort of goods as Budd's, which brought them into rivalry in various markets; but that didn't trouble them, for the world was big, and there was no limit to the expansion of production. Lanny didn't sit in at these conferences, but he heard some of the casual talk and gathered that the German capitalist was much less optimistic than the American. Johannes had had to work for his money, and knew what it was to face adversity; he wouldn't expect to have summer weather during his entire cruise on the ocean of big business.

Robbie, on the other hand, was sure that for America, at least, the problem of permanent prosperity had been solved. He had got the ideal President of the United States this time; the Great Engineer, who didn't have to be told what to do, because he understood the business machine in every part and knew exactly how to help American industry and finance to conquer the world. Just look at the way things were booming, orders piling in from every land! Budd's had such a backlog that it could be sure of dividends for a couple of years if it never booked another order. Robbie said that the choicest stocks were now acquiring a scarcity value; people were putting them in safe-deposit boxes, and they no longer came on the market. "Don't sell America short!" said one half of "R and R" to the other half.

There was only one cloud in Robbie's sky, and that was his personal trouble with the business in Arabia. They talked about that at much length. Johannes advised Robbie to take his loss and get out; the place was too far away, and the factors beyond control. They had more than got back their investment, so why not call it a day? But Robbie was stubborn; it was a matter of principle. Johannes smiled and said: "I cannot afford to have principles. I am a businessman!"

All his life Lanny had sat and listened to such conversations, and learned how the world was run and how the wires were pulled. What firm of lawyers one had to employ in Washington if one wanted the American State Department to get busy with the British government and demand protection for an American oil property! What detective agency one employed if one wanted to be sure of keeping labor organizers out of a great manufacturing-plant! Or, if it was Germany, what Cabinet member one dealt with in order to get promptly the supply of rationed raw materials that one needed for export products! How to put one's earnings back into new plant in such a way as to avoid income taxes! There were no laws that shrewd businessmen couldn't find some way of getting round—and it was a good thing, because what was going to become of industry if governments kept on encroaching on all opportunities of profit?

The firm of "R and R" talked frankly in the presence of Lanny, because they didn't take any of his "radical" ideas seriously; and maybe they were right about it. Johannes looked upon the Redness in his own family as a sort of measles, German measles, perhaps, which young people had, and the earlier they had them the quicker they got over them. Robbie told how Budd's had put the Communists out of business in Connecticut, and Robin told how they were still doing it in Germany. They were using those Nazis—a dangerous weapon, but there appeared to be no other at hand. The steel and allied interests of the Fatherland were now paying a regular tribute of one-half of one percent of all their earnings into the treasury of

Adolf Hitler's party, and Johannes was paying his share; not that he liked to do it, but the emergency was extreme and a man couldn't separate himself from all his associates.

A part of that money had to be spent for arms, and Johannes had used his influence to have the Nazis purchase several thousand submachine guns which Budd's had made for the United States government during the war and which Johannes had bought at a great bargain, using cash put up by Robbie. That was the way capable businessmen took in money with both hands! Those little guns were marvels—they could be carried in one hand and fired from the shoulder like a rifle; they had been brought in through Holland canals, marked as agricultural implements, and unquestionably they had been the means of turning the tide of battle for the streets of Munich and Berlin.

VII

Esther asked Lanny to come to her room; she wanted to have a chat with him. Quite a change since he had last been in this home; then she had been relieved to see him go, but now she wanted his help. Esther wasn't the kind to be impressed by a rich marriage, but she had come to realize that while Lanny's moral code was different from hers, he had one and he lived by it. He had been right about Bess, and as a result had won Bess in a way that Esther had failed to do. Life was puzzling, and no matter how hard one tried to do right, one often blundered.

Esther was worried about her husband. She had always thought that he drank more than he should, and now he drank more and more. No one ever saw him drunk, but he depended upon liquor to sustain him, and it couldn't fail to harm him in the end. Lanny said he had seen a great deal of the same thing among the French people; they rarely got drunk, but many kept themselves mildly pickled all the time; their systems seemed to get used to it. Lanny said that Robbie drank because he was under too great a strain; he worried about his business affairs, some of which hadn't gone so well. Esther said he undertook too much, and what was the sense of it? They didn't need so much money; she saw to it that they lived within their means, and the boys had learned to do the same.

Lanny replied: "It's a kind of a game with Robbie, and he plays it too hard. It's too bad that he hasn't got some hobby."

"You don't know how hard I've tried to interest him and to help him; but there must be some lack in me. I really believe that you have more influence over him than I have."

"I don't think so, Esther." He had decided to address her thus; he couldn't very well call her "Mother" while Beauty was in town! "I have never heard Robbie speak of you except with affection and respect."

"He doesn't give me his confidence, and he resents being criticized."

"Most of us do, Esther. Robbie is proud, and he doesn't like to admit mistakes. If he takes an extra drink it's always a special case, and he wouldn't admit to himself that it's become a habit."

"That's the way men drift into it, and why I hate it so. I've tried my best to impress it upon the boys, but I don't know if I've succeeded—drinking at Yale is simply frightful."

"The boys look all right." Lanny sought to console her. They had both left for Yale a day or two ago—Junior for the law school. "The Prohibition experiment doesn't seem to have turned out very well," the stepson added.

"I hoped so much from it. Millions of women thought it was going to be the saving of our happiness; but nobody seems to pay any attention to the law."

"How does Robbie get his liquor?"

"It's the old story; 'right off the boat.' You hear the men all talking about it; each one is quite sure that his has come direct from Canada, and they swap references of their bootleggers—but how far can you trust men whose business is breaking the law?"

"Not very far, I should think."

"Robbie is careful enough when he deals with a banker, or somebody who is trying to sell him a few carloads of metal; but some plausible young fellow turns up with a tale of having just run a bargeload of Scotch into the river last night, and all the businessmen in town swallow the tale and the liquor; they bring the stuff into their homes and serve it to their families and their guests, and no one ever thinks of having a chemist analyze it!"

"They're afraid of what they might find," smiled Lanny.

"It's made the most frightful corruption in our city affairs. The bootleggers seem to have more money to spend than anybody else in town."

VIII

Esther talked for a while about Lanny and his bride, and asked about their plans. But it wasn't long before she brought back the subject of her husband. Another thing was worrying her—Robbie's playing the stock market.

"He's always done that, hasn't he?" asked the son.

"He would do what he called taking a flier; but now he plunges. He doesn't tell me about it, but I pick up hints—the way he looks at the paper, things I hear him saying over the phone. He's made a great deal of money, apparently, but at the expense of his peace of mind. And why, Lanny, why? We don't need it, and what are we going to do with it?"

"We can't stop men from taking risks, or from challenging one another. If they haven't got a real war they make an imitation one. I try to think what Robbie would be like if he wasn't playing some money game. What would he do with himself?"

Esther answered, out of her troubled soul: "There's something wrong with our education. We try to give our young people culture, and it doesn't take."

Lanny saw the traces which anxiety had left in his stepmother's features, so smooth and serene when he had first become acquainted with them. Her straight brown hair was now showing signs of gray, and there were lines about her eyes and mouth. She was a conscientious woman, and tried to play the game of life fairly; had others been unfair, or was it that the spirit of her time was too strong for her? Certainly she wasn't happy, and Robbie wasn't happy.

Had she been too strict with him? Had she resented his youthful error and punished him in her heart for it, and in so doing punished herself? She had this beautiful home, managed it efficiently, played the part of a perfect hostess, a great lady of society, a benefactor to the poor, a leader of useful civic movements; but she wasn't happy. Lanny wondered how many of these elegant homes in what were known as "exclusive residential sections" held tragedies of this slow-burning, secret kind. Lanny would have liked to ask some intimate questions: "What is your love-life with Robbie? How much trouble do you take to hold his interest? How much do you know about how to hold his interest if you want to?" Alas, he could talk about such matters with his irregular mother, but never with his tight-laced and rigid stepmother!

IX

The guests of the yacht *Bessie Budd* packed up their belongings and prepared to be transported up Long Island Sound to the richest city in the world. Her owner had business there, and Zoltan Kertezsi had arrived and was expecting Beauty's help in promoting the Detaze show. Of course, Zoltan hadn't failed to hear that the stepson of his painter had got married, nor did he overlook the advertising value of that event. He telephoned, suggesting a larger appropriation for grander show rooms, to accommodate the crowd which he felt sure would come, if only in the hope of catching a glimpse of the stepson's bride. He chuckled over Irma's having bought some of the paintings. "Tell her she wouldn't have got them so cheaply if I had known!"

Lanny bade farewell to his old Connecticut family, and prepared to meet his new Long Island one. Mrs. Barnes had returned from Europe and was waiting at their country place; to delay too long to pay his respects would have been a failure in tact. Mr. and Mrs. Dingle were also invited, but Beauty pleaded the pressure of duties in connection with the exhibition. She had lived a long while in the fashionable world, and knew when people wanted her to accept an invitation and when they hoped she'd have sense enough to decline.

She and her husband would stay in a hotel, and while he looked up the meeting-places of the God-seekers, she would renew acquaintance with the many New Yorkers whom she had met on the Riviera in the course of the years. The yacht was returning to Germany with the Robin family, where Johannes had his business and the young people their various tasks to resume. They had all had an enjoyable holiday, and promised themselves others of the sort.

Lanny and Irma were met at an East River pier and motored out to a South Shore estate for whose grandeur the bridegroom had been inadequately prepared. At last he was going to learn how really rich people lived! "Shore Acres" the place was playfully named, but it might have been called "Shore Miles." The whole great expanse had a steel fence around it, twelve feet high, with inhospitable spikes pointing outward. The buildings stood on a bluff looking out over the sea; they were of red sandstone, an adaptation of the Château de Chambord which had been built four hundred years ago for King Francis I. They had a great number of turrets, gables, and carved chimneys; in the American replica these latter had no openings, the house having a central heating system. The fastidious Lanny didn't like buildings that were too big for comfort, and he thought more of the people who had created a type of architecture than of those who "adapted" it.

The place was only about ten years old, but already the interior had been redecorated—just a few weeks before its owner had dropped dead. The entrance hall was finished in white Vermont marble, and would have served any moderate-sized city for a railroad waiting-room. The flunkies didn't line up to receive the bride and groom as they would have done at Stubendorf, but perhaps that was because Lanny's new mother-in-law hadn't heard of the practice. Over this royal domain the large stout widow of the electricity king presided with admirable energy. The place now belonged to her daughter, but she ran it, and strode through the echoing corridors smoking her large dark cigars and keeping track of everything that went on.

Lanny had heard about living *en prince*, and now he had to do it and like it. He had a suite of apartments, with a four-poster bed in which several princes had been born. (Its pedigree was on the headboard.) His upholstery was of such exquisite silk that he was embarrassed to sit on it, and certainly he would never put his feet on the sofa. His bathtub was sunk in the floor and he descended into it by three wide steps, having ruby-red lights set into the rises so that he could see where he was going. The walls, floor, and tub were of the most wonderful green marble he had ever beheld, and all the fixtures of the tub and the plumbing, at least to the point where they disappeared into the floor, were of silver, and it wasn't plated. When you turned the faucets, the water shot into the tub as if from a fire-hose. Irma's apartment, which adjoined his, had similar equipment, but her marble had the pale pink tinge of la France roses and the fixtures were of fourteen-carat gold. You might refuse to believe it, and if you had done so during the life of the owner, he would have given you the name of the concern which made them. This particular suite had belonged to J. Paramount himself, and he had been a gay dog; the first time Lanny sat on the toilet seat he was startled by pretty little chimes ringing behind his back, and they didn't stop until he got up.

A more than life-sized portrait of the financial genius confronted you in the entrance hall, and the young art expert studied it attentively. It was the work of a popular painter, who had made an honest effort to report what he saw. "J.P.," as he was still referred to, had been a robust man and a fighter; he had that sort of jaw and eye. Hair and eyes had been black, and if he had grown a mustache and beard he might have made a pirate of the Jolly Roger epoch. His look was grim, but you could imagine the eyes lighting up, and you had to imagine a persuasive tongue, which had convinced the guardians of treasure that he was the wizard who could take one dollar and put it together with another dollar, and cause a brood of baby dollars to come into existence in a few days or weeks. He had performed that biologico-financial miracle over and over—he had never failed a single time. The huge corporation pyramids which he had constructed still stood, and "the Street" was convinced that they would stand forever as monuments to this master manipulator.

Another monument was this palace; and confronting the lifelike portrait Lanny wondered, was this hard-driving spirit watching him somewhere in limbo? Challenging him, perhaps: "By what right do you sleep in my bed and splash in my bathtub and listen to my chimes?" Would he consider Lanny Budd a proper successor, fitted to wear his heavy armor and draw his mighty bow? Certainly the young master didn't fancy himself in the role. Lanny hadn't yet found out just where Wall Street was situated!

X

Irma, having spent half her life in this palace, took it as a matter of course; so Lanny must try to think of it as home. Talking to him in London, the majestic Mrs. Barnes had urged him to do this; she had made it plain that she was prepared to accept him and do her best to make him happy. Not an easy speech for a domineering woman to make; but she was the dowager, and had to humble herself. Never again would Lanny hear that dreadful word "bastard." He had won the fight; he might take charge of the mansion, or he might carry Irma away. It was the mother's hope that the pride and glory of the great domain would capture the young man's fancy and win him away from the insane idea of taking Irma to inhabit a "cottage" in that pathetic little property on the Riviera.

This conflict of purposes became more plain as soon as Fanny Barnes made certain that her daughter was pregnant. Then it developed into a struggle over a grandchild, and it was going to be waged not merely between Lanny and his mother-in-law, but between two mothers-in-law. Each had a home which she wished to offer to the heir-apparent; and who was going to decide which was the better? Who was going to find any fault with the manner of Lanny's upbringing? Let that rash one keep out of Beauty's way! On the other hand, what would be said to that depraved person who might hint that Irma was anything short of perfect? Look at her! Ask the world about her!

Lanny's intention was to wait until after the exhibition, and then take his bride by the first steamer that was properly equipped for the transporting of a princess. Take no chance of delaying until someone could argue that her condition made travel unsafe! She had told him that she would prefer Juan over any other place to live, and so Juan it was to be. Meanwhile he would be the soul of politeness, and accept with gratitude whatever courtesies might be offered. But he wouldn't change his plans.

On this huge estate there was no useful thing that a young master could do without trespassing; but there were innumerable forms of play. He and Irma might ride horseback, something which he had enjoyed in England now and then. They might play tennis on beautifully kept clay courts, or, when it rained, on an indoor court with a wood floor. They might swim in a well-warmed indoor pool. There were a "game room" with pool and billiards, a bowling-alley, a squash court—also a man in attendance who apparently had nothing to do until someone came along to play. There was a music room with a magnificent piano, and a smaller one had been installed in Lanny's apartment. All these cabinets full of scores—had they been here in J.P.'s day, or had Mrs. Fanny instructed some music-store to send out one thousand of the world's masterpieces for the pianoforte?

The only trouble was that Lanny had no time to make use of these treasures. The establishment was built for company, and Irma's young friends came pouring in to welcome her and to satisfy their curiosity about the lucky man. Lanny had to be on hand, have on the right clothes, and take his part in whatever was proposed: riding or motoring, tennis or squash parties, a sail if the day happened to be warm and the breeze right. There were teas and dinners and dances in honor of the bridal pair; and always reporters hanging onto the skirts of these events, seeking interviews and writing up the gossip from which tens of thousands of debutantes would learn how to do the right thing in the right way, and millions of salesladies and stenographers would have their imaginations fed with dreams of luxury. The time was past when Lanny Budd could amuse himself by talking to any stranger who came along. From now on he must remember that the stranger might be a newspaperman or a spy—for any item about what the husband of Irma Barnes was doing or saying might be sold to one of the "tabs" for five or ten dollars.

XI

Lanny's position was that of a prince consort, such as the husband of Queen Victoria. He had performed his first and principal duty, he had planted the seed, and now he had to watch and tend it carefully. He would escort his bride wherever she wished to go; unthinkable that he should refuse to do so—it would have started a scandal in no time. He was a member of the "younger set" of Long Island, and would learn to know a large group of handsome and fashionably clad playboys and girls, most of whom would never grow up. He would listen to their eager chatter, having to do for the most part with themselves and their playmates. He would learn to know the various personalities, and be able to understand the jokes having to do with Aggie's recent motor mishap or Tubby's excess of *embonpoint*. They drank a great deal, but rarely lost their ability to get out of the cabaret and tell the chauffeur where to take them. They had built a play world, and were gay in it, persistently and conscientiously. There was nothing they resisted with such determination as the impulse to take anything seriously.

Also Lanny had the duty of meeting two new families, that of his mother-in-law and that of his deceased father-in-law. He had to be polite to them all, and try to satisfy them as to Irma's future. J.P.'s younger brother Joseph was important, because he was one of three trustees who under the terms of the will had the handling of Irma's estate. She got the income, but couldn't spend any of the principal without their consent. The other two trustees had been confidential employees of the father, and all three of them had full-time duties. Just to keep track of twenty-three million dollars and its earnings was quite a business, and the estate had a large suite of offices. The duties of the trustees consisted of clipping coupons and depositing dividend checks, keeping books and rendering elaborate quarterly statements, which Irma turned over to her mother unopened.

Mr. Horace Vandringham was the gentleman who had sent the cablegram to his sister in Cannes. Thanks to Emily Chattersworth, Lanny knew the text of that message; but not a word was said about it now, and Uncle Horace would do his best to atone for his excruci-

ating error. He was older than his sister, and was an "operator" in
Wall Street; that is, he not merely bought stocks and waited for
them to go up, but he got other people interested with him, they
formed a "syndicate," and Uncle Horace caused the stocks to move
in the direction he desired. If he was "long" on the stock, he would
circulate rumors of mergers, stock dividends, and "split-ups"; if he
was "short," he would cause the public to hear that the company
was in trouble and that the next dividend was to be passed. If his
judgment was good he made a "killing"; and apparently it had been,
for he lived lavishly and talked money in large quantities. Robbie
knew about him and said he was a "shark," which wasn't necessarily
a term of reprobation in Wall Street.

To Lanny this new uncle presented himself as a "character." He
was big and burly, bald on top, and the top was as rosy as his face.
He was full of energy which could not be repressed. When he
walked you got the same sort of surprise that you would from
watching an elephant in the forest; you wouldn't have imagined that
such a bulky body could move so fast. He swung his arms vehe-
mently, and rocked from side to side even as he strode across a
room. He ate violently, laughed loudly, talked a great deal, and was
positive in his opinions. He was evidently trying to be agreeable to
this new nephew, who might be in position to turn his sister out of
her home; he would ask what Lanny thought about some matter,
but it was no good trying to reply, because Uncle Horace couldn't
help interrupting and telling him. Lanny gathered that these big
Wall Street men were used to having their own way.

Gradually the bridegroom discovered the situation between the
two families which he had acquired. The Vandringhams were real
aristocrats; that is to say, they belonged to the old Dutch New
Yorkers who had had money for generations. But they had lost most
of their money, and Fanny had married the upstart Barnes and been
unhappy. Now she looked down upon all the Barneses, and favored
her brother, who was the real gentleman. She wanted Irma to be a
Vandringham and not a Barnes; if ever Irma manifested any tend-
ency of which her mother disapproved—which happened not infre-
quently—that was the evil Barnes blood showing itself. The mother

resented the indignity of the estate's having to be handled by the Barneses and not by the Vandringhams. How much more money Horace would have made for them!

Also Lanny had to meet the dependents, a matter calling for tact. J.P. had been charitable, and his widow carried on the tradition. Irma's former governess and the master's former confidential secretary enjoyed a sort of demi-status; they dined with the family except when there was company, and then they whisked themselves out of sight without having to be told. An older maiden sister of Fanny and two aunts had what you might call a three-quarter status; they disappeared only when there was important company.

Also there lived in various quarters on the estate a number of what you might call half-servants, elderly retired attendants who performed light services when occasion arose. One of Mrs. Fanny's many tasks was to find things for them to do—for she said she hated to see people idle or things going to waste. She would set them to performing offices for one another; if one man had to be taken to the dentist, another drove him; if one woman fell ill, another nursed her. It might be that the pair hated each other's guts, but they would do what they were told. One and all, these persons desired to be of service to Lanny, and their humility, their gratitude for being alive, seemed pitiable to him. They didn't fall on their knees and put their foreheads in the dust when he passed, but it seemed to him that spiritually they did this, and it was one of the reasons why he found being a prince consort so dubious a satisfaction. But he was in for it. He couldn't change the world, or the fact that he was Mr. Irma Barnes!

37

Café Society

I

THE Detaze show opened in the second week of October, and Lanny owed it to Zoltan and his mother to be on hand. Irma was pleased to accompany him, for she had found the London show amusing, and had met a number of distinguished persons. It is the pleasantest time of the year in New York; the weather is at its best, the theaters are opening, "everybody" is back from the country or from abroad.

The business manager engaged the most expensive suite in the most expensive hotel. Impossible to live any other way, and it would have been unkind of Lanny to suggest it. Was his wife to change her system of living just because he was a poor man? Here was a smooth-running machine ready to carry him through life, and all he had to do was not to interfere with the experts who were running it. The rooms were engaged and the bill sent to Shore Acres, and Irma wouldn't even know what was being paid.

She had learned to do things in a certain way, and he was expected to do the same and forget it. She carried little money in her handbag, just enough for tips and such small items. For the rest she said: "Charge it." In restaurants and hotels she signed slips, and bills were mailed to the estate and the manager attended to them. Now it was Lanny's duty to sign slips, because it took one more burden off his wife's hands, and incidentally it looked better. Under this arrangement he would never spend any money of his own unless he was away from her—and she didn't want him ever to be away.

How silly to bother about such matters, or to try to discuss them! She had told him that she cared nothing about money, and she

775

meant it; why couldn't he mean it? She had got the money by accident, and she had to spend it, because there was nothing else to do with it. His happiness was hers, they had promised to be one in all things, and didn't that include money? Let things "ride," and talk about something worth while!

At home it had been one of Lanny's pleasures to drive his own car; and that was all right at the estate, there were plenty of cars, and one of the best was called his. But in the city you had to have a chauffeur to drive, or where would you park? If you drew up in front of a hotel and it was raining, you and your wife wanted to step out under the porte-cochere and forget the car until it was time to leave. Lanny had to learn to sit in the back seat and make himself agreeable to the ladies.

So, in one way after another, Irma's money functioned as a steamroller, making a path for itself and flattening out everything that stood in its way. Did Lanny have any idea about privacy? Did he want to be let alone? When their manager engaged rooms in a hotel, the hotel manager at once notified the press, because it would mean advertising for the hotel; so when the princely pair arrived, the photographers were waiting. Would they kindly oblige just for a minute? It would have been ungracious to say no.

And then the reporters, wishing to know what were their plans, why had they come to town? As it happened, Lanny had come to promote a showing of his late stepfather's art. That was a worthy and dignified purpose, so he told for perhaps the thousandth time the story of a French painter who had had his face burned off in the first year of the war, and had sat in his studio and painted his greatest pictures wearing a silk mask. That was a good story, and the papers would use it; but also their readers wanted to know, what was Irma wearing, how did Lanny find it in America, and how did he enjoy being the husband of a glamour girl? He said that he enjoyed it greatly, and forbore to mention being a Pink, or to record any objections to living in the royal suite of the Ritzy-Waldorf.

II

The show opened, and it was what New York called a "knock-out," or, if you wanted to be elegant, a "wow." It had everything that New York required; real art, which was in the Luxembourg and had received the *cachet* of the leading critics in Paris and London. The melodramatic story attached thereto served for the journalists to write about and for people to tell to one another as they looked at the pictures; it was like having an exciting program for a musical composition. Also, there was the painter's fashionable but slightly risqué widow, with two portraits hanging on the walls; his stepson and the latter's bride—they weren't hanging on the walls, but were an important part of the show nonetheless. Back of all this was the shrewd and skillful Zoltan, working to make the utmost of each of these various features.

The crowds on the opening day included a great part of the distinguished names in the worlds of both art and fashion. The press treated it like the opening night of the opera, when they publish two articles, one telling about the music and the singers, and the other about those present, their diamond corsages and ruby tiaras and double ropes of pearls. The critics said that the landscapes of Detaze represented a conventional but solid talent, while his later work, the product of the stresses of the war, could fairly be described as revelations of the human spirit. They called *Fear* a masterpiece, and said that *Sister of Mercy* contained real nobility combined with those elements of popularity which had caused it to be likened to Whistler's painting of his mother.

The result was that on the second day of the show Zoltan reported to Beauty an offer of fifteen thousand dollars for this picture, and a few days later the bidder, a great copper magnate, doubled his offer. It was a sore temptation for Beauty, but Lanny said no, he would never part with any of the paintings of his mother. Beauty didn't overlook the fact that they constituted an inexhaustible source of social prestige; she had had such a good time showing them and being shown in Paris and London, and she looked forward to Berlin and Munich and Vienna, Boston and Chicago and Los Angeles—perhaps even Newcastle, Connecticut, who could say?

They had greatly increased the prices of the paintings since the success in London; but it made no apparent difference to the public. New York was full of people who had money, and who felt about it as Irma did—what was it good for but to spend? It was the theory upon which the whole economic system was based; the more you spent, the more you made. It worked for the community, in that it kept money in circulation and goods pouring off the transmission belts of the factories. It worked for the individual, in that it brought him to the front, made friends for him, showed that he was on top of the wave, that his business was flourishing and his credit good. The maxim that nothing succeeds like success was old, but it never seemed so true as on the island of Manhattan in October of the year 1929.

The paintings were selling. Pretty soon there wouldn't be any left, and there couldn't be any more exhibitions! Zoltan raised the prices all the way down the line; presently he raised them again; but still they sold. People wanted to pay high prices; it was something to brag about. "You see that Detaze? I paid ninety-five hundred for it at the one-man show last year. Widener offered me twelve thousand a few days later, but I said no." The bank president or cement magnate would puff on his fat cigar and expatiate: "There's no better investment than a great painting. I keep it insured, and it's as good as cash in the bank. It may be worth more than my whole business some day. You know about that fellow—very tragic story— he had his face burned off in the war, and he used to sit on the Cap d'Antibes, wearing a mask, and paint the sea and the rocks." It wasn't quite so, but that didn't matter.

Irma's rich and fashionable friends—she had no others; how could she?—all came to see the pictures. All wanted to hear Lanny tell about them, and all said pretty much the same things. When Irma got bored, the pair would go out and have tea at one of the smart hotels, and dance for a while, and perhaps give a dinner party, and afterward return to the show rooms, because Zoltan had mentioned some important person who was coming. Irma might bring her dinner guests, for it was very "smart" indeed to be associated with paintings which caused the whole town to be talking about her husband and his mother. The glamour girl enjoyed being admired, and had sense enough to know that it was better to be admired for something else than her father's money. The town was "lousy" with rich people—such was the language of the younger set—but not many of the lice had a genius in the family. Also it was a good way to meet the whispers about "bastardy"; what was a social disgrace in America became romantic when associated with the art life of Paris.

III

After the show the happy young couple would repair to one of the night clubs. These had become elaborate establishments, decorated in gay modernistic style and serving every kind of liquor, just as if there was no such thing as Prohibition. In some you couldn't get a table unless you were considered a person of consequence, and you paid a "cover charge" as high as twenty dollars. There was a band of jazz musicians, and a clever and sophisticated master of ceremonies conducted what was called a "floor show," with singers and dancers who received high prices. From time to time the patrons danced; the saxophone moaned, the trumpets squealed, the drums thumped in desperate efforts to wake them up, but they danced monotonously like people walking in their sleep. Lanny had a feeling of pity for the entertainers, who worked so frantically to keep things going, to produce what was called "pep." The jaded patrons must continually have a new stimulus, otherwise they might stop to think—and what would they think?

When Lanny and Irma entered one of these places it was by appointment, and the moment they appeared the spotlight would be turned upon them, telling everybody in the place that celebrities were arriving. When they were seated, the master of ceremonies would make a little speech about them, and they would be expected to arise in the white glare and "take a bow." If they had been actors or people of that sort they would have made a little speech; but haughty society people, not knowing what to say, stood upon their dignity. After that the singers would sing to them, the comedians would interpolate a kidding remark or two, the Mexican guitar players would come and serenade them, the Gypsy dancers would ogle Lanny and display their seductive curves; the darlings of fashion would remain the center of proceedings until a movie star or a champion pugilist appeared.

The best of the show was reserved until after the theaters let out, when the place became crowded. Many people ate their principal meal of the day then, and paid the highest prices for the fanciest foods. There would be a great deal of drinking and excitement, and now and then a row, which was handled swiftly and efficiently by experts. Shootings were rare, and if you thought otherwise it was just because they got the headlines. Mostly it was what New York called fun, and it went on until the small hours of morning; free and easy, promiscuous, and democratic in the sense that if you had the "mazuma" you were as good as anybody who had no more. It was "café society," and in the public eye and in public esteem it had entirely replaced the old, dignified, and exclusive "Four Hundred" of pre-war days. The latter kind still existed, but no one paid any heed to it; its members might as well have been so many mummies in the Metropolitan Museum of Art.

Lanny, who knew life in France, now observed it in the land of unlimited possibilities. He remembered how he had met Olivie Hellstein, daughter of a great Jewish banking-house; what formalities had been necessary, what careful inquiries had been made. But in New York he might have been introduced to the heiress of the Barnes fortune by almost anybody in a night club. If he had had the nerve he might have come up to her and said: "Hello, Irma, I'm Lanny Budd—don't you remember me?" She couldn't be sure whether she remembered him or not, for she met so many young men, and if one was handsome and presentable it would be too bad to hurt his feelings. Any young man who had the right clothes and could make witty remarks might become a café celebrity, and have no trouble in finding some lady who had money to burn and would be glad to have him tend the fire. And it wasn't only in New York;

it was said that there wasn't a town of ten thousand inhabitants in the United States that didn't have a night club.

Lanny's duty as the guardian of the seed was to see that Irma ate the proper food and didn't drink too much. Also it was advisable for him to be right there at her side, leaving no space for any other male to slip in between. If he danced with some other girl, right away some agreeable youth would take his seat and begin what was called "making a pass" at Irma. Unless he was drunk, he wouldn't say anything offensive; on the contrary, he would be as charming as possible. He would make joking remarks about marriage, notoriously a tiresome and trying affair, a theme for banter on stage and screen; he would try to find out whether Irma was in love with her husband, or whether she was disposed to play with the idea of an adventure. If she showed herself reserved, all right, he would move on to the next young matron. Nobody took offense, for it was a game that all were playing. What was your money worth, if you couldn't have any fun?

IV

Lanny and his bride would return to their royal suite at two or three in the morning, and sleep until ten or eleven. Then they would have their baths, and have breakfast brought to them, also the morning papers. They would look first to see if there was anything about the show, and themselves as part of it; after that they would read about their friends in the society columns, and about the figures of stage and screen whom they had met or were planning to meet. Irma would want to know about the line-up for several of the football games in which friends were playing; and that would be all for her. Lanny would have liked to know about the war in China or the senatorial election in France, but it would be hard to find out without being rude, because Irma wanted to talk about the people they had met the night before, especially the dashing young man of fashion who had made a "pass" at her. If Lanny didn't listen, she would begin to think that the jokes about marriage had some basis in reality.

"Feathers" would come—that was Miss Featherstone, the social secretary—bringing a list of appointments made and requested. Then it would be time for the dressmakers and the *marchands de modes*— an urgent matter, since Irma had fallen behind on account of having eloped, and being on a yacht, and visiting at Newcastle. The urgency was the more extreme because the changes in style were so drastic. There was a great deal of complaint about them in the newspapers, and among the so-called intellectuals, who had fought hard for the emancipation of women and now saw them slipping backward. Some were saying they wouldn't stand for such absurdities; but the makers of fashion smiled, knowing that women would wear what they were told to, because there wouldn't be anything else in the stores.

But could you imagine that, ten years after women had got the ballot, after they had established their right to smoke in public places, to have their hair cut in men's barber shops, and to drink in men's bars—they would be going back to wearing skirts that touched the filthy sidewalks? And a thing called a "bertha," a deep lace collar, almost a cape, sewed to the neck of one's dress and hanging down to one's elbows! And "stays," a polite name for corsets, tight at the waist and restricting one's breathing! Up to recently a woman's whole summer costume might weigh as little as twenty-two ounces; but now there were going to be bows and ruffles and "princess slips," and eleven yards of material to a gown instead of four. Hats were going to be large, gloves long—and hair also. Back to Queen Victoria!

Most women went to their dressmaker, but not the heiress of the Barnes fortune. The "creator" whom she favored had a living model as much like Irma as possible, and fitted the "creations" on her. The work had begun as soon as Irma reached home, and now *couturier* and model would come to her hotel, and the finished product would be put on the model, and Irma would recline on a chaise-longue and survey the effect. It cost money to get your clothes that way, but it saved time and it got you the best. Each costume had a name of its own: Antoinette, Glorieuse, l'Arlésienne, and so on; each was sold with a guarantee that it would be unique. Of course others would steal the idea as soon as Irma appeared in it, but that wouldn't matter, for by the time that duplicates could be made, Irma would be done with hers and have passed it on to her subordinates.

It would have been unkind if Lanny had failed to assist in these habilitating ceremonials. He had such good taste, and so much experience at that kind of thing, ever since he was a small boy. He didn't approve of the new styles, but it was no good trying to fight them; if you didn't wear them it meant that you hadn't been able to afford new things—that was what "styles" were for. The steamroller passed over Lanny Budd again, and in the evening he escorted to the Detaze show room a lady with an elaborate lace train which compelled all the picture lovers to stop looking at pictures and look at her—if only in order to keep from treading on her train!

Such was the life; and Lanny was settled in his own mind that they were going to get out of it. He had the excuse of her pregnancy; surely she couldn't expect to wear "stays" after this fourth month! Later on, he would try to get her to nurse the baby, as Beauty had done with Marceline. But what after that? She wouldn't go on having babies indefinitely, not even to oblige the president of Budd Gunmakers. Would this crazy cabaret world continue to draw her like a moth to a candle-flame? He saw how excited she was over it, what pleasure she got from the spotlight, from seeing people turn their heads to stare when she entered a hotel lobby or any public place. She enjoyed giving interviews, and he saw that she was toying with the idea of having ideas; she would ask her husband: "Do you think I ought to say that people attach too much importance to money?" He advised her to go further and say that people were drinking too much, and that she herself was ordering mineral water. In her innocence she mentioned a certain brand, and Uncle Horace was amused, and told her that the manufacturers would pay her several thousand dollars for permission to publish that statement. A funny world to be in!

V

Lanny Budd, desiring to be known as a proper and dignified husband, satisfactory to Budds, Barneses, and Vandringhams, guarded his words and actions carefully. But he was living in a pitiless glare, and in spite of his best efforts he was drawn into a disagreeable bit of publicity. He escorted Irma into her favorite night haunt, and when they entered, a man sprang up from a table and came to them, calling Lanny's name, and then Irma's. At first Lanny didn't know him, but then realized that it was Dick Oxnard, the society painter whose villa he had visited on the Riviera and found inhabited by so many fair ladies. Nearly six years had passed since then, and it was hard to imagine such a change in a man; the fair blond giant no longer looked young and godlike, he looked middle-aged and decayed; half his curly hair was gone, and his face was bloated—he evidently had been drinking heavily.

But he still had the charm of manner, the gay laugh, and the prestige as a member of one of New York's old families. Everybody loved him, because he had been so generous and kind. "Well, well, Irma!" he exclaimed. "So this is the lucky fellow!" He caught her by the hand—evidently he knew her well, perhaps since her childhood. He caught Lanny with his other hand. "You lucky young devil, I spotted you for a winner, and now you've drawn the *grand prix!* Come over to my table and meet my friends!"

It was a public scene; the spotlight was on them. Lanny might have withdrawn his hand and said: "Excuse us, but we have other guests." It happened, however, that they didn't, and Irma appeared quite ready to go with her friend, drunk or sober. The husband followed, and came to a table well supplied with liquor, though it was decorously poured from a teapot into cups. There were three young ladies seated at the table, refined in appearance and elegantly dressed—but that didn't mean much. Was this free-and-easy painter intending to introduce Irma to some of his tarts? If he had said "Mary, and Jane," and so on, in his offhand manner, Lanny was prepared to lead his wife away. But no, all three had proper names. There was a vacant chair alongside the host's, but when Irma started to slip into it he exclaimed: "No, don't sit in that. Gertie has wetted it, the little bitch!"

Such was conversation among the smart set in their teacups. Lanny flushed with annoyance; but evidently Irma was used to the vagaries of the boys when they were "well lit up"; she laughed with the others, and a waiter hurriedly pulled the chair away and put another in its place.

"Why haven't you been to my studio?" demanded the painter, of Lanny.

"Have you a studio in New York?"

"A fine way to treat your friends! Tell him, Irma, have I a studio in New York?"

"Indeed you have, Dick; a grand one."

"I have painted some screens that will put your eyes out."

"I'll come," said Lanny, "as soon as the Detaze show is over."

"I've been meaning to get around to it. But there's so much they call art in this damned town. Irma, have you heard about the new bathroom I've painted for Betty Barbecue?"

"No, tell me."

"I've made her the finest sunken bath in the modern world. You're in a grotto at the bottom of the sea that seems made of precious enamel, all turquoise-blue and Nile green. Brilliant sea anemones grow up from the floor, and the crimson starfish and spiny sea creatures swim or crawl on the walls—by God, when the hidden lights are turned on it takes your breath away!"

"Well, I surely want to see it if she'll let me in."

"She's got to let you in! It's part of the bargain; she has to let anybody see it at any time."

"Even when she's in the bath?"

"She doesn't get in the bath. Would she take the risk of splashing the finest piece of interior decoration in New York?"

Oxnard was all right while he talked about art, and all right while he talked about Lanny. He made a joke of the fact that Irma's husband had come to his home and been so shocked that he never returned. He told Irma that if a good moral boy was what she wanted she had got him; the prettiest little blondine you ever saw had tried to ride off in his car and he had turned her down cold. Irma looked at Lanny affectionately and was glad to have this excellent report.

But then matters became less pleasant. The unfortunate female creature who went by the name of Gertie showed up at the table, which apparently she had left in a hurry. Dick Oxnard was in the midst of quaffing a cup of champagne when he espied her, and he set down the cup with a bang. "You dirty little bitch, get out of here!" he shouted. "Go on home to your kennel and don't come out till you're house-broke!" The poor child—she was little more than that—flushed in an agony of humiliation; tears came into her eyes, and she fled, followed by a stream of the foulest language that Lanny had ever heard in English. He knew a lot of it in Provençal from having played with the fisherboys; but he assumed that Irma didn't know it in any language, and being a good moral boy he didn't care to have her learn it.

He rose from the table and said: "Come on," and took her by the hand and led her to a remote part of the room. It meant that he had to summon the head-waiter and ask for a table; a conspicuous action, and a blow in the face of his host.

"Disgusting!" he exclaimed, when they were alone.

"Poor fellow!" said Irma. "He doesn't know what he's doing. He's drinking himself crazy, and nobody can do anything for him."

"Well, we couldn't stay there and let him drag us through such scenes."

"I suppose not; but it's too bad we have to do it in such an open way. He's furious about it."

"In the morning he won't know it happened," said the husband.

VI

They were seated, and ordered their supper, and Lanny was prepared to put the alcoholic unfortunate out of his mind. But Irma was so placed that she could watch him, and she said: "He's just sitting there glowering at you."

"Don't let him see you looking."

Their supper came, and they were supposed to eat it, but Irma had lost her appetite. "He's still not doing a thing but just sitting there."

"Pretend you don't see him, please."

"I'm afraid of him."

"I don't think he could do much damage in his condition."

A minute later the girl exclaimed: "He's getting up, Lanny! He's coming over here!"

"Don't pay any attention to him."

It took some nerve to sit with one's back turned and pretend to be eating supper, but that was what Lanny thought the situation called for. When the glowering blond giant was within a few feet of him, Irma stood up and put herself between them. Of course that made it necessary for Lanny to rise, too.

"So you think you're too good for me!" exclaimed the painter.

"Please, Dick, please!" pleaded the woman. "Don't make a scene."

"Who made a scene? Haven't I got a right to send a little bitch away from my table if I want to?"

"Please don't shout, Dick. We're old family friends and we don't want to quarrel."

"You were my friend before you ever met that damned little sissy. You come back to my table and let him stay here."

"Please, Dick, he's my husband."

"A hell of a husband!"

"Please be a gentleman and do what I ask. Go back to your own table and let us alone."

A critical moment. Some men would have pushed a wife aside and let the fellow have one on the point of the chin; but Lanny was sorry for this wreck of a man, and didn't wish to forget that he was or had been a genius, and had given Lanny a beautiful and valuable painting which was hanging in Bienvenu.

The drunken man raised his arm as if to push Irma away; and of course if he did that Lanny would have to stop him somehow. But at that moment Providence intervened in the shape of two husky gentlemen, one on either side of the belligerent painter. Some such form of *deus ex machina* has to be at hand in places where liquor is sold; in fashionable night spots they are immaculately clad, and never do any more damage than necessary, but they are capable, and the bulges of their shoulders are not cotton stuffing.

Lanny was relieved, and said: "Will you kindly ask this gentleman to leave our table and stay away?"

"Please, Mr. Oxnard, come back to your own table," said one of the "bouncers."

"So the little skunk has to holler for help!" exclaimed Oxnard. The men began to impel him, gently but firmly; apparently he had sense enough to know that he had to do what they told him—doubtless he had had experiences of the sort before. He made just enough noise to let the diners know what he thought of Lanny Budd, but not enough to cause the bouncers to "give him the works." They escorted him to his table, and one seated himself alongside and continued to speak soothing words. That was better than throwing him out, because he had many influential friends—and also he owed a considerable bill.

It was the thing known as a "scene." The spotlight had not been turned on it, but many people had watched it. The general opinion was that Lanny hadn't played a very glorious part, and so it appeared in the tabloids and the radio gossip. He tried not to let it worry him, and was satisfied that Irma appreciated his self-restraint. His comment was: "I wish we didn't have to go to those places." Furthermore he said: "I'll sure be glad when we return to Bienvenu and can get to bed before morning."

VII

Letters came to Lanny, reminding him of the life which he had lived, and which now seemed far away. Bess wrote, telling him of their rather stormy voyage and enclosing the program and press notices of a concert at which Hansi had played the Mendelssohn concerto with great *éclat*. "Hansi says he was playing it at Juan when Uncle Jesse came in and made a Red out of him!" How many ages ago had that been?

Rick wrote to say that he had found a small publishing-house that was willing to bring out his unorthodox book. He reported that Marceline was thriving, and enclosed a few lines from the child. Rick and Nina promised to come to Juan after Christmas as usual. Continuing, Rick referred to an event of the date on which he was writing: Ramsay MacDonald, for the second time Prime Minister of

Britain, was sitting on a log in a camp at Rapidan, Virginia, discussing peace and disarmament with President Hoover. Rick said he hoped they were getting somewhere, but he was losing faith in politicians. Even if Ramsay knew what to do, would Herbert let him?

Then a letter from Kurt in Stubendorf. He had a second son, and enclosed a snapshot. He was working hard on his first symphony, and sketched the opening theme, resolute and bold, *alla marcia*. He congratulated Lanny on his marriage, and hoped it would bring him happiness; he added that such great amounts of money put a heavy strain on the strongest character. Kurt might have said: "I know that yours will be equal to the test." But Lanny knew that Kurt didn't think that. Lanny himself wasn't sure about it, and he hoped that German newspapers didn't report the doings of café society in New York.

Kurt wrote: "I have just come back from Munich, where I met our Führer and heard him deliver a most inspiring speech. I have no hope that it will do any good to tell you about it, but mark my word that we have the movement of the future, and the man to lead Europe out of its present mess. If you don't find what you are looking for among the New York plutocracy, bring your wife and spend Christmas with us, and give Heinrich a chance to tell you about the youth movement he is helping to build." Lanny thought about that in the brief intervals when he had time to think about anything; he certainly wasn't satisfied with what he was finding among the aforesaid "plutocracy."

Also a letter from Lincoln Steffens, who was in San Francisco, writing his autobiography. Stef wrote notes to his friends in a tight little script that was as good as a crossword puzzle; if you once got going you might have quite a run of luck, but if you stopped for any single word you were lost. Stef said he had just met his little boy after quite an interval and found it exciting. He advised Lanny to have a boy as soon as possible. He said that he had known J.P. very well in the old days, and was indebted to him for taking him on the inside of the "merger racket." He concluded by saying: "If you are in the market, take my advice and get out, for the tower is now so high and leaning so far that one more stone may send it toppling.

You are too young to remember the panic of 1907, but after it was over a friend of mine explained it by saying: 'Somebody asked for a dollar.' Wall Street is in a condition now where it would break if somebody asked for a dime."

Lanny wasn't "in the market"; he was in pictures and matrimony, and that was enough. He forwarded this letter to his father, with a transcription written on the back. Robbie's reply was: "Just to show how much I think of your Red friend's judgment, I have purchased another thousand shares of telephone stock. It was up to 304 and I got it at 287½, which looks mighty good to me!"

That was the way they all felt, and the way they were acting; it was a phenomenon currently known as the "Great Bull Market," and people laughed at you if you tried to restrain them. Everywhere you went they were talking about stocks; everywhere they told about profits they had made, or were going to make next week. There was a "Translux," a device by which the ticker figures were shown on a translucent screen, in nearly every branch broker's office; such an office was to be found in most of the hotels where the rich gathered, and you would see crowds of men and women watching the figures. If it was during market hours, one after another would hurry off to a telephone to give an order to his broker. It was the same in every city and town; hardly one without a broker's office, and market quotations were given over the radio at frequent intervals. Farmers and ranchers were phoning their buying and selling orders; doctors and lawyers and merchants, their secretaries and errand boys, their chauffeurs and bootblacks—all were following the market reports, reading what the newsapers told them, eavesdropping for "tips" or following their "hunches." The country had got used to hearing about "five-million-share days" on the stock exchange, and took that for "prosperity."

VIII

Irma had become rather tired of listening to people saying the same things about the paintings of Marcel Detaze; and so, to tell the truth, had Lanny. One morning Irma said: "Mother's on the way to town and we're going to see what's in the shops. Would you like to go with us?" Lanny replied: "What I want is to take a long walk and look at New York. I don't see enough from the window of a limousine."

He set out from that temple *de luxe*, the Ritzy-Waldorf, in the direction where he knew the sun rose, though he couldn't see it from the bottom of these artificial canyons. He had learned how one half lived, and now he would observe the other half. In London it was the East End, here it was the East Side. What tropism guided the poor toward the rising sun? Was it because they got up early and saw it, while the rich didn't begin life till afternoon?

Anyhow, here were swarms of people; in O. Henry's day the Four Million, now the Seven Million. What was the limit to their crowding onto this narrow island? What was the force that would stop them? Fire, or earthquake, or bombs, perhaps? Or just plain suffocation? Some wit had said that the aim of every country boy was to get enough money to go and live in New York so that he could get enough money to go and live in the country.

Baghdad on the Subway! Lanny had read stories about it when he was young, and now he looked for the types, and it seemed to him that all were types. Nearly everybody walked fast; to stroll meant either a down-and-out or a policeman. Everybody was intent upon his own affairs, and stared straight ahead out of a thin, pale, intense face. If anybody bumped into you he didn't have time to excuse himself, he just dodged and went on. If you were in trouble, and stopped somebody to ask the way, he would come out of his trance of money-making, and tell you in a friendly enough manner where you were and how to get to the place of your desire; but as a rule it was understood that nobody had time for politeness.

Lanny came to the river, which he had seen from the deck of the *Bessie Budd*. The frontage had been given up to dingy tenements and sheds, but now the rich were taking sections for their penthouses. It made an immediate and rather startling juxtaposition of riches and poverty. Not so wise of the rich, Lanny thought—but doubtless they would get the poor cleared out very soon. If they wanted anything, they took it. What else did it mean to be rich?

He turned back into the interior and strolled south. Block after block, and they all seemed alike; mile after mile of dingy houses with brownstone fronts; if it hadn't been for the sun, and the signs at each corner, he might have thought he was walking in circles—or, rather, in rectangles. Everywhere streets crowded with traffic, sidewalks swarming with humans. How did they live? How could they bear to live? Why should they want to live? Indubitably they did all these things. You saw few faces that indicated happiness, but nearly all revealed an intense determination to live. It was the miracle of nature, repeated over and over, in antheaps, in beehives, in the slums of great cities.

So mused the young philosopher; an elegantly dressed philosopher, wearing the proper morning clothes, with only one button to his coat, and a small gardenia on the large lapel—it was one of the duties of the hotel valet to provide it. In the old days the saunterer would have been jeered at as a "dude," and some small boy might have shied a stale turnip at him; but now the boys were all in school, and anyone who had ten cents could see people like Lanny in a near-by motion-picture theater. No longer was there anything strange or annoying about a slender, erect figure with regular features, a little brown mustache, and clothes from Savile Row, London.

There was an Italian section, and stout brown women chaffering for dried garlic and strings of red peppers in front of tiny shops. Then it became a Jewish city, with signs in strange oriental characters. The tenements were obviously of the oldest, covered with rusty iron fire-escapes having bedding and wash hanging on them. The streets were filthy with litter—what taxpayers would consent to keep such streets clean? Old men with long coats and long black beards stood in the doorways of the shops, and the curbs were lined with little pushcarts having neckties and suspenders, hats and slippers, cabbages, apples, and dried fish. Women with baskets poked into the merchandise, examining it and bargaining in Yiddish, a kind of comical German of which Lanny had learned many words from his friends the Robins. Certainly everybody here was determined to live. How they did hang on! With what ferocity they asserted their right not to go under!

IX

Lanny knew that somewhere in front of him was the City Hall district, now at the height of a hot election campaign; also the Wall Street district, where for days the market had been in a state of instability. Lanny had started out with the idea of seeing these places, but they were farther away than he thought. He knew that there were subways by which, for a nickel, he could be whirled back to the hotel district in a few minutes; so he was in no hurry. He thought it might be interesting to talk to some of these people, to find out what they thought about the state of the world, and of their confused and bewildering city. People who didn't know that he was Mr. Irma Barnes!

A vague discontent had been in Lanny's mind; he was missing something in New York, and now, wandering among these dingy tenements, he realized what it was; he had no Uncle Jesse here, no Longuet or Blum, no Reds or Pinks of any shade. Nobody to point out to him the evils of the capitalist system and insist that it was nearing its collapse! Not even a Rick or other intellectual to tell him in highbrow language how wasteful was the system of competitive commercialism, and how diligently it was digging the foundations from under itself! Lanny had learned to require this mental stimulus, as much so as his glass of orange juice in the morning and his glass of wine at lunch.

There were bound to be some Reds in New York; where would one look for them? Lanny's thoughts turned to his old friend Herron, who had died a couple of years ago in Italy—one might say of a broken heart, because he could no longer bear the aspect which Europe presented to him. But his spirit lived on in a Socialist school which he had started in New York, with money left by the mother of that wife with whom he had fled from America. This had happened more than twenty-five years ago, while Lanny had been a toddler on the beach at Juan. Herron had told him about the school, but the young visitor racked his brains and couldn't remember its name.

It occurred to him that there must be a Socialist paper of some sort in this great metropolis, and a neighborhood like this would be the place to look for it. He stopped at a stand and inquired, and a copy of the *New Leader*, price five cents, was thrust into his hands. In format it was different from *Vorwärts*, *Le Populaire*, and the London *Daily Herald*, but its soul was the same, and Lanny, strolling along and looking at the headlines, was comforted at once. An editorial on the front page denounced Mayor Walker, Tammany candidate for re-election, as a waster and corruptionist, a frivolous playboy, a night-club habitué. Large headlines described a mass meeting at which Norman Thomas, the Socialist candidate, had promised to reduce the price of milk.

Lanny examined the few advertisements, and, sure enough, there was a box reporting the activities of the Rand School of Social Science. He recalled the name at once; Carrie Rand had been the name of Herron's wife. They were having lectures, courses, meetings of various sorts. Lanny walked to the nearest north and south avenue, hailed a taxicab, and got in, saying: "Seven East Fifteenth."

The driver gave him a second look, and grinned. "You a comrade?"

"Not good enough for that," was the modest reply; "but I know some of them."

"Fellow-traveler, eh?"

"I believe that's a Communist term, isn't it?"

"That's what I am, buddy."

So the ice was broken, and all the way up Third Avenue the driver would turn and explode his ideas at his fare. There is nobody more free-spoken than a New York taxidriver, and he doesn't have to be a Red, though of course that helps. His license on the dashboard has his photograph on it, so that you can look and make sure that he is the licensee; it is supposed to help control his driving, if not his tongue. This driver told Lanny about Tammany, and the crookedness of its politicians; also of the labor-skates and others who rode on the backs of the workers. "Incidentally, between you and me," said he, "that bunch at the Rand School are yellow labor-fakers. You don't have to believe what I tell you, but look out for yourself."

Lanny didn't object to these opinions; quite the contrary, they made him feel at home. It was the old phonograph record scratching away! "I've an uncle in Paris who's a Communist," he said. "His girl has a younger sister who is married to a Paris taxidriver, and he talks just like you."

"Naturally," responded the other.

"The party line," smiled Lanny. He would have enjoyed an argument with this lively chap—but only if he would stop the car somewhere. Weaving in and out among the iron pillars of the Third Avenue El, whizzing past a street car, missing another taxi by six inches, or maybe only one—Lanny found it difficult to concentrate his mind upon the problem of expropriating the expropriators. However, this was New York, and you lived dangerously if you lived at all.

X

Seven East Fifteenth Street proved to be a moderate-sized building with a brownstone front, having a proletarian drabness; it had once been the Young Women's Christian Association. Lanny gave his driver half a dollar for the cause, and received the reply: "Thanks, Tovarish." He entered and strolled into a bookstore provided with the familiar literature, including some from abroad, of which he bought a few specimens, smiling to himself at the thought of how they would look in the royal suite of the Ritzy-Waldorf. Then he asked for someone who could tell him about school courses, and was introduced to a young intellectual with fair hair and alert sensitive features.

"I'm an American who's been living abroad," said Lanny. "I'm not a party member, but I knew George D. Herron in Paris and Geneva, so I'm interested in the school."

There couldn't have been a better introduction. The two sat down, and Lanny gave his name as Budd, shivering a little inside, hoping the young comrade didn't read the capitalist press. The comrade gave no sign of having done so. Lanny knew enough about Socialist affairs by now to realize that there was one invariable rule, whether it was in Paris, London, or Berlin, in Rome, Cannes, or New York; all Socialist enterprises were running on a shoestring, and a party official who met anybody who might have money was driven automatically to think: "I wonder if he will help us!" Lanny preferred to get that part over with quickly, so he said: "I'll be glad to make a small contribution to the work of the school, if I may." Comrade Anderson graciously said that he might.

Seeing that the young official was well informed and companionable, Lanny remarked: "I've been taking a walk and I've got up an appetite. Would you have lunch with me?"

"We have a cafeteria in the building," replied the other; so they went into the basement, and Lanny chose from some dishes on a counter, and had a whole meal for less than he would have paid for. his small glass of iced tomato juice at the Ritzy-Waldorf. "Comrade Budd" was introduced to several young people, and they all talked about the state of the world, and presently Lanny observed that a bright-faced Jewish girl was staring at him rather hard, and his skin began to crawl and the blood to climb into his face, for he knew that he was being recognized, or at any rate suspected. They would put it in the *New Leader*, and from there it would break into the "tabs." Unquestionably the prince consort was committing a major indiscretion!

But he stayed on, because Comrade Anderson was talking about the state of the market. There had been a slump in prices of late, and he said that stocks had been selling at from thirty to fifty times the amount of their normal earnings, whereas the proper ratio was less than half that. Anderson was giving a course of lectures on the present business and money situation, and had all the figures at his fingertips. "Do you realize, Comrade Budd, what the practice of installment buying has done to the country's finances?"

"I never thought about it," Lanny admitted.

"The American people owe seven billion dollars in the form of installment payments at the present time; and see how that has mortgaged the buying power of the country! It means that the manufacturers have got several years' business in one year; and where are they going to find new customers? It's the same as a man's spending several years' income in one year; what's he going to do the rest of the time?"

This gave Lanny a warm feeling. It had become an intellectual necessity for him to hear someone damn the capitalist system. He had fared so well under it himself that the world considered his attitude a perversity, but to Lanny it was a moral action, a tribute to the common humanity. Was he, living in the royal suite, to forget the existence of the millions in the tenements? His reason told him that the modern business structure was a house builded upon quicksand; he lacked the courage to start tearing it down—even if he had had the power—but he liked to hear some young intellectual start condemnation proceedings in the name of the working masses.

XI

After the lunch had been eaten and paid for, Lanny took his companion aside and gave him a hundred-dollar bill, perhaps the first such document that Tom Anderson had ever seen. "No, I won't give you my address," Lanny added. "I'll stop in some day when I'm in town." He made his escape quickly, because he saw the bright young Jewish girl whispering to one of her fellow-pupils, and he was pretty sure she was saying: "That must be the husband of Irma Barnes! Didn't you see his picture in the papers?"

Lanny strolled to Fourth Avenue and stepped into a taxi, saying: "Ritzy-Waldorf," and this time the driver didn't call him "Tovarish." He went into the hotel and found his wife and mother-in-law in the tea-room, having avocado salad and a fruit cup. "Where on earth have you been?" said Irma.

"Oh, I had a long walk. I saw the town."

"Where did you go?"

"All over the East Side, and away downtown."

"What on earth made you do that? There's nothing over there."

"I saw a lot of people, and they interested me."

"Don't you want some lunch?"

"I ate in a cafeteria. I wanted to see what it was like."

"What funny things you do think of!" exclaimed the wife; and then: "Oh, Lanny, Mother and I saw the loveliest diamond brooch!"

"Are you hinting for your husband to buy it?"

"I know you don't like diamonds, but I've never understood why."

"It's an out-of-date way of showing one's wealth," explained the bridegroom. "One has so much nowadays that one couldn't put it on, so it's more *chic* to look down upon the practice. Don't you think so, Mother?"

Mother was wearing a small diamond brooch and a large solitaire ring. She wasn't sure whether this strange new son-in-law was spoofing or scolding her, so she changed the subject. She had been looking at the market figures, and said that the break had become serious. She hoped Horace wasn't in the market too deeply. Was Lanny's father in?

Lanny said he was afraid so. He added that a break was to be expected, because stocks were selling at from thirty to fifty times their normal earnings, and that was twice too high.

"My brother has a different opinion," remarked Mrs. Barnes.

"Has he considered the effect of installment buying on our business situation?" inquired the son-in-law. "We have seven billion dollars of such obligations outstanding, and that is bound to cut down consumer power in the near future."

"Where on earth do you find out about such things, Lanny?" said his wife, with admiration in her tone.

38

Humpty Dumpty Sat on a Wall

I

THE day after Lanny's slumming expedition was Saturday, the nineteenth of October. The Detaze exhibition had been running for ten days, and was such a success that they were continuing it for another full week. Saturday being an important day, Lanny had promised to come over early; but first he stopped to look at the Translux —a habit more easy to acquire than to drop. It was not quite eleven o'clock, and he saw that the slump of the previous afternoon was continuing. He became worried about his father, and went to a telephone booth and called his office in Newcastle. "Robbie, have you seen the ticker?"

"Oh, sure," replied the father. There was one in the Budd office, and Lanny had observed that the carpet in front of it was well worn.

"Aren't you worried about it?"

"Not a bit, Son."

"Are you long or short?"

"I'm long on everything in the good old U.S.A. Believe me, I know what I'm doing. We had several bear markets like this last year; we had them this spring, and they were fine times to pick up bargains. The market drops ten points, and then it goes up twenty."

"Yes, Robbie, but suppose it changes about, and goes up ten and down twenty?"

"It can't, because of the underlying business conditions. Look at the orders piling up!"

"But orders can stop coming, Robbie; they can even be canceled. Do you realize that the American people owe seven billion dollars on installment-buying contracts? How can they go on ordering more things?"

Robbie wasn't so easily impressed as Irma. "Have you been talking to some of your Reds again?" He proceeded to turn the conversation around, urging his son against getting mixed up with such people in New York. Lanny was married now, and had responsibilities; he couldn't afford to make any more scandals!

"The Reds have got nothing to do with the question," insisted the younger man. "Anybody can look at prices and see they are too high —thirty to fifty times normal earnings of the stocks! How can that go on?"

"Because everybody knows that their normal earnings are bound to increase. Because we've got an administration that has sense enough to let businessmen alone and give them a chance to increase production, employment, and wages, all at one lick. Because nobody is listening to the croakers and soreheads—the people who tell us to sell America short!"

Lanny saw that he was wasting his time. He said: "Well, I wish you luck. If you run short of cash let me know, for we're banking some every day."

"Take my advice and buy Telephone this morning," chuckled Robbie. "My brokers have an office in your hotel."

II

Lanny and Irma went over to the show rooms. Phyllis Gracyn was coming; she was about to open a new show—it had just come in from a "tryout" in Atlantic City, and they had run into her at a night club. Lanny had told Irma about this adventure, now so far in the past, and Irma, who had curiosity about love affairs past or present, had been interested to meet the actress. Gracyn came, splendid in new silver-fox furs and the certainty of having another "hit" in the offing. But it turned out that she wasn't interested in Detaze that morning—she spoke of the market, and when she heard that Lanny had just been telephoning to his father, she wanted to know what that solid man of affairs thought about the situation. She had let a friend talk her into buying a thousand shares of Radio, and it was a lot of money for a poor working girl!

So it went, one person after another. Zoltan and Lanny were the only two of their acquaintance who were content to buy good stocks and put them away, and so didn't have to worry about the fluctuations of the market. Lanny was having to do a lot of arguing to keep his mother from being drawn into the whirlpool of speculation; everywhere she turned, people were telling her such marvelous stories—and offering her tips free of charge! One gentleman's butler had made three hundred and fifty thousand dollars by playing the information he had picked up at his master's dinner table; another's office boy had retired, having cleared forty thousand by following his own hunches. How could you lose, when everything was on the up and up?

Irma and Mrs. Fanny were going to a musical comedy matinee, so

Lanny had a "bite" with his mother and Mr. Dingle, who dropped in now and then at the show, but carefully kept out of everybody's way. If the man of God knew that a stock market existed, he never let on; he told them that he had found what he believed was an extraordinary medium: another of the poor and lowly, a Polish woman who sat in a dingy little parlor upstairs over a Sixth Avenue delicatessen shop, and charged you only two dollars for a séance, no matter how long it lasted. She wore a dingy Mother Hubbard wrapper, and her voice was frequently made inaudible by elevated trains roaring madly past the window; but her "control," an Iroquois Indian speaking with a powerful man's voice, declared that all the spirits of Parsifal Dingle's deceased relatives and friends were standing by, and Parsifal declared that they told him things which he himself had forgotten. If spirits were really there, it was important; possibly even more so than the question of whether the agent representing the Taft family would purchase two of the highest-priced Detaze seascapes.

The exchange closed at noon on Saturday, and after luncheon Lanny got an afternoon paper and read that the closing prices had "revealed great weakness." He went back to the show room and made himself agreeable to visitors, and later met his ladies at the hotel. Irma was giving a dinner party, and he had to advise her whether to wear the old Antoinette, which had made such a sensation, or the new Cerulean, which had been delivered that morning. Already there were imitations of Antoinette in the night clubs, but still it was lovely.

At the dinner party all the young people talked about the sensational market. Apparently there wasn't a single man or woman who wasn't "in"; some told what they had lost and some what they had gained, and all said what they thought was coming. It seemed to Lanny that they didn't really know anything, but were repeating what they had picked up here and there. The same thing was true of himself—the only difference was that they got their ideas from the New York *Herald Tribune*, while he got his from the Rand School of Social Science. To believe that prices were going up was patriotic, while to believe that they were coming down appeared slightly disreputable; so for the most part Lanny permitted his wife's guests to express themselves, which they gladly did, especially after the champagne had started flowing into the teacups.

III

Sunday was bright and warm, so they motored out to Shore Acres to play golf on their private course with friends who came in. At luncheon there was more discussion of the everlasting "market." Uncle Horace was there, bursting with energy and talking exactly like Robbie Budd; when stocks went down was the time to buy; don't lose your nerve, don't sell America short. Mr. Vandringham named the best of the "blue chips," from American Telephone and Telegraph down to Western Union and Westinghouse. There were more than twelve hundred stock issues listed on the Exchange, and as many more on the Curb, and no matter which one you mentioned, this vigorous operator knew all about it, the number of shares, common and preferred, the various classes of issues, A and B and so on, the number of shares outstanding, the prices and fluctuations as far back as had any meaning. Really, he was a walking *Moody's Manual;* he would say: "General Lawnmowers? Oh, yes, that's old Peter Proudpurse's merger, but the Fourth National crowd have got hold of it now, they've put Smith and Jones and Brown on the board, and they're taking in Amalgamated Carpettacks."

Lanny had spent his life learning the names of music composers and their opera, of authors and their books, of painters and their pictures. In the course of seven or eight years he had acquired a truly extensive knowledge of paintings and what they were worth. But now he saw that, if he was going to live with his wife's relatives and friends, he would have to learn about American corporations and their securities; if you had ears and a memory you just couldn't help it; and certainly you didn't want to be a dub, and cause chuckles as Lanny did when he assumed that Seaboard Air Line was an aviation concern, instead of a railroad to Florida. After all, there was a snobbery of the intellect as well as one of the purse, and it was no use overlooking the fact that these giant corporations were remarkable creations, dominating the age in which Lanny had to live.

So he questioned this large and voluble gentleman about what was going on, and received copious replies. He decided that his new relative wasn't such a bad fellow, in spite of being a "shark." Uncle Horace reported that three and a half million shares had been sold on the exchange in the two hours of Saturday, which was very nearly an all-time record. He said it was the result of the activities of a group of bear operators who had been pounding the market for weeks. As a result of such treatment it had revealed itself to be "spongy"; when the specialist at a certain trading-booth offered, say, one thousand Allied Chemical, he discovered that there was nobody wanting to buy Allied Chemical, there was just a blank space where there ought to have been customers. The order might be to sell "at the market," but there wasn't any market, and the broker had to go on offering at lower and lower prices, which was very bad indeed for morale.

Among those at the luncheon were two very wealthy ladies who had been invited to discuss possible operations for the morrow. Uncle Horace was proposing to form a "pool"; he explained that if stocks continued to decline, the bear interests would start to realize on their victory, and a shrewd operator, watching the signs and possibly having inside information, would step in and pick up some bargains. The market would undoubtedly rally, and he would make a "cleanup," all in a few hours.

Lanny learned from this conversation that his mother-in-law invited people to her daughter's home in order that her brother might get their money for his gambling operations. But that was all right, it was the way the game was played; they were all friends—at any rate so long as they made money. Lanny had been brought up in a home to which generals and cabinet ministers were invited so that they might order machine guns for their countries; in which a countess or other great lady would accept presents for acting as a "puller-in" for the munitions industry. For that matter, wasn't he using his wife's prestige to help sell his former stepfather's paintings? Perhaps when the Great Bull Market started its next upswing, he might be selling paintings to the ladies who had dipped some money out of Uncle Horace's pool.

It was a system of "you scratch my back and I'll scratch yours." Mr. Vandringham suggested that Lanny might put a little money into the pool; the prospects looked exactly right for a "killing." Perhaps it would have been good business for Lanny to do so, for his new relative might have been of use to him in various ways. But he excused himself by saying that he knew only one thing, pictures, and thought it wiser to stick to that. Uncle Horace said he respected Lanny's caution; certainly there was nobody more foolish than the untaught amateur trying to outguess the big fellows who devoted their lives to the Wall Street game. Having spoken, this particular big fellow bade farewell and hustled his bulky but vigorous self out to his car, to see some other persons who were going to fish in his pool next morning.

IV

Lanny and Irma drove back to the city. Lanny had got interested now, and watched the market from time to time on Monday. The same brokers who had a branch office in Newcastle had one in the Ritzy-Waldorf, and here on a translucent screen figures were continually appearing, from which you would learn what had happened on the trading-floor of the New York Stock Exchange a few seconds earlier: one thousand shares of Telephone stock had been sold at $276\frac{1}{4}$ per share, then two hundred shares of General Motors had brought $67\frac{5}{8}$. On one side of the offices was a large blackboard with many small squares, and boys hung up cards having figures on them, while well-dressed ladies and gentlemen sitting in rows of chairs studied them attentively. Many customers remained through the five hours that the Stock Exchange was open; they had nothing to do but study these figures, and then go off and talk about them, and try to guess how they would move on the morrow.

The figures behaved exactly as Mr. Vandringham and Robbie had foretold. There was heavy selling early in the day, and prices dropped several more points; but after lunch there was what was called "strong support," and the market rallied. Lanny took this to mean that the shorts were covering, as Uncle Horace had said they would; Lanny assumed that Uncle Horace would be among the buyers, and later on he learned that it was so. The shrewd operator had bought at the moment when his chosen stocks were lowest. His pool, representing a million dollars in cash, had helped to check the drop; others had rushed in, sensing the turn of the market, and had forced the price up in the closing hour. In the last few minutes Uncle Horace had sold out, and had the pleasure of reporting gains of more than four hundred thousand dollars. Good news indeed for ladies who had come to Sunday luncheon at Shore Acres, and they hoped that Fanny Barnes would invite them soon again.

Profits in this nationwide gambling game were made several times as fast for the reason that you didn't have to put up the whole price of the stock; the buying was done "on margin." You put up twenty percent, and your broker deposited the stock at a bank which lent the rest of the money. The colossal scale on which these operations were being carried on was indicated by the fact that brokers' loans for that day were well over six billions of dollars. The thing called "Wall Street" was a machine of marvelous intricacy through which many millions of shares could be bought and sold between ten o'clock in the morning and three in the afternoon; the machine would arrange for the recording of all these transactions, the transfer of shares, the payment of the money, the deduction of commissions. Memberships in the New York Stock Exchange, which carried the right to operate on that trading-floor, represented a cash value of more than half a billion dollars. Lanny, introduced suddenly into the midst of this cosmic machinery, was quite awe-stricken by the spectacle. Events had happened so precisely according to the prediction of his relatives that he conceived a new respect for their judgment. The stocks of the Rand School of Social Science went down many points, and Lanny was sorry that he hadn't put a few thousand dollars into his new uncle's pool. Perhaps he'd come into the next one!

After his fashion, he tried to understand the meaning of the events he was watching. Uncle Horace and his friends had gained a lot of money which they hadn't earned. Who had lost that money? Lanny took it for granted that what one person gained another must lose; but the operator insisted that this wasn't so; the long-range trend of the market was upward, and thus millions were enriched without anyone's losing. Lanny wished he had had Stef here, so that he might ask him about that. After a while he decided that it was stupid not to think things out for himself, and so he went about with brow furrowed, resolutely trying to penetrate the mysteries of his country's financial system.

The greater part of the country's business was carried on by means of credit. People trusted you because they believed you had the money. So long as they believed, you could spend, and in this way a huge structure of speculation was built up; everybody counted upon having more, and so everybody spent more, and in such a world it was no longer possible to tell the difference between what was imaginary and what was real. But suddenly one man began to doubt, and he asked for a dollar; the other fellow didn't have the dollar, so he rushed off to get it, but he couldn't find anybody who had one; the demand for the dollar spread through the community, and was called a "panic." Thinking thoughts such as these was like walking on what you took for dry land, but suddenly you began to feel it heaving and shuddering, and you realized that it was a field of ice, and the hot sun was shining on it, and it was growing "spongy."

V

Parsifal Dingle had his own ideas of the difference between what was imaginary and what was real in this world. Mr. Dingle had made up his mind that his spirit was eternal, and on that basis the importance of what happened to it here and now could be mathematically determined. What was the relation of twenty-four hours to eternity? Or of threescore years and ten to eternity? This arithmetical problem has haunted the souls of mystics since the dawn of thought; for what shall it profit a man, if he shall gain the whole world, and lose his own soul?

Beauty's husband had become interested in certain souls which had "passed over" into that realm of eternity. He heard his wife and his stepson talking about who were buying Detaze pictures and what prices they were paying, but the sounds passed in one ear and out the other. Mr. Dingle was on the verge of making discoveries so important that he could think about them anywhere, whether he was in the Detaze show rooms, or in a hotel restaurant, or in a motor-car stalled in Fifth Avenue traffic.

To his wife he said gently: "I have learned through Madame Zyszynski that Marcel is waiting for you." So Beauty had to tear herself away from the elegant and famous persons who wanted to look at her and compare her with the two portraits on the walls— and allow her man of God to take her in a taxicab over to a dingy Sixth Avenue neighborhood, where poor down-and-outs stood in front of blackboards telling them that a cook was wanted in a lumber camp in Maine, or a dishwasher in a Bowery eating-joint at twelve dollars per week and two meals. The most elegant of ladies alighted in front of a delicatessen shop which had a cold turkey and half a boiled ham in the window, entered a narrow hallway lit by a dim gas-jet, climbed some creaking stairs, and entered by a door having the sign, "Madame Zyszynski: Medium."

The Polish woman had apparently got a new and clean gown in Beauty's honor; it was black, and had gold stars sewn on it. The medium herself was elderly, stout, and pudgy, with a kindly face, but entirely devoid of color, so that it looked like soft dough; her straight black hair was tied in a knot on top of her head and she was wholly devoid of charm. She said, in uncertain English, that the visitor would oblige her by sitting quietly while she went into a trance, and afterward until she came out. The name of her "control" was "Tecumseh," and the visitor might ask him questions, but please be polite to him and not excite him. After which she seated herself in an armchair, laid her head back, and presently began to moan and snort and jerk in a most disconcerting way.

Then she became still, and began to speak in a voice that was much deeper than her own, but still foreign. The voice said that a man was there, and he gave the name of Marceau, and he was happy, and he made pictures here also, and he still loved her—he said things that possibly might have been embarrassing to the new husband, had he not known that in the other world there is no marrying or giving in marriage, and no sense of possession. The messages went on and on, and Beauty began to shiver, for it seemed to her that Marcel was really speaking, and it was the same as in the old days. She was such a worldling that it had really never occurred to her that death might not be the end, and now she was so excited that the tears ran down unchecked and stained the front of the very lovely crape dress that she wore.

VI

Of course Lanny had to hear all about that experience. He had to consider every sentence that Beauty could remember, and say whether that didn't sound like Marcel. Lanny couldn't be sure, because his mother had been asking questions, and how many hints had she given? The Polish woman claimed not to know a word of what she was saying in her trance; that might be so and again it might not. But Beauty wanted it to be so, and was a little provoked that Lanny wasn't as enthusiastic as herself. She wanted him to go and have a try, and he promised that he would go after the show was over—they really owed it to Zoltan to stick by him in these crowded closing days.

But Mr. Dingle had time for God, and for all God's children in God's heaven; he had standing appointments with the medium twice every day, morning and afternoon; and right while the stock market was throwing all New York into convulsions—going down twenty points and going up ten—the very day after Uncle Horace had made his "killing," Lanny's stepfather came to him, saying: "There is a message for you, my son."

"Indeed?" said the son. "Who from?"

"The name wasn't given. But your name was."

"Have you ever mentioned me to Madame Zyszynski?"

"I have been very careful not to. I thought something might come through for you."

"Did you receive the message yourself?"

"No, a manicurist got it."

"A manicurist!" Really, that seemed too funny.

"A young woman had a séance early this morning, before she went to her work, and she wrote the message down. Madame kept it by her and asked all her clients if it meant anything to them. It is supposed to be in French, and neither Madame nor Tecumseh nor the manicurist knows any French. Tecumseh repeated it three times, and the girl wrote it the way it sounded." Mr. Dingle handed his stepson a scribbled piece of brown paper.

There was a trick sentence which Lanny had learned as a boy, and which he used to write out for his American and English friends to puzzle them. It is a sentence made of French words, *"Pas de leur Rhône que nous,"* and people would say it over and over, thinking French, trying to make it mean French, and failing to realize that they were speaking an English sentence. Now the trick was reversed; an uneducated girl had written something in American, and it was supposed to be read as French: "Brig addy ay voo zavvy rays on."

Lanny read it two or three times. He said it fast, the way you are supposed to say French; and suddenly he began to turn cold, and the strangest feeling ran over him—no, it wasn't entirely strange— he had had it once before in his life. Twelve years ago, but it was like yesterday in his memory; the hour just before dawn, when he had lain in his bed in his father's home, and had seen the first faint traces of light gather together and form an image of Rick, standing at the foot of his bed, mournful, silent, with a red gash across his forehead. Rick still bore the scar of that wound, which he had got when his plane crashed in France and left him at death's door, a cripple for the rest of his life. That had been Lanny's first contact with the supernatural—or at least what appeared to be the supernatural. Now here it was again; and here was that same creepy, crawly, cold feeling!

"Brigadier, vous avez raison!" It is the refrain of a humorous French ballad about a cavalryman who always agrees with what his riding companion says, no matter what may be the nature of it. It had

been in some book of Denis, *fils,* or Charlot, in that first happy summer when Lanny had gone to the Château de Bruyne, trembling a little over the strangeness of *la vie à trois* and wondering how he was going to make out in it. Such a good time they had all had—and that refrain had been one of the jokes with which they had amused themselves. All families develop such passwords to intimacy; and Lanny thought, suppose that Marie had wished to say to him: "I am here, waiting for you"—what could she have contrived that would tell him more certainly than the foolish little verse, which had not crossed his mind in so many years? *"Brigadier, vous avez raison!"*

VII

Lanny dropped the picture business and the stock market, and took his stepfather's appointment for the next morning. He sat and watched the pudgy old woman go into her trance, and listened with strained attention to every word that was spoken by the alleged Tecumseh. The visitor came away in that state of tormented uncertainty which dogs the lives of so many truth-seekers in those dim regions of the subconscious. "Marie" had given her name; but then it was a common name, and how could he be sure that his mother or his stepfather had not spoken it in some unguarded moment? And what about the stories of spiritualist mediums making elaborate notes and exchanging data about likely prospects? What Marie said to him through the voice of Tecumseh was what she would have said; but then it was what any woman would have said to the man she had loved and left behind. She wished him happiness in his new love; but wouldn't any woman in the spirit world do that?

Also there was the possibility of what people called telepathy; "mental telepathy," they said, meaning to distinguish it from American Telephone and Telegraph! Of course nobody knew what telepathy might be or how it would work; it was just a word, but it helped you, because it seemed easier to believe that somebody might dip into your subconscious mind and pick out something—than that the universe was full of spirits, whispering messages to an Indian, to be spoken by the vocal cords of an old Polish woman for a price of two dollars. If the spirit of Marie had wanted to talk to Lanny, wouldn't it have been easier for her to do it that night when he had come back to her home and lain in her bed?

Lanny voiced this idea to Parsifal Dingle, who replied: "Suppose that a hundred years ago somebody had told you that it might be possible to send messages under the ocean, would you have believed him?"

"I suppose I'd have been dubious," admitted the other.

"Suppose someone had said: 'It will not be possible to send the message through the water, but only through a copper wire wrapped in the extract of a tropical tree'—that would have sounded rather odd, too."

Lanny admitted that it was all rather odd; in fact, he had been finding life that way ever since he had begun to think about it instead of just living it. Now he had a new oddity to put with the many others. *"Brigadier, vous avez raison!"*

VIII

Lanny's mother-in-law resented the trustees of her late husband's estate, but she had to manage to get along with them. Mr. Joseph Barnes had come out to Shore Acres to call on the bridal pair; but the other two trustees, Mr. Marston and Mr. Keedle, having been employees of J.P. most of their lives, were not sure of their social status and were awaiting an invitation. Irma had promised to take Lanny to the office to meet them; but it was such a dull duty that she kept putting it off. Now the mother telephoned, saying: "Really, dear, it's a great discourtesy." So Irma said to Lanny: "Let's go this afternoon and get it over with."

Accordingly, Lanny phoned to Uncle Joseph and made an appointment. The office of the estate was in one of the great office buildings on lower Broadway, and they motored down through heavy traffic; the pressure was such that the chauffeur would have to go a considerable distance to park, and when he came for them he would have to drive round and round the block until they appeared. A car had become more of a nuisance than a convenience on this jam-packed island of Manhattan—which had been bought from the Indians for twenty-four dollars, but now you would pay that price for as much space as the tip of your finger would cover. Now upon this soil had arisen the most amazing of the works of man: a congeries of buildings, from fifty to a hundred stories high, turning the streets into narrow canyons or clefts of granite. If all the people who worked in these warrens had come out of them at once, they would have filled the streets several layers deep. You entered an express elevator, a little silent cell; when it started you felt your entrails sink, and when it stopped they surged up against your heart and lungs.

Uncle Joseph was a tall, distinguished-looking gentleman, like his deceased brother; always well dressed, rather pompous in manner, but friendly enough when you knew him. He had an odd hobby of collecting specimens of the old-time American dime-novels upon which he had been brought up; since Lanny was also a lover of literature, this was a bond of fellowship between them. Uncle Joseph had been a sort of chief clerk for the more brilliant and daring elder brother, and now it was a religion with him to see that Irma's capital was properly guarded. What she did with the income was none of his business—unless she would permit him to reinvest it in "blue chips." He hoped that Lanny would be on his side in controversies over this subject, therefore he cultivated the young man with extreme politeness. His suavity was that of the head-waiter in the main dining-room of the Ritzy-Waldorf, and both of them appeared to Lanny as priests who worshiped with the utmost devotion a wooden idol with no brains in its head.

Irma's father had bequeathed an annuity to Mr. Marston and Mr. Keedle, the other trustees, in order that they might devote their time to watching each other. They were, if possible, even more anxious to please than was the uncle; they bowed and beamed, and told how honored they were, and escorted the young couple through the rooms and showed them typewriters and adding-machines and filing-systems, and introduced them to the head clerk by name, and to the other clerks by a wave of the hand. To Lanny it would always be embarrassing to be mistaken for divinity, but he had to learn to look as if he didn't mind it. He and his wife sat down in Uncle Joseph's private office and permitted the three gentlemen to explain upon what principles and by what methods they managed the property. Now and then the bridal pair would nod gravely, expressing their satisfaction.

IX

Lanny, really trying to understand the great metropolis and the things that went on in it, perceived that these three conscientious gentlemen lived and operated in a world entirely controlled by pieces of paper. Not motor-cars and jewels, not even palaces and land were the basis of the Barnes fortune, but a few pieces of paper called "securities," which were worth more than their weight in anything in the world, even radium. In the estate office were other pieces of paper, a cardfile which listed all the facts about each of the precious ones. Yet other pieces called dividend checks came at regular intervals, and Uncle Joseph signed some more called receipts—and so it went on, day after day, and would go on, world without end. Uncle Joseph knew that it would, because he had the right to name his successor, and was training his oldest son in the office, and had named him in proper legal form—on a piece of paper.

For the keeping of the securities, Irma's father had found a place where surely neither moth nor rust would corrupt nor thieves break through and steal. It was a private compartment in the vault of one of the three biggest Wall Street banks, where all the resources of modern science had been utilized to contrive a really secure hiding-place for treasures of this sort. Uncle Joseph invited them to inspect it, and Lanny thought it would be interesting, or pretended to. Irma's father had shown it to her, but she went along for politeness. The great bank was only a few doors away. Their coming was announced by telephone, and they were escorted to the office of the great financier who presided over the institution and who assigned one of the thirty-seven vice-presidents to conduct the distinguished visitors to the vaults.

You descended in an elevator, for they were a hundred feet or more below the surface, cut into the solid rock of Manhattan Island. They were, in effect, a steel box as big as a good-sized house; or rather, a series of boxes, such as the Chinese make, each fitting inside the next. The outermost box was of concrete, and the others of steel. Into the space between two of the steel walls one could, by pressing a lever, introduce hydrocyanic gas, which would instantly kill any living thing. Into the layer next to the concrete a heavy stream of water could be poured, filling it entirely, and flooding any hole or passage which might be dug. In the innermost of the surrounding spaces was a walk, and a man paced round and around it, and there was an arrangement of mirrors whereby he could see all four walls of the vault, and under it and over it. The man was locked in at closing time with a time-lock and could not get out until his time was up; he paced around and around looking into the mirrors, and each time he completed a round he pressed a button, and if he failed to press it within a certain time an alarm bell rang in the nearest police station.

Thus Uncle Joseph thought that the Barnes fortune was safe from mobs and marauders. He wasn't worried when the price of stocks went down, for what the estate owned it owned outright; the stocks were a share in the producing power of America, which couldn't fail for long. However, the conscientious Mr. Joseph Barnes had worried a great deal over the fact that the heiress of this tremendous fortune went out so freely into a world consisting largely of night clubs, where she met handsome young men, a percentage of whom were scoundrels and an even larger percentage wasters. Uncle Joseph's heart had been in his mouth when he received word about the elopement; but now he was relieved, for this seemed to be a fairly decent sort of young fellow; rather airy, one might say flighty, but well meaning and apparently open to instruction. The keeper of the treasure was watchful and attentive, and took every occasion to impress upon Lanny the gravity of his responsibilities as bearer of the seed and maker of the future.

X

The next day was Wednesday, the twenty-third of October, and Lanny went over to the show room, where he heard the good news that the Taft family had purchased the two seascapes. At lunchtime, when Lanny looked at the Translux, he found that the market was beginning to slump again. Mrs. Barnes had come to town; she had had a call from her brother, who was getting up another pool, and she was putting in her "pin-money," a matter of ten thousand dollars. Irma was tempted, but she had given her father a solemn promise that never in her life would she buy a share of stock on margin, and when·she heard about the Dingle family's experience with the spirits, she was more than ever afraid to break her word. Lanny saved her from temptation by inviting her to come to the show rooms and meet the Honorable Winston Churchill, who was reported to be coming.

When they came out, in the latter part of the afternoon, the newsboys were shouting: "Panic in Wall Street!" Lanny read more talk about sponginess, avalanche of selling orders, Niagara of liquidation, complete absence of support. The ticker was two hours behind the market. The bond ticker was giving selected prices for some of the "blue chips," and showed losses around twenty points, most alarming. Lanny stopped at the hotel for a look at the Translux, and found that he couldn't get into the room; it was packed with men and women, and on the edges he noticed the worried faces and heard the anxious talk. The closing hour had been terrible, and nobody knew yet what had happened.

Irma's smart friends talked about nothing else at teatime, or at dinner, or in the evening. Nobody cared what the Right Honorable Winston Churchill had said about Detaze, nobody cared whether Lanny had had a message from his *amie* in the spirit world. A six-million-share day—think of it! And what was coming tomorrow?

Mrs. Fanny had been trying to get in touch with her brother, but his line was constantly busy. She knew that her money had been put in; had it been got out again? Lanny phoned to his father at dinnertime, and learned that he was still at the office, which in itself meant that he was worried. Yes, he admitted he was in the market rather heavily; but it was all right, he was sure that prices would rally. Low prices always brought out the people who bought for investment. Don't sell America short! However, Robbie added that he was arranging to have cash in hand in case of need. Lanny said: "If you get in a jam, let me know."

Mrs. Fanny heard from her brother at last. He hadn't been able to close out his pool; the bears had had everything their own way. But prices were sure to rally in the morning. Uncle Horace had invested a couple of million dollars on a twenty-point margin; that is, he had bought ten million dollars' worth of stocks. If the price continued to drop, his brokers would call for another ten percent, so he would have to have a million dollars in a hurry; better be on the safe side and have it ready. Would Fanny get her share to him the first thing in the morning?

Fanny didn't have it, and came to Irma, who said: "Of course," and wrote a check for five thousand dollars. Irma didn't often write checks, it was too much trouble. She had promised Mr. Slemmer, her business manager, that she would never write a check of any size without letting him know; he kept no large balance, because the banks paid only two percent on checking-accounts, whereas good investments paid six or more. Mr. Slemmer was a very careful man, and insisted on saving money for Irma, whether she wished him to or not. The girl said to Lanny: "It's a nuisance, but I promised him, so you'd better phone him."

Lanny called the manager's home, on the Shore Acres estate, and was told that he had gone to the city and hadn't returned. Lanny left the message, and Irma remarked: "I wonder if he's in the market, too." She said it casually, rather taking it for granted that he would be. Everybody was.

They talked about little else but stocks. Irma couldn't understand panics, and Lanny had to explain them. It was hard for the Barnes heiress to comprehend why everybody didn't have plenty of money, and why, if more was needed, the government didn't print it. Absurd for people to be in want! Lanny tried to explain that if it were not for the poverty of the poor, the riches of the rich wouldn't be of much use to them. Irma said: "Lanny, you're just trying to make me a Pink like yourself!"

Anyhow, she didn't approve of panics; everybody worrying and rushing about, trying to get money in a hurry. She refused to have anything to do with them, even as a spectacle, like a storm on the ocean, to be watched. Uncle Joseph had suggested that Lanny might be interested to come down some day and see the Stock Exchange in action, and now Lanny said: "Tomorrow would be a good day. Wouldn't you like to be there at ten o'clock, to see what happens when the gong sounds? It ought to be a show."

"For heaven's sake!" exclaimed Irma. "Get up and go downtown at that hour, just to see a lot of brokers buying and selling stocks?" She was being fitted with her winter wraps, and that was important. However, she said, obligingly: "You go, if you really want to see it, and I'll have them wait until you get back. You won't stay long, I'm sure."

"I'll take the subway," he replied. "They tell me it's a lot quicker."

Irma declared that he'd have the breath crushed out of him; but Mrs. Barnes said no, the laboring classes traveled at seven, the clerks at eight, the businessmen at nine, and by nine-thirty the subway was quite comfortable. Many impatient people rode down for a nickel instead of using their cars. She had done it herself.

Thus reassured, Lanny called Uncle Joseph at his home, and that obliging gentleman agreed to meet him in front of the Exchange building promptly at five minutes to ten. Incidentally he said: "I hope that Horace isn't in the market too deep, for things look very serious." Then he added: "Irma and Fanny will be glad that the estate is not involved."

Lanny answered: "They ought to be!" He had to be careful not to reveal any secret from one clan to the other.

Uncle Joseph said: "Be sure to be on time. I'll have the admission cards ready."

Lanny hung up the receiver, smiling. More pieces of paper! What would they do when they got to the pearly gates, and St. Peter asked them for their admission cards?

39

Humpty Dumpty Had a Great Fall

I

THE large and splendid building of the New York Stock Exchange on Broad Street had a great crowd in front of it that Thursday morning: persons who had no way to get cards of admission, but must be content to stand in the street and try to imagine what was going on inside. The visitors' gallery was large, and crowded by several hundred selected persons. One of the first whom Lanny saw was the Honorable Winston Churchill, a pudgy but energetic gentleman whom he had first come to know at the Peace Conference, where he had labored to persuade the Allies to make an end of Bolshevism and the Bolsheviks.

The gallery looked down into a vast hall, having on one side so many tall windows that it was practically a wall of glass. The north and south walls had giant blackboards divided into squares, one for each of more than twelve hundred brokers; each broker kept one eye on his square, and when his number showed up he knew that his office wanted him on the phone. Under the board behind brass rails was an enormous telephone exchange with a row of operators; it was not supposed ever to happen that a broker would not be able to reach his office at once. Fortunes were at stake, and the fraction of a second might mean the difference between success and failure.

The obliging Mr. Joseph Barnes explained the mechanism of this great institution. On the trading-floor had once stood what were called "posts," at which certain stocks were dealt in. In those days a broker had made his memoranda in a notebook; but now the business had grown so that each broker had to have a clerk, and trading-posts had been replaced by horseshoe-shaped booths, with a shelf inside at which clerks could work recording orders. These clerks were required to wear uniforms, so that by no possibility could any one of them ever impersonate a broker. There were great numbers of boys serving as messengers, but they weren't big enough to impersonate anything except monkeys, said Uncle Joseph.

Nowadays the greater part of the trading was in the hands of so-called "specialists," men who stayed at one trading-booth and dealt in one particular stock. That made it easier for everybody, because you knew where to make a bid or to look for one. You could tell the specialists because each carried under his arm a peculiar sort of book, eighteen inches long and only three inches wide. Its pages were numbered according to the prices of the stock in which he traded; if U.S. Steel moved to 205, the specialist would turn to that page and see instantly what customers had ordered him to buy or to sell at that price. Steel might stay there for only a second or two, but that was longer than it took to act: the calling of an offer by one man and a sign of acceptance from another.

Ordinarily the elderly and more important brokers sent their subordinates to the trading-floor, but now everybody sensed a crisis, and the big men were on hand. The floor was crowded; every eye was on the great clock; you could see the hand slowly moving, and when it neared the moment, people seemed to hold their breath. Suddenly there was the crash of a gong; then—Lanny had read many times about "pandemonium breaking loose," but the first time he ever saw it was at ten o'clock on the morning of the twenty-fourth of October in the year 1929. More than twelve hundred men leaped into action at the same instant, all yelling at the top of their lungs. The sound of it shot up to the visitors' gallery, hit the high ceiling and bounced back, and from that time on there were millions of sound waves, clashing, mingling, beating one another to pieces. It was like no other volume of sound in the world; it couldn't be compared to a stormy ocean, because there are different waves and you hear each one, but you never heard any particular shout, no matter how loud it might be. The medley did not diminish while Lanny stayed in the gallery, and when he went out into the street he heard it there, though all doors and windows of the building were closed, the ventilation being from the roof.

Swarms of men jammed around each of the trading-booths, all raising their hands and waving them, dancing about. They were offering either to buy or to sell stocks; and of course whenever one bought, another had to sell, and vice versa. If buyers and sellers were equal in number, sales could be made quickly, and without excitement or strain. The frenzy meant a great excess of buyers over sellers, or the converse. Which was it? Not merely those in the visitors' gallery but all America waited for the answer.

At five places on the floor sat men at a sort of overgrown typewriter, and the moment a sale was made the clerk carried a record of it to one of these men, who typed it on his machine, and by an ingenious mechanism the results of all five of these typings were combined in one stream of figures on a ticker tape. Three underground floors of this great building were full of electrical apparatus of unbelievable complexity, whereby this precious stream of figures was sent out with the speed of lightning to three thousand places in the financial district, and by Western Union to four thousand other places scattered over the United States. Above the call board in the trading-hall was a big translucent screen, and the figures appeared here, so that both brokers and visitors could see them. The first sales were big, and the first prices were down; somebody was dumping blocks of ten and twenty thousand shares onto the market.

Twenty thousand shares of some "blue-chip" stock which is selling at 400 is eight million dollars, and that is big business on any trading-floor in the world. It couldn't be the bootblacks and messenger boys, the maidservants and farmers' wives who traded through the "odd lot" houses; it could only be the great banks seeking to protect their position, the operators who had got a fright, the investment trusts, of which there were five hundred, grown overnight like mushrooms, all assuring the public that their function was to "stabilize the market" and protect investors by spreading their holdings among the best stocks. Now they were dumping their stocks, and it was a panic.

I I

The specialist in U.S. Steel who had orders to sell "at the market" had no choice; he had to go on offering. He shouted 200, and if no one answered he had to shout 199, and then 198; it seemed like the end of the world to him, but presently he would be shouting 190, and no takers. The specialist would hardly dare to open his book, for he knew that he had "stop loss" orders by the score and perhaps by the hundreds at those different prices, and what was he going to do with them all? When he made a sale, he could see that it didn't appear on the Translux; he saw there sales that he had made ten minutes ago, half an hour ago, so he knew that the ticker was overwhelmed by the rush of selling. He no longer knew where he was or what was happening; it was like having the earth drop out from under his feet.

The ticker designated the different stocks by key letters: X for U.S. Steel, R for Radio, GM for General Motors, WX for Westinghouse, and so on. The sales recorded showed that Radio had lost one-sixth of its value in the first hour; General Electric, which had been over 400 a few weeks ago, was dropping under 300. Uncle Joseph shouted into Lanny's ear: "I never saw anything like this in my life." Lanny shouted back: "What is going to happen?" The answer was: "I can't imagine."

Irma had said that it would be monotonous, listening to brokers shouting; and so it was after a while. There was no change, except that the clamor grew even louder, the signs of confusion greater. There was no way to find out the prices actually prevailing on the floor. Lanny began thinking: "What is happening to Robbie?" He shouted: "Let's go," and they went out, and right away there was a mob around them, crying for news of what was going on. They answered as well as they could, and pushed their way onward.

"The worst panic in Wall Street's history," said Joseph Barnes; "at any rate, the most sudden."

"I must call my father," said the younger man. "Shall we go to the office?"

The street was so packed that it was a job getting through, even in the middle. Lanny, being more active, said: "Excuse me if I run." Others were doing the same, without making any excuses. He arrived breathless at the estate office, where everybody fell upon him. "What is happening?" They were all excited, whether they were "in" or not.

Lanny put in a phone call for his father's office, and got the reply: "The line is busy." It was that way everywhere, Mr. Keedle said; you couldn't get anything in Wall Street, you could hardly get a broker's office anywhere in the United States.

It was easy to imagine what was happening. Wall Street had built the most perfect machine in the world to enable the American people to buy stocks, and now the American people were turning the machine around and using it to sell stocks—or to try to. The opening prices had appeared on many thousands of ticker tapes and illuminated screens; they had gone out over scores of radios. There were three hundred million shares of stock held on margin, and most of the owners had the same impulse at the same instant—to pick up the phone or rush to the telegraph office and put in an order: "Sell at the market!"

Uncle Joseph arrived, breathless. He had just learned from a friend that Telephone was below 270—the stock which Robbie Budd had been so happy to get for 287½. Lanny tried again, and was told that the trunk lines to Newcastle were all busy. He decided that there was no use sitting there waiting, what was needed was action; his father might be wiped out in the next few minutes. The brokers called on you for more margin, and if you didn't put it down on the counter, they sold you out. In a time such as this, influence, even friendship, counted for nothing; either you went down or your broker did, and no brokers were going to fail in this panic.

Lanny wrote out a message for his father. "I have three hundred thousand dollars in the bank and I am going to get a certified check and take it to your brokers' office in the Ritzy-Waldorf and have them notify your Newcastle office that they have it. Also take my stocks which you have. Borrow on them or sell them if you need to." Uncle Joseph promised to deliver this message as soon as the call came through.

III

Lanny made a dash for the subway, glad enough of this plebeian, five-cent form of transportation. The money he had was what Zoltan had deposited from the picture sales, after deducting his own commission. By right only one-third of it was Lanny's, but he had the handling of it, and he would act first and justify afterward. When the subway train came to Grand Central station he darted out, and into a taxi which took him to the bank. He gave the driver a dollar, and said: "Wait for me," ran into the bank, wrote the check payable to the brokers, and presented it to be certified. It was a world in which you wrote three hundred thousand dollars or three million as casually as you wrote three; the bank officer would step to the books to make sure you had it, and then write the bank's certification on it, and it was as good as U.S. currency. "Pretty wild times, Mr. Budd," the man remarked, sympathetically. Lanny, having been in New York for three weeks, replied: "You said it!" and was gone.

"Ritzy-Waldorf," he ordered the taximan, and gave him another dollar and dashed to the brokers' office. The place was packed to the doors; if he had been an acrobat he could have gone all the way to his goal on the shoulders or the heads of other men and a good many women. Prices were being shouted in horrified tones. The market level was down twenty points and some stocks had lost thirty to forty. Radio had lost a full third of its value. It occurred to Lanny that there might be a private entrance to the brokers' office—he was used to being taken in at such places. He found it and banged and kicked until it was opened; then he put his foot in it and waved his check—another piece of paper, and a good one. He asked for the manager, and went right after him without waiting for permission. Easy to recognize him by the fact that he sat at a desk with five telephones, trying to use them all at once.

Lanny slapped the check in front of the man and said: "I am Robert Budd's son and this is for my father's account. All I want is for you to notify your Newcastle branch that you have this money."

"I'll do my best, Mr. Budd," replied the man, who had beads of perspiration dropping from his brow.

"That isn't enough," declared Lanny. "You've got to do it."

"Here," replied the man, in between sentences of another conversation. He shoved Lanny a phone which didn't happen to be ringing. Lanny took it and put in a call for Newcastle, and for at least half an hour he sat there, worrying the operator, and between times learning about the life of a branch manager of a brokers' office. It consisted of saying: "I am sorry, we had to sell you out," or else: "I am sorry, we will have to sell you out unless you produce more margin before noon."

The telephone operator kept saying: "All trunk lines busy, sir." Apparently she wasn't allowed to say anything but a formula, no matter how mad you got or what you said. Whatever panics might do to Telephone stock, they were not permitted to affect telephone service.

Finally she said: "I'll give you the supervisor," and Lanny fussed at this official, who promised to try for him. So finally he got the brokers' office in Newcastle, and Lanny demanded the manager, and told his story, wondering if this man also was talking through five phones at once. He got the two managers together, and heard the New York one state that he had three hundred thousand dollars for the account of Robert Budd. That was all; they didn't tell him anything about the state of Robbie's account. "I hope everything is all right," said the New York man, and then started saying into the telephone: "I am terribly sorry, Mrs. Archibald. You will have to have a twenty-percent margin here in the next half-hour, and be prepared to put up another twenty percent if the market continues to drop. We may be demanding seventy-five-percent margins before closing time. This is the worst in my experience and we can make no exceptions."

IV

Lanny went upstairs to his rooms. How funny to find his wife reclining in a chaise-longue looking at the art creations of Bernice, *robes et manteaux,* and waiting for Lanny to come and tell her whether black furs or brown were more becoming to her warm brunette coloring! "There's a frightful panic in the Street," he said. "Everybody we know may be wiped out." That scattered them. Madame Bernice and her two assistants rushed off to find a telephone and put in their "stop loss" orders; meanwhile Lanny sat at his own phone and put in a call for Newcastle. The same reply: "All trunk lines are busy. We will call you."

He did what he had done before, made a fuss; of course he was gumming up the telephone service, and thousands of others were doing the same; it was *sauve qui peut.* Finally he managed to get his father's office, only to learn that Robbie was out; the secretary said he had gone to see Mr. Samuel Budd. Lanny could guess what that meant: Robbie was trying to scrape up some cash. The secretary said, very discreetly, that Mr. Robert had not told him anything about his position in the market. Lanny told what he had done, and asked the secretary to get the brokers' office and get a confirmation of the receipt of the money. He added: "Tell my father to call me at my hotel. I'll wait here in my room."

Then Lanny telephoned his mother at the show rooms, and asked her to come to him. She had heard that there was a panic; one could have told that by the way the crowd had melted away from the show. She said: "Is anything wrong with us, Lanny?" He wouldn't talk over the phone. "Take a taxi and come at once."

It was between twelve and one, the worst hour of the panic. The blue chips were tumbling, several points at a time, and one time right after another. The worst of it was that the ticker was an hour and a half behind the market, and there was a spread of thirty points between the prices quoted and those actually prevailing. So no one knew what to believe or to expect. Everybody you knew was in, and every last one of them might be ruined. Irma's large and majestic mother was pacing the floor in an agony of dread because she couldn't get into touch with her brother. "Feathers," the elegant secretary, was pale, but silent, not telling anybody what her losses were. Parsons, Irma's maid, was weeping silently in a corner because she had put all her savings into Montgomery Ward and the chamber-maid had just told her that it had gone from 83 to 50.

Beauty came in, and Lanny took her into his own room and shut the door, and told her what he had done. She went dead white, except for her war-paint. "Oh, Lanny, how *could* you!"

"Think it over, old girl," he suggested. "You and I have lived off Robbie for thirty years. You have had a thousand a month, which makes three hundred and sixty thousand."

"But a third of that money belongs to Marceline!"

"Marceline has lived off Robbie since long before she was born. Maybe Marcel never lived off him, but his *amie* and his wife did, which is the same thing. We simply had to save Robbie if we could."

"What will we live on, Lanny? I have only a few hundred in the bank."

"I have some money in Cannes; and we still have a lot of pictures."

"Will anybody ever buy any more pictures? There'll be nobody in the rooms except poor artists and others who just want to look."

"I'll find a way to make money, Beauty, and I won't let you suffer. Also, Robbie will come back, no matter what happens; the family won't let him go down. I'm sorry to have acted without your consent, but I knew that it might be a matter of minutes. Fortunes are being wiped out wholesale."

"I don't understand it, Lanny. How can such things happen?"

"That's a long story, and we'll know more about it later. The point is, I had to do what I could for Robbie, and I want you to tell me that I did right."

"I suppose you had to; but, oh, how perfectly horrible! Why, nobody can ever be sure of anything again! Do you think you saved him?"

"Our money may be only a drop in the bucket to him. The brokers can demand any margin they think necessary. If you have bought on a twenty-percent margin and the stocks drop that amount, your margin is wiped out, and you have to put up another bunch of money; and so on, as long as prices go down. Any time you aren't there with the cash, they sell the stocks for what they will bring, and you start life over again."

"Lanny, it's like a buzz-saw!"

"Well, thank me for keeping you out of it. And as for Robbie, from now on we can consider that we've done our duty; if he gets in again, it's his own funeral."

V

Beauty went off to her hotel to weep alone. No use going to the show rooms, ever again—there was nobody there who mattered, nobody worth exhibiting yourself to! Lanny stayed by the telephone, which rang frequently; various friends of the family calling, to impart dreadful news and exchange futile words.

The young man's thoughts were on the situation in Newcastle. Grandfather Samuel, the stern old Puritan, had never gambled in his life; would he forgive his son for gambling, and put up money to save him? Or would he say: "Whatsoever a man soweth, that shall he also reap"? Would Robbie's brothers help him—or were they too in the market? All the country club set was in, Lanny knew, and many of the businessmen, for he had heard them talking. Now they would all be scurrying, trying to beg or borrow cash. Esther's father was president of the First National, a Budd bank, and doubtless he would do all he could, but he wasn't allowed to lend money without security. Lanny thought: "Of course I might ask money from Irma." But he said to himself: "No, if that's the only way, Robbie will have to take the count."

There were plenty of other people whose thoughts turned to Irma, and who had not the same scruples. Lanny discovered her at the phone in her room, saying to one of her intimates: "But, my dear, I have no such sums in cash; my own mother is in difficulties, and maybe my uncle, and I have to help them first." Most embarrassing to have your best friends crying over the telephone, and thinking that you were stingy and selfish, you with all that fortune salted away—how could you? It wouldn't be long before they would be coming in person, weeping and having hysterics. Yes, Irma Budd was going to know there was a panic, and she couldn't keep it from making a difference in her life!

Horace Vandringham burst in at a little after one. The bright red color which he usually wore had faded to yellow, and he looked as if he had been put through a clothes-wringer. He had put up every share of stock he owned, and unless his sister and his niece would save him he was absolutely cleaned out. He didn't know what the market was doing, or what it was going to do; he had to have cash and more cash, they must go downtown to the vault with him and take out a bundle of their stocks and let him take them to the bank. They must do it now, instantly!

Fanny said: "But, Horace, you know the trustees won't allow that. It is expressly forbidden in the will."

"Well, you must make them consent. This is an emergency. For God's sake, Fanny!"

The mother called the estate office, and ordered Mr. Joseph Barnes to take the subway express and come to the hotel at once. Apparently he had been expecting the call, for he argued. The others couldn't hear what he said, but evidently he was laying down the law, for Fanny flushed as red as her brother no longer was. "Come up, Joseph; we can't discuss these matters over the phone."

Uncle Horace wanted to know how much cash Irma had. The mother produced the last statement of Slemmer, which showed only a couple of hundred thousand dollars on hand. "I can't tell what checks he has drawn," said Fanny.

"Well, get him and find out!" fumed the brother.

Slemmer still hadn't returned to Shore Acres. They got the name of his hotel, and phoned him there. He said that the bank balance was about seventy-five thousand dollars; the rest of Irma's money was in the hands of the trustees, who had reinvested it.

"Well, surely *that* money belongs to Irma!" insisted Horace to his sister. "All the income is her property, and is not subject to the provisions of the will. She has a right to sell such stocks, or hypothecate them—whatever she pleases. Let Joseph keep his nose out of it!"

VI

Lanny perceived that there was going to be a jolly row between the two families. His own attitude was that of the pioneer settler who came home to his cabin and discovered his wife in conflict with a bear, and who stood his gun by the fence and said: "Go it, woman; go it, bear!" Lanny had a ringside seat and he stayed, and learned more about the manners and morals of the rich. Money is supposed to improve the former if not the latter; but Mr. Horace Vandringham, of one of the old New York families, hurled his great bulk back and forth across the room and called his brother-in-law a yellow skunk and a dirty double-crosser, and the brother-in-law replied that he was a damned fool and crazy as a bedbug. Incidentally Mr. Joseph Barnes said something which interested Lanny: "My brother always knew that this thing was going to crash; he said it was jerry-built, and he wrote his will to provide for this very day."

They tried to get Lanny into it. Uncle Horace turned to him and inquired: "What do you say?" But Lanny just wasn't going to get in. He replied: "I notice that it hasn't occurred to any of you to ask what Irma thinks."

"Well, Irma?" demanded Uncle Horace. "Are you going to let me go to the wall?"

Lanny was learning about his wife as he went along. She was just twenty-one, and she was learning in the same way as her husband. She said: "Uncle Horace, I have been thinking it over, and I've decided that I don't like the business of gambling in stocks."

Uncle Horace gave a gulp. His face showed his surprise, and so, perhaps, did Lanny's. The new husband had been doing a great deal of talking to his wife and in her presence, but she hadn't given much sign that she was paying attention; however, the word "gambling" was Lanny's word, and certainly not Mr. Vandringham's.

"Uncle Horace," continued the girl, "I am sorry about this trouble you are in, and I'd like to help you, but it's no good if you're going back in, because it'll be the same thing all over again. So it's up to you to say whether you're willing to get out and stay out."

"But, Irma, it's my business!"

"I know, and you're free to go on with it, but not to come to me when you get caught. If I help you, it will have to be on condition that you'll find some other business but buying and selling stocks on margin."

She said it quietly, and having said it, she stopped. She was no longer the princess but the queen. "My lords and gentlemen, it has pleased us to decree," and so on. Lord Horace gulped again, and looked helplessly at his sister, who appeared as much taken aback as he was. He began arguing and pleading, and talked for quite a while, but Irma only said: "I'm not going to change, Uncle Horace."

So finally he gave up. "All right, Irma. I have no choice."

She turned to the other uncle. "How much stock have you invested from my income?"

"A little over three millions, at yesterday's prices."

"Well, let him have enough of it to protect his margins. But when the panic stops, he's going to sell and get out."

"I may not have anything left!" exclaimed Uncle Horace, with agony in his face.

"I'll stand part of the loss. Anything so long as we don't have this kind of thing again. You must get your affairs on the same basis as the estate—what stocks you own you own outright, and you can put them in our vault and forget them."

VII

When this Homeric battle was over and the two warring gentlemen had hurried out to obey their orders, Lanny said: "I've got to drive down to Newcastle and see my father. Would you like to go along?"

"Indeed I would," replied the young wife. "Anything to get out of this madhouse."

"I'm afraid we'll find another one there, only smaller," he remarked.

"Feathers" was instructed that, if the call came through, she was to tell Mr. Budd that the pair were on their way. They gave the chauffeur a chance to go and watch the ticker, and set out with

Lanny driving. He had told her what he had done for his father, and
it had impressed her tremendously. He really didn't care for money
after all! So now, while they were speeding up Park Avenue, she
said: "You know, of course, I mean to help your father if he
needs it."

"Thank you for the offer, Irma; but it's up to the Budds to look
after their own."

"But maybe they can't. Maybe they're in, too."

"Maybe so; but I told you I wasn't going to have anything to do
with your money——"

"That's all ancient history, Lanny. You're my husband, and your
father means something to me, just as my uncle does." When he
started to argue, she said: "Let's forget it. We'll see what position
he's in, and what he has to say. If he needs help, I mean to give it."
Again, the queen speaking!

Out on the highway that follows the shore of the Sound, Lanny
said: "You know, Irma, it's odd; what you said to Uncle Horace is
just what I've been getting up steam to say to Robbie."

"I never gave much thought to it before," she responded, "but this
day has opened my eyes. I see what my father meant, and how wise
he was. How I wish he were here now!"

She started asking questions about the stock market, and about
business and finance; it was a primary-grade course which she should
have had in school. "Where on earth does all the money go?" she
asked, and he explained to her the nature of credit; the money didn't
go anywhere, it just ceased to be. She tried earnestly to understand
the strange idea, and the conversation was so different from her usual
gossip, her boy and girl friends, their clothes and their games and
their love affairs, that Lanny thought, perhaps this "shakedown"
mightn't be such a bad thing for the idle rich after all!

She made the suggestion: "You might tell your father that you
can't get help from me on any other terms than those I laid down for
Uncle Horace." Lanny wondered, was she finding the exercise of
power a pleasant thing? She could hardly be the daughter of her
mother and her father.and not find it so.

The drive to Newcastle was a matter of two or three hours.

Lanny made it as fast as the law allowed, and now and then a bit faster. Passing through the towns you could tell where brokers' offices or newspaper bulletin boards were by the crowds in front. It was a little before six when they reached Newcastle, and there, too, were crowds on the main street, one in front of the brokers' and another in front of the *Chronicle* building. Lanny stopped at the former, for there was a chance that his father might be inside, and if not, he wished to phone and find out whether he was at the office or at home.

Impossible to get into the brokers'; but from the crowd outside he learned that the closing prices had still not come in. The ticker had fallen more than four hours behind, and it would be after seven when anxious customers all over the country could know what had happened to their holdings. Lanny felt pretty sure that his father wouldn't be at home under such circumstances, so he called the office, and at last, to his relief, he heard the familiar voice.

"How are you, Robbie?"

"I'm still alive—that's about all."

"You're not wiped out?"

"I have a call for more margin in the morning."

"You got word about the money I deposited?"

"I did, and I don't know how to thank you. It saved me for the moment."

"You're going to be at the office for a while? Irma and I will come right over."

VIII

How different the world had been when Lanny had driven his wife through those gates just a month ago! Now the genial and self-confident Robbie looked ten years older; he was so harassed that he couldn't make any pretense, even before the daughter of the Barneses. He told in a few brief sentences what his position was. His father had refused to lend him a dollar. All his life Robbie had insisted upon having his own way, and now he must pay the bill. There would always be a position in the firm for him and a good salary on which he could live; but oil ventures and stock gambling were equally sinful in Grandfather Samuel's eyes, and what had happened was the promised judgment of the Lord.

Robbie's brother Lawford was in the market too and, anyhow, he wouldn't have helped Robbie. The other two brothers didn't have much money, and they too were "in," but concealing the fact. Robbie had got a hundred thousand from one of his uncles, but that was a mere drop in the bucket. He had pledged all his own securities, even his Budd stock; also he had put up Lanny's securities, as Lanny had authorized. The father started to make apologies for this, but Lanny cut him short. "Forget it; we want to see you through, and we want to know what we're up against. Don't hide anything from us."

"No use trying to. I admit it's got my nerve. You and your Red friends can have your way from now on."

Robbie went to the ticker, which wasn't tired in spite of working so long overtime. The prices of the last hour were now coming in. "Things seem to be holding better," he said. The tape was giving only the final figure of the stock price. So you read: "R 6½ 6¼ 6⅜ 6½"; from this you understood that Radio was now holding its own, but you wouldn't know whether it was at 46 or 36. Robbie had been keeping track, and had notes of the various prices in which he was interested.

He showed a memorandum which his secretary had got by telephone from the *Chronicle* office some time ago. In the course of the afternoon a group of leading bankers had met in the House of Morgan and agreed to put up a fund of two hundred and forty million dollars to stabilize the market. Such was the story which would be in the afternoon papers throughout the country, and it was hoped that it would check the rush to unload. "If I can only have a little time," said Robbie, "I can make arrangements and save the situation." Lanny must have heard a score of people saying those same words in the course of the day.

Irma spoke up: "I have promised to help Uncle Horace out of his trouble, and I want to do the same for you, Father Budd."

"I can't let you do it, Irma!" The once-proud father-in-law started to protest, but her majesty cut him short.

"Lanny heard me tell my uncle what I was willing to do, and he will explain it to you. But hadn't we better go home where we can be comfortable? There's nothing more can happen tonight, is there?"

"I was waiting to get the closing prices," said the exhausted man; "but I'll have my secretary phone them to the house."

IX

There was a duel coming, and Lanny had been bracing himself for it. He wanted to be kind, but also he wanted to have his way. He guessed that his father wouldn't have any interest in dinner— better get it over and done with, get the load off both their minds. So he left Irma and Esther to exchange notes on the sufferings of womankind in panics, and took his father into the latter's study.

"First, Robbie, I want to tell you, Beauty approves of your having that money. She agrees with me that you've done everything for us, and we owe you all we have."

"You're both going to get it back, Son, if I live."

"All I say is, forget it for the present. We love you, we want you to be happy; we both think you haven't been for a long time. What I ask you is, have I earned the right to talk to you straight?"

"Yes, Son—go ahead!"

"Neither Beauty nor I can see what you are trying to accomplish in this scramble for money. You're wrecking your health and your happiness; you're making us miserable, and Esther—the whole family. Nobody needs the money, nobody wants it; there isn't a single one of us who wouldn't vote against your plunging in the stock market, now or any time. You know that Bess would back me up if she were here. Do you think the boys would like it if they could see the state you're in tonight?"

"You've got me licked, Son. I have to take it."

"It's not a question of taking anything. It's a question of getting our lives on a sane basis, so that we can get some happiness out of life. Do you think the boys are so keen to be millionaires? Ask them which would they rather have, their father or his money? They are able-bodied, and why shouldn't they work and make their own way in the world? Do you admire the idlers at the country club so much that you want to add two more?"

"Just what is it you want of me, Son?"

"I want of you what Irma asked and got from her uncle. I want you to promise never again to buy or sell a share of stock on margin. It's the damnedest trap for human happiness that I've ever seen, and you know I've watched a lot of them up and down the Riviera. I want you to get out, and do it tomorrow morning."

"But at these prices it would mean the loss of practically everything I have."

"All right, take the loss; there isn't one of us that won't gladly pay his share, just to know that you're out, and to be able to breathe freely again, and not think maybe you're getting ready to shoot your head off."

"I'm not going to do that, Lanny."

"How could I know what you'd do—stuck down there in New York and not able to get you on the telephone? There'll be lots of businessmen jumping out of their office windows tonight, or into the river—and I'd just like to be sure that my father isn't one of them."

"You have my word as to that."

"I want more. I can't see you go down without going down too, and why should you drag me into a gambling-game that I despise? Beauty, Marceline, Esther, Bess—all of us have to be in it with you. I'll send telegrams and get up a round robin of protest if you want me to."

"I'll do what you ask, Son; you have a mortgage on me. But I can't possibly get out tomorrow; if I can hold on for a few days, until the market rallies——"

"There you go! It's what every gambler says—my luck is bound to change!"

"But, Lanny, you see what has happened—the big fellows are coming in to stabilize prices."

"Oh, my God, Robbie Budd, you tell me that—you swallow that bait for suckers! You're actually believing that a bunch of Wall Street bankers are worrying about the public? They're going to do something to help humanity for the first time in their sharks' lives?"

"But they have to save the market in order to save themselves."

"So they tell the suckers. They're in, and of course they have to stop the panic long enough to make a market in which to sell out. After they've done that, the market can go to hell and the investors along with it. For God's sake, Robbie, have as much sense as they have! Put in your selling orders for tomorrow morning, and take your losses, whatever they are. I'll gladly chip in everything I own to help you; I'll start life over again, and you do the same. We don't any of us need so much money. You go take a long rest—go hunting, the way you used to, or come over to Juan and go sailing with me. You used to be such good company when you had time to think about something else but the rascals who were trying to get the better of you. And yet you go on putting yourself in their clutches. You're just as helpless in that market as any hayseed being taken in by a shell-game at a county fair. Turn your back on it and walk away!"

"That's what you want, Son?"

"As sure as there's ground under your feet! Let Irma and me go back tonight with peace in our souls! Let Esther get some sleep, instead of pacing the floor all night in an agony of dread. If I've ever done anything in my life to earn your respect, do that favor for me! Sell at the market, and wash your hands of Wall Street!"

"All right, Son, it's a deal."

X

Driving back to the city late at night, Lanny described that scene to his wife, and remarked: "You and I are the gamblers now. If the market takes a turn upward, our elders will blame us all the rest of their lives!"

"Do you think it'll do that?"

"You might as well ask me what will happen if you toss a coin. That's just the hell of it. All we can do is hold our breath."

"Well, I'd rather put up a lot of money than go through things like this," declared Irma.

It was the opening Lanny had been waiting for. "I think we've both had enough," he said. "Let's get out of it—right away. I think about Bienvenu, with the sun shining in the patio—and not so many telephone calls. Surely this New York life can't be very good for a baby, born or unborn."

"I'll go any time you say, Lanny."

"There's a steamer for Marseille next Wednesday."

"All right. I'll tell Slemmer to get the tickets."

"And tell him we don't have to have the most expensive suite. Let's do a little economizing—at least until we know what's happened to our families and friends."

"All right." She was a well-tamed heiress at that moment. All the rich of New York were in the same mood. Wouldn't it be nice to go off on a farm somewhere, and grow our own vegetables, and have fresh milk, eggs, and butter, and live the simple life!

Lanny continued: "Robbie argues that this panic won't hurt business. He says it's just paper profits that have been lost, and that business is still sound. But that seems nonsense to me. The crowd that came up from Wall Street every night, flushed with victory and thinking it owned the world—it may have had only paper profits, but it bought real goods with them; and now it's going to stop spending, and that's bound to cause a slump."

"It's wonderful the way you understand these things," said Irma. Lanny felt a glow of pride, and didn't consider it necessary to mention that he had heard Stef and his Uncle Jesse saying these things, or that he had been reading them in *Le Populaire* and *L'Humanité*, in the *Daily Herald* of London and the *New Leader* of New York. He had been hearing them for so long that they were his own ideas now!

40

Tomorrow We'll Be Sober

I

THE next morning was Friday, and Lanny read the papers, each of which gave three or four pages to the panic and its ramifications. They reported that there had never been a day in the history of the Exchange when so many accounts had been dumped overboard; they estimated that, including the Curb market, thirty million shares of stock had changed hands in the United States and Canada. But, one and all, the editors and writers did their best to sound courageous and hopeful; they made all they could of the heroism of the House of Morgan and other banking heads who had stepped forward to save the financial structure of the country. President Hoover, Great Engineer by whom Robbie swore, issued a statement that the business of the country was fundamentally sound. The chairman of the powerful National City Bank, who had come from Europe a few days before and told the country that the market situation was healthy, now repeated his assurances, and nobody reminded him of his previous slip. Not merely the speculators, but the great substantial financial houses, the insurance companies, the investment trusts, were coming into the market this Friday morning to pick up the bargains which had been scattered along the roadway during the rout.

Lanny went downstairs to the brokers' office to get the opening prices, and it appeared that the writers were justified: the panic was over. If you wanted to sell stocks at reduced prices, you could do so, and if you had any margin left your brokers would pay it to you. Also, it was possible to communicate promptly by telephone. Robbie was at the office of his brokers in Newcastle, and Lanny called him there, and learned that he was carrying out his promise and selling; there was a tone of anguish in his voice, and once or twice he hinted for Lanny to let him off for just a day or two more, so that he might recoup some of his terrific losses. "I'm going to be out several million dollars, Son."

"Will you have a couple of hundred thousand left, do you think?"

"Yes, I'll have that."

"All right, that's fine. We can all get along."

"I'll have to ask you and Beauty to wait a while for what I owe you."

"So far as I am concerned, you can consider that I've paid for a part of what you've done for me. As for Beauty, she can learn to wear last season's dresses. Forget it, Robbie, and go and play golf before the weather gets too bad." So he talked, as cheerful as any financial writer on the New York *Times* or *Herald Tribune*. But inside him he was shivering. "Good Lord, suppose it *does* go up again!"

Irma was in the same state. Uncle Horace was begging almost on his knees for three days—only two days and a half, counting Saturday but not Sunday—in which to rehabilitate his affairs. The market was absolutely certain to rebound; all the authorities agreed about it, and to sell now was suicide, it was a crime. The head of the Vandringham clan sat before his niece with tears running down his sagging cheeks—he had lost ten or twenty pounds in the last couple of days, for he had been running about, perspiring, and had forgotten to eat and perhaps even to drink. "Irma, for God's sake!" He cursed Joseph Barnes because he was daring to misinterpret Irma's orders and not give him enough stocks to keep him safe for the two and a half days that were really necessary to the selling-out process.

Lanny tried to keep out of the fight; but when Irma asked him, he repeated what he had said. "It's a toss-up. You can be sure of this: if the market does come back, and Uncle Horace makes money, he'll be right where he was before; he'll say he was right and you were wrong, and he'll be independent of you, and he'll be in the market again, and the next time there's a smash, you'll have to go through the same scenes."

"I'll have given him fair warning, at any rate."

"No, you'll have taught him that you don't stick by what you say."

In spite of this advice Irma gave way. It was really hard for her; she was young, and didn't know the world, and her mother was putting pressure on her to save the dignity and credit of the great family whose blood she shared. It might have been different if Lanny had said: "I am sure." But how could Lanny say that? If he said it and turned out to be wrong, what would become of his standing as a husband? By God, you were in the market whether you wanted to be or not! A fish might as well talk about refusing to have anything to do with the ocean!

II

More and more clearly every hour Lanny realized this truth. When he came up at noon from watching the market, he found the family in a state of excitement. A check which Irma had written for her uncle had "bounced"; the bank had called up to inform her that she had no funds. The check had been written right after Slemmer had told her that she had seventy-five thousand dollars to her account; but Mr. Slemmer had been mistaken, said the seventeenth vice-president of the Seventh National Bank; on that date there had been only about one hundred dollars in the Irma Barnes account. (She still kept her maiden name in business affairs, it being one of power.)

So Irma had to phone Uncle Joseph and tell him to sell some of her stocks and put the money to her account; after which began a search for Slemmer. He had checked out of his hotel in the city, and he hadn't showed up at Shore Acres, and he didn't show up at either place or any other. Very soon there was a scandal, the police having to be notified, the district attorney's office sending a man up, and newspaper reporters and photographers coming to the hotel.

The most conscientious and efficient of business managers had been playing the market, like everybody else; and he had got caught, as the saying was, with his pants down. He had drawn out Irma's money in an effort to save himself, and when she had called him, he had realized that the jig was up and had disappeared. Had he tied a stone around his neck and jumped off one of the piers? It was a considerate way of behaving, but not all were considerate—they shot themselves in hotel-rooms, which was bad for business, or they jumped from windows and messed up the sidewalks. Or had Slemmer taken a train for Mexico or Canada? No one would ever know. He left behind him a wife and two children, who never heard from him—or if they did, they kept the secret. There they were, weeping hysterically, and what could Mrs. Fanny do—order them out of the estate with cold weather coming on?

That was one story out of thousands. If you were in a prominent position, like the Barneses, you couldn't help hearing many such. Your friends came in and wrung their hands and harrowed your soul —sometimes they actually didn't have money for food. You just had to give them small checks to tide them over. No matter what your resources were, you could be sure that the demands would exceed them. New York had become a torture house, and you couldn't bear to look at the faces of people in the streets. All sorts, rich and poor, had suffered, and would go on suffering for a long time. Lucky indeed you were if you had the price of steamer tickets for the warm Mediterranean route! Lucky if you could afford to have a baby, and not have to get rid of it by the abortion route—a well-traveled highway at all times.

III

Trading was gigantic in volume that Friday, but the market was orderly from bell to bell. The red-eyed and exhausted brokers could catch their breath, and let their hoarse throats heal, and eat a little food; their clerks and office workers could dig out from under the avalanche of paper which had overwhelmed them. There was a story of a broker who remembered a waste-basket under his desk, into which he had been stuffing bundles of orders which he was unable to handle. Now the storm was over, and everybody was saying: "Don't sell yet; wait for the rise; it's sure to come." There were signs of it all day Friday; the market had what the papers called "strong support," and the names of the great bankers were freely used to convince everybody that securities were as secure as ever.

But Robbie Budd was a man of his word; he had said that he would get out, and in the afternoon he reported to his son that he did not own a share of stock on margin. He had many pawned at the First National Bank of Newcastle, including Lanny's; now the only danger was that the bank might have to have more collateral for its loans. Lanny said: "Sell some of them now, Robbie—sell at market, and pay the bank off. Get yourself in the clear." Robbie said again: "Is that what you want, Son?" and the answer was flat: "It is."

There might have been sons who would have got pleasure out of giving such orders to their fathers, but Lanny was surely not among them. He had the right to do it, because part of the money was his and his mother's; but he hated the responsibility—the more so because he had so little assurance of being right. But he had acquired a sort of phobia on the subject of this stock market, dating from the hour when he had watched the frenzied brokers down in the trading-pit; they had seemed to him like the damned souls in Dante's inferno. It made no difference whether Satan had sentenced them to behave like that or whether they were slaves of their own greed—they were just as pitiable human victims.

So Robbie sold; and when he got through he said that he had redeemed Lanny's stocks and put them back in the vault where they belonged; now he had just about enough money to repay the three hundred thousand which Lanny had handed him. Lanny said: "Give us three notes, one for Beauty, one for Marceline, and one for me, and we'll put them away. If you can ever pay them off comfortably, all right, and if not, we'll forget them. Now take my advice and go home and sleep twelve hours. And you and Esther make your plans to come and visit us at Juan after Christmas."

A funny thing, which Lanny had been gradually coming to realize. Bienvenu would now be a completely respectable place! Mr. and Mrs. Parsifal Dingle, Mr. and Mrs. Eric Vivian Pomeroy-Nielson, and Mr. and Mrs. Irma Barnes! Three sinless couples, each with a marriage certificate! And four children, and another on the way! The "faintly incestuous atmosphere" would be dissipated entirely, the strict Miss Addington would be happy, and any daughter of the Puritans could be invited for a visit! Surely the last trace of suspicion that Esther might have harbored concerning Mabel Blackless, alias Beauty Budd, must have been dispelled by her behavior during the last couple of days!

IV

One thing the panic had done: it had knocked the picture business flat. Plenty of people came to the show rooms to look at Detazes and talk about them, but not one bought anything, and few even asked the prices. Zoltan continued to play the perfect host; loving good art as he did, he was able and willing to forget the commercial side; the rooms had been paid for in advance, so those last three days might be taken as a gift to the public, a solace to those in trouble, a reminder of higher and better things than stock prices.

Lanny realized with a pang that in the turmoil of these days he had completely forgotten the existence, or whatever you might call it, of Marie de Bruyne. Suppose—just suppose—that she had been trying to communicate with him, and that he had failed to give her a chance, what would she think? Did they know about Wall Street in the spirit world? Seeing that the market held steady on Saturday, and knowing that his father was safe, Lanny decided to take another of his stepfather's appointments with the Polish medium. He went to the apartment and watched her go into the trance, and sat and waited for Tecumseh to tell him what else his *amie* might have to communicate.

But it wasn't Marie who "came through" this time; it was a strange creature who said that her name was "Roberta," and that she had gone very, very young into the spirit world, but that now she was happy here with "Madeleine." Lanny couldn't think of any Madeleine, and said so, but Roberta refused to be disconcerted, she said that she knew Lanny well, and watched him with love, and that her life-span had been short; also that Madeleine wore a white uniform here also, and that her hands were very gentle, and that she no longer felt any of the pain of the accident—a whole lot of stuff like that, and Lanny was bored, because Tecumseh was off the track, but you couldn't tell him so because Madame Zyszynski had said you must be polite to him, because if he got angry it made her ill.

So Lanny paid his two dollars, and went home and told his mother about this futile business; but to his great astonishment Beauty began to tremble, and turned pale, and exclaimed: "Oh, my God, Lanny, my God!" When he asked her what it was, she hid her face in her hands and began to weep, and said she couldn't tell him, she couldn't bear to think of it. Finally, when he insisted, she blurted out: "Lanny, you might have had a little sister! It was when you were only two years old, and I wanted her so much, and I thought it would be a little girl."

"What happened?" he kept asking, and finally she said: "I didn't dare to have her. I thought that two accidents were too much for one *amie*, and I was afraid Robbie would stop loving me. I never told him about it, but while he was in the States I went and had an abortion. You know, Lanny, you can't blame me—women do it."

"I know."

"I never knew if it would be a little girl—I don't know if it's possible to tell, the doctor never said. But I had imagined a little girl, and I was going to call her Roberta, after Robbie. And maybe it was a girl—and, oh, God, do they have souls when they aren't anything?"

"I don't know," Lanny answered. "Was there a Madeleine?"

"Madeleine was the nurse who attended me in the hospital. She was so kind, and I used to say that her hands were gentle. I brought her to Bienvenu for a while."

"And what became of her?"

"She was killed in a motor-car accident a year or two later."

"Really, that's extraordinary!" Lanny was quite awe-stricken for a while, and pictured the air around him filled almost solid with spirits. But then again came the idea of that thing called telepathy. Had the medium been dipping into Beauty's subconscious mind, pulling out memories that she would have been glad to banish? In any case, it was something to think about.

"Lanny," said the mother, "it really seems too bad to go off and leave that woman and not find out what else she can tell us."

"It does," he agreed. "I wonder if we couldn't take her with us."

"Oh, do you suppose we could afford to?"

"It oughtn't to cost so much. She can't be making a fortune at two dollars a sitting."

"Parsifal and I have been talking about it; but I feel so terrified over this panic, and Robbie losing all his money."

"Robbie's a businessman, and he'll make more. Go have a talk with Madame and find out if she'd like to come. We can put her up at the Pension Flavin, and pay her a little in addition. Offer it to her in francs—a thousand a month will sound like a fortune to her."

Lanny went away thinking: "Bienvenu will be a queer place after all!" He wondered which would be worse—sexual irregularity or the presence of disembodied spirits?

V

It was most inconvenient for Irma, not having any business manager; and just while she was getting ready for a voyage. She had to make all sorts of decisions, and Lanny had to help; so he learned a lot about the burdens of royalty. Uncle Joseph, that penurious person, had to be forced to sell more stocks on a very depressed market, in order that Irma might be able to sign checks for the many friends who were about to be turned out of their homes. Feathers had to write the checks and keep account of them—for the disagreeable experience of having one "bounce" must surely not recur.

Feathers would have to assume a lot of new duties; but she was so well terrified by her financial losses that she had dropped every trace of that great lady attitude which "social" secretaries are supposed to wear. She begged Irma not to leave her behind, and Irma agreed to take her on condition that she would become a plain ordinary secretary and do whatever she was told. There wouldn't be much social life for Irma, on account of her advancing pregnancy. The haughty Miss Featherstone, who was a college graduate and daughter of a decayed "old family," promised to make herself useful, even if she had to "mind the baby." That became one of the jokes in the establishment; any time there was something unusual for Feathers to do, it was called "minding the baby."

Irma and her mother drove out to Shore Acres on Sunday. Irma wanted to say good-by to her family and friends. Lanny wasn't needed, so he went by train to Newcastle. Esther was happy, smiling through her tears; her gratitude to Lanny was touching. Robbie said nothing about the market, but Lanny knew what was in his thoughts. If he had waited until Saturday morning he might have got more than he got on Friday! If there was another rise on Monday, he would be wishing he had waited until that day. Uncle Horace had been allowed to wait—why not Robbie? But he would be a good sport and not say it to his son. That book was closed, and Robbie would forget his dream of becoming a really rich man; at least, he would forget it for a while.

Lanny went to say good-by to his grandfather, who was failing, and who said: "My boy, you will probably not see me again in this world." Lanny would have liked to tell him about his research into the next one, but he knew that it wasn't entirely orthodox, and so wouldn't please the president of Budd Gunmakers. And anyhow, it might be only telepathy! But Lanny thought, what a funny thing; the good Christians were all taught to believe that your soul survived, and yet they ridiculed the suggestion that after a soul had got settled in the beyond, it might have a desire to get in touch with those whom it had left behind. Didn't they really believe what their church taught them? Or did they think that the souls would forget everything? If a soul did forget, what would be left of it?

Lanny's steamer was making one of those midnight sailings; and it happened that Phyllis Gracyn's new play was to open on that evening. Lanny said to his father: "You remember the last time we sailed—how we went to see Gracyn?" December of 1918, nearly eleven years ago; right after the actress had jilted Lanny, and he was feeling that he had made a mess of his life. Now he was supposed to be sitting on the top of the world, and if it turned out to be the top of a volcano, he was still expected to enjoy it. Irma was intensely curious about Gracyn, and wanted to see how she made love—which of course she would have to do in any play. Did Irma expect to get points from her? Anyhow, they were going to the opening; and Lanny said, wouldn't Robbie and Esther drive down and join them?

They'd have dinner at the hotel, and go to the show, and thence to the steamer, and Robbie and Esther could spend the night in New York and drive home in the morning.

Esther had always refused to see the actress whom she considered the seductress of her stepson. But now she had decided that she mustn't be so strait-laced, she must try to get along with the people in her world; show her gratitude to her stepson, and do what she could to divert her husband's mind from his troubles. She agreed to come, and Lanny, knowing it was an effort, gave her a kiss and called her a good sport.

VI

So many interesting and important things in New York, and Lanny had missed them, on account of the Detaze show, and Irma and her smart friends, and the panic, and the spirits! But he didn't want to leave without seeing the great art collection at the Metropolitan. Zoltan said it was an "old fogy sort of place," but it had a few new things—and Lanny hadn't seen the old ones for eleven years. Zoltan couldn't go because he had the job of getting all the pictures packed—they were going on the same steamer to Marseille. Irma couldn't go to the museum, because she had ordered some dresses which she had to pay for, and they had to be fitted. Lanny went alone, and spent a happy morning looking at Egyptian mummies, Greek sculpture, and early American painting. He could never get through such a place as this, because he would run into something that held him too long.

Having promised Irma to be back for lunch, he rode down on a Fifth Avenue bus. He passed one of the great hotels which had a brokers' office on the ground floor, and there was a crowd of the sort which had become familiar. He thought: "Good Lord, what is happening now?" Lanny was a natural-born optimist, but he had to be a "bear" on this market for the sake of his reputation with all three of his families. On the other hand, if it was another slump, that too was serious, for this was the day when Uncle Joseph was scheduled to be selling out.

Lanny couldn't wait to reach his own hotel, but hopped off the bus and joined the crowd. One glance was enough—he knew by the faces that it was another panic! The excited people on the edge of the crowd were saying that this time was worse than Thursday; the bottom had dropped clean out from under the market. Every figure on the Translux showed a drop, and the ticker was again way behind.

Lanny took a taxi to his hotel, and there were Fanny and her brother; tears streaming down Uncle Horace's flabby cheeks, and his hands shaking as if he had the palsy. "Irma, for God's sake, it means everything I have in this world!"

"I gave you your chance," the girl was saying. "I begged you to get out. Father Budd did so, and he's all right; but you had to hold. on, you were the one that knew all about it—and how could I fight you?"

"But, Irma, if I can only hold on through today——"

"I know—one day, and then one more day. But I'm not going to dump any more stocks at panic prices."

"You don't have to sell them, Irma; it's enough if you deposit them with the brokers."

"I know; and when the market drops again, I deposit more."

Lanny wanted to say: "Stand firm, Irma." But he saw that he didn't have to; she was remembering the things he had explained to her on the drive to Newcastle. She'd be quite a businesswoman before she got through.

Uncle Horace's pleading was in vain. "You had your chance; you had what you asked for." Such was her majesty's decision.

The burly and once so energetic man sank into a chair with his bald head in his hands. "What is going to become of me?"

"You don't have to worry, Uncle Horace. You know I'll always take care of you. I'll set you up in some other business; but stock-gambling is out, so far as my money is concerned."

So that was the end of one "market operator." Lanny had learned enough about New York to imagine the rest. Horace Vandringham would become an insurance broker, and peddle policies to Irma's friends; if he failed at that, he would become one of those querulous old folks at Shore Acres. Already there were too many of them, and this panic, or series of panics, would increase the number; Lanny remarked that the place would become another Hampton Court—and when Irma asked what that was, he told her about the aged servants of the British royal family, who lived out their appointed days looking out upon beautiful formal gardens.

Lanny hadn't been there, and couldn't say what they talked about, but he knew how it would be with the pensioners at Shore Acres. Thursday's panic had filled New York with people who had formerly boasted of how much they had gained, and were now almost as proud of their heavy losses. "Cleaned me out!" you would hear one exclaim. "Gutted me like a fish! I lost half a million that first day!" Now there would be a new lot, ready to chime in: "It was Monday that finished me. I played the market for a comeback, and I saw three million blow away in an hour!" As with fish stories, the biggest fortunes got away; and contrary to the laws of perspective, the farther they receded into the distance the bigger they grew.

VII

All that day the tormented city was in an uproar. It had been as Lanny had foretold—the "big fellows" had "protected the market" just long enough to get out from under. They had done their unloading on Friday and Saturday, and now, on Monday, there was nobody to buy anything. It was like the collapse of a house of cards. General Electric, the greatest electrical manufacturing concern in the country, lost 47 points that day; Western Union lost 39; Telephone, which Robbie had bought at 287½, closed the day at 232. The exhausted brokers and clerks and messengers and secretaries and bookkeepers, who had been working day and night over the weekend, now faced a sixteen-million-share day, breaking all records, surpassing all nightmares. It was estimated that the value of securities in the United States shrank fourteen billions of dollars in five hours; and it wasn't the end.

There was nothing that Irma or Lanny could do about it. A dreadful world to be in, but they hadn't made it and couldn't change it. Lanny had no more money to give, and Irma had to choose between giving away all she had or hardening her heart and closing her purse. Her friends didn't show up very well in this crisis; they wanted all they could get, and it was more than Irma owned. No use blaming them too much; they were people who had never learned to do any useful thing in their lives, and the prospect of being without money broke their nerve. Lanny, whose money had come too easily, was harsh in his thoughts of them; he remembered the conversations he had been forced to listen to, the derision with which his words of caution had been greeted. Also he remembered the unborn baby, and he said: "Let's take a drive and get away from the telephone."

Feathers assumed the duty of answering calls, and Lanny took the car and drove his wife up the valley of the Croton River to the great dam. In the lowlands the autumn foliage was still on the trees, and it was a sight you didn't see on the Riviera. Lanny tried to interest her in nature, but it wasn't an easy feat of the mind. What was she going to do about that huge country place? Would she be able to keep it up if her stocks went on tumbling to nothing? Would there continue to be dividends? Lanny wasn't sure.

They came to a swanky roadhouse, and went inside and had dinner. In between the numbers of the floor-show there were bulletins about the end of the world. Reports came over the radio; the ticker was hopelessly behind, but the bond ticker gave samples of the closing prices, and some people listened and went out without dining, because what they had in their pockets was all they had in the world.

Lanny said: "Let's not go back to the hotel tonight. You'll just get yourself in for a lot of grief."

"Oh, I have so many things to attend to before we sail!"

"Attend to them by mail after you get to Juan. Most of them will have settled themselves before that."

She gave way, and they drove over to the Hudson, and up to one of the towns where there was a good hotel. "They'll think we're not married, because we have no baggage, Lanny." He answered that they wouldn't send them to jail. He wrote "Mr. and Mrs. L. P. Budd," and was glad that the name was obscure.

Irma phoned to her secretary and learned that her mother had taken Uncle Horace to Shore Acres. "I suppose she's afraid he'll shoot his head off," Irma said to her husband. "I fear she'll never forgive me for having let him down. Do you think I could have saved him, Lanny?"

"Look at the market," he answered. "One might as well try to guess about a bolt of lightning."

He called Robbie at his home—and this time Robbie was there. "Well, what do you think of it?"

"You win," was the father's answer.

"What are you doing?"

"Esther and I are playing bridge with Jane and Tony—" that was Esther's sister and her husband. "We have lost a couple of dollars and are worried."

Lanny didn't say: "Aren't you glad you're out?" He said: "Well, see you Wednesday. I'm going to keep Irma on the road till then."

VIII

The New York papers leave the city soon after midnight and you can have them on your breakfast table if you are anywhere within a couple of hundred miles. So Lanny and Irma sat up in bed and read three or four pages of details about the dreadful events of the day before. Pleasant indeed to be comfortable while you learn about other people's misery—provided, of course, that you are without heart. Lanny, carrying that handicap, felt all his Red impulses reviving; he put on the old phonograph record, and heard his Uncle Jesse declaring that it was the downfall of the capitalist world. Very monotonous, the scratching of that old record; one had to remind oneself that a statement didn't cease to be true when it became trite.

The papers agreed that this was a "rich man's panic." The big investors, the speculators, had been hit, and many of them knocked flat. Lanny could believe it; but he knew also that millions of little people had been in that market, and had been the first to be swept away. Anyhow, when the big fellows were suffering, it didn't take them long to pass it on to others. Lanny knew that when the rich stopped buying luxuries the salesclerks would lose their jobs, and before long the workers who made the goods would be turned off also.

If Irma's income dropped, wouldn't the pensioners at Shore Acres suffer? Wouldn't some of the servants have to be turned out? It was clear to his mind that a great business recession must be on the way, and he decided to warn his father about it. This time Robbie would listen!

Lanny persuaded his wife to go on driving. What could they do in New York? Stand outside the brokers' offices and watch the tortured faces? He had seen enough of them to last him the rest of his life. Or go up to their rooms in the Ritzy-Waldorf and hear their friends crying over the telephone? Tell them for the hundredth time that Irma had very little cash, that her business manager had absconded, that her estate was tied up, that she had to help her mother and her uncle and many others? Here was New York state, which Lanny had never seen, and the sun was shining on it, the tang of autumn in the air and every turn of the winding roads a picture for a lover of art and nature. Lanny poured out his treasures of understanding and love, and beguiled his young bride farther from the great massacre of human hopes.

IX

More than once during the cruise of the *Bessie Budd* Irma had said: "I wonder if we are really married." Each time Lanny had answered: "We'll do it again some day." It might be that if it ever came to a test some stern English judge would decide that they had not been bona fide passengers of the *Plymouth Girl*, but had been perpetrating a fraud upon the Archbishop of Canterbury. More than once during their sojourn in New York Lanny had thought of suggesting another marriage; but the trouble lay with Irma's so notorious name. If they were to have another ceremony, who would believe that they had been married before? And what a juicy morsel for the "tabs" and the radio scandal-mongers!

But now the people they knew were so busy with the panic that they wouldn't pay any attention to a hundred marriages. Lanny said: "I hear it's very easy to get married in Jersey. How about crossing over there and hunting up a preacher?"

"Oh, Lanny, should we dare?"

"We can find some small village where there wouldn't be report-ers. Anyhow, let's have a look."

They crossed the Hudson by the Poughkeepsie bridge and drove south. When the road signs told them that it was the state of New Jersey, they turned back into the well-wooded hills and began look-ing for a village of sufficiently humble appearance. The first one had no church, and when they found one with a church it had no preacher. At last, however, they found an aged Methodist minister about whom it seemed a safe guess that he had never been in a night club or listened to radio gossip; he was a bit tottery and his voice quavered, but his white-haired wife was spry, and she hurried next door for a neighbor to serve as the second witness. The three of them were so kind and sweet that the young people were embar-rassed, as if they were perpetrating another fraud.

However, it was all right; this was the sweet land of liberty, and if you wanted to get married in every state of the Union, it was your privilege. In this particular state there were no banns and no bars; you weren't asked anything about your parents' consent, your re-ligious faith, the state of your health, or even whether you were sane. All you had to give was your name, which might be fictitious, and your address, which might be the same, and your age, which fre-quently was. These were duly noted in a record book, and signed by the preacher and the witnesses, who could see that this was a rich young couple, but gave no sign of ever having heard the name Irma Barnes.

The old gentleman went to a clothes closet and got out his best frock-coat, badly in need of brushing, and put it on. He took up the printed word of God, which he held as a sort of fetish, though he didn't need to consult it. He took his stand in front of them, coughed once or twice, and proceeded in a very solemn tone to invoke the blessings of Almighty God upon what he was about to do; then he did it, and after he had done it he wrote a certificate and gave it to Irma for her future protection. She took the document quickly and stepped back, because she had heard somewhere that it was the cus-tom for the preacher to kiss the bride and she didn't want it. Lanny provided a diversion in the shape of a ten-dollar bill, probably the largest sum the man had ever received for such a service during his long pastoral career. The two young people gave their thanks, said their hurried farewells, and made their escape. "What a funny thing that that should make us husband and wife!" mused Irma.

X

When lunchtime came they stopped in a town, and in front of a newspaper office was a bulletin board, from which they got reports of the morning's events in Wall Street. This Tuesday, the twenty-ninth, proved to be the worst of all. Apparently the entire stock-owning population of the United States was telegraphing or tele-phoning orders to sell at the market, and Europe and the rest of the world were joining in. The slaughter of prices affected the bond market, the grain market, even real estate; bankrupted people had to have cash, no matter at what price. The horrified brokers on the trading-floor could hardly credit what they heard. There was a story of one who was trying to dispose of a block of sewing-machine stock which had been selling at more than 40; he was calling for a bid, and a messenger boy had the bright idea to offer one dollar, and he got the stock. It had been sold "at the market."

That afternoon Lanny was driving his wife through the lovely scenery of the Catskill mountains. The air was exhilarating; they got out and walked in the sunshine, and sat for a while listening to the babble of a mountain stream. Irma developed a real appetite, and that was a good thing for the expected baby, which she was begin-ning to feel.

At dusk they drove into a town, and in the lobby of the hotel sat and listened to a radio telling of the wreckage of men's fortunes that day. Another record-breaker—seventeen million shares on one ex-change. The ticker was again hopelessly behind, but the radio gave sample prices, from which it appeared that the entire list of United States stocks had lost nearly half their value. After dinner, they lis-tened again, along with a miscellaneous crowd—traveling-salesmen, hunters, farmers, small-town merchants—who talked freely about their troubles. Misery loves company, and men took a perverted kind of pride in telling of their ruin. They had swallowed the bait which Wall Street had fed to them through newspapers and radios and "market reports"; they had refused to "sell America short," and now it was they who had been "sold down the river."

This was the real America, of which Lanny hadn't seen very much. Nobody shed tears—they preferred making "wisecracks." Lanny was interested to note that every last man took it for granted that stocks would come back; what fortunes would be made by the lucky ones who were able to hold on for a few days!

Presently one of the "newscasters" came on the air: a pert, aggressive gentleman, speaking with a swift staccato style; everything was "Flash," and there was a clicking of a telegraph key to suggest that he was getting it right off the wire. He told about the market crash, the prices, and who was said to be down and out, and what bears had managed to coast on top of the avalanche. Then came news of café society, the gossip of personalities which had made the man famous. "Flash! Your reporter is informed that Mr. and Mrs. Lanny Budd are expecting a little bundle from heaven some time next March. They were married in June—no time wasted. She is Irma Barnes, the glamour girl of Broadway last season. It is possible that the glamour will need polishing up after the events of the past five days. Irma's father, the great J. Paramount Barnes, took no chances with his holding companies, but put his money into blue chips. Hold onto them, Irma, they'll be worth something some day!"

There sat the glamour girl and her glamour boy, blushing and stealing uneasy glances at the people in the crowded lobby. But nobody looked at them; nobody had looked at the hotel register; nobody was thinking about anything but the closing prices—and, besides, it couldn't have occurred to them as a possibility that the greatest of café celebrities might be sitting alongside them in this remote hotel.

XI

In the morning the young couple had the papers, and read the details of that desolating day. American Telephone and Telegraph, the security upon which Robbie Budd had staked his fortunes, was down eighty-three points from the price that he had paid. Lanny, who had cast in his lot with the bears, need never again worry about his standing as a Wall Street authority! "I believe I've lost half my money," said Irma. He told her to cheer up; they would survive.

She wanted to see her mother before sailing, so they drove back to the city and out to Shore Acres. They found Uncle Horace pretty well calmed down. He no longer interrupted Lanny when he spoke, but listened politely. He had to admit that he was glad he hadn't been in that market; but, oh, if only Irma would let him get in *now*, what a killing he and she could make! Poor derelict, he would sit in the brokers' offices and watch the prices, read the gossip of the "Street," make his predictions, and see himself fail over and over again; for that Great Bull Market went on sinking, sinking —like one of those Spanish bulls when the matador has pierced him through the heart, and he stands rocking unsteadily, his great head drooping inch by inch.

Fanny Barnes wept, and agreed to forgive her daughter, and the daughter promised to come home before too long. All the dependents shed dutiful tears as the fortunate young couple drove away. Their belongings were packed for them, and a truckload of baggage was taken to the steamer. Robbie and Esther arrived, and father and son went down to the brokers' office and joined the customers, sitting with their hats tilted back on their heads and watching the Translux, far behind after another day of turmoil. But prices were firmer, and once more the market authorities were emerging from their cyclone cellars; once more leading bankers and statesmen were assuring the American people that business conditions were fundamentally all right. The Great Engineer said it, and "John D." and his son told the world that they were buying sound securities. The rest of the people would have felt better if they had had any means of

knowing which securities these were; also if they had had the
Rockefellers' money to buy with.

Mr. Dingle, being uninterested in worldly shows, had assumed the
duty of getting Madame Zyszynski to the steamer. She had been
booked in the second cabin, where she would feel more comfortable,
along with Irma's maid. Lanny hoped that the spirits would take
note and not be left behind. He had to stop and remind his materi-
alistic self that spirits do not exist in space—and, anyhow, maybe
they are just telepathy! Funny thing, if the subconscious mind
was playing games like that, creating imaginary beings, fictional or
historical, or a combination of both! The lover of art reminded himself that that was what all great artists did, and it was called genius.
Maybe Madame was some kind of genius; or maybe it was Lanny's
own mind which was doing the tricks. For some reason it hadn't got
properly harnessed up for creative labor, like Kurt's and Rick's.
Why that was, Lanny didn't know; but Zoltan said: "You are too
comfortable, my boy!"

They had dinner at the hotel, a party of six: Lanny and his wife,
Robbie and his, and Zoltan escorting Beauty. Robbie and the three
ladies were driven to the theater in Irma's car, and after that the
chauffeur would go to the hotel and take the secretary and the maid
to the steamer, and then return to the theater for the party, and
afterward drive the car back to Shore Acres. Lanny and Zoltan
chose to stroll to the theater, and have a chance for a good-by chat.
Zoltan was sailing for England in a few days, to see if anybody there
would buy pictures; he had had word from two of his patrons in
New York that they would be glad to sell the old masters which
they had purchased. Art prices were on the way down, and Lanny
would have to learn a new schedule!

XII

Phyllis Gracyn, alias Pillwiggle, was starring in *The Golden Lure*,
a drama in three acts. It might have been the story of Irma Barnes
when she was seventeen, a girl in school, naïve and trusting—if Irma
ever had been that. Her father was a traction magnate, playing the

political game in the large-scale crooked style. He was a widower and had a mistress, a golden blonde, and both magnate and mistress were tied in a net of intrigue, with a corrupt district attorney trying to get the magnate on a charge that would have sent him to Sing Sing. The stage Irma learned about the mistress, Gracyn, and went to her, asking her help in saving the father. The stage Irma thought that the stage Gracyn really loved the father, but she didn't, she had been planted there to get evidence on him. But of course she had a heart of gold, and was so touched by the daughter's plea that she told the stage Irma a secret which would save the father, and helped the stage Irma to foil the crooked district attorney in a sensational third act.

Of course it was "hokum" of the crudest sort. But Broadway had a technique for dressing up what it knew was hokum in modern costume, flavoring it with a dash of cynicism, sprinkling it liberally with wisecracks, and building it up to what was called "the big punch." There was a large and fashionable audience; some people still had money for theater tickets—or was the house mostly "paper"? There were some references to the stock market, doubtless put in at the last moment, and these got a great "hand." Gracyn carried off the honors; she wasn't the old-style slinky vamp, but the gay and smart kind that you met in the night clubs nowadays. Evidently the play was a "hit," and she would have a chance to recoup her financial losses. The real Irma didn't recognize her stage self or her father, but she thought that Gracyn was "a darling," and whispered to Lanny that she didn't mind his having been in love with her—but a long time ago, and there must be no more of it!

They were driven to the Hudson River pier and boarded the great steamer. There was music and laughter and singing—people were always a little "high" at that hour of the evening. Several of Irma's young friends had come, and they were higher. When the time came for the partings, those who were sailing threw down rolls of colored paper tape, holding one end, so that they made lines connecting them with the friends on shore. When the steamer was warped from the pier these lines were broken, and all felt sad. You stood waving and shouting, but mostly you couldn't make the right person hear you. The Budds all had tears in their eyes, for they had been through strenuous hours. Beauty had rarely been so happy, for at the last moment Esther had pressed her hand and said: "I have misunderstood you all my life, and I am sorry." Another blond mistress with a heart of gold!

Out in the river you could tell what had been happening in the Wall Street district, for at that late hour every window in every building was ablaze with light, and the same was true for many of the midtown office buildings. If you didn't know what was going on inside, it was a lovely spectacle, a dream city rising from the sea. Lanny and Irma watched it fade into the distance. Behind them, in the saloon, a party of young people were pounding the piano and singing college songs, hurling defiance at all panics:

> "For tonight we'll merry, merry be,
> For tonight we'll merry, merry be,
> For tonight we'll merry, merry be;
> Tomorrow we'll be sober."

Lanny and Irma moved over to the starboard side. There was Bedloe's Island with the Statue of Liberty. Lanny remembered how he had stood by the rail of the ship eleven years ago and watched the great tall lady at this same late hour. She had come from France, and he had been going home, and she had waved her bright torch as a sign of greeting. Now he was going again, and she waved it still more vigorously; she was singing: "I've been drunk for a long, long time—tomorrow I'll be sober!"

BOOKS BY UPTON SINCLAIR

WORLD S END
THE JOURNAL OF ARTHUR STIRLING
MANASSAS, A NOVEL OF THE CIVIL WAR
THE JUNGLE
THE OVERMAN
THE MILLENNIUM
THE METROPOLIS
THE MONEYCHANGERS
SAMUEL, THE SEEKER
THE FASTING CURE
LOVE'S PILGRIMAGE
SYLVIA
SYLVIA'S MARRIAGE
DAMAGED GOODS
THE CRY FOR JUSTICE
THE PROFITS OF RELIGION
KING COAL, A NOVEL OF THE COLORADO
  STRIKE
JIMMIE HIGGINS
THE BRASS CHECK
100%—THE STORY OF A PATRIOT
THEY CALL ME CARPENTER
THE BOOK OF LIFE
THE GOOSE-STEP—A STUDY OF AMERICAN
  EDUCATION
THE GOSLINGS—A STUDY OF THE AMERI-
  CAN SCHOOLS
MAMMONART

LETTERS TO JUDD
THE SPOKESMAN'S SECRETARY
OIL!
MONEY WRITES!
BOSTON
MOUNTAIN CITY
MENTAL RADIO
ROMAN HOLIDAY
THE WET PARADE
AMERICAN OUTPOST
UPTON SINCLAIR PRESENTS WILLIAM FOX
THE WAY OUT: WHAT LIES AHEAD FOR
  AMERICA
I, GOVERNOR OF CALIFORNIA
THE EPIC PLAN FOR CALIFORNIA
I, CANDIDATE FOR GOVERNOR AND HOW
  I GOT LICKED
WHAT GOD MEANS TO ME: AN ATTEMPT
  AT A WORKING RELIGION
PLAYS OF PROTEST
CO-OP: A NOVEL OF LIVING TOGETHER
THE GNOMOBILE
NO PASARAN!
THE FLIVVER KING
OUR LADY
LITTLE STEEL
YOUR MILLION DOLLARS
EXPECT NO PEACE

Plays

PRINCE HAGEN
THE NATUREWOMAN
THE SECOND STORY MAN
THE MACHINE
THE POT-BOILER

HELL
SINGING JAILBIRDS
BILL PORTER
OIL! (DRAMATIZATION)
MARIE ANTOINETTE

CPSIA information can be obtained at www.ICGtesting.com
Printed in the USA
LVOW082329301211

261769LV00001B/364/A